Then he sighed and looked back to her. "But damn if I don't feel responsible for you."

"Well, ye needn't be," Cait said. "I can take care of myself."

"Not from what I've seen. And now, thanks to me, you're even less equipped physically to deal with men like the Gothards."

"What d'ye mean, thanks to ye?"

He frowned. "Surely you realize you fell down the stairs as a result of my intervention? And 'twas my sword that cut you. Accidentally—I was not even holding it—but 'tis my responsibility nonetheless. I insist you accept my help."

"I'd say you've helped me quite enough already." This man was out of his mind. "This kind of help I dinna need."

He opened the door. "I'll check on you in the morning. If your head still aches, we'll have a doctor in to examine it."

Caithren was so confused and frustrated that if she'd had the energy, she would have kicked the door shut behind him. As it was, it closed softly.

Did he think she was there for his bidding? *I'll check on you in the morning.* Not if she had anything to say about it.

EMERALD

Lauren Royal

A SIGNET BOOK

SIGNET
Published by New American Library, a division of
Penguin Putnam Inc., 375 Hudson Street,
New York, New York 10014, U.S.A.
Penguin Books Ltd, 27 Wrights Lane,
London W8 5TZ, England
Penguin Books Australia Ltd, Ringwood,
Victoria, Australia
Penguin Books Canada Ltd, 10 Alcorn Avenue,
Toronto, Ontario, Canada M4V 3B2
Penguin Books (N.Z.) Ltd, 182–190 Wairau Road,
Auckland 10, New Zealand

Penguin Books Ltd, Registered Offices:
Harmondsworth, Middlesex, England

First published by Signet, an imprint of New American Library,
a division of Penguin Putnam Inc.

First Printing, October 2000
10 9 8 7 6 5 4 3 2 1

Printed in the United States of America

PUBLISHER'S NOTE
This is a work of fiction. Names, characters, places, and incidents either are
the product of the author's imagination or are used fictitiously, and any resemblance to actual persons, living or dead, business establishments, events,
or locales is entirely coincidental.

For my mother, Joan Falbaum Royal,
who taught me how to read and write

and

For my father, Herbert Charfess Royal,
who taught me to appreciate and
respect all genres of literature

With my everlasting love to you both

Acknowledgments

I wish to thank:
My husband, Jack, for loving me in spite of this madness called writing; my children—Brent, Blake, and Devonie—for putting up with a mom who lives half her Waking Hours in a different world; my critique partner, Terri Castoro, for wisdom and patience and always being there to laugh instead of cry with; Joan Royal and Karen Nesbitt, for driving me all over England and stopping at every village and hamlet and pile of rocks without too many audible groans; Irm Jawor, for the book of Scottish granny sayings that inspired Cait's annoying—um, endearing—habit; Amy McBay Stiles, for incredible two-way brainstorming; Ken and Dawn Royal, for feedback on first-draft synopses; Della Floyd, RN, for expert medical information; the UK contingent of the Opposite View e-mail list, for answering all of my very off-topic questions; my foreign fan club "presidents"—Karen Nesbitt in Canada and Jane Armstrong in England—for seemingly telling every single person in their respective countries about my books; my free-but-worth-it-at-ten-times-the-price publicity team: Debbie Alexander, Dick Alexander, Robin Ashcroft, Joyce Basch, Alison Bellach, Caroline Bellach, Diana Brandmeyer, Carol Carter, Terri Castoro, Vicki Crum, Elaine Ecuyer, Dale Gordon, Darren Holmquist, Rhonda Johnson, Taire Martyn, Cindy Meyer, Lynne Miller, Amanda Murphy, Romain Nayal, Karen Nesbitt, DeeDee Perkins, Nancy Phillips, Jack Poole, Herb Royal, Joan Royal, Ken Royal, Wendi Royal, Sandy Shniderson, Diena Simmons, Connie Story, Julie Walker, and Stacy Volpe (whew! do I have a lot of wonderful friends and relatives, or what?) . . . and, last but not least, every reader who has ever written me a letter or e-mail. Thanks to one and all—your friendship and support make it all worthwhile.

Chapter One

Chichester, England
Thursday, August 1, 1667

"Jason, you cannot mean to kill him."

Jason Chase stopped short and wrenched from the grasp his brother Ford had on his upper arm. "By God, no. But I'll know why he did this and bring him to justice if it's the last thing I do." He shifted a glance over his shoulder toward the man in question. "I can still see sweet little Mary lying still as death, and her mother's torn clothes and bruised face as she chanted Geoffrey Gothard's name, over and over." Trembling with rage, his hand came up to worry his narrow black mustache. "My villagers." He met Ford's gaze with his own. "My responsibility."

"You've plastered the kingdom with broadsides." Ford's blue eyes looked puzzled, as though he were unsure how to take this new side of his oldest sibling. "The reward will bring him in."

"I'm bloody well satisfied to bring him in myself."

Jason turned and continued down East Street to where Chichester's vaulted Market Cross sat in the center of the Roman-walled town. The most elaborate structure in all of England . . . but the beauty of its intricate tracery was at odds with the evil that lurked inside.

An evil that Jason intended to deal with.

Scattered businessmen, exchanging mail and news beneath the dome, paused to glance his way. He recognized the Gothard brothers from the descriptions his villagers had given him: Geoffrey, tall and slim, with a stance that bordered on elegant; Walter, shorter and rawboned. Jason's footsteps echoed as he strode through the open arches, his own brother following quickly behind. In their wake, people seemed to stream from all four corners of town, hurrying to catch the show.

Walter Gothard scurried back like a frightened rabbit. With a click of his spurred heels, Jason came to a halt and drew an uneven breath. He pinned Geoffrey Gothard with a determined gaze. "I'm taking you to the magistrate," he snapped out, surprising even himself at the commanding tone of his voice. For a fleeting moment Ford seemed dumbfounded, then he stepped away and motioned back the crowd.

Jason's hand went to the hilt of his sword. "Now, Gothard."

The other man's gaze held hard and unwavering. "My nearest and dearest enemy," he drawled. A line Jason recognized from Shakespeare. The man was not uneducated, then—indeed, his bearing was aristocratic, and his clothes, though rumpled from days of wear, were of good quality and cut.

Confusion churned with the anger in Jason's stomach. "What mean you that I am your enemy?"

Gothard's gaze roamed Jason from head to toe. "The Marquess of Cainewood, are you not?" The insolent words seemed to spew from the pale lips set into his squarish head.

"I am." Jason's words were clipped, through gritted teeth. He wanted nothing more than to go home to his calm routine, back to his estate, his life. But he could think only of little golden-curled Mary following him around the village, begging him for a sweetmeat, her blue eyes dancing with mischief and radiating trust.

Blue eyes that might never open again.

And there stood the man who had battered her, shadowed by the pale limestone of the Gothic structure overhead.

"I've done naught to draw your ire— we've never met." Jason squinted at the man in the shadows. Gothard and his brother were pale, with the type of skin that burned and peeled with any exposure to the sun—and it looked as though they'd seen much exposure of late. "Stand down and consign yourself to my arrest."

The man's blue eyes went stony with resentment. Jason blinked. He seemed to know those eyes. Maybe they *had* crossed paths.

"To the devil with you, Cainewood."

Jason squared his shoulders, reminding himself why he was here. For justice. Honor. The questions could wait—for now. He slowly counted to ten, focusing on the fat needle of a spire that topped the old Norman cathedral across the green. As responsibility weighed heavily on his mind, his hand tightened on the hilt of his sword.

Father would have expected this of him. To defend what was his, stand up for what was right—no matter the personal cost.

Deliberately he drew the rapier from its scabbard.

"Damn you to bloody hell." Gothard pulled his own sword with a quick *screak* that snapped the expectant silence. "We will settle this here and now."

Jason advanced a step closer, slowly circled the tip of his rapier, then sliced it hissing through the air in a swift move that brought a collective gasp from the crowd. The blade's thin shadow flickered across the paving stones. His free hand trembled at his side.

With a roar, Gothard lunged, and the first clash of steel on steel rang through the still summer air.

The vibrations shimmied up Jason's arm. Muscles tense, he twisted and parried, danced in to attack, then out of harm's way. His heart pounded; blood pumped furiously through his veins. Like most noblemen, he'd been taught well and spent countless hours in swordplay, but this was no game. And his opponent was trained as well.

Gothard was fleet, but Jason was faster. They scrambled down the steps, and the crowd scurried back. Gothard was cornered, but Jason was incensed. He edged Gothard back beneath the dome, skirting the circular stone bench that sat in its center as they battled their way to the other side of the octagonal structure. Gothard took sudden advantage, and Jason found himself retreating as their blades tangled, slid, and broke free with a metallic twang.

His arm ached to the very bone. Perspiration dripped slick from his forehead, stinging his eyes. But the other man's breath came ragged and labored.

All at once, a vicious swipe of Jason's sword sent Gothard's clanging to the stones, skittering down to the cobbled street, far from his reach.

Jason's teeth bit into his own lower lip. "I came not to kill today, Gothard, but merely to see justice done." He sucked in air, smelled the other man's desperation. "Are you ready to come peacefully?"

Sweat beading on his sunburned brow, Gothard stepped back until his calves hit the round stone bench. Frantically he scanned the mass of people still pouring from the surrounding establishments. Three more men stumbled out of a taproom and crossed the dusty street to the dome, the bright rainbow colors of their clothing marking them aristocrats.

They wove through the crowd. "Come along, Leslie!" one of them yelled as they pushed their way to the front.

Gothard's eyes narrowed. In a flash of movement, one of his arms snaked toward the newcomers, the other down to the wide cuff of his boot, where the curved handle of a pistol peeked out.

Jason's jaw tensed; his knees locked. Time seemed to

slow. His surroundings seemed impressed on his senses: the heated babble and musky scent of the excited onlookers, the cool dimness in the shaded dome, the bright green grass and streaky sunlight beyond. As Gothard stretched from his crouch, Jason rushed headlong, his sword arm rigid. Simultaneously, Gothard jerked the newcomer in front of him as a screen.

Jason tried to check his momentum, but his blade forged ahead, piercing satin and flesh with an ease that came as a shock to a man unused to killing. As long as he lived, he would never forget the astonished look in the man's hazel eyes.

The sword pulled free with a gruesome sucking sound that brought bile into Jason's throat. The man collapsed, his eyes going dull as his bright blood spurted in a grotesque fountain that soaked Jason's shirt and choked his nostrils with a salty, metallic stench.

Stunned, he watched the blood pump hard then slow to a trickle—a spreading red puddle seeping into the cracks between the stones. The dead man's face drained of color, to match the pristine white lace at his throat. Geoffrey Gothard raised his arm, cocked his flintlock, and pulled the trigger.

The explosion rocked the Market Cross, momentarily startling everyone into silence. "I'll see you at the gates of hell," Gothard muttered into the void. He turned and pushed through the crowd, signaling his younger brother to follow.

Ford Chase rushed forward when his own brother, the thirty-two-year-old Marquess of Cainewood, clutched his chest and crumpled to the ground.

Surely he was in hell.

Crackling sounds slowly filtered through his consciousness. A grunt. A dull thud.

His eyes slit open, and his head split in two. Or it felt like it. Hell.

Wincing at the brightness, he forced his eyes open wider. Shiny dark red curls swam through his vision as his sister Kendra moved to toss a log onto the already blazing fire. Another thud, and waves of heat washed over him. Hell. It was hot as hell in here.

He blinked once, then again. "Where—where am I?" he stammered out.

Kendra whirled. "At Cainewood, Jason. Home." She rushed to his bedside, swabbed his brow with a warm, damp cloth. Her familiar lavender scent wafted around him, and her light green eyes were filled with concern. Kendra, his sweet, exasperating sister Kendra, so full of life—but her expression worried him. And the heat.

"Damn, I'm hot." He pushed at the covers—two thick quilts and a velvet counterpane—and tried to sit up. Pain knifed through his body. He fell back, touching his shoulder and chest gingerly. Thick bandaging. "What happened?"

A quick frown marred her wholesome features, then was gone. "Do you not remember? You were shot."

It all came screaming back: the limestone Market Cross, the weight of the rapier in his hand, the shock as it sank into flesh. Gothard, that whoreson, pulling a man from the crowd to use as a shield. "Holy Christ," Jason whispered.

He'd killed an innocent man.

"You're going to be fine," Kendra rushed to reassure him. " 'Twas naught but a shoulder wound, and the ball came clean. The surgeon said you'll be fine."

No, he would not. He would never be fine again. Jason shut his eyes and turned his head to hide the hot, unmanly tears that threatened. He was always so levelheaded; whatever had possessed him to take the law into his own hands?

Rage, that's what. Black, unreasoning rage. The sight of Clarice Bradford's ghost-white face and her motionless, bruised young daughter. Just remembering made his blood seethe anew.

"Mary?" he croaked.

"She still lives. But she's no better." Kendra smoothed her lemon-yellow skirts, a cheery color that seemed to clash with the sadness that clouded her expression. She put a hand to his forehead. "You don't feel hot. You're not feverish." She swiped at her own damp brow. "How are you feeling?"

"Like hell. 'Tis hot as hell in here."

"The surgeon said to keep you warm."

"Surely you took him too literally."

She bit her lip in a rare show of uncertainty. "I'll go get Ford." Giving his hand a quick squeeze, she sighed, then hurried from the room to fetch her twin.

Jason lay still, staring at the familiar stone walls of his ancestral home. Colorful tapestries lent the cavernous chamber an intimate feel and kept the drafts to a minimum. Cainewood Castle had always made him feel safe, peaceful. But not today.

Pangs of guilt overcame him in waves, only to be replaced by anger over Geoffrey Gothard's actions. 'Twas no longer only about Jason's villagers; now the coward had used a blameless man as a shield. A man who would live today if Jason had just waited for the authorities. But damn it, he'd not gone there to kill Gothard, let alone an innocent bystander. He'd intended to see Gothard detained, brought to justice . . . The pain in his head intensified.

He knew also that Gothard would have been long gone had he not acted immediately when he heard word of the man's whereabouts. Law enforcement in these parts was sorely lacking.

He raised a hand to his aching head. Why the devil did Gothard think him his enemy?

Ford sauntered in at Kendra's heels, flashing a hopeful smile. "How do you feel?"

"Like hell," Jason and Kendra said together. Wincing, Jason pushed the long black hair from his eyes.

" 'Tis the laudanum." Ford stated the facts like the analyst he was. "The surgeon gave you enough to fell a middling-size horse. Said you would need it to make the trip home, but that it may well give you a headache."

"He may well have been right." Jason closed his eyes, sucked in a steadying breath, opened them again. The candlelight seemed brighter than usual. Too bright. He blinked up at the cobalt blue canopy overhead. "What day is it?"

"Friday. Evening." Ford cleared his throat and leaned against one carved, twisted bedpost. "You were out over twenty-four hours. Damn, 'tis hot in here."

Kendra glared at her twin. "I'll open a window."

"The door as well. And for God's sake, bank that fire." Ford turned to Jason, sharing a smile at their sister's overzealousness. Then his smile drifted away. "I believe Gothard thinks you are dead. You were covered in blood—"

"That of the man I killed." Jason's chest constricted painfully. "Who was he?"

Ford blinked. "I know not. I rushed to care for you, and when I looked up, he was gone."

"He was with two men. They must have taken him. We'll have to make inquiries—"

"In due time." One hand on her hip, Kendra frantically fanned the door open and closed. "Cooler now?"

Her face was flushed to match her dark red hair. Jason smiled, though even that movement hurt his head. "Sit down, Kendra."

The bed ropes creaked as she sat carefully on the mattress beside him. "I rode into the village this morning." One of her fingers traced idle circles on the blue velvet counterpane. "I talked to Clarice."

"She's talking?" He struggled up on his elbows, ignoring the pain in his shoulder, the throbbing in his head.

After the incident, Clarice had uttered nothing but Gothard's name. He had to go to her, see if he could do anything for her daughter, get the answers to his questions—

"Take it easy," Ford warned.

Ignoring his brother's protest, Jason tried to swing his legs off the bed, then stopped with a defeated groan. "I'm not going anywhere," he muttered, his head dropping back to the pillow. "What have you learned?" He looked to Kendra. "How did Clarice know Gothard?"

"She'd seen him around the village."

"He made no attempt to hide his identity." Frowning, Jason steepled his fingers atop the counterpane. "The brothers registered at the inn. They talked to people; I was able to get descriptions for the broadsides and the sketch from Martinson." The blacksmith was known for his clever characterizations.

Ford paced the carpeted floor. " 'Tis clear they did not come here intending to do this."

Kendra nodded. "Clarice said that when all was said and done, they were both furious with the other. And frightened at the consequences. That's why they ran before finishing the . . ."

"Rape," Jason ground out. "You can say it, Kendra. Thank God at least Clarice was spared that." She'd been badly hurt, though, and his hands clenched as he vowed no one would ever hurt another woman like that while she was under his protection. "But why did they do it?"

Kendra's gaze dropped to her folded hands. "Clarice said he told her . . ."

"If he'd not have your castle, then at least he'd have your woman," Ford finished for her.

His woman. Jason's head felt blank, until suddenly it dawned on him. "My mistress?" he said incredulously. "He thought Clarice was my mistress? A villager?"

"She's pretty enough." Ford shrugged. "He saw you

hugging Mary and handing her to Clarice. He believed she was your daughter."

"My daughter?" Marriage and family were so far off in Jason's plans, his mind boggled at the mere thought. "How . . . how did Mary come to be hurt so badly?"

"She wouldn't stay quiet." Kendra's eyes turned misty. "Geoffrey threw her against the wall to shut her up. Forever, it seems. The doctor says she will never wake."

"Holy Christ." He could picture her, the sweet girl he'd come to know, limp and motionless, slipping into death.

And somehow, he was responsible.

Chapter Two

"**M**arried? I dinna want to get married!"
The last strains of the funeral bagpipes were still echoing in Caithren Leslie's ears when she found herself facing the family lawyer across her father's desk. "Have I misheard ye?"

Lachlan MacLeod sighed and ran a hand through his grizzled hair. "There is nothing wrong with your hearing, Miss Caithren. All of Leslie is Adam's that is, unless you see fit to wed within the year. Then the larger portion that came through your mother will revert to you and your husband. In which case you will provide for your brother, of course. The minor lands that are entailed with the title are not sufficient to support a man."

"At least not in the style to which Adam is accustomed," her cousin Cameron put in dryly.

"God forbid my brother should put Leslie before pursuing his own pleasure," Cait said, pensively twirling one of her dark blonde braids. " 'Tis been five years since he's been home for more than a visit." She closed her eyes momentarily, then focused on the lawyer. "This cannot be."

"It can be, Miss Caithren, I assure you." MacLeod's arthritic hands stacked the papers on the desk. "While 'tis rare for a daughter to hold title, 'tis not unprecedented. 'Twill stand against a challenge."

"Nay, 'twas not what I meant." Caithren stared at her father's desktop. It had always been littered with papers, reflecting the goings-ons at busy Leslie. Now it was neat. Too neat. Her heart ached at the sight. "Da told me that if Adam didn't mend his ways, one day Leslie would be mine. That part is not surprising." She looked toward Cameron for strength, feeling a bit better when their hazel eyes met. He'd always been there to lean on. " 'Tis the marriage requirement I cannot ken."

Taking her by the shoulders, Cam gently pushed her across the flagstone floor and into a brown leather chair. He perched himself on the arm and looked toward the lawyer expectantly. "Mayhap if ye read that wee portion of the will again. I . . . I dinna think Cait quite heard it."

MacLeod shuffled pages, then cleared his throat. " 'I am sorely sorry for this requirement, daughter, but it is my hope that you will grow to understand my position. As you're twenty-one already—' " The lawyer paused and tugged at one pendulous earlobe. "He wrote this last year, you understand, before he—"

"Aye, while I was naught but a bairn." Caithren crossed her arms and legs. Beneath her unadorned black skirts, the leg on top swung wildly up and down as she talked. "Now, having attained the advanced age of twenty-two, I imagine I'm a confirmed spinster—"

" 'As you're twenty-one already,' " MacLeod rushed to continue, " 'I find myself concerned for your future. In addition, I promised dear Maisie on her deathbed that I would see you safely wed. Since you're hearing these words, it is apparent I lived not long enough to do so. Caithren, my love, you cannot but admit to a certain streak of stubbornness and independence, and bearing such, have left me no other avenue to make certain your dear mother's wishes are granted. I know you will do right by your mother, myself, and your own life, rather than see Leslie fall into your brother's incompetent hands. Please forgive me my duplicity and know 'tis for your own good.' "

Silence enveloped the small study, the pitter-patter of the rain unnaturally loud against the window. Caithren stared up at the timber-beamed ceiling.

Cameron's hand brushed her arm. " 'Tis sorry I am for ye, sweet. This is a hard day for ye, I know."

"Da suffered. 'Tis a blessing he is gone. Did everyone not tell me that today?" But despite having decided she was done crying, her throat seemed to close painfully, and something in her eyes was blurring her vision.

She blinked hard. "I have no intention of marrying."

Cameron rose to stand before her. He wiped his palms against the dark blue and green Leslie kilt he had dressed in for the funeral. "Never?" His eyes skeptical, he ran a hand back through his straight, wheaten hair.

"Ever," Cait assured him. She tightened her arms around her laced bodice, hugging herself.

"But—but so many have courted ye," Cam sputtered. "Surely there must be one man . . ." He blinked, then focused. "Duncan. Mayhap ye would consider Duncan? He has land of his own, and the village maidens are forever titterin' over his good looks—"

"He's a fool." When Caithren stood, Cam stepped back in self-defense. "He'd be no better for Leslie than Adam. And he'd never let me have a hand in running things, or ye, for that matter."

Cameron blinked. "James, then. James is no fool."

"Aye, you've the right of it there. But James is not one for the land. He has his nose in a book all the day. He'd be no better than Adam, either."

Cam walked to the window and gazed out at the pouring rain. "Surely there must be someone." His voice bounced muffled off the uneven glass. "What sort of life would ye live, then? Your folks were so happy . . . d'ye not want as much for yourself?"

She joined him there, watched familiar gray clouds

glide slowly over the green rolling hills where her family had lived for generations. Beyond a stone wall, the ponies that she and Cameron were breeding fed in a nearby field, swishing their long tails. Tenant farmers worked in the distance—people she knew as well as her own family.

She'd lived her entire life in this fortified house that looked like a wee, turreted castle. Da had built it for her mother—he'd always treated Mam like a queen. *Love overcomes the reasons o' mind,* Mam used to murmur when she walked up the path to her home; *the heart always rules the head.* But she'd said it with a laugh and a blush of pleasure. Aye, Mam had been loved.

But she'd still been the property of a man.

"For all Da loved her, Mam had nothing to call her own. I want to be independent, free to run Leslie—with ye, the way we've been doing it since Da fell ill. Together. Any husband of mine would inherit my property upon marriage, and no man would allow ye an equal partnership." One of her fingers traced the crooked line of a raindrop as it trailed down the pane. "We would never realize our grand plans. Even my own dear father plotted to manipulate me from the grave. All men are the same."

"Not all men, Cait." When she turned to him, Cam's eyes held a challenge.

"Mayhap not all," she conceded. "Not ye." Turning back to the window, she traced another raindrop . . . two . . . three.

Then hope leapt in her breast as it occurred to her. "Ye!" She whirled to face him. "I shall marry ye. Leslie should be yours in any case—how many times have I said it?"

Cameron stared, incredulous. "Me? Are ye daft? We're kin."

"First cousins. The kirk would never allow it." Mac-

Leod's voice came stern across the room. Caithren had forgotten all about him.

Cam was still sputtering beside her. "Besides, I . . . I love ye, but not that way. More like a sister."

"I kent as much." She paused for a breath. "And my love for ye is much the same. I never expected to wed at all, much less for romantic love." She felt a lump rise in her throat as her excitement gave way to defeat. " 'Tis hopeless."

Her fingers went absently to play with her laces, and she wandered back to MacLeod, tears swimming in her eyes. "Is there no other way? Must I wed or see it all go to Adam?"

"Well . . ." The family lawyer met her gaze, then looked away.

"Aye? What are ye thinking?" Slapping her palms onto the desk, she leaned toward him. "You've an idea, d'ye not?"

MacLeod glanced heavenward. "May your father forgive me for circumventing his plans." He took a deep breath and straightened his fine wool doublet. "If you could convince your brother to sign over his rights—"

Caithren's heart galloped in her chest. " 'Twould work? Such a paper would be legally binding?"

"I cannot see why not. 'Twould not be signed under duress . . . who would there be to challenge? I assume, in exchange for a fair allowance for his keeping, that Adam would jump at the chance to relinquish his responsibilities. If I know your brother at all—"

"Aye, ye do," Cameron said in wry confirmation. He walked over to Cait. "Though he would still have the title. Sir Adam Leslie, Baronet. Not that he deserves it."

"I care not about that." Caithren turned around to think. "Then I must go to Adam." She spun back to her cousin. "My letters never seem to reach him, and he may be off to India soon."

"India?" Cameron frowned. "Do you know where he is now?"

"A letter came just yesterday." She hurried to the desk and pulled out a sheet of parchment. "He mailed it the first of August, from Chichester." She scanned the single page. "He said he was in the company of two friends on their way to West Riding near Pontefract, where Lord Scarborough had invited them hunting. Then to London for Lord Darnley's wedding on the thirtieth. And he hopes to make it home for Hogmanay, but there is talk of a voyage to India." She looked up. "He should still be at Scarborough's. Pontefract is about halfway to London, is it not? Not so far."

"I will go."

"Nay, Cam. I must ask this of Adam myself."

"Ye dinna trust me to ask him to sign a piece of paper?"

Caithren winced at the hurt look that crossed her cousin's face. " 'Twould not be the same request, coming from ye." Setting the letter aside, she put a hand on his arm. "I do love him, ye ken, but I also see him for what he is."

Cam's hand covered hers and squeezed. "Then I'll accompany ye, Cai—"

She pulled away. "Nay, 'tis here ye are needed. The harvest approaches." She held up a hand to stem his next protest. "Ye may see me to Edinburgh and put me on the public coach, but then 'tis back to Leslie where ye belong. I can deal with Adam." A wee tingle of fear was fluttering in her stomach, but she ignored it. "We can hire a chaperone in Edinburgh. Ye may choose her personally, if it will make ye feel better."

When Cam's shoulders slumped, she sensed her victory. He took her chin in one hand and tilted her face up. "There is no arguing with ye, is there, sweet Cait?"

"Nay, and there never was." She went up on her toes

to kiss him on the cheek. "I'm thinking 'tis about time ye learnt it, cousin."

He gave a wry shake of his head, followed by a speculative smile. "D'ye ken, I reckon ye may be right."

"Aye?"

"There may be no man willing to take ye to bride, ye stubborn lass."

"Be off with ye!" She swatted at him playfully. "Ye know what Mam used to say."

"I cannot wait to hear this one."

"Ha freens and ha life."

"Good friends make a full life," Cameron murmured.

She locked her gaze on his. All she had left to love were Cameron and Leslie. She would not lose either. "You're a fine friend, Cam. The best. Leslie will fare well in our hands."

Hurrying into the Edinburgh room she and Cameron had taken overnight, Caithren opened her satchel to add the ribbons she'd just bought.

"What took ye so long, lass?" Mrs. Dochart, the chaperone Cam had chosen, clucked her tongue. Her three chins wobbled, and one foot tapped against the bare, wood planked floor.

Cam grinned at her. "I'd wager ye five to one she got lost on her way back," he teased. "What happened, Cait? Did ye go to Whiteford House instead of White Horse Close?"

"Worse," she muttered. She tied two black ribbons on the ends of her braids, then lifted some clothes to slip the rest underneath, lest they get tangled. "I was wandering around Brown's Close. I remembered 'twas a color, but forgot which one." She fished out her money pouch and added the coins she'd received as change. "And I set down my hat, then couldn't find it."

Cam laughed, then clamped his lips when she sent him

a scathing look. "How is it that anyone as efficient as ye can be constantly misplacing her hat?"

"They're just hats, not all that important. I usually have much more pressing matters to worry about. The Widow MacKenzie's health, or the proper time to shear the sheep."

"We'll have to advance our schedule by half an hour from here out." Mrs. Dochart brushed at the mustard-colored cloth that laced over her pillowish bosom. "One cannot be late when the public coach is running." Her beady black eyes honed in on Caithren's open satchel. "What have we here, lass? Men's clothing?"

Cameron nudged aside Cait's hands as she went to shut the bag. He pulled out a couple of garments. "Breeches? A shirt?"

"I may ride a horse at Scarborough's. Adam went there for hunting, ye ken." She pushed him away and stuffed the clothes back inside. "I'm unused to riding in skirts."

The chaperone pursed her lips. "You're off to England, lass. Not the wilds of Scotland." She bundled up in an ugly mud-colored cloak that reached to the floor, covering her uglier calico skirt. Caithren thought she looked like a lumpy brown mountain. "Women in England ride sidesaddle, garbed in riding habits."

"Mrs. Dochart's right, sweet. You'll not be on your own land where ye may act as ye choose and none will say nay. Those Sassenachs are *civilized*." He pronounced the word with more than a modicum of distaste. "I will tote the breeches back home for ye." He snatched his woolen plaid off a hook on the plastered wall, wrapped himself in it, and jammed his hat on his head.

"I want to bring them." Cait took tiny framed paintings of Da and Adam off the table and snuggled them on top of the clothing. She shrugged as she fastened the closure. "Whether I wear them or not remains to be seen."

While she donned her own tartan wrap, Cam hefted the satchel. "You're the one has to carry it. Bring what ye wish." He handed it to her, failing to hide his amusement when she strained under the weight.

Squaring her shoulders, Caithren followed Mrs. Dochart from the room and down two of the five narrow flights of stairs before Cameron caught up and took the satchel from her. "I'll miss ye, Cait."

She managed a brave smile. No matter what she'd said last week in Da's study, 'twas a scary thing to be going to England alone. "I'll miss ye, too. But I'll not be staying in Pontefract long, not with Adam off to London for that wedding. I cannot believe I had to wait a whole day just to leave here."

Cameron laughed. "My impatient Cait. The coach only runs once a fortnight." He pushed open the inn's door. "Ye were lucky, sweet."

Caithren touched the emerald amulet she wore on a chain about her neck—her good-luck charm. She sighed as she stepped into the gray Edinburgh day. A persistent drizzle kept the cobblestones wet and shining. Canongate teemed with coaches, horses, and humanity, and Holyroodhouse loomed in the background, tall and imposing. 'Twas as different from peaceful Leslie as Caithren could possibly imagine.

She drew her blue and green plaid tighter around her shoulders. "I can only hope there are no more delays, or I'll miss Adam for certain. Then I'll have to go all the way to London." She paused for a breath. "Michty me, I'd prefer not to even consider that possibility."

"Me neither." Cam chuckled as he handed her satchel to an outrider and watched him heave it onto the coach's roof. "I cannot imagine ye making it all that way without getting lost."

Mrs. Dochart paused on the coach steps. "Worry not on that account, lad. I'm goin' all the way to London, and if need be I'll make it my business to see she gets there on time and in one piece. 'Tis what ye hired me for, after all."

Cait watched the woman's ample rear disappear into the coach. "God alone knows how I'll survive the eight days to Pontefract with that old bawface, let alone nine more to London if need be. Already I cannot abide her, and I only met her this morning."

"She's exactly what ye need, sweet cousin. I hired well." Cameron carefully counted eight pounds to pay the two women's fares. "I can only pray Adam will do as well finding a chaperone for ye on the other end." He glanced at the slate sky, then drew off his hat and settled it over her braids. "Here, I dinna want to see ye go hatless."

She looked up at the plain brown rim, then grinned. "D'ye think I look bonnie?"

"Oh, aye." His eyes lit with humor. "A man's hat suits ye." His expression sobered as he rooted under his plaid and pressed a pistol into her hands. "And I want ye to take this as well."

"Da's gun?" It felt heavy and vaguely menacing, the dull metal pitted, the wooden grip worn smooth from years of use. "But why?"

"I dinna trust the English. Short of accompanying ye myself, I'd at least send ye with some protection."

"But I know not how to use it."

He handed her a heavy little pouch and a flask of gunpowder. "Pour a wee smidge of powder into the muzzle, then wrap a cloth patch around a ball, ram it—"

"Nay, 'twas not what I meant. I've seen Da load this pistol hundreds of times. But I've never shot at anything, Cam."

"Damn, I wish I'd kent that. I would've practiced with ye." He took back the pouch and flask, hesitated, then reached beneath her plaid and stuffed them into her skirt's deep pocket. "Take it anyway. You're a bright lass, Cait. If need be, you'll figure out how to use it."

Slowly she slid the pistol into her other pocket. The weight of it did make her feel somewhat safer. And she'd seen Da shoot it often enough; she reckoned she could do it if she had to.

"Take care, Cait." Cameron leaned to kiss her cheek.

She blinked back the tears that threatened, lest her cousin see them. Thankfully he couldn't see her heart racing in her chest, or tell that her stomach rebelled at the mere thought of traveling so far with naught but a stranger for company. She forced a smile. "I'd better go afore the old bawface starts in yelling at me."

With a laugh, Cam helped her up the coach steps.

"Damn, it will take three days to cover Cainewood in this bloody creeping carriage. Pass me that journal, will you?"

"Clever change of subject." Kendra handed over the leather book and one of the pencils made from the graphite mined on the property. She hitched herself forward, frowning at Jason seated across from her in the carriage. "You're not well enough to go. 'Tis been barely more than two weeks."

"I'm not waiting much longer." He flipped open the estate journal and made a note to have the Johnsons' roof rethatched. "The reward I posted is not bringing in Gothard. I've killed an innocent man, thanks to him."

"Thanks to Gothard? 'Tis yourself you're blaming." As usual, Kendra was too observant for his comfort. "Someone else is hurt, and naturally, 'tis all your fault."

Ignoring her sarcasm, he scribbled reminders to buy another bull and see that Mistress Randall's spinning wheel was repaired. "Not hurt, Kendra—killed. And poor Mary fares no better. 'Tis a wonder she still breathes." The attack on Clarice and Mary might not have been premeditated, but the episode at the Market Cross proved the brothers were cornered. Dangerous. He rolled the pencil between his hands. "I'd have left

already if only I had some clue as to the Gothards'
whereabouts. They seem to have disappeared."

"They'll resurface. And the reward you've posted will
ensure you'll hear of it."

"When?" He banged the journal closed and slammed
it onto the seat. "When will I find the whoreson who
made me kill an innocent man? How many others will
die before his capture?" His fists bunched between his
spread knees. "And who died at my hands? The least I
can do is send condolences to his family, make some
reparations. Where the hell is Ford?"

Kendra stared at him. "He's working on it," she said
carefully.

Her pale green eyes looked so troubled. He con-
sciously relaxed his jaw and, with a sigh, reached to put
a hand on her shoulder. "I'm sorry. I know not what's
come over me." He glanced out the window at the green
fields of Cainewood, struggling for the calm that usually
came to him so easily. "I feel so damned powerless."

Kendra's gaze followed his and caught what he'd
missed in his blind fury. "Look, he's back." She leaned
to watch her twin gallop up the lane.

Jason knocked on the roof to stop the carriage, then
threw open the door. "News from Chichester?" he
asked. "Do we know who I killed?"

"No." Breathless, Ford shook his head. "Whoever he
was, his friends bore him away without so much as re-
porting his identity. That's not what I rode out to tell
you, though." He swept off his hat, dragged a hand
through his wavy brown hair. "There's a man waiting at
home to see you. From the stables. Two of your horses
have been stolen."

A hard ball of anxiety hit Jason in the stomach.
"Not Chiron?"

"No. Pegasus and Thunder."

"Thank God for small favors."

Although he was relieved his favorite mount had been

spared, he still cursed the slow carriage a hundred times before it finally rolled over the drawbridge and through the barbican into Cainewood's grassy quadrangle. A man waited on the wide steps that led to the castle doors, cap in hand and a crude blood-stained bandage tied around his head.

With an agility that wrenched his shoulder and made him wince, Jason leapt from the carriage and made for the double oak doors. He gestured the stableman into the entry. "Porter, come in, will you?"

The man frowned and touched his fingertips to his forehead.

"Come in," Jason repeated. " 'Tis no longer bleeding. These floors have seen their share of blood through the centuries, in any case."

With obvious reluctance the man climbed the steps after Kendra and Ford. He drifted inside, staring up at the slim pillars that supported the Stone Hall's vaulted ceiling, and seated himself gingerly—not in one of the carved walnut chairs that Jason indicated, but on one of the iron treasure chests instead, no doubt figuring 'twould be easier to clean.

Impatiently Jason followed Porter's awed gaze as it swept the entry, taking in the intricate stone staircase, crowned at intervals with impressive heraldic beasts. "Who?" he asked. "Who has stolen my horses?"

The man dragged his gaze back to Jason's. "Those men, my lord. The brothers. The ones on the broadsides."

"In stark daylight?" Jason's jaw dropped open in astonishment. "Right from under our noses?"

"They knocked me out." Slowly Porter shook his injured head. "I'm sorry, my lord. I didn't hear much, and I couldn't seem to move."

"What *did* you hear?" Jason crouched at the man's feet and peered into his apprehensive eyes. "Anything. Anything you can remember, I want to hear it."

The groom fiddled with the cap in his hands. "The one was saying he didn't want to take the horses." He set the cap in his lap. "I couldn't hear what the other said."

Reeling with confusion and frustration, Jason touched the stableman on the knee. "Anything else?"

"They did mention another man's name. They were headed to Lord Scar—" He stopped and squeezed his eyes shut for a moment. "I cannot remember," he said at last. "Lord Scar-something. He said his brother was entitled to whatever this other lord has. And they were going to take the horses and go to get it."

"Gothard." Jason stood and cursed under his breath. "Cuthbert Gothard, the Earl of Scarborough. Why did I not think of that connection?"

" 'Tis a common name," Ford said. "You had no reason to think the Gothard brothers were connected to Lord Scarborough."

But he should have. 'Twas his job to eliminate any threat to his village. "I could have sent a letter of inquiry to Scarborough, asking if they were relations and what he knew of their whereabouts." He paced the three-story chamber, his footsteps echoing off the vaulted stone ceiling. "Now it is too late—the brothers are on their way already." He paused midstep. "If I hurry, I can reach Scarborough before they do and give him fair warning. Then lie in wait."

"Lie is right." Kendra slanted him a look of utter disbelief. "You'll end up lying in the road somewhere. You'll never catch them if you're riding in a coach, with them on the backs of your fine horses. And you cannot ride Chiron such a distance in your condition."

Had his father not told him to stand up for what he believed in? Even without his personal responsibilities, common decency would demand he warn the earl.

"I can ride Chiron, and I will." He turned to Porter. "I thank you for a job well done. They'll doctor you in the kitchen. Tell Ollerton I said you may have the day off."

"Thank you, my lord." Porter stood and bowed, but Jason's attention was already elsewhere.

"Ford, ask Claxton to bring a portmanteau to my chamber. I'm off for West Riding."

"No, you're not!" Kendra ran after him up the wide stairway, turned the corner, and jumped ahead of him as he entered his chamber. "You were shot two weeks ago, for God's sake!"

Shouldering her out of the way, Jason strode to his chest of clothes to choose a few of his plainest shirts. " 'Tis not serious; the surgeon said so himself. The first days found me groggy from the laudanum, and I've let you coddle and care for me since. But now the bastards have stolen my horses, and I've a lead where they're headed. Nothing you say will keep me here. Lives may be at stake, and apparently, for reasons I cannot fathom, I am involved."

Ford came in with Claxton, who had brought the portmanteau and moved to pack it. "This is no ordinary trip," Jason told him. "I'd best choose my wardrobe myself."

His manservant blinked. "Then I shall go ready myself for a journey."

Jason shook his head. "I go with no valet, but alone, dressed as a commoner. If Gothard thinks I'm dead, it makes no sense to call attention to myself."

"Alone, Jason?" Kendra railed as Claxton left the chamber. "Who will care for you?"

He walked to the bed, opened one of the two leather bags, and tossed in the shirts. "The shoulder doesn't pain me much," he said, stretching the truth, "and there's no sign of infection." That at least was fact. And if his siblings were looking at him like he'd gone around the bend, so be it. He would do what was expected of him. What he expected of himself.

Kendra pulled the shirts back out and folded them neatly. "You should have let Claxton pack."

"I may be surrounded by servants, but I am capable of caring for myself." Bending over his chest, he selected two fine lawn shirts and a snowy cravat, depositing them into his sister's outstretched hands. He threw open his tall, carved clothes press and took a dark blue velvet suit from a hook. Three pairs of his plainest breeches and a couple more workaday shirts found their way into his bag. The boots on his feet would do.

"Geoffrey Gothard must be stopped." Jason paused in his packing to gaze out the diamond-paned window. In the sunshine beyond lay his land, his people. "I cannot face my own villagers until it is done."

"You sent broadsides near and far," Kendra argued. " 'Tis common knowledge Gothard is a wanted outlaw. For the hundred pounds you've offered—"

"—that MacCallum woman will see it is done," Ford finished for her.

"Emerald MacCallum? That fabled Scot who wears men's clothing and carries a pistol?" Jason blinked and dragged his gaze from his land, back to the dim room. "Tell me not that you've fallen for that claptrap. A woman tracking outlaws for the reward, why you'd have to be maggot-brained to believe such fancies—"

"Then someone else will see it done." Kendra crossed her arms.

Jason could feel his face heating. Part of him agreed with her, but the expectations he'd been raised with overrode her cool logic. "I cannot wait for *someone* to see it done. Since King Charles abolished Cromwell's Major General districts, there is no central authority of any kind." His sturdiest stockings joined the pile of clothing. "For God's sake, did you not see it with what happened in Chichester? A man was killed, and no one even knows who he was."

"Charles was right to abolish the districts," his brother

protested. "Their main activity was to tax us Royalists."
Ford raised a finger to make another point, then shook
his head as if realizing this was not the time for their
old argument. "Jason, think about what you're doing."

"I've thought of little else. England has never seen
such lawlessness." Jason paced the red and blue carpet,
snatching up an ivory comb and his shaving kit as he
moved past his dressing table. "There is no provision for
passing vital information from one county to another.
Depending on a reward offer—someone's greed—in
order to see this man put away . . . no, I cannot do so."
He dropped to sit on the bed, fought to marshal his
temper. "I killed an innocent man. I will never be able
to live with myself until Gothard is behind bars, never
to murder again. And I'll hear from him just what he
thinks my part in this is."

Kendra came to stand before him. "I've checked the
church's birth records, and, contrary to popular belief,
your middle name is not 'Responsible.' " She smiled, a
gentle smile that tugged at his heart. "Gothard is gone
from this area—you can be sure of it. You're injured.
You've people here, people who need you. And family.
Jason—"

"That is it, Kendra." He couldn't let her sway him.
Rising from the bed, he grabbed a ball of hard-milled
soap from his washstand, threw it into the portmanteau,
flipped the bags closed, and secured the latches. "No
more arguments." He went to his sister and gave her a
hard hug, ignoring the jolt to his shoulder. "They've sin-
gled me out—how can I turn away? What kind of man
would that make me?"

Kendra opened her mouth, but Jason cut her off.
"You cannot stop me, Kendra sweetheart." He smoothed
her dark red curls. "Just wish me Godspeed."

"If you'll not wait to heal, then at least wait an hour
or two for Ford and myself to get ready." She held her-

self stiff and uncompromising. "You've never gone off without us before. I can care for your wound . . ."

"This is not a holiday, Kendra. You would slow me down."

He felt her take a deep breath, and then the fight drained out of her. When she pulled back and nodded up at him, he turned to Ford. "Find out who I killed, will you? Ask around again in Chichester. *Someone* must know the identity of his two acquaintances. Then locate them, follow up. Send word to Pontefract if you hear anything."

"Jason, 'twas not your fault."

"Do it," he ordered. He jammed his sword into his belt, tucked a small pistol into his boot top, lifted the portmanteau. "Watch over Cainewood for me. God willing, I'll not be long."

"And then we can lay this nightmare to rest?" Kendra asked.

He stared at her a long time whilst the chamber filled with an oppressive silence. Then, unable to make that promise, he kissed her cheek and strode from the room.

"Godspeed," she whispered after him.

Chapter Three

Her back to the other passengers straggling in and queuing to rent rooms, Caithren stared at the innkeeper in disbelief. "Are ye telling me there are no horses for hire in this town?"

He rubbed a hand over his bald head. "That is what I am telling you, madam."

Mrs. Dochart took Cait by the arm. "Come along, lass. Mayhap the situation will change on the morrow." With her other hand she set down her valise and dug inside for coins. "We'll take a room upstairs, Mr. Brown."

Caithren shook off the woman's hand and leaned farther over the innkeeper's desk. "Are there no hackney cabs, either?"

"No hackney cabs."

"But Pontefract is a stage stop!"

"We've extra horses here for the public coach, naturally. But they're not for hire."

Behind her, Caithren heard impatient feet shuffle on the gritty wood floor. "Hurry up, there," someone grumbled.

"Hold your tongue," Cait shot over her shoulder. "I've spent eight days shut up in a hot coach"—with a crotchety, meddling old woman, she added silently—"just to get here and visit my brother at the Scarborough estate in West Riding."

Rubbing his thin, reddish nose, the innkeeper slanted her a dubious look. "The *Earl* of Scarborough's estate?"

"Aye, the same."

He shrugged. "You can walk. 'Tis nice enough weather and naught but a mile or so." The man opened a drawer and pulled out a thick, leather-bound registration book. "Out there, then head east. The road will take you straight past the Scarborough place. You'll find it set back on the right side, perhaps a quarter mile from the road. A huge stone mansion—you cannot miss it." With a dismissive thump, he set the book on the desk and opened it to a page marked with a ribbon. "You may leave your satchel if you'd care to. Should Scarborough invite you to stay"—his tone betrayed what he thought were the chances of that happening—"I reckon he'll send a footman calling for it." After pausing to give Caithren one more considered look, he waved her aside and the next person forward.

"Come along, lass. We'll be losing the light soon." Mrs. Dochart set her own bag alongside Cait's behind the desk. "Unless ye'd prefer to wait for the morn?" she added hopefully.

Cait reached up a finger to twirl one of her braids. "Nay, I wish to go immediately." *Without* a chaperone. "But I'm . . . I mean to say . . . well, I expected we'd part company here. Not that I haven't enjoyed yours," she rushed to add, waiting for a lightning bolt to strike with that lie. She couldn't remember ever uttering a more blatant falsehood.

The old bawface looked dubious, but 'twas clear she'd no wish to tramp over the countryside. "Your cousin hired me to look after ye, lass, and—"

"Only so far as Pontefract. He was well aware I was getting off here, ye ken. My brother will hire a chaperone for the return trip."

Mrs. Dochart sniffed and patted her gray, coiffed head. "If you're certain, then—"

"I'm certain." For want of another way to end their association, Caithren executed a little curtsy. " 'Tis pleased I am to have met ye, Mrs. Dochart, and I thank ye for keeping me company." That lie might have topped the first one; she wasn't sure. Feeling a great burden had been lifted from her shoulders, she crossed the inn's taproom and headed out into the waning sunshine and down the road.

She'd not progressed ten feet when the woman's voice shrilled into the quiet street. "Ah, Caithren, lass!"

With a sigh, Cait composed her face and turned back to the inn. "Aye, Mrs. Dochart?" The bawface stood framed in the doorway. A cracked wooden sign swung in the light wind, creaking over her head. "I told ye I shall be fine."

"But the innkeeper said east. 'Tis west ye're walkin'."

"Oh!" Her cheeks heated. "Right."

"Nay, left."

"Right. I mean to say, aye. Left, east." She hurried past, murmuring "Thank ye" over her shoulder. Though she'd have sworn she heard the woman muttering under her breath, she was soon relieved to be out of earshot.

The evening was warm, and the slight breeze felt wonderful after the stuffy, confining coach. 'Twas passably pretty country, the land green and flatter than at home. She much preferred the harsh contours of Scotland—the beautiful glens, the blues and purples of the wooded mountains, the little lochs and streams and waterfalls everywhere. But after all, she didn't have to live here. She could enjoy the land for what beauty could be found.

Her heart sang to be free at last, on her way to meet Adam, perhaps rest a few days, depending on the returning public coach's schedule. In two weeks' time she'd be back at Leslie, signed papers in hand, giving Cameron the tongue-lashing he deserved for saddling her with that irritating old woman.

Glancing down, she spotted the distinctive red-green leaves of meadow rue poking from the edge of a ditch. With a gasp of delight, she knelt to pick some, wrinkling her nose at the strong, unpleasant scent. Bruised and applied, it was good to heal sores, and difficult to find near home. Pleased, she tucked it into her pocket and continued on her way.

She rubbed a hand across her forehead and tried not to think of how tired she was. Following what promised to be her first decent meal in weeks, tonight she'd luxuriate in a big tub of clean, steaming water. She couldn't wait to wash off the dust of the road. And she couldn't wait until tomorrow morn, when she'd be snug in a soft feather bed at Scarborough's, imagining the public coach rattling down the road toward London with that bawface tucked inside. The thought was so vivid and appealing, she almost missed the gravel drive that led to a yellowish stone mansion in the distance.

The sun was setting, and she tucked her plaid tighter around her black bodice and skirt. When Adam saw her dressed in mourning, he'd understand right off how completely he'd neglected his family and home. 'Twould be a simple matter to convince him to sign the papers Mac-Leod had drawn up.

In the fading light she hurried along the path, marveling at the way 'twas so raked and pristine. Scarborough must employ an army of servants.

But . . . they weren't here now. The mansion was shut up tight as a jar of Aunt Moira's preserves! The sun sank over the horizon as Caithren stared at the heavy, bolted oak door. She heard the call of a single hawk overhead, apparently the only living creature in the vicinity.

So much for her happy daydreams. Caithren stifled a sob. She would have to stay the night in Pontefract, steel herself to climb back on the coach in the morning, then somehow survive the nine days it would take to reach London.

She counted on her fingers. She should arrive on the day of Lord Darnley's wedding, just in time to present herself as an uninvited guest. 'Twas the only place she knew for certain she'd be able to find Adam. Touching her amulet, she prayed there'd be no summer storm or anything else to delay the coach, because God only kent where Adam would be headed the morning of August thirty-first.

A scuffling sound on the roof made her glance up. Probably some sort of wee animal. Or rats.

Cait shuddered. "Set a stout heart to a steep hillside," she said aloud, imagining her mother saying the words. She squared her shoulders and was turning back toward the road when there came the snort of a horse and an answering neigh.

Horses meant people. Her spirits lifted. Mayhap Adam and his friends were here after all, and they'd just been out hunting. Even were it strangers, mayhap they could spare her the long walk—

She heard a muted *thump* and the crunch of gravel, as someone apparently dropped from the roof. Then another *thump*.

"Sealed up. Cannot even get inside and take a few trinkets to pay our way. Damn it to bloody hell." Coming from around the side of the mansion, the man's voice was cultured. But he was cursing a string of oaths the likes of which she'd never heard. She scooted into the archway that housed the front door and pressed herself against the cold stone wall.

"I'm glad 'tis sealed up." The second man's voice was whiny and none the more pleasant. "I don't fancy taking things, Geoffrey."

"Everything here is ours, Wat. Or should be. You crackbrain."

The man called Wat didn't respond to the insult. "But Cainewood's horses? What about those?"

"These are rightly mine." The first man kicked at the ground, or at least Caithren thought he did. 'Twas difficult to tell from around the corner. "We had to take them. We were low on funds with no way to get here. Can you not get that through your thick skull? Did you want to walk? Sleep in the open and beg for our supper?"

"We could have found work."

"Work? When hens make holy water. Should we stoop to chopping wood for a living? Baking bread? Shoeing horses?"

"Geoff—"

"Enough!"

Caithren heard the crunch of gravel beneath someone's shuffling feet. "So. Lucas is gone. What now, Geoffrey?"

"He'll be at the London town house, I reckon." Cait heard the sound of pacing, then a prolonged silence, followed by a low whistle.

"What are you thinking?" Wat sounded wary. "I care not for the look in your eyes."

"We will go to London." There was a significant pause. "And we will get what belongs to us."

A chill shot through Caithren, though the night was still warm. Apparently Wat felt the same way. "You cannot mean to hurt him?"

"Whatever it takes. He's got it coming, and you're next in line. When you're the earl, we'll be sitting pretty."

"When I'm the earl?" Caithren could hear her heart pounding while Wat mulled that over. "Geoffrey," he said slowly, "you're not . . . you're not talking . . . murder?"

"Maybe I am."

They were planning to *murder* someone? Cait's breath seemed stuck in her chest.

"You would kill him?" Wat squeaked.

"I don't believe it will come to that. Besides, 'twould be his fault for kicking us out. Just as it's his fault we're in this trouble. And his money we'll be using to get out of it."

Wat had nothing to say to that. Or mayhap he was shocked speechless.

"With Cainewood's death on our hands, we've nothing to lose," Geoffrey growled. "Come along."

Cait began to tremble as she listened to the noises of men mounting horses. 'Twas not long before they rode around the corner of the mansion at a slow walk, heading straight past the front door where she hid. She scurried into a corner of the arched entry.

"I cannot do it." Even through Cait's fear, Wat's whine was grating on her. 'Twas a wonder the one called Geoffrey didn't put killing him next on his list of misdeeds.

Evidently Geoffrey chose not to listen, because he ignored the protest. "We've coin enough left to pay for one night at the inn. We'll let everyone see us."

"See us?"

"We'll leave for London come morning. People will remember us here, and if we ride like the dickens, no one will believe we could have gotten there in time. We'll not be suspected of hurting our dear brother."

"But Geoffrey . . ." Wat's voice was so drawn out and plaintive, Caithren almost felt sorry for him. As they rode before her and then past, she risked inching forward to get a look at them.

Two men, both rumpled and sunburned. They spoke like quality, and looked it, too—overly proud, even if their clothes could use a washing. But they were robbing, murdering scum. English scum. Cameron had been right about Englishmen.

Though the men's voices were fading as they moved down the drive, what she heard did nothing to calm Cait's heart rate. "Now let us find some women." The last of Geoffrey's words drifted back, faint but intelligible. "That new kitchen maid that was hired on before we left—she was a comely one, was she not? If she's not visiting her mama while Lucas is gone, she must be staying in Pontefract."

Women. The scum were in search of women. Caithren hugged the tops of her crossed arms in a futile attempt to stop herself from shaking.

England was as evil a place as she'd always heard. What was she doing here all alone? She should have let Mrs. Dochart accompany her out here to Scarborough's. Or Cameron—she should have let Cameron make the trip. In the name o' the wee man, this certainly had been an ill-conceived undertaking.

Though she couldn't hear another word the men said, she was still shaking when they disappeared from view, still shaking when she started the long, lonely walk back in the dark. Still shaking after she'd reclaimed her satchel, paid for a room at the inn and extra for a bath, and trudged upstairs to wash off the dust of a week's travel.

She slipped into her plain room, shut the door and leaned back against it, a palm pressed to her racing heart. She had to get herself in hand.

Nothing—leastwise a couple of scummy Englishmen— was going to stop her from finding her brother.

Jason slowly slid off Chiron, feeling stiff as a day-old corpse. It seemed the ache in his shoulder had extended to every bone in his body. He detached his portmanteau and set it on the stable's dirt floor, then stretched toward the rough-beamed ceiling, a delicious pull of his abused muscles.

"Will you be stayin' at the inn, sir?"

His arms dropped, and he looked down into the lined face of a gnarled old stableman. "Only to clean up. Then I'm headed to the Scarborough estate in West Riding. 'Tis nearby, no?"

"Aye, but no one is there." The little man's face split in the involuntary grin of someone imparting bad news. "Scarborough shut the house and made off for London. Two days past."

After six days of hard riding, would he be stopping here only to leave again? He could barely keep himself from groaning aloud. He forked some hay beneath Chiron's nose. Perhaps the man was misinformed. "How come you to know this?"

The smile turned self-satisfied. "Cousin Ethel's worked there thirty-odd years. She's staying hereabouts while the lord is gone—likes to stop by to pass the day." He puffed out his scrawny chest. "Servants, we know everything."

Jason rubbed his stubbled jaw. "Then old Cuthbert is gone?"

The stableman blinked. "Old Cuthbert is dead."

"Dead?" *Dead?* At the hands of his relatives, the Gothard brothers?

"A month past. He and Lady Scarborough—they died crossing the channel. Young Lucas is the new earl. 'Course he's not so young, exceptin' compared to me." He eyed Jason up and down. "About your age, I suspect." He bent to unbuckle Chiron's saddle. "Things over there be different now. Took 'im no more 'n a week to toss his brothers out on their ears, with naught but the clothes on their backs and some pocket change." With a little grunt, he lifted the saddle and hung it on a hook. "Deserved it, they did. Cousin Ethel tells stories . . . that Geoffrey tormented Lord Scarborough— the new one—from the day he was born. Geoffrey hated Lucas, he did, because Geoffrey was older but couldn't inherit."

Very interesting. The little man was a fountain of information, if only Jason could keep it flowing. "Why was
that?" He reached for a currycomb and ran it through
Chiron's glossy silver coat.

"Rumor has it he be Lady Scarborough's son from
another marriage, ye see." The stableman filled the
trough, and Chiron drank greedily. "That Geoffrey, he
had it in for Lord Scarborough—the new one—before
the lad was walkin'."

"And the younger son?" Jason probed. "Walter, is
it?"

"Wat? Dumber than a box of hair. Geoffrey led him
around by the nose since he teethed his first tooth. Two
against one it was, and Lord Scarborough—the new
one—just waitin' 'til the day came he could toss them
out. 'Course 'tis sad 'twas sooner rather than later."

"Does everyone in the village know all this?"

"All I know is what Cousin Ethel's told me." The
man looked up from where he was crouched, cleaning
Chiron's hooves. "But I know how to keep my own
mouth shut. You can lay odds on that."

"Be an interesting wager." Jason lips twitched beneath
his mustache. "Geoffrey and Walter, they're in the
area?"

"Nah." He dropped a hoof and moved around to lift
another. "Disappeared the day after the funeral, and
I've yet to set eyes on 'em since."

If anybody would know the brothers had returned, it
would be this man. Some of the stiffness left Jason's
shoulder as he relaxed. "I think they may have found
trouble," he said carefully. "Talk has it there's been a
reward posted for Geoffrey."

"That so?" The man's eyes lit up. "Well, then, I'm
hopin' he'll come back and that Emerald MacCallum
woman after 'im. A Scottish lass taking our own son,
born and bred. Now that'd be a sight to see, here in
little old Pontefract. We'd be talkin' about it for years."

"I imagine you would." If the rumors of Emerald MacCallum were any more than fanciful nonsense. Jason leaned to hand him the comb. "I reckon I'll be staying the night here, after all." Fetching his pouch from his coat pocket, he pressed a silver coin into the groom's age-spotted hand and patted the horse's flank. "Keep an eye on him for me, will you? His name's Chiron. Appreciate the chat."

He lifted the portmanteau and headed from the stables. Now he knew why the Gothards had it in for their brother . . . but what they had against *him* was beyond his comprehension.

Jings, but it felt good to be clean, Caithren thought, even if she'd had to fold her knees up to her chin in order to fit into the inn's small wooden tub. She tipped the wee bottle of oil she'd pressed from Leslie's flowers, pouring a few more precious drops into the bath. Scooping a palmful of the lukewarm scented water, she smoothed it over her shoulders. It smelled like Scotland. Like home.

When the water grew cold, she donned the clothes she had brought for riding: soft brown breeches and a coarse white shirt, castoffs outgrown by Da's stable lad. After plaiting her dark-blonde hair, she piled the braids on top of her head and jammed Cameron's hat on to cover them. There was no mirror in her room, but hopefully she looked enough like a boy that the men downstairs would leave her alone. She'd had her fill of Englishmen tonight already. Just her luck, the scum brothers would be staying at this inn. And in search of women.

She ducked out the door, paused, and went back in, then pawed through her satchel to find her father's pistol in the bottom. 'Twas an ugly thing of cold, mottled steel, made for naught but utility. It felt heavy in her hands—heavy and surprisingly reassuring. Bless Cameron for making her bring it; how had he known how alone and out of place she'd feel so far from home?

Remembering how Da had done so, she made sure the pistol was loaded, then half-cocked it and stuck it in the back of her breeches. She dug her plaid out of the satchel to cover it. Unlike the English cloaks, a plaid was neither masculine nor feminine; Cam's looked exactly the same as hers. With any luck she might pass. As an afterthought, she tucked both the miniature of Adam and his letter into her breeches pocket, then headed downstairs to the taproom, doing her best to swagger like a man.

The paneled room was lit by oil lamps burning cheerfully on each of the round wooden tables. Pewter spoons clinked on pewter plates, and the buzz of leisurely conversation filled her ears. Homey scents of meat pie, fresh-baked bread, and brewed ale hung in the air. Cait's stomach growled.

She made her way to the taproom's bar. "Mr. Brown?"

"Yes?" The innkeeper looked up from wiping the counter. His brow creased, as though he were wondering how she kent his name. So he didn't recognize her; her disguise must be working.

She felt better already. "I'm looking—" She cleared her throat and deepened her voice. "I'm looking for my brother, an Adam Leslie. He was staying with Scarborough this week past."

"Adam Leslie?" The man set down his fistful of rags and wiped his hands on the front of his breeches. "I do not recall a man by that name."

Caithren's heart sank. Adam was fond of frequenting public taprooms, so she was hoping the innkeeper would know where he had gone. Mayhap she would not need to travel all the way to London.

The man ran a hand across his bald head. "What does he look like?"

"Tall, fair, longish blond hair . . ." She dug in her pocket and brought out the portrait. "Here," she said, holding forth the wee oval painting. "I'm wondering if he told anyone where he was headed next—"

Brown took it and considered, frowning. "I'm sorry, but I recall no man named Adam Leslie, nor anyone who looks like this picture." He handed it back. "Is it a decent likeness?"

She nodded.

"I have a good head for people, sir, er . . . madam?"

"Aye." Caithren sighed. Her disguise wasn't working after all.

Mr. Brown piled some discarded trenchers on a tray and lifted it to his shoulder. "I'm sure I would have remembered your brother had I seen him."

Blast it, another lump was rising in her throat. She'd never been a crybaby, and she didn't intend to take up the practice now. She pulled the letter from her pocket and unfolded it, scanning the worn page. "He was traveling with two other gentlemen, Lords Grinstead and Balmforth. Might you have seen them?"

"I'm afraid their names are not familiar, either."

"Oh . . ." A burst of laughter in the background seemed to mock Caithren's distress. Her hunger had faded . . . although she could very much use a mug of ale.

"I'm sorry," he repeated.

" 'Tis no fault of yours." Slipping the letter and painting back into her pocket, she glanced about. She couldn't face the other travelers eating and socializing in this room—she'd spent the best part of a week with some of them already, with more forced togetherness promised to come.

And what if Mrs. Dochart came downstairs? The old bawface knew not that she was back yet—with a quick escape and any luck at all, she could spend one night alone in her peaceful, solitary room.

She turned back to the innkeeper. "Might ye have some supper sent up? Room three."

"Certainly, Miss . . . Leslie, is it not?"

"Aye. Thank ye."

"No trouble a'tall." With another appraising glance, he disappeared into the kitchen, and she turned to head upstairs.

"Thank you kindly." Jason pressed a coin into the serving maid's hand and settled back with his ale. Taking a swallow, he watched her sway from his shadowed corner into the lamplit center of the taproom. A nice sway she had, too, but he had neither the stamina nor inclination to pursue her right now. He rubbed his tired eyes. God knew he wasn't good for much more than people-watching this evening.

He downed a second gulp as a boy, tall for his age, turned dejectedly from the taproom's bar and made his way to the stairs. Jason smoothed his mustache, ran a thumb over his unshaven chin. The lad was overly pretty, way too thin, and young—not even shaving yet. Strange to find him in a taproom alone, but perhaps his folks were waiting upstairs. Jason hoped so—he knew what it was like to be young and alone, and he wouldn't wish it on anybody.

He massaged his sore shoulder and took another sip. 'Twas aggravating to find himself so worn out, weeks after the injury. But having pushed himself to the limits to beat the Gothard brothers here, he was relieved to find he had managed it. Obviously they weren't over-working his horses. When they arrived, tomorrow or the next day, they'd be in for a rude surprise. He'd get the answers to his questions, and this chapter in his life would be closed.

Or almost. No word had come from Ford as to whom he had killed.

He took another sip of his ale. At the same time the

boy started up the bare wooden steps, two men came down and met him halfway, on the staircase's tiny landing.

Geoffrey and Walter Gothard.

Jason bolted up, his heart beating a wild tattoo. The poor lad began visibly shaking the moment he set eyes on the brothers. When they blocked his way up, he tightened the blue and green shawl he had wrapped about his shoulders.

As Jason watched, the boy squared his slender frame. "I ken who ye are." The words were delivered loud and bravely in a distinct Scots accent, even if the lad's voice went high as a girl's with tension. "Ye will not get away with your wicked plans."

The wean sounded like he meant it. Halfway there to intervene—not to mention capture Geoffrey Gothard once and for all—Jason froze. Was the boy after Gothard as well? After all, there was that hundred-pound reward—an absolutely vast sum to someone like this lad.

The boy took a step back down the stairs, then suddenly reached beneath the plaid wool and pulled something out, brandishing it daringly.

The soft glow of metal spurred Jason into action. No matter how bone-tired he was, there was no way he could allow a lad to become Gothard's next victim. A wild bellow rose from his throat as he drew his rapier and reached the stairs in four running strides. No doubt drawn by the racket, Geoffrey's eyes met his and went wide with recognition. He turned and bolted up the steps.

Jason shouldered the boy aside. "Send for the authorities!" he yelled, reaching to snag Geoffrey by the arm and whip him back around. He dropped his sword; another death was not the way to end this. Instead, his fingers closed around Geoffrey's throat and squeezed as the sword slid clattering down the stairs. Walter tried to sidle past, but Jason shot out a foot and tripped the younger Gothard, who thumped down, whining loudly, to be held hostage with a well-placed boot pressed into his gut.

A sickening crunch and a short, sharp cry of pain and surprise drew Jason's attention to the bottom of the stairs. He looked down, startled to see the lad had fallen sometime during the scuffle. And even worse, his rapier lay dangerously nearby, and a bright splotch of blood stained the boy's shirt. The lad was still as death, lying face up amidst the tangle of his unwrapped plaid shawl. His hat had fallen off . . . no, *her* hat.

Hell and furies, 'twas a woman! A woman with long, tawny braids. Disoriented, Jason's fingers loosened. He half-turned to get a better look, and Walter squirmed from beneath his foot and stumbled down the stairs.

" 'Tis the ghost of Cainewood!" he yelled as he reached the bottom and ran for the door.

"Dunderhead!" Geoffrey rasped, one hand flying up to cradle his abused throat. Murder in his eyes, he dealt Jason a mighty shove that sent him to his knees and clunking down two steps. While Geoffrey pushed past to follow his brother to freedom, Jason righted himself and made his way down the stairs after them.

But the woman moaned softly at his feet. With a quick, regretful glance at the door, he knelt by her side. Blood still trickled from the cut on her shoulder—a cut from his own sword that had tumbled downstairs in her wake. A negligible injury, but his fault nonetheless.

"Wake up!" Jason shook the woman's other shoulder, but her eyes refused to open. How in God's name had he ever thought she was a boy? She was a woman, full grown, with a woman's bosom that heaved beneath her man's shirt. Smallish, perhaps, but a definite bosom nonetheless.

He rubbed the back of his neck. Why, that sorry excuse for a disguise wouldn't fool a living soul . . . well, perhaps only someone as single-minded as he had been these days past. The lingering pain from the pistol wound must be muddling his brain. He glanced back down at the woman and wondered at the boy's clothing.

It hit him like a bolt of summer lightning. She was after the reward, and she was—

He rose, shoved the rapier back into his belt, and bent to try to rouse her once again. No luck.

A pair of dusty shoes strolled into his vision, stopping by the woman's head. Jason straightened. "Did you send someone to fetch the authorities?"

"The magistrate's in Lancashire. Visitin' his sick mother." Typical, Jason thought in disgust. The inn-keeper, a wiry, balding man, rubbed his nose. He stood with his other hand on the newel post, eyeing the woman with sympathy. "She took room three. If you'd not mind bringing her up."

"I expect 'tis for the best," Jason agreed gruffly. He grabbed the woman's pistol off the floor—the oldest, ug-liest gun he'd ever seen—and lifted her into his arms. A limp bundle she was: slim, soft, and smelling of flowers. He stared at her, picturing Geoffrey Gothard already miles down the road.

Damnation. Gothard had gotten away again, and all because of an incompetent Scottish reward hunter who would certainly bungle the capture, if she didn't get her-self killed outright.

He'd laughed at the ridiculous rumors, but the joke was on him . . . because here was Emerald MacCallum, right in his arms.

Chapter Four

With a grunt, Jason laid Emerald on the bed, then lit a candle and set it on the plain wooden table beside her. Rubbing his aching shoulder, he stood staring at her chalk-white face. The flickering flame cast a sense of movement he knew was naught but an illusion. He lifted one slim wrist and let it drop back to the bed.

Limp and deathly still. Just like little Mary.

A strange hollowness opened in his gut. He reached to feel for the pulse in her throat, relieved to feel it warm and steady beneath his fingers.

He drew a restorative breath and untangled the plaid shawl. As he tossed it over the spartan room's only chair, the woman's soft floral scent wafted to his nose. Though he was no stranger to undressing women, he couldn't remember ever stripping one he'd never laid eyes on before. The room seemed suddenly short of air. He drew off her shoes and dropped them on the planked wood floor, then rolled her stockings down shapely calves and off her small, arched feet. He'd never noticed a female's feet.

Clearly it had been far too long since he'd had a woman. Of late, his responsibilities to the estate and as a father figure to his siblings allowed precious little time for pursuing personal pleasures.

Shaking off the unwelcome twinge of desire, he hurried to find the damage from his sword. He loosened the laces of her shirt, eased it down, and brought the candle close to her shoulder. The cut was tiny and shallow, the blood already clotted against her creamy skin. His heart calmed somewhat, then speeded again as he tried to ignore the expanse of silky, bare flesh. Unbidden thoughts came scurrying back when he caught himself studying the top halves of her breasts. Breasts that looked as though they were made to fit in the palms of his hands.

With a muttered oath, he set down the candle and pulled the shirt back into place, noticing an unusual pendant that nestled in her cleavage. He lifted her head and drew off the necklace. Warm from the heat of her body, an oval green stone—an emerald?—shone from an ornate gold setting embedded with tiny red and blue jewels and small round pearls. The simple link chain had obviously seen much wear. Candlelight glinted off the rubbed gold surfaces.

An emerald. Emerald MacCallum.

He set the necklace on the bedside table with a little click that seemed to reverberate in the quiet room.

A soft moan from the woman lifted his hopes and drew his gaze back in her direction. Not beautiful in a classical sense, Emerald looked sweet and unspoiled. Like a dairymaid, truth be told, since she'd braided her hair to conceal it under her hat. Not at all like he'd pictured the fabled Emerald MacCallum, but then, 'twas not as though anyone knew what she looked like. Drawings on broadsides were of the outlaws, not their pursuers.

But the thought of a petite woman like this capturing outlaws was laughable. The breeches left little to the imagination, and he couldn't help but notice her feminine curves were thinner than the current fashionable ideal. Someone needed to feed this woman. Guilt lodged in his stomach as he rubbed a thumb along her cheek, glancing at her long, full lashes and wondering what color her eyes were. Her pert nose was a bit upturned; her wide mouth looked kissable.

With a huff of impatience, he jerked his hand away
and rolled her onto her stomach, then wrestled the thin
quilt from beneath her and settled it over her back. Gingerly he explored her head for the lump he knew must
be there, given that she'd been knocked unconscious. He
winced when he found it, hard and large and warm to
the touch. The tight braid on that side couldn't be comfortable. He set to undoing it to relieve the pressure.

Long and shimmering, hair every hue of blonde and
brown slid between his hands. When the first side was
loose, his fingers lingered at the place where her straight,
white part ended at the nape of her neck. Baby fine
hairs glimmered gold in that spot. No matter that the
woman was Emerald MacCallum; the downy little hollow looked innocent and vulnerable.

Anger fired up his system. At himself, at the world.
He'd thrown down his sword to avoid bloodshed, and
now someone else was hurt. His fingers absently loosed
the second braid while he seethed at the whole situation.
He tried to block a vision of poor little Mary, but the
unsuccessful effort only led him to picture this woman
in the same condition. The thought made him shake.

Damn if those bastards hadn't gotten away. Again.

He rose and paced around the room, lighting more
candles and cursing himself. He should have gone in
with loaded pistols and blade at the ready, prepared to
handle the brothers once and for all, with no thought to
fairness or avoiding violence.

Father would have done it that way.

"Father would have handled it," he muttered in self-
disgust and walked across to the window.

Hearing a voice, Caithren shifted on the bed, her head
in a painful fog. The voice had been a dark, harsh whisper. She just was unsure if she'd actually heard it, or if
it had been part of her disturbing dream. When she tried

to move, her head hurt, and she moaned, struggling against the nausea.

Swift footsteps approached. "You're awake, then?" 'Twas the same man's voice, but rich, comforting, and laced with relief. Cait tried to roll closer to the sound, but the man held her in place with a large, warm hand. "For God's sake, be still." Tinged with worry, his voice wasn't quite as nice. "You bumped your head but good."

She was lying face down with her nose mashed into the pillow. She couldn't breathe properly.

The man's hands gripped her shoulders, gently helping her turn. "Are you dizzy?" he asked, moving to arrange her aching head on the pillow.

When he came into view, her answer got lost somewhere between her mind and her mouth. Clear green eyes—eyes too beautiful for a man—were studying her. His shadowed jaw and fine tanned features were framed by long, wavy raven hair that was prettier than her own. Bent over her as he was, the ends threatened to tickle her cheeks.

He looked frustrated and concerned. And she didn't have a clue who he was.

"Can you talk? Emerald, are you all right?"

"Emerald?" she echoed. She supposed she was all right, if she didn't take into account her aching head and the fact that her gaze was riveted to a faint dimple in the stranger's chin. There was only one thing she was certain of in that moment. "I-I'm not Emerald," she managed.

"Oh?" Under a narrow black mustache, his chiseled lips tilted a bit, but not in humor. "You're Scottish," he said, as though that explained everything.

"You're English," she countered, batting his hair from her face. He straightened, and his spicy scent wafted away, leaving her head a little clearer. The room swam into view. She lay beneath not the dusky rose canopy of her bed at home, but a utilitarian beamed ceiling, the plaster cracked and at least a century older than Leslie Castle.

She was somewhere in England, and Da was dead.

Disoriented, she raised herself to her elbows, then flopped back to the pillow. A fresh burst of pain detonated inside her head, forcing a moan out through her lips.

"I told you to keep still." With a gentle hand, the man swept her hair off her face.

He'd unplaited her braids.

She pushed away his hand and fingered the ends of her hair, confused. Her other hand drifted up to touch the side of her head where the pain was the sharpest. "I'm not Emerald."

"You're Scottish"—he held up a palm to stop her words from tumbling out—"you're wearing men's clothes, you're carrying a pistol, and you're after a wanted outlaw. Now tell me you're not Emerald MacCallum."

"I am not Emerald MacCallum."

His mouth curved as though he were amused. "Did the knock on your head damage your memory?"

"My memory is intact, thank ye. But my name isn't Emerald." Despite her denial, her brain seemed impossibly muddled by the throbbing pain. " 'Tis Caithren," she managed finally. "Caithren Leslie. Not Emerald."

"Hmm . . ." The man raised one black eyebrow. "If you're not Emerald, then can you explain what you're doing here?"

Her brain might be muddled, but she knew an accusation when she heard it. "Why should I not be here?" she asked on a huff. "Is there some law against my visiting your country? England and Scotland share a king, the last I heard. Though not for long, I'm hoping."

He crossed his arms while one booted foot tapped against the wooden floor. Obviously he was waiting for her to explain herself. Arrogant cur. She wouldn't look at him, then. Her gaze swept the room, taking in the plain whitewashed walls, a simple wood cabinet, a utilitarian washstand, a small tub full of dirty bathwater that should have been carried away.

Pontefract. She was in her room at the inn in Pontefract.

She was here in Pontefract . . . She squeezed her eyes shut tight, blocking out the man so she could concentrate. "I've come to find my brother," she said at last, opening them in relief.

"Hmm, is that so?" he challenged in a calm voice that betrayed a touch of irony. "Then I suppose you can explain to me how you know Gothard."

She stared at him blankly. "Gothard?"

"Geoffrey Gothard. The man you tried to shoot in order to collect the reward. I'm not a half-wit, Emerald."

"I'm not Emerald. And I'm not a half-wit, either, but you're certainly making me feel so, since I haven't the slightest notion what you're blethering about."

He sat at the edge of the bed and studied her for a while, as though trying to gauge her sincerity. The mattress sagged under his weight, rolling her too close to him for her comfort. The queasiness clawed at her stomach again. She was alone with a strange man. A strange *English* man. Her mouth went dry, and she licked her lips.

His eyes darkened, making her nervous. With a sigh, she reached up to fiddle with a braid, then remembered her hair was undone. She fisted her hands atop the bedcovers.

" 'Tis God's own truth I'm telling ye, Mr. . . ."

His mouth twisted up in a hint of a smile. "Chase. But you may call me Jason."

"I may, may I?" Stuffy, these English. Well, 'twas not as though Cameron hadn't warned her. She took a deep breath and decided to try again. "D'ye believe me?"

"I think not." His sarcastic tone grated on her. "What is your brother's name?"

She struggled against the pain in her head. ". . . Adam."

"And why do you have cause to think he'd be here?"

"He was visiting . . ."

As she strained to come up with the name, he shook his head, sending the glorious hair swinging. "You'll have to invent these lies more quickly if you expect them to sound believable."

"Scarborough," she gritted out.

"The *Earl* of Scarborough?" A sparkle came into his eyes, as though he were entertained by the thought of someone related to her visiting an earl. Just like the innkeeper downstairs. By the wee man, did she look that provincial? Her clothes were in decent condition. Her father had been a baronet.

"I'm surprised at you, Emerald." His mocking voice interrupted her musings. "You've a reputation for being the cunning sort. Surely you can come up with something better than that. It must be the knock on the head."

How this man could think her someone else was beyond her. Exasperated, she slammed her hand against the mattress, wincing when it jarred her body. "Bile yer heid."

"Pardon?" Clearly amused, he raised a brow. "Are you suggesting I boil my head?"

Clenching her teeth, she looked away. Her plaid was tossed over a chair, her shoes and stockings on the floor. Alarm shot through her. "Did ye undress me as well, then?" She thrust her hands under the bedclothes to see what else he might have taken off of her.

That eyebrow went up again. "I reckon you'll find you're still decent. Bloody hell, woman, what do you take me for?"

"An Englishman." Her clothing was all in place, although the laces on her shirt had been loosened. She gave them a vicious tug, then looked down and gasped.

"There is blood on my shirt." She felt for the source, but it didn't really hurt much.

"You were cut. Nothing serious."

Slackening the laces, she peeked beneath. He was right. The meadow rue she'd picked would heal it in no time.

" 'Tis why your shirt was unlaced," he continued. "I . . . checked." When she looked up, his face was red. A proper gentleman he was, then, but he was still an Englishman.

He just stared at her. Caithren bit her lip and felt for her good-luck charm.

And her hands closed on air.

"Where is my amulet?" she squeaked in a panic. She struggled up on her elbows again, felt the dizziness rush back.

"I have it right here." He reached to the bedside table, lifted the amulet, and dangled it over her head by its chain. The emerald swung in a hypnotizing pattern. "I'm hardly in the habit of stealing from unconscious women."

"Well, I dinna know ye, do I?" She snatched it to her chest.

"But you know Geoffrey Gothard, do you not?"

Jings, the man was persistent. She shot him a peeved look and slipped the chain back over her head, feeling better when the amulet was settled in place. She wrapped a hand around it. That Geoffrey he was talking about, she remembered who he was now—the murdering cur she'd overheard at Scarborough's and met again on the inn's staircase. That terrible, horrible man and his scum of a brother. Englishmen. She shivered, tugging up on the thin quilt.

And here she was, alone with another Englishman, a strange man in a strange country. Well, at least this one Englishman was looking out for her, even if she didn't care for him badgering her with questions. And though he was plainly annoyed, he'd yet to raise his voice to her.

"Thank ye for your help," she said softly by way of apology. She tried to smile, and his eyes softened; he leaned closer and brushed the hair from her face. One warm finger trailed her cheek; he was staring at her mouth, looking as though he wanted to kiss her, like that bampot Duncan had looked at the village dance last month.

What a daft thought. The Englishman, kiss her? He didn't even believe who she was. The knock on her head must have been harder than she'd supposed for her to think something like that. And he was vexed with her, although she'd done nothing to warrant it. Nothing she could recall, anyway.

She squinted up at him. "Why are ye so vexed?"

"I had a job to do, and you got in the way," he said with a sigh that, if she didn't know better, she might take to be apologetic. "No fault of yours." He waved a dismissive hand. "Stay away from Gothard, Emerald. He's a dangerous man."

"I saw that for myself." Despite his annoying use of the wrong name, Caithren's heart melted a little. He had rescued her downstairs, and now he was warning her of danger, trying to protect her. She sought to reassure him. "He's unlikely to be a danger to me, seeing as he's on his way to London."

"London?" His body tensed. "How come you to know this?"

"I . . . overheard him and—his brother, aye? When I went out to Scarborough's to find Adam." Because he seemed concerned for her welfare, she added, "They didn't see me."

The Englishman's green eyes narrowed on hers suspiciously. "Why are you telling me this? To send me off in the wrong direction?"

"Pardon me?"

He stood abruptly. "Just stay away from Gothard. Find yourself another reward to collect." The candle flames flickered as he strode to the door, disturbing the room's musty air. His gaze settled on her emerald amulet for a moment, then he pierced her with those incredible eyes. "I admire your persistence—it puts me in mind of my family—but I cannot see why you refuse to own up to who you are."

"Ye know what my mam would have said?" Caithren crossed her arms beneath the quilt. "Telling it true, pits ain in a stew."

He paused with his hand on the latch. "I cannot understand you."

"Then permit me to translate. Telling the truth confuses your enemies."

"I am not your enemy." He blinked several times. "Why of a sudden does everyone think me his enemy?" He said it to no one in particular, and his eyes rolled toward the blackened beamed ceiling, as though he were looking for the heavens to send down an answer.

"I should be on the road after Gothard," he mused to himself. Then he sighed and looked back to her. "But damn if I don't feel responsible for you."

"Well, ye needn't be," Cait said. "I can take care of myself."

"Not from what I've seen. And now, thanks to me, you're even less equipped physically to deal with men like the Gothards."

"What d'ye mean, thanks to ye?"

He frowned. "Surely you realize you fell down the stairs as a result of my intervention? And 'twas my sword that cut you. Accidentally—I was not even holding it—but 'tis my responsibility nonetheless." She heard a click when he pushed down on the latch. "I insist you accept my help."

"I'd say you've helped me quite enough already." This

man was out of his mind. "Your kind of help I dinna need."

He didn't seem to hear her, or else he simply dismissed her opinion. Either way, his ignoring her rankled. "Get some sleep," he said, "but make sure you awaken. The last thing I need is another Mary."

Mary? Who the devil was Mary?

He opened the door. "I'll check on you in the morning. If your head still aches, we'll have a doctor in to examine it."

Caithren was so confused and frustrated that if she'd had the energy, she would have kicked the door shut behind him. As it was, it closed softly.

Did he think she was there for his bidding? *I'll check on you in the morning.* Not if she had anything to say about it.

The silver blade flashed, vibrations sang up his arm, and the man before him crumpled to the ground. Blood pumped, sickeningly slick and bright—

His heart racing, Jason sat straight up in bed, sweat breaking out to coat his clammy skin. His breath came in short, hard pants.

Who was this man he'd killed? Had he been a husband, a father? Certainly he'd been a son. How many lives had Jason ruined with that fateful thrust of his sword?

Hopefully not as many as when his own parents had been slain on the field of battle. God forbid he should put another family through a hell like that. Not even, as his parents had, for reasons of honor.

Senseless honor. They had died fighting for the King, yet Cromwell had prevailed.

He raked a hand through his hair and swung his shaky legs off the bed. Dust motes floated in the brightness that streamed through the crooked shutters. Sunshine.

Daylight. He'd overslept. Another restless, too-short night, like they all seemed to be since he was shot.

He stumbled to his clothing, pulled out his pocket watch and flipped open the sapphire-adorned lid. Almost noon. Damn, Gothard would be long down the road by now.

And Emerald after him. Cunning Emerald, the woman Jason had found himself absurdly tempted to kiss. He was the one who ought to have his head examined. He threw on a shirt and breeches, then padded across the hall to knock on her door.

Silence. He tried the latch, and the door swung wide to reveal an empty room.

Cursing at himself, he went back to his own room and pulled on his boots. His family had been right—he had no business going after Geoffrey Gothard. But it had nothing to do with the state of his health; the fact was, he belonged behind a desk or riding his land. He had always valued peace and tranquility; he knew not how to do this. He was botching it good and proper.

Downstairs in the taproom, the early dinner crowd was much too cheerful for Jason's mood. A quick glance failed to reveal Emerald among the diners. The harried innkeeper was rolling a fresh barrel of ale into place behind the counter. When he paused to mop his red face, Jason jumped behind to help him upend it. It settled into place with a *thump*, displacing more than its share of dust.

Jason coughed. "Know you where I might find the woman who was injured last night?"

The man wiped his shiny brow with a handkerchief. "She left this morning. Took the public coach."

"The coach? Not a horse?"

"No horses available in Pontefract. Told her that yesterday when she wanted to hire one."

"She had no horse of her own?"

The innkeeper shrugged. "She arrived on the coach."

Jason rubbed his aching shoulder. One didn't track outlaws while riding public transportation. If Emerald had arrived here looking for a horse, something must have happened to hers. She must be on her way to the next town to find herself another.

His hand dropped. "The coach toward where?"

"London."

"London? Are you certain of that?" Surely she'd gone in another direction; she'd only said London to confuse him, had she not?

But the old stableman had told him Scarborough was in London. The Gothards had come to West Riding to speak with their brother—to get something from their brother—it made sense that now they would be headed to see him in London instead. And of course Emerald would go after them.

The man dabbed at his dripping nose. "London, yes. 'Tis Thursday, no? The coach leaves for London at eight every Thursday."

"Eight. Damn." She had a four-hour lead. But the public coach was slow as a condemned man mounting Tyburn gallows, and Chiron, Jason's silver gelding, had won his last three races in Sussex. If Emerald hadn't found a horse yet, he might be able to catch up to her. "How much do I owe for the room?"

He slapped coins on the counter and ran upstairs to fetch his belongings, then headed back down to the stables. Blasted woman thought she could fool him, did she? The Gothard brothers were riding for London, and here she was, going after them at her first chance. She knew their relationship to Scarborough as well, even if she'd tried to cover that slip with a story about her brother.

She was Emerald MacCallum, all right, no matter the lies that tumbled from her enticing lips. And he had to keep an eye on her, lest she get to Geoffrey first—because she was bound to get herself killed in the process.

She might have a reputation for tracking men—indeed, she'd done a credible job of it so far, tracing the brothers to here—but she'd never come up against the likes of Gothard before. The man was evil.

And now she was injured, thanks to him. He owed it to her to follow her, watch over her. Protect her. Besides, they seemed to be heading in the same direction.

'Twould be no trouble.

Chapter Five

Jason caught up to her coach—at least he hoped it was her coach—in Doncaster. The passengers had already disembarked. A few walked along Church Street or Greyfriars Road, stretching their legs while the horses were changed.

Emerald was nowhere in sight. He tethered Chiron and poked his head into the coach's cabin, finding it empty. Neither was she inside the Greyfriars Inn, where other passengers were taking refreshment.

Bloody hell, she must have hired a horse and left already.

Frustrated, he paid for an ale and paced Church Street while drinking it. Perhaps he should be relieved . . . it would have been hell following a public coach. Too damned slow. Once he found her—assuming he could—it would be much better with her on horseback. He could follow surreptitiously and keep her safe without worrying about the brothers getting too far ahead.

Yes, it really was quite a relief. Anxious to get on the road after Emerald, he tilted his head back and drained the rest of the ale. And looked back down to see a woman across the street, disappearing as she rounded the corner of the Church of St. George.

A woman who looked suspiciously like Emerald MacCallum.

Jason took off jogging after her. Instead of breeches, the woman was wearing a dark green skirt over a long-sleeved, high-necked shift, topped by a brown laced bodice that looked like it belonged in the previous century. He'd not really caught sight of her face. But the sun had glinted off dark blonde hair plaited into two braids. He'd thought Emerald had only braided her hair yesterday in order to hide it under her hat, but he could have been wrong in that assumption. Absurd hairstyle for a grown woman.

There she was, standing by the double doors of the majestic medieval building. Stopping in a graveyard a safe distance away, he concealed himself behind a monument and watched.

It was definitely Emerald. Apparently she only dressed like a man when her quarry was in range. Or maybe she hadn't found time yet to mend her shirt where his blade had slashed it.

Gazing up at the massive planked doors, she reached a finger to trace a section of their scrolled ironwork, then her hand closed over the latch. She stopped short of opening it, instead heaving a visible sigh and then wandering around the other side of the church, toward another graveyard that looked ancient compared to the one where he was standing. Idly she bent down to pluck off part of a small plant and slipped it into her pocket. Strange woman.

It hit him then. As in Pontefract, there had been no horses available here in Doncaster. She was only biding her time until the coach was ready to leave.

Damnation. He would have to follow the coach after all, until Emerald was successful in finding herself a horse. And risk Gothard getting to London ahead of him, potentially endangering other people there and along the way.

He had no choice.

He groaned aloud at the thought, then set the empty tankard atop a gravestone.

*   *   *

Tilted, mossy stone markers were spaced unevenly on the green grass. Caithren strolled the crooked rows, touching one here and there. The same names appeared over and over through the centuries. Mowbray, Southwell, Hodgkinson.

She shivered as she touched the rough headstone of two Southwell bairns. They'd been dead over two hundred years, one at the age of four, the other simply listed as "infant daughter." Her throat tightened at the thought of losing family. Like she had just lost Da.

"Boarding!"

Startled, she glanced around the kirk toward the Greyfriars Inn. She'd enjoyed her solitude 'til the last possible moment, but now the coach had pulled up before the rounded corner of the red-brick building, fresh horses in place, and the first passengers were climbing aboard, that old bawface Mrs. Dochart among them. With a sigh, she looked down at the sisters' tomb, crossed herself, and turned to make her way from the graveyard and back to the inn.

The sun went behind a cloud and suddenly the cemetery, shadowed already by the soaring walls of the kirk, seemed eerie and forbidding. A soft wheezy sound set her heart to pounding. Spooked, she froze in her tracks. 'Twas the wind, she told herself, whistling through the old kirk. Cameron always said she had too active an imagination. But her fingers flew to her amulet as her body tensed, ready to run.

A footstep sounded behind her, and a hand clamped on her shoulder. Whirling, she let out a little shriek.

"Whoa, there," said the man in front of her. "You look like you saw a ghost." Beneath his wide-brimmed hat, he looked puzzled and apologetic.

Then the face registered, and Caithren's jaw dropped open. Her hands went to her heaving chest. It took a moment to find her tongue, but when she did, she let loose.

"Ye!" The Englishman had said he felt responsible, but she hadn't figured he was insane enough to follow her. "Ye scared me half to death."

"I'm sorry. I meant not to frighten you, only—"

"What the devil are ye doing here?" Still trembling, she leaned on a gravestone. Last night's confusion came rushing back. "Did ye follow me? I told ye I dinna want your help."

He shrugged in answer as he gazed around the cemetery. "You're shaking still. I suppose you believe in ghosts?"

"I've yet to meet a Scot who doesn't," she said shortly.

His lips curved as if he found that amusing, then he motioned his head toward the gray stone kirk. "Why did you not go inside?"

She glanced helplessly from him to the building, then back. "Ye were watching me?" The thought was disturbing. She'd wanted to explore the elaborate medieval kirk, not to mention pray there for the stamina to put up with Mrs. Dochart for eight and a half more days. Lord knew she needed some help. But she'd been afraid the coach would leave without her, so she'd stayed outside instead.

And he'd been watching her. A vague sense of unease stole over her. Her hand went into her pocket, feeling for the familiar comfort of Adam's portrait she'd put there to remind her of her goal. "I-I must go. Please, just leave me alone."

" 'Tis a beautiful building." He gestured at the bell tower, where no less than sixteen pinnacles crowned the battlement.

The sun came back out, dispelling her nervousness. He was only a man. A misguided one. "I haven't the time to go inside. The coach is leaving."

He nodded. "I'll walk you through."

"There is a door on the other side?" She frowned,

but followed him willingly, dimly wondering why she was cooperating with an Englishman. But she supposed in his quaint way he was trying to help.

'Twas cool inside and deathly quiet. Deserted as well, at two o'clock on a Thursday afternoon. The flames of votive candles made shadows dance in the dim light that filtered through the kirk's beautiful stained-glass windows. Silently she paused to admire the ancient grandeur, loath to disturb the utter peacefulness with unnecessary words.

With a tug on her hand, he urged her down a side aisle.

"Last call!" The driver's voice managed to pierce the thick stone walls. Looking up, Cait could see that some of the colorful windows were old and broken, no doubt letting in the sound, as well as the wind that had frightened her in the first place.

"I must go," she whispered, trying to pull from the Englishman's grasp. He had no business touching her.

He held tight and continued doggedly toward a small private chapel that projected outside the main wall. It would be near Church Street and the inn. That must be where the door was.

But when they stepped through an archway and inside, a scan of the wee chapel revealed only a single wooden bench and a simple altar with three small burning candles. Afternoon sun shone through a cracked window, projecting brilliant colored patches on the stone floor.

Alarm skittered through her. "There is no door."

"I never said there was a door."

She stifled her urge to yell—she couldn't be making a racket in the kirk. "I must *go*."

"I think not."

He wanted to *keep* her here? She moved for the main sanctuary and front door, but he was faster and blocked her path. Losing patience, she shoved at his arm. "Please move out of my way."

"I'm not going to hurt you." He wedged himself into the archway, spreading his feet at the bottom and his hands at the top. "I want only to protect you."

Protect her? The man was daft. She beat one fist against his chest, but he was solid and immovable. Through a high cracked window, she heard the call of her name. Panic welled in her throat. She needed to be on the coach. Her future depended on finding her brother. She had not the time for this stranger and his accusations and claims of responsibility.

She gave him another shove and kicked at his shins, but he stood firm, his mouth a straight line beneath his thin mustache. She almost wished she hadn't left Da's pistol in her satchel on the coach.

When she heard the creak and groan of the coach departing, her confusion blended with white-hot anger. Frantically she tried to duck under his arms, through his legs, and finally turned her back, sputtering incoherently. Only when the sound of the wheels faded into the distance did he step from the archway.

No matter they were in a kirk—she whirled and slapped him hard on the face.

"Holy Christ!" His hand came up to cover his cheek where her finger-shaped imprints were already making a blotchy, red presence. "You've got a hell of an arm, Emerald."

"Dinna ye blaspheme in the kirk!" she yelled, bringing up her hand again.

Neatly he caught her by the wrist. "Once, you're quick. Twice, I'm stupid," he said drolly.

"You're stupid, all right! I missed my coach!" She wrenched free and shrank away from him, backing toward the sanctuary.

"There is nowhere for you to go," he said calmly. "I won't hurt you."

"Why should I believe ye?" But she did, though it made no sense. "How in the name of the saints am I going to get to London?"

"There will be another coach."

"In three days! And I must be in London by next week!"

He rubbed his injured cheek. Absurdly, she noticed he still hadn't shaved. He must have been in a hurry this morning.

"Next week," he mused, as though to himself. "What for?" He came close, his hand dropping from his face to clamp her shoulder, holding her from bolting. As though she had anywhere to go. "Why do you need to be in London? Think fast—I'm sure you can come up with a good one."

"My brother is expected there." She twisted from his grip. "I told ye I'm looking for him. I need him to sign some papers."

"That story's getting old, Emerald."

" 'Tis God's truth!" Tears threatened, but she blinked them back. She didn't know if she were more angry that he'd detained her or that he insisted on calling her Emerald. Both made her spitting mad. "If I miss him in London, he might go to India. And then how will I find him, I ask ye? What will I do then?"

"India? You are even more creative than I credited you with." Wincing, he bent to rub one of his shins, and she was gratified to think she'd damaged him. "India," he muttered, his voice unmistakably disgusted.

The tears did fall then, fast and furious. All she'd wanted to do was find Adam. It had seemed such a simple matter to go to him and have him sign the papers; now everything had gone awry.

"I must get to London!" The Englishman's face looked all blurry through the tears. "Why did ye keep me here?" she wailed. "Whatever for?"

He opened his mouth, then closed it. Then opened it again. "I told you last night. I feel responsible—"

"I am not your responsibility!"

"—for seeing to your safety," he continued unperturbed. "I only hoped to delay you a few days, so that I can take care of Geoffrey Gothard before he can do you harm."

"Gothard again?" She stamped her foot, hard. It seemed the candle flames wavered, but the Englishman didn't budge. "I hate ye!"

"You're not my favorite person, either. I'm only trying to help you." He shook his head. "India." The sigh that escaped his lips was so elaborate it ruffled his long black hair.

She sat down, right there on the bench, and dashed impatiently at the wetness on her cheeks. Wheesht! She rarely cried at home, but here she was a veritable fountain. England was a very nasty place. Cameron didn't ken the half of it.

"What am I supposed to do now?" Her shoulders trembled. "Will ye take me back to the coach?"

"Forward to the coach. And the answer is no." His black boots shuffled on the stone floor, then he plopped to sit beside her. "Please don't cry." His voice sounded miserable.

He hated tears, did he? Good. She let loose a particularly pathetic wail.

He scooted to the far end of the bench. She angled toward him so he could see the tears run down her face to full effect. He rose and walked away, paced the breadth of the wee chapel and back again. When he came to stand before her, arms crossed, she dropped her head into her hands and sobbed uncontrollably.

Or at least she hoped he thought so. She had to convince him to take her to the coach.

"I'll take you to London," he muttered.

Tears forgotten, her gaze shot up. "If ye think I'd go wi'—"

"Look, I have to go to London regardless." He frowned at her puzzled glare. "To find Gothard. I can protect you this way. I don't suppose it will be too much trouble to take you along."

She rose and stepped before him, so she could stick her face near to his. "Oh, aye?" He flinched, but she only pushed her nose even closer. "Thanks to ye, I dinna have any clothes or money—'tis all on the coach. I-I dinna even have a hat! I expect you'll be sorry afore this is over."

His face turning red, he swept off his hat and stuck it on her head. "I'm sorry already."

She tipped the hat's brim and swiped the tears from her cheeks as she pulled back. As soon as they caught up with the coach, she'd be off, and best of luck to him in foiling her plans again. Fool her once, he was quick. Twice, she was stupid.

And Caithren Leslie was far from stupid.

Jason sat Emerald before him on his horse, and they rode two long hours before she said a word. But when he guided Chiron through a stand of trees and turned back onto the Great North Road, she uttered a single sentence, grudgingly.

"Dinna think I haven't noticed ye took the long way 'round to avoid the coach."

He snorted. "To the contrary, I'm quite certain you notice everything, Emerald."

"I'm *Caithren*." She leaned back to glare up at him, bumping her head on his sore shoulder. He grunted and scooted back in the saddle. Christ, the wench smelled good. Like a heady mix of wildflowers. His arm tightened around her waist, and he left it that way, even though the close contact reminded him of all his aches and pains. Bloody hell, was there anyplace she hadn't kicked or hit him?

"How did ye find me?" she asked in a peevish tone.

It had been blind luck—if you could call it that—but in his present mood he couldn't resist needling her anyway. "For a tracker, you're not very good at covering your own."

"I'm no tracker, whatever that might be."

"You trail outlaws and bring them in to collect the rewards." His gaze kept returning to that vulnerable little hollow at the nape of her neck. "Perhaps the Scots have a different word for it, but we call that tracking."

"D'ye mean to say ye think I do this regularly? Not just for this Gothard fellow, but for others?"

" 'Tis exactly what you do, and we both know it. See here, Emerald, you're becoming legend. There are few hereabouts who know not what you do, and I'll not have you telling me you're one of them."

She huffed and jerked on the reins, jarring his bruised body and causing Chiron to shy. Jason hadn't considered how the two of them would get to London on one horse. Truth be told, he'd not considered much of anything related to this misadventure before coming up with this harebrained scheme to detain her —to insure she couldn't do anything foolish that might get her killed.

As though she could possibly do anything more foolish than he had. How he'd ended up taking her along was beyond his comprehension. A woman's wiles at work.

The end of one of her braids flew back on the breeze, tickling his face. Damn woman kept wiggling against him. 'Twas uncomfortable in more ways than one. Before they left Bawtry tomorrow, he would have to buy another horse. Hopefully he would have better luck than she had finding one.

His stomach growled, and she deigned to grace him with another sentence. "Hungry, are ye?"

" 'Tis long past time for dinner." He knew not which

hurt worse: his poor abused body or his empty belly.
"And I left without breakfast this morning, thanks to
you."

"Thanks to me? This wasn't *my* idea."

He didn't rise to that bait, and they rode for a while
more in uneasy silence. He wondered if he should just
give in and return her to the coach. But then he noticed
her fingering her amulet. Emerald. He remembered her
nick from the scuffle with the Gothards and stiffened
his resolve.

She had no business chasing after them.

"You'll thank me for protecting you later," he murmured under his breath.

"You're not doing this out of responsibility and kind-
ness." Emerald's smug words held a challenge. "Did ye
really think I'd fall for such an unbelievably noble excuse? Ye want to kill this man Gothard, and you're
afraid I'll get to him afore ye do and steal your reward
out from under ye." Evidently proud of her powers of
deduction, she leaned back with a grunt of satisfaction,
jabbing her shoulder into his wound.

He opened his mouth to argue, then thought better of
it. Let her believe that nonsense, if it pleased her.
Though she could hardly have come up with a more out-
of-character assertion, 'twas not surprising that a woman
like Emerald would find such a motivation acceptable.
Telling the truth, that he was concerned for her life, had
apparently insulted her independent nature. Her explanation suited his purposes perfectly.

For the first time in days, he found himself pleased by
a turn of events.

Chapter Six

That evening, the clink of cutlery on pewter and the buzz of ale-lubricated conversation filled Caithren's ears as her gaze wandered the well-lit taproom of the Crown Hotel in Bawtry. She inhaled deeply of a steaming chunk of meat pie before popping it into her mouth. "Not bad for English food," she said around the bite. "Hunger is the best kitchen."

Mr. Chase set down his tankard and steepled his fingers. "Translate?"

"Food tastes better when you're hungry. English food, at any rate."

Ignoring the barb, the Englishman lifted his spoon. She watched him, remembering when she'd first set eyes on him and thought he was so handsome. Now he just looked stubborn and irritating. Imagine finding oneself attracted to a man who had the gall to keep her off a public coach.

She deliberately looked away, out one of the Crown Hotel's large, fine glass windows. Across the street and to the right, candles glinted through the mottled windows of a nice, small plastered inn called the Turnpike. Down on the left sat the Granby Inn, a squat, square building that looked perfectly acceptable.

The Englishman had certainly chosen an enormous, expensive hotel. She wondered if he had money. He didn't look it. But she felt like she were staying in a private mansion. In the name o' the wee man, there were *marble* pillars in the entrance hall. And the hotel had fifty-seven rooms. Fifty-seven! She wiggled on her chair, which was plush and upholstered, sighing at the luxury. At home they had only plain wooden chairs around their table. After spending half the day on horseback, the padding was welcome.

"You'll get to London much faster on horseback than by coach," the Englishman said, interrupting her musings. "This arrangement will actually work to your benefit."

"Aye?" Her hand went to her emerald amulet. With any luck, "this arrangement" would be over come midnight or so.

"Yes. We'll make it there in five or six days instead of nine. Long before the coach. And hopefully before Gothard."

She took a dainty bite of her pie. "Gothard?" Of course she knew who he was talking about, but she couldn't resist baiting him.

His face slowly turned pink. "Geoffrey Gothard," he clarified and stabbed his spoon into his own pie.

"Oh, him." On impulse, she reached across the table to touch the Englishman on the arm. "You'd best go faster if you're planning to catch him. He was fixing to 'ride like the dickens,' whatever that means." She sat back with a smug smile.

"It means like the devil." He polished off the last of his bread, studying her with a calculating green gaze. "How come you to know this?"

Cait sighed. "I *told* ye I heard Geoffrey and Wat talking, when I was looking for my brother at Scarborough's place."

"Well, we made decent time today." He flexed his shoulder, and a pained look came over his face. "We shall ride like the dickens, then, and God willing, I will find the bastard right off."

"God willing, is it?" Toying with the handle of her

dull pewter tankard, she drew a deep breath. "Ye can assist God by looking for Gothard at the home of someone named Lucas."

He stopped in mid-chew. "Pardon?"

She took time for a sip of ale, half hoping he would choke from curiosity. "The Gothards are going to London to get something from this man Lucas." She sipped again. "If he fails to give them what they want, they're going to murder him."

"Lucas Gothard? They plan to *kill* the Earl of Scarborough?"

Caithren shrugged. "Is that Scarborough's given name? Adam never said."

"What—how—"

"Lost your powers of speech?" She took another delicate bite, chewed, and swallowed.

"What else did they say?" One black eyebrow cocked, he stared at her expectantly.

"Ye cannot expect me to remember an entire conversation."

He said nothing, but she saw a muscle twitch in his jaw. Uncomfortable under his gaze, she reached into her skirt pocket to touch the miniature portrait of Adam. Her one memento of home, and the only thing she had to her name right now, save the clothes on her back.

The Englishman was studying her, his eyes narrowed. "Why did you let the Gothards get away?"

"I told ye—"

"No, 'tis a nice story. Very well done of you. But for you to know this much, well, 'tis perfectly clear you're none other than Emerald MacCallum, and not a chance you'll convince me otherwise. Are you going to eat that?" He indicated her bread.

"Help yourself." As she watched him reach across and break off a piece, Cait struggled for calm. She'd given him the silent treatment earlier, but it had been at least as hard on her as it had on him. No sense continuing the unpleasantness when she'd never see him again after tonight. Although if he called her "Emerald" one more time, a swift kick where it hurt might be in order.

He washed down a second piece of her bread with his ale. "Tell me why you're looking for your brother."

His amused tone, as though he were trying to pacify her, would annoy her if she let it. But she wouldn't. Considering, she tangled her fingers in the end of one of her braids. Mayhap if she told him more of her story, he would come to believe her. "My father decreed that Adam will inherit all of Leslie, unless I marry within the year."

Plates rattled and diners chattered in the background. "And . . . ?"

"Marriage is out of the question. Men are too demanding and controlling." She flashed him a bright, facetious grin.

He appeared to be coughing up his ale.

"Is something amiss?"

"No." He thumped himself on the chest, then winced. "Continue."

"Well, Adam isn't fit to run Leslie. A restless sort, Adam is. And since I dinna plan to marry, I need his signature on some papers relinquishing his rights to the property." She fixed him with her best accusing glare. "The papers are in my satchel on the coach."

"I'll have another set drawn up in London." He blotted his mouth with his napkin. "At my expense."

"Your generosity knows no bounds."

Apparently unaffected by her sarcasm, the Englishman stared at her supper. "Are you going to finish that?"

She shoved her half-eaten pie in his direction. "By all the saints, you're a bottomless pit. 'Tis a wonder you're not fat as old King Henry."

"Runs in the family." With a scrape, he pulled it closer.

"As the sow fills, the draff sours."

"Pardon?"

She watched as the pie methodically disappeared. "The more ye eat, the less ye enjoy your food."

"Another of your mother's pearls of wisdom?"

"Aye, her words are wise."

"In this case, her words are wrong." He washed down the last of her supper with the last of her ale, then stood. " 'Twas quite enjoyable. Now I must dash off a note and post it to Scarborough, to warn him of his brothers' intentions. And another note to my family. They'll be wondering where I am." He rooted in his pocket and came out with a key. "Would you like to go up? The innkeeper had naught but a single room, but I'm certain we'll fare well together."

"Ye are, are ye?" Fifty-seven rooms and only one available? She didn't believe him for a moment. He planned on keeping his eye on her.

"Yes," he said, so tolerantly she gritted her teeth. "Room twenty-six, upstairs and to the left. I will meet you there in a few minutes." Handing her the key, he started out of the taproom, then turned back, weaving his way past other guests.

"I can trust you to wait?"

The key's hard metal edges bit into her clenched fist. "I'm not going anywhere," she assured him blithely.

Not yet, anyway.

Caithren headed up the fancy wrought-iron staircase, fuming as she looked for number twenty-six. 'Twas clear the Englishman didn't like her, yet he expected her to share his room tonight. She was glad she'd be rid of him soon. She would never figure him out. Most especially, she would never figure out what it was about him that made her want to goad him.

Or what is was about him that made her want to touch

him. If she were to be honest, that was the most puzzling thing of all.

Reaching the end of the corridor, she turned in disgust. She must have gone right, not left.

The Englishman was standing at the other end of the hall, watching her. "Are you lost?" he called.

"Nay." She hurried toward him. "I only wanted to have a wee look around."

One eyebrow raised, he took the key from her hand and fitted it into number twenty-six's lock. When the door swung open, she stood eyeing the room with trepidation, then turned and pinned him with an accusatory glare. "There is only one bed."

"I told you there was only one room. 'Tis no fault of mine it came with only one bed. We will manage." He prodded her inside and set his portmanteau on the bed in question. "I may be an Englishman," he said dryly, "but I'm not in the habit of forcing myself on unwilling women."

"I didn't think ye would." With a start, Caithren realized 'twas the truth. As infuriating as he was, she felt safe in his presence. It made no sense.

He removed his surcoat and tossed it over the back of a lovely carved chair, then went around the room lighting candles. She wandered over and fingered the fabric of his brown coat. Fine stuff, even though plain. Neat stitching that would have rivaled her mother's.

"Mam always despaired of my sewing talents," she blurted. What an inane thing to say. As though he cared. But she'd never been good at controlling her mouth when she was jumpy like this.

"Did she now?" He shut the door, blocking out the noises of other people in the hallway and downstairs.

"Aye, said I'd never make a proper wife. Never mind that I am capable of seeing to the health and provisioning of everyone at Leslie."

He moved an extra candle to the dressing table. "At

Leslie, huh?" From his leather bags came two shirts and
a pair of breeches, which he left in an untidy heap on
the bed, then an ivory comb, a razor, and a ball of soap.
"If you can do all that, I cannot see whereas sewing
would make much of a difference, one way or the
other."

"Dinna ye need a wife who can sew?"

He raised an eyebrow and heat rushed to her cheeks.
Jings, she couldn't stop blethering.

"I do not need a wife at all." He set the implements
on the dressing table and examined himself in its fine
mirror. "My sister, Kendra, takes care of running my
household."

"How about after she marries?"

His eyes met Cait's in the silvery surface. "Not bloody
likely. Anytime soon, at least." His gaze held hers for a
moment, and her stomach fluttered. Perhaps she wasn't
as safe with him as she'd thought. He stroked his mustache, then sighed and set to work with the brush and
soap, making a fine lather.

When he started brushing it onto his face, Caithren
walked to the window and drew aside the drapes. 'Twas
pitch-black behind the hotel, and she couldn't see a
thing. With a sigh, she let the curtain drop and ran a
hand down the wall beside the window. It had wallpaper—thick sheets nailed to the wall, with flock printing.
The paper's pattern felt velvety under her fingers. She'd
heard of wallpaper, but she'd never actually seen any
before.

The blade made a small scraping noise that sounded
loud in the silence. Despite herself, she snuck a glance
in the mirror. She'd not seen him clean-shaven, and devil
take it if her fingers didn't itch to touch the newly exposed smooth skin. Wishing she could convince herself
otherwise, she went to the bed and started folding the
clothes he'd left there, but her gaze kept wandering to
the emerging planes of his face.

He dipped the brush again, rubbed white foam in a wide arc beneath his nose, caught his upper lip with his teeth—

"What are ye doing?" she burst out.

"Removing my mustache." Calmly—as he did everything else—he drew the razor over a section, rinsed it in the washbowl, shaved the next patch. And on, until many black hairs floated on top of the water, and the space above his lip was bare and paler than the rest of his face.

He rubbed it ruefully. "Feels odd," he said, flashing her a grin full of straight, white teeth she hadn't noticed before. And those chiseled lips. Michty me, if he didn't have a beautiful mouth. Her own mouth gaped open as she laid the second shirt on the bed and sat herself at the edge, her hands clenched in her lap.

"What do you think?" he asked.

She finally found her tongue. "Ye look young."

He laughed. "And just how old did you think I was?"

"I dinna ken," she hedged, mentally kicking herself for making such a brainless comment in the first place. "Thirty, mayhap?"

"I'm thirty-two." He looked back in the mirror, turning his head this way and that.

"That old? But ye look—"

"I know. 'Tis why I grew it sixteen years ago. I was handed a lot of responsibility at an early age, and I thought if I looked older . . ." His fingers moved to stroke the absent whiskers, then jerked away. "I miss it already," he said.

"I thought ye wore it in imitation of the King." She gestured at the gorgeous long hair that reached to the middle of his chest. "Ye look like a Cavalier."

"My family did support Charles in the War," he said distractedly. One hand went up to stroke the wavy mass. "Well, there's nothing for it," he announced in resigned tones.

Puzzled, she cocked her head. "Nothing for it?"

"The hair." He reached for his knife. "It must come off as well."

She leapt from the bed, reaching to still his hand. "Why?" she breathed.

His eyes crinkled with humor in response to her horror. "Same reason I shaved the mustache. Gothard knows I'm alive now. I'd prefer he not notice me following him. I'll look different, yes?"

"Aye." Suddenly she realized she was touching his hand voluntarily, and she pulled back. "Ye look different already," she declared.

He glanced in the looking glass again. "Not different enough." Holding the end of a hank of the beautiful black silk, he measured it against his shoulder and hacked off a hunk. Crookedly.

She winced. "You're going to look like a wally-draigle."

His expression changed from pained concentration to definite amusement. "A what?"

"A most slovenly creature." She moved closer. "I'll cut it for ye," she said, "if you'll go down to the kitchen and ask to borrow some scissors."

Relief relaxed his features. "Done."

He left the room before she quite digested the offer she'd just made. Cut the man's hair? She wanted nothing to do with him. What had she been thinking?

She paced around the large chamber. The carved oak furniture all matched, and the counterpane and bedhangings looked to be of silk. Once again, she wondered how he could afford such a place. But apparently he'd been thinking ahead. He'd needed a mirror to do this job, and not many small inns would provide one.

She jumped when he barged back in, holding forth a pair of scissors. "Did you think I was a ghost again?"

"Nothing that benign." She dragged a chair over to face the mirror and waved him into it. He sat and grinned at her reflection in the glass, handing her the scissors over one shoulder.

"Go ahead," he urged.

The black waves felt soft in her hands. With a wince, she measured and cut, measured and cut, a wee bit at a time. Soon she was engrossed in the careful work, but not so much that she didn't steal glances at him in the mirror. His striking features were even more arresting without the mustache. She'd not noticed the long black lashes that crowned his clear, leaf-green eyes. A spicy masculine scent permeated his hair and skin. With her hands on him like this, he didn't seem so irritating and dangerous. As his dark locks slipped through her fingers, it seemed like a different man was emerging. Surely not, but she felt differently toward him all the same. And chided herself for it.

He was studying her in the mirror as well. "What color are your eyes?" he asked.

"My eyes?" She clipped, then glanced up. "Hazel. Why?"

"They looked green earlier today, but now they look blue."

She frowned. "Well, they're hazel." She laid the last silky sheared hank on the dressing table and stepped away to assess her handiwork. His hair now neatly skimmed his shoulders.

"Thank you," he said softly. " 'Tis a much better job than I would have done."

She glanced at his knife on the table's marble surface, and a wry smile teased at her lips. "I expect so."

Despite all her reservations, she was feeling rather kindly toward him—until he stood, stretched, then unlaced the top of his shirt and pulled it free from his breeches.

"What are ye doing now?" she burst out.

He sat back on the chair to pull off his boots. "Getting comfortable for bed. We've a long day ahead of us tomorrow. We're planning to 'ride like the dickens,' if you remember."

"I remember," she said. "But—"

"Are you not going to take off your outerclothes?" His second boot fell to the floor with a loud *plop*. "I'm not planning to attack you."

"I have nothing else to wear, thanks to ye. My night rail is in my satchel. In the—"

"—public coach." He peeled off a stocking. "I know. That thing beneath your bodice, the garment that looks like a blouse? I'm no expert on women's clothing, but 'tis quite long, is it not? A shift, is it called?"

"Aye, 'tis a shift." She plucked distractedly at its sleeves. "Not that it's any of your concern." She stalked to the bed and tucked his clothes that she'd folded back into the portmanteau, then moved it to a table. Pulling back the lovely counterpane, she found a thick quilt resting beneath. She lifted one corner and climbed into bed. "Sleep well," she said, in a tone meant to speak of finality.

He rose and moved to look down on her. "You're going to suffocate," he predicted. "At least loosen your bodice."

When she made no move to do so, he threw back the quilt, leaned over her, and made quick work of untying the bow at the top of her laces.

"Unhand me!" she squeaked in disbelief. He was tugging at the laces before she collected her wits enough to bat his hands away. "I-I cannot believe what ye are doing! No man has ever loosened my clothing—"

"A pity, sweetheart," he interjected smoothly, finishing the job he'd started. One long fingertip trailed softly alongside her face. "Though I find that difficult to believe with a woman like you. Don't you fret—I may be the first, but I can assure you I'll not be the last."

She felt a flush crawl up her neck, heating her cheeks.

She opened her mouth to say something, but nothing coherent came to mind.

"There they go again," he said. "Your eyes were just green, and now they've turned blue." He reached for her amulet.

"That stays," she said firmly, finding her tongue. "I never take it off."

He only raised a brow and moved to the foot of the bed to pull off her shoes. "Now you'll rest easier." Caithren was still sputtering when he flipped the quilt back to cover her.

Glaring at him, she lay silent as he walked around the room snuffing the candles. In increments, the room descended into darkness. He slid in on the other side of the bed, his substantial weight depressing the feather mattress and making her almost roll into him. She gripped the blanket in tense fists, holding herself in place.

"Sleep well, now," he called in a voice that was annoyingly unperturbed. Apparently giving him the evil eye had had no effect on him at all. "We've a long journey ahead of us still."

He leaned to blow out the candle atop the small table by the bed, and Caithren raised herself to an elbow to do the same on her side. Her heart pounded hard in her chest as she lay back down and stared into the darkness. It didn't seem as though he planned to attack her, and yet . . . she realized suddenly that her pulse raced not from fear, but from something else.

Da had fed and clothed her, Cameron had offered protection and companionship, and more than one suitor had connived to press his lips to hers. But no man had ever made it his business to care for her in a physical sense. The Englishman's hands on her had felt different than Da's or Cam's or those fumbling courting lads'.

She wasn't at all sure whether or not she cared for the feeling. And why did it matter, aye? Her hand went up and wrapped around her amulet. She'd be rid of him after tonight.

Rigid, she lay beside him, willing herself to stay awake while her eyes adjusted to the darkness. Had they crossed their arms across their chests, she imagined she and the Englishman would resemble one of the marble effigies in her village kirk, a lord and lady frozen together in time. But she was no titled lady, and the Englishman was certainly no lord. He wasn't even a gentleman.

She had to get away from him. Back to the coach, where she hoped and prayed they were still carrying her belongings. 'Twould be a miracle should her money still be intact, but she couldn't worry about that now.

It seemed like forever before his breathing evened out in sleep. She waited a few minutes until she was sure, then jogged his shoulder to double-check. He groaned as though in pain, then settled down with a soft snore. She leaned over him, remembering the other moments he'd seemed to be hurting. Suddenly she wondered if *he* could have been injured last night as well. Helping her.

Rising, she swept her shoes off the floor and continued to stare. She couldn't let herself be swayed, even if he had been hurt. 'Twas no fault of hers. Slowly she backed away, then turned. Her decision had already been made.

With one last glance over her shoulder, she slipped into the corridor and quietly closed the door behind her. Leaning against the wall, she straightened her bodice and relaced it snugly. Then she slid into her shoes, marched downstairs, through the taproom, and out into the night, trying her best to look as though she hadn't a care in the world.

'Twas chilly and drizzling. She had no money to hire a horse, no alternative other than to start walking. But there loomed a long night ahead. The coach had stopped in one of the towns they'd passed, and if she followed the road, surely she'd get back to it before morning.

* * *

"Mama, must ye go? You've been home nary a month."

"I must, wee Alison." Flora MacCallum moved to her youngest's bed and bent to kiss her little forehead. She smoothed the fine, chestnut hair from her daughter's face. "Mayhap, with any luck, this time will be the last."

Malcolm crawled over his sister and down to the floor to hug his mother around the knees. "Are ye going to be Emerald again?"

"Aye. I'm going to be Emerald one more time."

"But 'tis the middle of the night."

"Nay, dawn approaches, and others are no doubt on the Gothards' trail already." She knelt to give her bonnie lad a fierce hug, breathing in his scent to sustain her through the days and weeks ahead. Soap and milk, underscored by a faint trace of the clean dirt she could never quite get out from under his fingernails. She wished she could bottle the aroma and take it with her.

Unwinding his small arms from around her neck, she stood to shrug into a man's surcoat.

" 'Tis lucky ye two were of a height." Hearing her mother's voice, Flora turned to see her leaning against the door that separated the two rooms of their cottage. "Not many women can wear their husband's clothes, ye ken?"

"Aye?" A strand of long gray hair had escaped her mother's braid; Flora walked over and pushed it behind her ear. " 'Twas the only lucky thing between us."

"Now, Flora—"

"Dinna go defending him, Mama." Her words were firm, but she pressed a kiss to the top of her tiny mother's head. All of Flora's height—and she was the tallest woman in all of Galloway—had come from her father. "I will never forgive my husband for pledging our home in a game of dice and then getting himself killed in that border raid. Damned hallirackit."

"Wheesht! The bairns are listenin'."

"And right they should be." She twisted up her unruly red hair and jammed her deceased husband's hat on her head. " 'Tis fair they know why I have to leave them."

"Flora—"

"Just give me peace 'til this is finished, Mama. One last time. With the reward posted for Gothard, I can pay off Kincaid and then some. We will be able to breathe. Concentrate on the farming. Mayhap even get wee Alison her own bed. Will that not be nice?"

"Nice, Mama!" Alison repeated.

Flora's mother bent to sweep a length of broken reed off the floor. The roof needed replacing as well. "Damn your daftie of a father for ever takin' ye tracking," she muttered. "Thought ye were the son he never had."

"Neither of us chose our men well." Flora stuck a pistol into her boot top and snatched up the sword that was propped in the corner. "Still and on, if Papa hadn't taken me, I wouldn't be able to get us out of the mess we're in today." She kissed her mother's parchment cheek. "Take care of the bairns, Mama. God willing, I'll be back to stay."

Hard kisses for Alison and Malcolm, and she was off to do what needed to be done.

Once and for all.

Chapter Seven

Jason jerked awake. Emerald was gone. Again.

Dawn's hazy gray light seeped through the window. He slept soundly these days, the bone-deep weariness of a healing body coupled with hard hours on the road. But still . . . how was it that a woman could rise, dress herself, and leave without waking him?

Cursing himself—which was getting to be quite a habit—he pulled on his boots and went downstairs, hoping she had only gone in search of something to break her fast. But the Crown's cheerful taproom was eerily empty. Too early yet for guests to be up and about.

And Emerald was gone, really gone.

He winced at the thought of her out there alone. But there was nothing for it. He could ill afford to waste precious time searching for her, even supposing it were possible he'd be successful. It had been a different matter when she was on a lumbering coach taking a specific route. She could be anywhere by now, and he knew not the first thing about tracking a body—that was her forte, not his.

He would simply have to make it his business to get to London first. How long was her head start? Had she found a horse? With no money, she'd have a hard time of it—

Panicking, he pulled out his coin pouch and spilled the contents into his hand.

Nothing was missing.

Idiot woman.

Slipping the pouch back into his pocket, he tramped outside into the gray morning and went to wake the stable boy.

'Twas four hours since Caithren had seen a soul. Soaked to the skin, she shivered with a bone-deep cold. She'd passed through three tiny villages—if one could even call them that—but only one had boasted an inn, and no coach had been parked in its courtyard.

It felt as though she'd descended into an evil land where no one existed save herself. As dawn approached, a talkative family rumbled by in an ox-drawn cart. She would have loved to beg a ride, but they were going the opposite direction. Regardless, just the sight of them brought a tiny smile of relief.

Walking backward, she watched them fade into the distance, their cheerful voices becoming fainter and fainter until all was quiet, save for the steady beat of the rain. A lonely sound. Summoning her last reserves of energy, Cait turned and walked faster. She must be near to the coach by now. Squinting her eyes, she thought she could see a village ahead, a silhouetted irregular line of rooftops. A church spire, or mayhap 'twas only more trees. She couldn't be sure, and rain suddenly pelted from the sky, obliterating the hazy view and washing down the sloping road, hiding the deep, slushy ruts. She tripped into one of them and fell to her knees in the mud, wrenching one foot as she went. The tears that had been threatening all the long night pricked hot behind her eyelids.

No, not the tears again. Wheesht, she wouldn't let that happen. She took a deep breath and dragged herself up.

Though she'd only twisted her ankle, her whole leg throbbed. Her teeth were chattering, and the hand clenching her amulet was shaking and white-knuckled with strain. When someone approached from behind on horseback, she hadn't the strength to turn around and look. Mayhap the traveler would help her. More likely he'd simply ignore her.

Seconds later, she was wishing that were the case. She heard the heavy thud of a man dropping from his horse, and when she forced herself to turn he was leading an obviously ill-treated nag by the reins, his boots squishing in the mud as he trudged toward her.

"What have we here?" Black eyes leered wildly from a rough-hewn face, dark with unshaven stubble that didn't look anywhere near as bonnie as it had on the Englishman.

Caithren backed up a step. "I-I have no money," she managed to stutter out. To demonstrate, she turned her pockets inside out, revealing naught but the miniature portrait of Adam, which she hastily shoved back inside.

Undaunted, the man dropped his mount's reins and stepped closer. The horse looked too worn out to bother going anywhere. Even through the scents of rain and mud, the man's stale, liquor-tinged breath choked Cait as he came near and peered into her face. "Pl-please, sir. I haven't anything you'd want."

"We'll see about that." With a lunge, he plunged one grimy hand down her bodice, rooting around.

"I have nothing!" Shocked, she twisted in his grip. "Unhand me!" This man was sick, evil. Bile rose in her throat as panic tightened her chest. "Stop! Unhand me! Now!"

"No money in here?" The rough fingers shifted and clawed one breast in a painful squeeze. "Ah, but I would not say you have nothing."

Anger and indignation boiled up. Cait's hands went 'round his thick neck and squeezed in return, but though her vision blurred with the effort, he seemed not to notice. She yelled, kicking at his shins, but her injured ankle threw her off balance, and he was managing to back her up into the trees at the edge of the road.

His other hand reached down, hiking her skirt as they stumbled together in the mud, a writhing mass of combat. Gathering her wits, she brought one knee up—hard. With a stunned grunt, the man pulled away and hunched over. But she knew he'd be after her again. She'd never outrun him with her hurt ankle. If only she could get to his horse.

She sprang for the animal, but the man reached to snag her by the wrist. Thinking quickly, she gritted her teeth and reached her free hand to pat his body, searching for a gun, a blade—

Beneath his soggy, smelly coat, her fingers closed on the grip of a knife. As she tugged it from its sheath, the man growled in rage and wrenched himself upright.

"Keep back!" Bravely, she brandished the knife in his face.

And a gunshot rang out, the sheer shock of it forcing her to fall backward into the mud. Her breath expelled in a rush. It hadn't hit her. It had come from another direction altogether.

The man turned and bolted for his horse. Hammering hoofbeats were coming upon them—indeed, were it not for the pounding rain and the veil of her own fear, Cait knew she'd have heard the sound earlier.

The man was mounted and moving before her rescuer made it to Caithren and reached down a hand to help her rise.

The Englishman.

She stared at him in disbelief. No matter where she went, he insisted on showing up. But she found herself absurdly grateful he'd shown up now, even if she didn't understand him. At least he'd never tried to take advantage. Her hands went defensively to her chest, trying to erase the feel of the monstrous man who was riding away.

With a lingering glance at the man's retreating back,

the Englishman slid from the saddle and gathered Caithren into his arms. "Are you hurt?"

Shuddering, she shook her head. His body gave off signals of comfort, but his next words were laced with a quiet fury. "I can scarcely credit how much trouble you are," he mumbled under his breath.

She'd have felt better if he'd have just yelled at her. "Wh-what did ye say?"

"I said, are you hurt?"

That was not what he'd said, and they both knew it. "Nay, only shaken a bit." Though she'd like nothing better than to stand on her own, her hands gripped his shoulders convulsively. Her manhandled breasts burned beneath her bodice, and her ankle shot fire if she put any weight on it, but she wouldn't cry. She'd heard him mutter about her being trouble, and she knew he hated her tears almost as much as she did.

He gave her a few awkward pats on the back, then set her away. She blinked in dismay at his face: the clenched, chiseled jaw; the telltale red in his cheeks; the hard, accusing eyes. Predictably, though, his voice was calm as ever. Calm and berating.

"What the hell did you think you were doing wandering alone in the middle of the night?"

He had the nerve to be outraged on her behalf? Protective? The cur. Anger coursed through her. "I was going back to the coach! To get my things and complete my journey! I was almost there, too. Just leave me be!"

He stared at her, his mouth working as though he wanted to say something but couldn't think how to word it.

"I dinna need your help," she added, though she wasn't at all sure what would have happened if he'd not charged in on his silver horse. "I was taking care of myself just fine," she said. And she might have. The man had been huge and mean, but she'd had the knife.

"I can see that." He eyed the dull gray blade in her hand. "And I saw you, um . . . with your knee . . ."

"Um-hmm." She gave him a smug smile.

"But I would expect that from Emerald MacCallum."

She gritted her teeth decisively. "Very well, then. I appreciate your gallant rescue, but now I'll be on my way." Gathering what little was left of her composure, she swivelled and started limping down the road.

She could feel his eyes on her back. One, two, three steps . . . four, five, six. "Emerald." His voice wasn't reproving any longer, more mocking if she didn't miss her guess. "Oh, Emerald . . ."

She didn't stop. Her name wasn't Emerald. Nine, ten, eleven, twelve . . .

"You're walking in the wrong direction."

She dropped the knife in the mud. He was behind her in a flash, his hands large and heavy on her suddenly trembling shoulders. " 'Tis London ahead. We passed the coach. Most likely it stopped in Rossington, north of where we slept."

"I kent that." Staring into the distance, she rubbed a wet finger over the smooth oval of her emerald. "I wasn't walking north?"

"No." He came around to face her, seemingly at a loss for words. Tears welled in her eyes; she couldn't seem to stop them. Hopefully they were disguised by the rain. His hand went up to stroke his missing mustache, then dropped and clenched into a fist. "Did you not notice the landscape was different?"

"Different?" Her voice went higher than she would have liked. She struggled to control herself as she scanned the drenched countryside. " 'Tis flat, just the same as yesterday. All England is flat and ugly."

He shook his head and gestured at the gently rolling land. " 'Tween Doncaster and Bawtry, 'twas flat planted fields, bordered with trees. Here, there are hills used for grazing."

"Hills, hah!" By all the saints, he was right, though she shuddered to admit it. Oh, why did she suffer from such a terrible sense of direction? Why couldn't she just have normal faults, like normal folk? A lisp, or blotchy skin. "Where I come from, this is flat." She sniffed back the tears. "W-will ye take me there, then? To Rossington, where the coach is?"

She hated herself for the wobble in her voice.

"No."

She hated *him* for being so disagreeable.

"Why not? What d'ye want from me?"

"I haven't the time to backtrack. And I want to keep an eye on you." Rain was dripping off his nose and his wide-brimmed hat, but he didn't look nearly as miserable as she felt. "I cannot allow you to face Gothard alone."

'Twas the last straw; the tears overflowed and ran down her cheeks. "I dinna want this man Gothard," she wailed. "I want my brother, Adam! I want my bed at Leslie, and my cousin, Cameron. I want something—one thing!—to go right for a change! And my name is Caithren!" Her chest heaved with a sudden sob, and the Englishman reacted immediately, wrapping her into his arms.

"I hate ye!" Reaching up, she pounded on his shoulders.

With a grunt, he shoved her away. "Bloody hell, will you stop beating up on me? I told you I'd take you to London. I'll replace your clothes and your precious satchel and whatever else was inside. I'll repay your money, and should it turn out you really do have a brother"—his face showed what he thought were the chances of that—"I'll hire a solicitor to draw up your bloody papers. Just stop hitting me, damn it." He paused for breath. "I'm not out to hurt you. I want only to make sure I get to Gothard first."

His voice softened, almost to a whisper. "I cannot get

on with my life—whatever is left of it—until I do so."
The eyes that bore into hers were filled with pain. "Can
you not try to understand that?"

Despite herself, she nodded, hot tears streaming down
her face to mix with the cold rain. When she swayed, he
gathered her close once again, and the tears flowed
faster.

What would she have done if he hadn't come after
her? She was so far ahead of the coach now; with no
money, there was no way she could make it to London
by herself. Even if she did manage to figure out the
right direction.

But she hated herself for needing him, especially because his arms felt so reassuring around her. He was a
scoundrel who wouldn't believe her story. A scoundrel
who'd kept her off the public coach, endangering her
plans to meet Adam and stranding her with nothing. A
scoundrel who kept calling her Emerald.

And still, she felt safe in the circle of his arms. Beneath his chilly, wet cloak, his spicy, male scent warmed
her nostrils while rain pattered all around them.

"Have we a bargain?" he asked softly.

She nodded against his chest.

He stepped back and reached out a finger, lifting her
chin. "Was that a yes?"

"Aye, it was." She drew a shaky breath.

"And you won't disappear on me again?"

"I'll not try to escape ye."

"And you won't hit me again?"

A tiny smile threatened to burst free. "That I cannot promise."

He heaved an elaborate sigh. "I suppose I will have
to take what I can get, then."

"I suppose ye will." Her lips curved after all; she
couldn't help herself.

He was staring at her mouth. He moved close, placed
his hands on her shoulders . . . and still, he was staring

at her mouth. "Shall we seal this agreement?" he asked softly.

"Wh-what?" Was he fixing to kiss her? Nay, that couldn't be. She backed away. "I said we have a bargain, Mr. Chase."

He blinked. "Mr. Chase? Did I not tell you to call me Jason?"

"I haven't been calling ye anything. I've been trying my best to ignore ye, if ye hadn't noticed. Out loud, that is. In my head, I've been calling ye all sorts of things."

"I'll bet you have." He bent down and fished the knife from the mud, pulled out a handkerchief and wiped the blade. "I'm thinking you should have leave to call me Jason."

"Oh, aye?"

A gleam came into his eyes. "After all, we have slept together."

Her cheeks flushed hot. "Not exactly. *Ye* slept." She looked down and readjusted the soggy bow at the top of her laces. "I was taught to address my elders with respect."

"Your *elders*? Do you think me so old and decrepit?"

Cait's gaze shot up at the disconcertment in his voice. She wished she had the talent to paint; if she could capture his expression on canvas, she could laugh at it forever. "Very well, then. Since I've no other means to get to London—thanks to ye—I will stay with ye willingly. As your equal." He opened his mouth, but she rushed on. "And as such, I will call ye Jason. Out loud. I cannot promise what I'll call ye in my head."

Frustration and amusement mingled in his glance. "Here," he said gruffly, shoving the knife into his belt and then shrugging out of his cloak and settling it over her shoulders.

"You'll get wet," she protested, even as she snuggled into it. It felt heavy and blessedly warm from the heat of his body. But his brown surcoat was becoming peppered with the dark splotches of raindrops. "I am already soaked. 'Twill do me no good."

"You're shivering. It will cut the cold." He removed his hat and plopped it on her head as well. "I'll not have you catching a chill."

He'd tied his hair back with a ribbon, making a short, neat tail at the nape of his neck. She watched as it became soaked, too.

"Now we'll both be miserable," she said. "But I thank ye for your gallantry. Why ye deserve thanks is beyond my ken, but Mam always said 'guid manners suffer bad yins.' "

Thin rivulets of water ran down his expressionless face and dripped off the end of his nose. She saw a muscle twitch in his jaw while she waited for him to ask for a translation.

"Courtesy outshines poor manners," she finally said.

His eyes narrowed. Swinging her up into his arms before she could protest, he marched back to his horse and deposited her on the saddle with a bit more force than was necessary. She let out a little grunt.

"I'm sorry," he mumbled. "Are you all right?"

"I reckon I'll live."

He reached up to wipe one warm tear from her cheek, a futile gesture considering the continual rain. "Why did you not pull your pistol on that bastard?"

" 'Tis in my satchel, in—"

"—the coach." He sighed. "I know. My fault. I'm sorry." He reached down to draw a pistol from his boot. The smallest gun she'd ever seen, much fancier than Da's, with a brass barrel and a mother-of-pearl grip inlaid with brass wire scrollwork. "Here, take this one," he offered.

It looked very expensive. "Nay, I—"

"Take it. You should have something to protect yourself." When she didn't move to claim it, he took it upon himself to reach beneath the cloak and stuff it into her skirt pocket.

"Thank ye," she said stiffly, clutching the cloak closed in front with two cold fists. "Mayhap I will need it; there seem to be a high proportion of unscrupulous men about England."

He fixed her with an assessing green gaze, then mounted behind her. His arms came around her waist, altogether more comforting than she expected, and they took off at a decent clip down the muddy road.

"You seem to paint all Englishmen with the same brush," he said presently. "Tell me, Emerald, are there not bad people in Scotland, as well?"

"My name is Caithren," she snapped. "And we save our aggression for the English."

'Twas not even close to the truth, but it sounded good.

Chapter Eight

Seated before Jason in the saddle, Emerald's head bobbed as she drifted in and out of sleep. He found himself leaning close, hoping for a whiff of the flowery scent he'd already come to think of as hers. Whatever it had been—bath oil, perfume or the like; he was certainly no expert on women's toiletries—the rain had washed away every trace. But plain Emerald smelled almost as good.

He glanced at the sky, happy that the rain had let up. The road in this area was clay, normally stiff and easy to travel, but the miserable wet had turned it into a path of mud. On both sides of the slushy mess, barley fields glistened green in the dwindling drizzle.

When he stood in the stirrups to relieve his stiffness, Emerald came awake with a start. She might have fallen off if he hadn't managed to make a grab for her. She yawned into a small, dainty hand. Certainly not a hand that looked accustomed to holding a pistol.

"Tired, are you?" he drawled, resettling both her and himself and adjusting again to Chiron's rhythmic sway.

"I didn't sleep, if you'll remember."

"What I remember is waking up alone, wondering where you were and if you were safe."

"Ye mean wondering if I'd managed to get to Gothard afore ye could."

"I didn't say that, Emerald."

"How many times must I tell ye I'm not Emerald

MacCallum?" She twisted around to see him. "Why will ye not believe my story?"

"You do a pretty job of telling it, but it doesn't wash. For one thing, it hinges on you or your brother inheriting some land. Besides the fact that I cannot imagine you as a landowner"—that earned him a glare before she turned away, her chin tilting up—"you're from Scotland. Land there is not owned by individuals," he said smugly. " 'Tis owned by the clans."

"A fat lot ye know." Her voice was unmistakably scornful. "I'm from the east, not the northern Highlands. Can ye not tell from my accent?"

That lilting accent was affecting his thought processes. "You sound like a Scot to me." He guided Chiron back to the center of the road, away from the dangerous bogs that plagued the edges. "Scots are Scots."

Before him, her back went stiff. "Curious," she said softly. "Ye dinna strike an initial impression of an uneducated man, but ye seem to be unaccountably lacking in knowledge."

"And I suppose *you've* been to university?" The fact that he hadn't had always rankled him. After the Civil War, Jason had spent his early adulthood in exile with the King, and of all the Chases, only the youngest brother, Ford, had received a formal education.

"Close enough," she said. "I read all of Adam's books after he was booted out. Didn't want to see them go to waste."

"Tell me not they believe women should be educated in that wilderness you call a country."

Though he'd said the words in all good humor—he'd seen to it that his sister Kendra was educated, and he thought her the better for it—an outraged squeal came from before him. Emerald shifted, her elbow unintentionally lodging in his gut.

"Ouch!" He rubbed his ribs. "Sit still, will you?"

"Well," she huffed, "I'm thinking ye should buy another horse. Then ye wouldn't care how I sit. And we could go faster. The Gothard brothers are on two horses, ye ken."

"Don't I know it," he grumbled. *His* two horses. She had a point. But though he'd planned to buy another horse yesterday, today he was having second thoughts. With another horse, Emerald would have the means to run off on her own.

Besides, his complaining aside, he rather liked having her riding in front of him.

"This horse is faster," he said. "Even with us riding double."

"How can—"

"Take my word for it." He knew those horses; they were decent stock, but not in Chiron's class. The brothers had gotten a head start toward Pontefract, and even wounded he'd beaten them there. "I'm sure they're not riding any more hours than we are," he said, anticipating her next protest. "This road is plagued by highwaymen at night, not at all safe to travel. And besides, their horses need the rest; they've been riding them for weeks."

"They said they would ride like the dickens," she reminded him. "They could be changing horses."

"I've no fear of that. They haven't the money to be changing horses."

Beneath her borrowed hat, her braids swished as she shook her head. "If ye haven't the money for another horse," she said in a patronizing tone, "ye can just say so. 'Tis nothing to be ashamed of."

He smiled to himself, realizing she truly had no idea who he was. That was good—it was safer for them both if his cover of a commoner was convincing.

"Speaking of money," he said, "why did you not take some when you tried to leave? How did you expect to fend for yourself with no silver to pay your way?"

She was silent a moment. "Are ye saying I should have *stolen* from ye?"

"Some folks would not look at it as stealing." When Chiron started up a hill, Emerald slid back against him. Too close. "As you so recently pointed out, it's my fault you have no coin. 'Tis a dangerous world; you really should look out for yourself."

The road flattened, and it was a relief when she drew herself straight. "Two wrongs dinna make a right."

"Does your mother say that, too?"

"Everyone says that. Ye must have heard it afore?"

"I've heard it." Spotting a bridge up ahead, he tensed. "I just don't think it applies in this case." Deliberately he drew his gaze from the bridge, wondering how she managed on her own. As unpleasant as this association had been so far, he felt he'd be signing her death warrant to allow her to go it alone. His father would never have left a woman to cope by herself. "Have you ever considered there might be such a thing as being too honest?"

"Wheesht! Ye actually sound angry I didn't take your money."

"Not angry. Only concerned for you, with your habit of chasing all over England." The sun peeked through the clouds just as the road fed onto Bridgegate. "I'll not always be here to protect you."

"Chasing all over England? I've never been here afore. And 'twill be a long time afore I'm tempted to come back. *And* I can take care of myself."

He doubted that but let the matter drop, stopping at the bridge's end to wait for a cart and two mounted riders coming from the other direction. The River Idle sparkled in the new, bright light, and a brilliant rainbow arched from its center.

"Oh, the colors are lovely." Some damp strands had escaped Emerald's braids, and she pushed them off the side of her face. "But rainbows bring bad luck, aye?"

"You think so?" he asked, amused.

She nodded. "I ken a verse against it."

A carriage lumbered toward them across the bridge. "By all means, chant it if it would make you feel better."

Her chin went up. "Are ye mocking me?"

"Never." At the driver's wave, he smiled and inclined his head. "I'm waiting to hear it."

She cleared her throat.

> "Rainbow, rainbow, haud away hame
> A' your bairns are dead but ane
> And it lies sick at yon gray stane
> And will be dead ere ye win hame
>
> Gang owre the Drumaw and yont the lea
> And down by the side o' yonder sea
> Your bairn lies greetin' like to die
> And the big tear-drop is in his eye."

Finished, she waited expectantly. "What a long, bothersome charm that is," he said. Not to mention he had understood but half the words. "Can you not just cross the rainbow out?"

"Cross it out?" Chiron shifted, and she knotted her fingers into his mane. "What mean ye by that?"

"Hereabouts, folk place a couple twigs on the ground in the form of a cross, and lay four pebbles at the ends."

"I've never heard of such a thing." She cocked her head. "Will ye be doing it, then?"

"Hell, no. I don't fancy myself superstitious." Another rider was crossing the river. "Would you like to get down and do it?"

"Nay. The verse will do well enough." Chiron snorted and gave an impatient toss of his head, making Emerald sway. Jason steadied her. "Shall we cross already?" she asked.

A father and two sons were on the bridge.

"I just . . ." There was no way to hide it—they'd be crossing many rivers. He took a deep breath. "I prefer to ride down the center of bridges."

"Down the center?" He could hear the smile in her voice. "And ye say you're not superstitious."

"The bridge is now clear," he muttered, guiding Chiron onto it.

"Down the center," she repeated with a giggle. "I'd never have thought you'd keep a ritual like that. An unsuperstitious man who is not afeared of ghosts."

He kept his eyes trained on the other side of the river. "I'm pleased to entertain you."

Her shoulders shook with mirth, but she kept her counsel as they rode through the town to the square. The marketplace bustled with commerce. Sellers hawked wheels of yellow and white cheeses while buyers haggled over fresh produce. Cattle for sale crowded a smelly pen, and farm laborers stood around, waiting to be hired. Jason noticed one booth filled with a mishmash of household goods and thought he spotted a few garments in the mix. Hopefully a new skirt for Emerald.

Perched along one edge of the square, Ye Olde Sun Inn was a timber-framed building with a central chimney and a narrow upper story under a steeply sloping roof. "Olde" indeed. But delicious scents wafted out the open door.

"Damnation, I'm hungry," he said.

"When are ye not?"

"Since I met you? Never. You've a disconcerting habit of keeping me from my breakfast." As she drew breath to protest, he added, "I'll buy us a meal and take a room for a couple hours. You can wash off the mud and then sleep while I find you some dry clothes."

"Sleep," she breathed, apparently placated for the moment. "Oh, a wee sleep sounds heavenly."

"Emerald. 'Tis almost noon. Time to wake up."

"I'm not Emerald," Caithren moaned, batting Jason's

hand from her shoulder. Her nap had been entirely too short; after walking all night, she could have slept the day away and then some. But she forced open her eyes. There was no time to waste. No matter how tired she was, she needed to get moving in order to find Adam.

Dressed in clean, dry breeches and a fresh white shirt, Jason leaned over her, too close for her comfort. His broad shoulders blocked her view of the room, and suddenly she felt frightened, alone with this stranger. It had been different last night when she was planning to leave. Now she would have to forge some sort of relationship with him. Sharing a room at an inn was an intimidating way to start.

Even groggy, she was utterly aware that because her clothes were all wet, she was naked beneath the sheets, one breast already bruised with the marks of an Englishman's fingers. But she remembered Jason's pistol was tucked beneath her pillow. Proof that he'd not be taking advantage of her, because surely he wouldn't have given her the means to protect herself.

She drew a shaky breath.

"Emerald?" He leaned closer still, unsettling her even more. "I brought you something from the marketplace."

Yawning, she struggled to sit up and reminded herself they had a truce. Self-consciously she clutched the quilt beneath her chin with both hands, feigning confidence she didn't feel. "What is it?"

"A Shropshire cake." He held out a flat yellow pastry with a diamond pattern scored into the top. "Try it."

She stared at his hand, mesmerized by the sheer size of it for a moment, and told herself that a man this large could hurt but could also protect. A delicious scent drifted under her nose, shifting her gaze to the cake. "Very thoughtful," she allowed. She leaned forward to have a bite. "Mmmm. It tastes like shortbread."

"Well, take it."

Not wanting to disappoint, she bravely risked using

one hand to hold it and have some more. "*Scottish* short-bread," she said around a mouthful.

He smiled. "I'm glad you like it. I bought four."

The buttery pastry seemed to melt on her tongue. "Where are the other three cakes, then?"

With a sheepish grin, he pointed to his stomach.

"I see." She took another bite. " 'Tis honored I am that ye saved me one."

" 'Twas a sacrifice," he said solemnly. "And a peace offering."

That got her attention. "For what?" The last morsel went into her mouth, and she licked her fingers. "I thought we already had a truce."

"For this." From behind his back, he produced a large, soft packet, and set it on her lap.

Slanting him a sidewise glance, she used one hand to slowly unfold the paper. When it lay open across the quilt, she could only stare. "Ye dinna expect me to *wear* this, do ye?"

"This" was a bright red gown, complete with an indecently sheer chemise and an embroidered stomacher—a long triangular contraption worn on the front of the dress to cover the laces. Cait looked wistfully at her shift, skirt, and bodice where they hung on three wall pegs drying. Or rather, no longer dripping. They were far from dry.

" 'Twas all I could find," he said apologetically. He took the gown from her, shook it out, and held it up. "It is not all that bad." He frowned at what was surely a look of pained disbelief on her face. "Is it?"

" 'Tis fit for an English doxy."

"If you think that, I am forced to conclude you've never *seen* an English doxy." Despite what looked like a heroic effort to control himself, his lips twitched.

Cait closed her eyes and touched her fingertips to her forehead. "It will have to do, I suppose. Temporarily."

"I'll leave you to get dressed." Quickly he stepped outside, closing the door behind him.

Resigned, she rose from the bed, wincing as she put weight on her ankle. When she slipped the chemise over her head, it slithered down her body, feeling like less than nothing. The gown went on next. She tightened the laces, then stared down at her cleavage exposed in the deep, curved neckline. The chemise's lace trim barely peeked out over the edge. Unlike her shift, it was mere decoration, apparently not meant to preserve the wearer's modesty.

No chance was she going into public with half her bosom hanging out. She loosened the dress, wiggled out of it, took her shift off the wall and wrung it out mercilessly.

Jason's voice came muffled through the door. "Are you decent yet?"

"Just give me peace 'til I tell ye I'm ready," she called impatiently. She shook out the shift, wishing she had an iron. 'Twas more wrinkled than old Widow MacKenzie's haggard face.

Well, there was nothing for it. She pulled it on, shivering at the clammy dampness. Though she usually wore it open at the neck, she tightened and tied the ribbon so the collar was snug around her throat. After putting on the dress, she lifted the matching stomacher and stared at it stupidly, then, with a huff, limped to open the door.

"I cannot figure how to attach this."

Jason stood on the threshold with his mouth open, his gaze riveted to her rumpled shift where it covered her above the gown's plunging neckline.

"I ken the dress is too big," she said, although she knew full well he wasn't looking at the loose waist. "Dinna ye dare laugh," she added.

"I'd not think of it," he fairly choked out, reaching for the stomacher. He came into the room and shut the door without a single snort, which she imagined was some feat.

"Hold it here," he instructed, plastering the stomacher against her front. "And then you attach the tabs, like this—"

"I cannot breathe." The stiff stomacher flattened her belly and breasts, pushing the latter up even higher and making her even happier for the cover of her shift. Experimentally she leaned forward, grunting when the pointed bottom dug into her lower abdomen. "Michty me," she said, "what is in this thing? Wood?"

"Yes. Or bone."

She'd been half fooling, but Jason sounded serious. She watched his long fingers work. "Ye look quite the expert at this."

"You think? I never expected to be dressing a woman." Finished, he looked up and grinned. "I have more practice taking these off."

"I'll wager ye do." She recalled him loosening her clothes last night, blushing at the thought. Embarrassed, she lowered her gaze. "I dinna suppose ye brought me dry stockings?"

"Stockings . . . oh, hell, I—"

"No matter," she said quickly, not really wanting to discuss intimate clothing. "Mine are almost dry." While he made their damp garments into a bundle he could hang from his portmanteau, she pulled on the stockings and her garters, lifting her skirt as little as possible. 'Twas no easy task since the stomacher prevented bending over. "How is one supposed to sit a horse wearing this contraption?"

"Ladies generally ride sidesaddle—"

"Balanced precariously for miles and miles?" Finished, she stood straight and arched her back, her body protesting the anticipated hours on horseback already. "Not a chance. I'll manage."

Closing the portmanteau, he slanted her an assessing glance. "Achy, are you?"

"Nay, only practical." She stepped into her still-wet shoes.

He nodded thoughtfully. "Emerald MacCallum would be practical."

"Caithren Leslie is practical." Shooting him a scathing glare, she dug under the pillow and slipped his pistol and Adam's portrait into the gown's pockets. "Shall we go?"

Three tedious hours later, Jason smiled to himself when Emerald tugged up on the stomacher for the dozenth time. "All England is not flat fields," she admitted wonderingly. "We are actually riding through a forest."

The shadows of the leaves overhead made pleasing patterns of light and dark on the road. "Sherwood Forest," he told her.

"Oh!" Her cry of discovery delighted him. "Robin Hood rode here, did he not? I would like to stop and have a wee look around Robin's forest."

He sighed. "We are almost to Tuxford. We've no time for wee looks."

"By all the saints, first ye keep me off my coach, leaving me with no money or belongings so I'm stuck with the likes of ye." She twisted to shoot him a glare. "Now ye reckon ye can make all the decisions?"

Bloody hell, she made him sound—and feel—like a tyrant. He pushed her shoulder to face her forward once again. "We cannot afford to let Gothard get too far ahead."

"I wish to go into the woods." With a huff, she leaned back against him as she had for much of the ride, ostensibly to ease the discomfort of the foreign stomacher. "There could be plants there I may be needing. My box of herbs was left in my satchel—"

Understanding dawned, along with the realization that

his body was reacting to her close proximity. "Then that was an herb you collected by the church yesterday?"

"Aye. Featherfew, for the headache. I believe I feel one coming on." She gave an annoyed shrug, and the movement ran through him like a tremor. "Ten minutes. If I haven't found what I need by then, we'll be on our way. I am hoping to find something to help with the swelling of my ankle. And something to heal wounds."

He scooted back in the saddle, but it didn't help. "Wounds?"

"Like the one ye gave me with your sword," she said pointedly.

"Very well, then," he muttered, irritated at himself. She was entirely too talented at triggering his guilt—and his body's responses. "Ten minutes." He guided Chiron off the road and dismounted, tethering him to a tree, then reached to help her down.

"I can do it," she said, but after a few clumsy attempts, she folded her arms across her well-covered chest. "Nay, I cannot. How am I supposed to move with this board strapped to my middle?"

He hid a smile and reached for her again, catching a whiff of her rain-washed scent. As soon as her feet hit the ground he released her, grateful to break the contact.

Steadying herself with a hand on the horse's back, she flexed her knees, then stroked the animal's silvery mane. "What d'ye call him?"

"Who?" he asked, distracted.

"Your horse." She slanted him a look, took a few tentative steps, then headed off into the woods. Her limp did nothing to assuage his guilt.

"Chiron," he said, following her. "I call him Chiron."

A giggle floated back through the trees. "Think yourself the Greek hero, do ye?"

"A hero?" His answering laugh was humorless. "Not a chance."

"Jason, the Greek hero." She knelt to inspect some

small plants by the base of a tree, allowing him to catch up to her. "One-blade," she murmured, obviously pleased. "The Greek Jason's guardian was the centaur Chiron, aye?"

"Aye. I mean, yes. My sister loves the legends; it was she who named my horse." Leaning against the tree, he frowned at the top of her head, watching her pick a few blue-green leaves. She seemed surprisingly knowledgeable about plants. Knowledgeable about lots of things. "How come you to know that tale? A Greek myth. And the English tales of Robin."

She rose, slipping the leaves into her pocket, and wandered off, her gaze trained on the moist, dark earth. "Ye think I'm an ignorant fool then, do ye?"

"No." That was not what he'd been thinking at all. Far from being a fool, she was quick and creative, at least when it came to inventing lies. "I know not what to think of you," he said honestly, following her again. "Or what to do with you, for that matter."

Eyes wide with alarm, she whirled, and he almost ran into her. The dress she seemed to detest swirled around her legs. "What d'ye mean, what to do with me? Ye promised ye would take me to London."

"And I will—"

"This arrangement wasn't my choice," she said. She measured him for a few heartbeats, then lowered herself to inspect another bit of greenery. "But I dinna mean to be trouble."

Despite himself, his gaze was drawn to the nape of her long, slim neck. "Of course you're trouble." He shrugged uncomfortably, glad her eyes were on the plant. He didn't want to know what color the hazel had turned to now. " 'Tis no fault of yours. All women are trouble."

"All women?" The two words laced with challenge, she straightened to face him.

At the flash in her eyes, he took a defensive step back. "Are you not going to take any of that plant?"

" 'Tis useless. I was hoping it was moonwort, but of course it is too late in the year." With a look that said the conversation was far from over, she meandered along and knelt by another plant. "Surely your mother wasn't trouble?"

"Her above all." He sighed, his gaze scanning the fragrant forest but his mind far in the past. A past he preferred not to think about. "She deserted four children, effectively leaving me, the eldest, to raise the rest."

She looked up. "Deserted ye?" she asked softly.

He surveyed the trees, the cloudy sky, anything to avoid the pity in her gaze. The last thing he wanted was this woman's sympathy. "She died. Sixteen years ago. She insisted on following my father into battle against Cromwell. Not a woman's place, but—"

"Not a woman's place?" Shading her eyes with a hand, she sent him a glare clearly meant to intimidate. "Who are ye to tell us where our places are, Jason Chase?"

He blinked. "I imagine I should expect such an attitude from a woman who does a man's job."

"If running Leslie is a man's job, then aye, I do one." Fallen leaves crunched beneath her as she rose. "Given your attitude toward women, I suppose your three siblings are sisters?"

"Only one." Thinking of his sister prompted a smile. "But Kendra was enough trouble for three. And still trouble—she refuses to get married, at least to anyone remotely suitable."

"Poor, poor Jason." Her commiserating noises sounded less than sincere. "Imagine a woman wanting to choose her own husband." She came near, her skirts swishing again, drawing his attention to her body. "Imagine a woman wanting a husband at all. They're all like ye, thinking they can keep their women in place."

Those changeable eyes were green now. He backed up until he bumped smack against a tree and could go no farther, at least not without looking like more of a fool than he already felt.

She moved closer again, too close. " 'Tis sorry I am if your mam was a halliracket, but—"

"A what?"

"An irresponsible person." She fixed her gaze on his. "But *my* mam would say a scabbit sheep canna smit a hail herself."

He crossed his arms and stared back at her, his mind a complete blank when confronted with such gibberish.

"One evil person cannot infect the whole. Ye cannot judge all women by your own isolated experiences."

He cleared his throat. "I suppose your mother is an angel on earth?"

Shrugging, she looked away and lowered herself to inspect another plant. Her voice drifted up, surprisingly subdued. "She's an angel in heaven. Mam died when I was but twelve." Slowly she tilted her face until her gaze was locked on his. "And my da died earlier this month." A faint glaze of tears seemed to brighten her eyes.

He blew out a breath. "I'm . . . sorry." Though he didn't know how much of her story to believe, he found himself drowning in those eyes, wanting to reach for her and offer comfort.

Thankfully, she focused back down, fingering a small whitish leaf. " 'Twas a blessing." He watched her pluck it, her fingers both graceful and deft. "He had a fit last spring and couldn't move but to blink his eyes and swallow." She looked up again. "I wouldn't care to live like that."

"Nor I," he assured her, not knowing what else to say.

"Now my family is only Adam."

"Right, you told me about him." A few too many times. "Adam MacCallum."

"Adam Leslie." With a huff, she stood. "By all the

saints, ye have got to be the stubbornest man I've ever met."

"Runs in the family," he said dryly, watching her pull her amulet from under her shift and fold one hand around it. It looked ancient, and he wondered how many Emeralds had worn it over the years. "Have you no other family at all?"

"A cousin, Cameron." The necklace fell from her fingers. "Leslie," she added before he could suggest otherwise.

He was beginning to think he'd never trip her up; she was a bright one, all right. And she asked way too many questions. Personal questions. "What is that?" he asked, indicating the leaf in her other hand.

"Bifoil." She added it to her pocket. "Good for wounds."

He bent and touched the plant's second leaf. "Why do you not take this one?"

"I must leave some to grow and flourish for the next person who needs it. Removing too much is rude. We must respect Mother Earth if we wish her to provide."

She ambled off again, her gait made awkward by more than a twisted ankle. 'Twas clear enough she was suffering from the long ride. Though he'd felt the same his first few days on the road, he wouldn't tell her that, any more than she'd admit to her pain.

It struck him that in some ways they were all too similar. Not particularly good ways, either.

She paused by a tall plant with a spiky bush of pale flowers, but left the blossoms alone, plucking off their ash-colored leaves instead. "Snakewood," she told him, the word trailing off into a yawn that reminded him she'd had no sleep in two days, other than the short nap. He could see the weariness etched in her face, the dark circles under her eyes. Responsibility weighed heavy on his conscience, mingling with that tender feeling that he found so confusing and disturbing.

His stomach rumbled, and he remembered they were almost to Tuxford. "Your ten minutes are up. Are you hungry?" When she shook her head, his gaze raked her slim frame. "You need to eat more."

"The gown is too big." Her pert nose went into the air, a gesture so amusing it dispelled his strange mood. "'Tis no fault of mine if you're no judge of women's sizes." He found himself following her again when she hugged herself around her loose waistline and started back toward Chiron. "Ye shall have to find me some decent clothes, Jase."

"Don't call me that. Jase Chase. It rhymes. 'Tis disgusting. What were my parents thinking when they named me?"

The question was rhetorical, but she responded anyway. "Apparently they weren't thinking at all." She turned and walked backward, watching him avidly, her grin too fetching for his comfort. "Or mayhap they had a ripe sense of humor, Jase."

He growled deep in his throat. "Nobody calls me Jase."

At that, she turned back around. "I do," she called over her shoulder, sounding altogether more cheerful than she had since they'd met. "So long as ye call me Emerald."

Chapter Nine

"What are they gawking at?" Caithren said irritably a few hours later. Waiting at the end of the bridge into Newark-on-Trent, she yanked up on both the stomacher and her shift, giving the evil eye to the two shabbily dressed men who were crossing. "I am not wearing this doxy's dress again."

She smiled to herself when Jason guided Chiron down the exact center of the bridge. "Careful, you're going toward the right—I mean, left. Ye wouldn't want anything bad to happen should ye veer from the middle."

"Very funny." His tone was dry, but she thought she could feel him laughing behind her. "It's clouding up again. We'll stop here and try to make up the time tomorrow."

"Are you sure?" she asked. " 'Tis not yet dark. Though the thought of a bed is very appealing." Not to mention in the last twelve miles she'd seen the folly of turning down dinner in Tuxford. It felt as though there were a hole where her stomach should be.

The sky did look menacing. After the soft, rain-soaked road, Chiron's hooves sounded loud on the town's cobblestones as he carried them down Beast Market Hill and onto Castlegate. "If we are going to stop, then I see just where to stay," Cait teased. On their right, the street's namesake loomed over the riverbank. "Since ye seem wont to choose the most impressive place."

Now he laughed aloud. " 'Tis Newark Castle, and

after the War, Cromwell ordered it demolished. Fortunately, the people refused to complete the job, so the face of the castle remains. But behind it, nothing. I expect you would not be comfortable."

" 'Tis a beautiful facade." She mourned the loss. "We've many large castles in Scotland."

They jostled their way through Chain Lane, a narrow alley of a street lined with tiny shops of all sorts, and into the marketplace. Jason rode through an archway beside a large inn called the Saracen's Head. Caithren thought her knees would buckle when she slid to the cobblestones, but she sternly forced them to comply. Jason would not ken any weakness on her part; not if she had any say in the matter.

The Saracen's Head boasted fine stables. A liveried ostler came forward to take Chiron in hand, and Cait and Jason hurried toward the inn just as the first raindrops were falling. Spotting bright yellow by the windows, she paused to snap off a couple of marigolds.

Jason frowned. "I don't expect the proprietor will appreciate that."

"Earth's bounty is for all to share," she argued. "This is just what I needed for my ankle. I will ask for some vinegar to mix with the juice, and by morning I'll be right as rain."

"We'll both be *soaked* with rain if we don't get inside." When she would have reached for another flower, he took her by the hand and dragged her through the door and to the innkeeper's desk. He set his valise and their bundle of damp clothing on the floor. "One room," he said to the seated man, a large fellow with a huge smile and a pockmarked face. "If you please, Mr. . . . ?"

"Twentyman," the man said.

"Two rooms," Caithren corrected.

"One," Jason repeated.

With a huff of disgust, she decided he could handle this alone and wandered off to the taproom. Something smelled wonderful, and her poor belly was just begging to be filled.

"Good eve," a jolly, rotund woman greeted her. She had round red cheeks and a round brown bun that shone in the well-lit room. "We've a lovely mushroom pie this evening."

Caithren glanced toward the lobby. Jings, Jason owed her whatever she wanted to eat. And then some. "I'll try it, then," she said happily. "And a sallet. And . . ."

"Spice cake?" the woman suggested.

"Aye. And a tankard of ale. I thank ye."

"I thank *you*, milady," the woman said. "Seat yourself, if you please."

Milady. Though Caithren wasn't a lady, it was nice to be mistaken for one, after the treatment she'd received thus far in this country. Smiling at the woman, she seated herself at a fine, polished table. When Jason came in and asked what she wanted, she was pleased to tell him she'd taken care of herself already. He might think he was calling all the shots, but she would prove otherwise.

He ordered for himself and joined her at the table.

"Twentyman," she mused. "Where does one get a name like that?"

" 'Tis a story," the jolly woman said, coming up from behind Cait to set two ales before them. "My husband's family was originally called Lydell. Tradition states that one of the Lydells poleaxed twenty men, hence the name Twentyman." She walked away.

"Ye English are strange," Cait said flatly.

Jason just threw back his beautiful dark head and laughed.

Mrs. Twentyman had three serving maids to help her, but she made it a point to bring Jason and Caithren's supper herself. The pie smelled divine. Its flaky crust was filled with gingery mushrooms and melted cheese, and Cait was in heaven with the first bite.

"Delicious," Jason told their hostess. "Newark was Royalist during the War, was it not?"

Mrs. Twentyman took that as an invitation to seat herself. "Aye, we were. Hull, Coventry, and Nottingham turned against King Charles in the troubles, but Newark was a loyalist stronghold." Warming to her subject, she hitched herself forward. "In 1642 the King paid a visit here, and the whole town turned out to greet him. There are secret underground passages where the wealthy people deposited their deeds, jewelry, and valuables during the War for safekeeping. One from our cellar," she confided.

"Secret passages?" Her curiosity piqued, Cait focused on Mrs. Twentyman, stabbing blindly at her lettuce. "Where do they lead to?"

"They crisscross beneath the marketplace, connecting in various places. Besides stashing their treasures there, some Royalists used them to hide."

"Were they in danger?" Cait dabbed at her mouth with a napkin, took a sip of her ale.

Mrs. Twentyman looked around, making sure her serving maids were doing their jobs, then turned back to Cait with a wink. "Most certainly there was danger. As long as I live, I will never forget one morning in 1643 when their worst fears were confirmed. A party of Roundheads were spotted on Beacon Hill, waiting to attack."

Caithren toyed with her cake. "What happened?"

"My husband's grandmother brought an old army drum out of her house. Although the drum needed repair, her young grandson, my husband's cousin, managed to sound the alarm. Bravely the lad strode through the town beating the drum loudly and shouting 'Who will stand up for King Charles?' "

"And they did," Jason told Cait. "They supported him courageously."

"Yes, indeed. They had few guns but made a brave

show with their pitchforks and staves and whatever they could find. That day their luck was in. The Roundheads took one look at the advancing mob and made a hasty retreat. Thanks to the loyal citizens and their little Twentyman drummer boy, Newark was still free."

"But only for a while," Jason lamented.

"We withstood three sieges," Mrs. Twentyman said proudly. "Of course, I was but a babe at the time."

Feeling full after half her pie, Cait leaned back in her chair, lulled by the storytelling lilt of their hostess's voice and the quiet roar of the other guests eating and conversing around them. She yawned behind her hand.

Mrs. Twentyman looked over at her and began to rise. "Poor dear, you're sleepy. And here I am yapping away."

Cait shook her head. "Your stories are wonderful, really." When another yawn forced her mouth open, she blushed. "But I am tired." She glanced at Jason, then back to the nice woman. "D'ye think ye might spare a little vinegar?"

"Vinegar, milady?"

"To mix with the nectar from these." Caithren pulled the marigolds out of her pocket. "My ankle is a wee bit swollen, and it will help."

"Will it, now?"

"Aye."

Mrs. Twentyman started stacking the plates, and Cait noticed something on her hand. She reached across the table and touched the woman's thumb. "And if ye squeeze a wee smidge of juice from a dandelion stalk on this wart, 'twill clear up in no time."

A little gasp came from Jason at her forwardness, but the innkeeper's wife looked pleased. "I will try that, milady. First thing tomorrow."

Cait smiled. "I'd like a bath." She looked pointedly at Jason. "Assuming ye can afford it."

The minute the words were out of her mouth, she

regretted them. So far Mrs. Twentyman had treated them like husband and wife. She was mortified, thinking now the woman might realize they were sharing a room but not married.

Jason exchanged an embarrassed glance with their hostess. "I think I can manage that," he said carefully.

"And I'll . . . I'll be needing some decent clothes."

She wasn't really surprised when Jason didn't argue. "I'll do my best to find some while you bathe. Let me just see you up to the room."

"You'll be needing clothes?" Mrs. Twentyman asked.

"Aye. And a night rail. Mine went . . . missing," Cait explained feebly.

Mrs. Twentyman looked between them, obviously curious. "I can lend you one of my sleeping gowns," the woman said generously.

Jason eyed Mrs. Twentyman's ample form, but Cait kicked him under the table. "I'd surely appreciate it," she said.

"Then I'll fetch one and send it up along with a bath and the vinegar." With one last inquisitive glance, the woman smiled and took herself off.

Jason leaned down to rub his ankle, eyeing Cait's half-eaten pie. "Are you going to finish that?"

She shoved it toward him wordlessly. He ate three bites, then looked up enquiringly, and she passed over her leftover sallet as well. She sipped at the last of her ale while she watched him make her food disappear.

"If you're wanting to go upstairs," he said, "I'll be needing to keep the key." He eyed the remnants of her cake, then shook his head and sat back. "In case you fall asleep before I return."

'Twas a struggle to stay calm and not worry about sharing his room, but she kent she had no choice. Her gaze wandered to the door in the corner. She was exhausted, aye, but not quite ready to go upstairs and face the night. "D'ye think that leads to the cellar?"

His brow furrowed. "Probably. Why?"

"I've a hankering to check out those tunnels." She rose and started toward it.

"Wait." He leapt from his chair and caught her by the wrist. "I thought you were tired."

She shrugged. "I'm curious. Mayhap we'll find some treasure."

"I don't think the Twentymans would appreciate—"

"Wheesht!" She tried to pull away, but only succeeded in pulling him along with her. Other supper guests turned to watch. She lowered her voice. "Dinna ye have any sense of adventure?" She tugged open the door and started down the cellar steps.

Muttering to himself, he grabbed a candle off an empty table and followed. The door above them shut, and the flame pierced the sudden darkness. At the bottom of the stairs, she swivelled to face him. "D'ye always do what you're supposed to?"

"Pretty much."

"Boring," she pronounced. With a swish of her English skirts, she turned and looked around. The cellar's walls were lined with provisions, the air chilly. A shiver rippled through her, borne of the cold or a tiny frisson of fear; she wasn't sure which. But it felt a wee bit forbidden and exhilarating to be down here.

"Has anyone ever told you you're impulsive?" Jason asked. He looked annoyed and tense. And darkly handsome in the cellar's shadows, if she were to be honest.

"Cameron. Every day. He finds it endearing."

Jason's response was a muted snort.

A narrow wooden door was set into one corner.

"That must be it." Her voice trembled a little.

He moved between her and the door and folded his arms across his chest, looking much like the man who had kept her from the coach. "I really think we should go back upstairs."

"Ye dinna want to see the tunnels? There could be treasure—jewelry or money left since the War."

He widened his stance. " 'Twould not belong to you if you found any."

"Of course it wouldn't. I wasn't planning to keep it. But it would still be exciting to discover. Are ye not intrigued?"

"No."

With a small huff, she skirted around him. "Then I'll meet ye upstairs. Which room number?"

"Four. But—"

She pushed open the door.

A musty smell came from the cramped, dark passage beyond. A rush of excitement made her knees weak, forced a giddy chuckle through her throat as she stepped inside.

"Come along, then," Jason muttered, sidling past her and holding the candle high.

Smiling to herself, she followed him along the dank, earthen tunnel. The curved walls oozed with moisture, and the place had a mildewed odor that spoke of long disuse. Something scurried across her path, and she jumped and let out a squeak, reaching for Jason's arm.

Bobbling the candle, he turned to her and cupped the flame to prevent it from blowing out. " 'Tis naught but a mouse." His smile was disarming. "Ready to turn back?"

"Nay. I wasn't afraid, only startled."

"Very well." He cleared his throat and looked pointedly down at where her fingers were still clamped on his arm. When she snatched back her hand, he proceeded, his footsteps sounding loud on the deserted pathway.

After a few yards, he stopped and glanced over his shoulder. "See any treasure yet?"

"Nay."

He walked twenty more feet. "Any treasure now?"

In answer, she blew out an amused breath.

Ten more feet. "Now?"

She half-groaned, half-laughed. The candlelight disappeared as he took a sharp turn, and she followed him around the corner.

And caught sight of something over his shoulder that made her stop short.

Floating four feet off the ground, a solemn man in a hooded cloak stared at her, his eyes unbearably sad and hollow.

Even as a shocked gasp escaped her, he seemed to be fading.

"What is it?" Jason whirled around, his eyes wide with alarm in the semidarkness.

Shaking, she put a hand on his shoulder to steady herself. "Did ye not see him?"

"See what?" He turned to look, but the passageway was empty.

"He was there. I saw him, I swear."

"What?"

"A ghost! A man dressed in robes. But his feet didn't touch the ground. Then—then he just faded away, into nothingness."

"Calm yourself." He switched the candle to his other hand and curved an arm around her shoulders. "There is no such thing as ghosts. 'Tis spooky down here. You imagined it."

"I did not!"

"Very well, then, you saw something. But there must be a logical explanation."

"I want to go back."

"Fine." Brushing by her, he started down the passage. "I never wanted to come down here in the first place."

She hurried to catch up, then grasped his hand, not caring what he thought. As she ran to keep up with his long strides, she threw an anxious glance over her shoulder every few seconds.

The ghost didn't reappear, but she shivered anyway.

"D'ye smell something? The atmosphere down here is strange." Somehow, speaking aloud was reassuring. It blocked the echo of their footsteps and the eerie sounds that seemed to bounce off the walls.

Jason's hand tightened on hers, making her already high-strung nerves tauten a bit more. His voice floated to her, composed and reassuring. "We're almost there." He turned, walking backward and peering through the half-light to see her face. "Are you all right?"

Before she could answer, a blast of frigid air whooshed down the corridor and snuffed the candle.

Caithren screamed long and loud, ceasing only when Jason pulled her into his arms and her mouth was muffled against his chest.

"Hush." He rubbed her back in a circular motion. " 'Twas naught but a draft."

The tunnel was black as the Widow MacKenzie's ancient kettle. She heard the squeak of a mouse, a slow drip somewhere, the rapid beat of her own heart, the slower beat of Jason's. "I dinna like it down here."

"The door is not far." His words were measured and patient. "We'll just feel along the wall."

Gingerly she reached out, her fingers meeting grainy, clammy dirt. She jerked back.

"*I'll* feel along the wall," he amended, turning within her grasp. "Just hold onto my waist, and I'll have you out of here in no time."

They progressed a few feet, then stopped cold when light suddenly flooded the passage.

"I heard a scream." Mrs. Twentyman stood in the open doorway, a hand to her ample chest. "Oh, 'tis you two."

Cait hurried past her and into the cellar, dropping to sit on a sack of flour. She crossed her arms and hugged herself in an attempt to stop the trembling. "I saw a ghost down there."

"No, she—" Jason started, but Mrs. Twentyman interrupted.

"Gilbert," the woman said matter-of-factly. "Our resident ghostly monk. One of the passageways leads to the old friary."

Caithren looked at Jason, still standing in the open doorway. "I told ye he was wearing robes."

"Gray, with a hood?" The woman nodded sagely. " 'Tis Gilbert, all right. But don't you worry, dearie, he's never hurt anyone. Though he does move around bottles in here sometimes—the serving maids dislike coming down to the cellar alone."

Jason shut the door to the tunnel, and Cait let out a shaky breath. He came over and helped her stand, wrapping an arm around her shoulders. "I apologize," he said to Mrs. Twentyman, "for trespassing. My companion here was curious—"

"Bosh. Think nothing of it. You're not the first guests to take it in your head to go exploring, and I'd wager you'll not be the last." She smiled at Jason. "Certainly not the first man to bring a woman down here and scare her right into his arms."

Embarrassed, Cait jumped away from Jason's hold, just as he quickly dropped his arm. In the name of the saints, what must the Twentymans think of them? And her wearing an English doxy's dress.

The kindly woman turned to Caithren. "Your bath is likely getting cold, though, so you'd best run along."

She needed no more of an invitation to bolt up the stairs.

Jason's long legs took them three at a time, and he caught up to her handily before she reached the taproom. "I'm sorry she thinks that of us. I know it disturbs you." Low and tender, his voice made her remember the warmth of his body embracing her protectively. He reached for her hand, clasping it as he had in the tunnel. It felt warm and sent tingles up her arm. She wished he would hold her again . . . when she wasn't frightened of a ghost. Just thinking that made the blood rush to her face, and she brought her free hand to her cheek.

"Are you sure you're all right?"

"I'm fine." Falling in behind him on their way up the narrow staircase, she slipped her hand into the gown's pocket to touch Adam's picture. She needed to shake these thoughts. "Ye still dinna believe it, do ye?"

"That you saw a ghost? No," he said flatly. "I reckon someone was down there, just as we were. Perhaps taking a shortcut or searching for forgotten valuables."

"He was *floating*. If you'd seen him, you'd believe."

"But I didn't." Jason reached the landing, turned, and shrugged. "Can we agree to disagree? Though I fought going down there, I thank you for coaxing me. It was fun."

"Fun?"

He grinned. "I've not done anything impulsive in a long while. Maybe ever, it seems." His mouth reversed into a frown. "Other than taking you with me, that is."

"And you're not sorry for that either, are ye?"

"I cannot say that I am." He guided her down a short corridor. "Here we are. Room four." Releasing her hand, he unlocked the door and waved her inside. "I'll leave you to your privacy."

"And my bath." She clenched her other hand around the one he'd dropped, but it didn't feel anything like when he'd held it. "I can still smell the mustiness from the tunnels. 'Twill feel good to be clean."

"Oh," he said. "I almost forgot. I have something for you. From the marketplace this morning." He dropped the key back into his pouch and withdrew a tiny, corked ceramic bottle.

Puzzled, she took it from him.

"Smell it," he urged.

She pulled out the cork and waved the bottle under her nose, drawing a deep whiff of the fragrant scent.

"Flowers of Scotland," Jason said proudly. "Or so the woman at the marketplace told me."

Caithren was stunned. " 'T-tis lovely," she stuttered.

" 'Tis the oil you used in your bath, no? And to wash your hair?"

"Well, I'd pressed my own myself. But aye, from Scottish flowers. Flowers of Scotland." What a sweet gesture. From a man who had as good as abducted her. 'Twas confusing, to say the least. " 'Tis lovely," she repeated.

"I'll replace whatever else you lost, as well." He backed up, easing the door closed. "I never meant to cost you your belongings."

She gazed at him, mute, then nodded.

"I'm glad you understand, Emerald."

But she didn't. She didn't understand anything. Least of all why she found herself starting to like him when he was still calling her Emerald.

And he was staring at her amulet. He found a green stone more convincing than all her protests. "I understand," she said, although she was more confused than ever. With a small smile, she added, "Jase," and then shut the door in his face.

"Mary! No!"

At Jason's muffled yell, Caithren startled awake. Though the room had two beds and she woke in hers alone, she still found herself disoriented and dismayed to wake in a room with a man. Across the chamber, he jerked and twitched, his face slick with sweat although it wasn't overly warm—the fire had burned so low she had difficulty seeing him.

"No . . ." The single word was grated out through a mouth contorted in pain. "No, no . . ."

Her stomach knotted with compassion, and she rushed over, tripping on the hem of Mrs. Twentyman's much-too-long night rail. "Jason, wake up." She put a hand to his shoulder. When he only moaned, she shook him hard . . . harder. "Oh, please wake up."

He turned, half rose, and threw his arms around her. Her legs tangled in the night rail again, and she tumbled on top of his long, hard body.

She lay atop him in shock. The thick white night rail had a high ruffle around the throat, full sleeves to Cait's wrists, and enough fabric to wrap around her three times. But she could still feel Jason through the voluminous garment. His size, his warmth. His spicy male scent overwhelmed her. She felt lightheaded, like when she'd awakened in Pontefract. But she hadn't been hit on the head this time.

"Wake up," she repeated, her voice muffled against his chest.

He muttered an unintelligible response, his body trembling. When his arms tightened, her heart lurched madly, and she sank into the embrace, molding herself against him, reveling in the feel of his hard planes against her softer curves.

"Christ Jesus, you feel good." He buried his nose in her hair. "Smell good."

His mouth trailed from her hair across her cheek, settling soft and warm on her lips. The kiss was a sensuous, persuasive caress, nothing like the unschooled pecks she'd received from village lads. When his tongue sneaked out to trace her bottom lip, she gasped.

He bolted upright, and she flailed back, landing on the floor in a twist of night rail and limbs.

Above her, he blinked himself awake and stared at her on the floor, his eyes glazed with confusion. "I'm sorry." He ran a hand through his hair, staring at his fingers when it apparently ended way before he thought it should. "Bloody hell, I . . . did I wake you? I'm sorry. I . . . what did I say? Did I knock you over?"

She struggled to her feet. "Never mind."

"I was dreaming."

"I certainly hope so," she huffed, sitting primly on the edge of the bed. Though she was feeling anything but prim right now. It took everything she had to stiffen her spine. She felt boneless. "What were ye dreaming about?"

His heavy sigh pierced the darkness. He lay silent a moment, then words tumbled out, soft and rushed. " 'Tis always the same. I see Mary, little Mary, dying, lying still as stone. And then the scene changes, and I'm fighting. A duel, to the death. I run a man through with my sword. Not my enemy, but an innocent man. Accidentally. He dies." His voice hitched and dropped to a whisper. "I know not who he is."

She yearned to touch him, but instead clasped her hands together in a death grip. "How perfectly terrible," she whispered back, almost reeling from the pain that radiated from this man.

"All the more terrible for the fact that it is true." He reached a hand to pry hers apart and lace with one on top of the coverlet. "In pursuing Geoffrey Gothard, I did kill an innocent man. Gothard is to blame, and the reason I cannot rest until justice is served." His eyes searched hers in the dim reddish light from the dying fire's embers. "Would a woman like you fault me, Emerald MacCallum?"

Her heart squeezed in sympathy. He was needing forgiveness—from himself, not her—but she couldn't resist the pleading in those sleep-heavy eyes.

"Nay, a woman like Emerald wouldn't fault ye," she whispered. "And neither would a woman like Cait."

His fingers gave hers a little squeeze. Some of the tension drained from his body, and he rolled to his side, his eyes sliding shut. "Let us to sleep," he murmured. "The sun will be waking us soon. Time was lost yesterday, between the rain and your nap. We must make it up in the morning."

When his hand pulled from hers, she felt a little pang

of loss. He was disagreeable and overbearing, but his was a tortured soul, and he could be kind, too. He'd been a rock of security down in the tunnel.

She determined to give him the benefit of the doubt and start over in the morning. She'd let him call her whatever he wanted. She was stuck with him, and she had to get to London; she might as well make the best of it.

Besides, she couldn't remember ever before feeling quite like she had when Jason held her in his arms.

Her lips still burning from his kiss, she crawled into her bed and sank back into exhausted sleep.

Chapter Ten

Downstairs the next morning, Jason looked up from the news sheet he'd spread on the polished wooden table. "Coffee," he told Mrs. Twentyman. "And . . ." He hesitated. Emerald was still upstairs getting dressed. Though his sister drank chocolate with breakfast, perhaps a woman like Emerald would prefer coffee instead.

"Chocolate for the lady," he decided, looking back down to the paper as the cheerful woman nodded and hurried off.

He scanned the articles. England was receiving New Netherlands in North America in return for sugar-rich Surinam in South America, under terms reached at Breda. Jason smiled to himself as he remembered his brother Colin's secret participation in that treaty with the Dutch.

A man named Jean Baptiste Denis had succeeded in transferring blood from a lamb into the vein of a boy. Amazing.

And Christopher Wren had—

He looked up when two men sat down at the adjacent table, already deep in conversation.

The ruddy fellow leaned across their table conspiratorially. "Me cousin wrote from Cumberland to say that none other than the celebrated Emerald MacCallum is in the vicinity."

She's not in Cumberland anymore, Jason thought with a smug smile.

"Damn me, but how does your cousin know that?" The man's companion, a thin, pale fellow, shook his head. "This Emerald MacCallum is naught but a fetching rumor, to my mind."

Just what Jason had once thought. He opened his mouth to clear up the confusion, but as a serving maid arrived with two steaming tankards, he thought better of it. No sense making it known he had Emerald in tow; he'd be liable to attract an unwanted entourage.

The first man hitched forward, scraping his chair on the polished floor. "Me cousin talked to her."

"Surely you jest."

"God's own truth. He asked her why she does what she does." He ran a hand back through unruly reddish-blond hair. "Woman's got two little children to support, a boy and a girl, and her husband died leaving a mountain of debt."

"Emerald MacCallum is a mother?" the thin man mused.

Emerald MacCallum is a mother? Jason mentally repeated, stunned. Could that be true? It would certainly be an explanation for why she seemed much sweeter and more nurturing than he'd imagined Emerald would be. But a *mother?*

"He also said the woman is over six feet tall. Imagine that."

Imagine that, Jason echoed in his head, stifling a laugh. Here she came now, meandering down the stairs, all five-feet-four-inches of her.

Unless, as she kept claiming, she wasn't Emerald. His breath caught.

Impossible. He'd found her, a Scottish woman dressed in men's clothing, holding a pistol on a wanted outlaw.

As she came closer, he caught sight of the emerald on the gold chain around her neck. Emerald was fast becoming legend, he decided, and people always exaggerated legend. Look what they said about William Wallace . . . seven feet tall, indeed! As absurd as Emerald's being six feet, and probably off by a similar amount.

"Me cousin said she was friendly," the ruddy fellow added. "He was sufferin' from the sore throat, and she gave him some strange Scottish herbs and told him to boil them in wine and drink the lot down."

Now, that sounded like the Emerald that Jason knew. He resumed breathing and motioned her to the chair beside him, but she sat across instead.

"Hungry?" He slid a tankard in front of her. "I reckoned you'd fancy chocolate over coffee."

Cait breathed deep of the sweet steam. "Ye reckoned well."

"How is your ankle this morning?"

"Much better." Cupping the warm drink in both hands, she sipped. "I borrowed your comb. I hope ye dinna mind."

"Not at all." He raised his own tankard. "I paid Mrs. Twentyman for the night rail. Did you pack it like I told you to?"

"Aye. Thank ye for that. And for having my clothes laundered and pressed." She smoothed her hunter green skirts and grinned. "Even if they were tossed over that chair rather haphazardly."

"My pleasure." His eyes danced with good humor. " 'Twas the least I could do since I couldn't find you new ones." Sobering, he took a sip of Mrs. Twentyman's strong brew. "We can make it to London in four days if we hurry. I've a mind to make it to Stamford by nightfall. 'Twill not be easy." He measured her thoughtfully for a moment. "I want to thank you."

"For what?" Caithren couldn't imagine. So far as she could remember, she'd done little but complain.

His lazy smile made her stomach do a flip-flop. "Last night, when I—well . . . I meant not to disturb you with my nightmare, but 'twas nice to have you there."

She couldn't think of anything to say to that. 'Twas not as though she'd had a choice. And for her it had been nice in its own way as well . . . if one could call those feelings "nice." She wasn't sure how to describe them.

Her tankard made a swishing noise when she twisted it back and forth. "Who is Mary?"

"Mary?" He busied himself swallowing his coffee, folding the news sheet.

"Ye spoke of a Mary in the night."

"Ah." An enigmatic glint came into his eyes. "A girl I love."

"Oh." She studied her chocolate.

"A young girl, all of five years."

"Oh!" The feeling of relief took her by surprise. "What happened to her?"

"Geoffrey Gothard. He was intent on taking pleasure of her mother, and Mary got in the way. She still breathed when I left, but the surgeon said she'd not last the week."

"Michty me."

"Mary was an orphan, abandoned in London's Great Fire. I . . . found her a home in my village." His voice cracked, and he cleared his throat. "With the Widow Bradford—her husband had died in a mill accident; no fault of mine, but I felt responsible."

"Why?"

" 'Twas my mill," he said lightly.

His mill? Jason was a miller? She wouldn't have thought so, but then she hadn't thought at all of what he might do for a living. She'd been too busy being furious with him.

Or, since the wee hours of last night, wishing he'd kiss her again. To hide her suddenly burning face, she sipped.

"Mary was bright-eyed, intelligent. She loved to laugh. She used to follow me around the village, and sometimes I'd stop by the Bradford house and play with her—"

Her tankard clunked to the table. "Play?" Cait tried to picture Jason on his knees with a small child. The thought prompted a smile.

"Yes, play. Backgammon and the like. She is good with numbers."

"Ye play backgammon?"

"Why does that surprise you?"

She shrugged. "I cannot picture ye playing anything, is all."

"The man you've seen, Emerald, 'tis not me at all." He rubbed his smooth upper lip. "When Gothard came into my life—destroyed people I cared for . . ."

"What of the mother?" She ran a fingertip around the rim of her tankard. "D'ye love her, as well?"

He drank leisurely, delaying his answer. "No, but I feel responsible for her." He lowered the tankard, steepled his fingers, and studied her across them. "Why do you care?"

"I'm stuck with ye, Jase. I'm trying to puzzle ye out." A vast understatement. But a slow smile dawned on his face, and he hadn't winced at the nickname. She decided to push her luck a little. "Who *do* ye love?"

"What I'd love right now is breakfast," he said cagily. "And here it comes."

And that was that for now, she supposed, as Mrs. Twentyman set a plate before each of them. But he wouldn't keep her in the dark once she got it in her mind to figure him out. He'd never met the likes of her before.

With a secretive smile, she watched the man across from her begin to eat. He did love to eat. Now she just had to figure out the rest.

"Tell me another," Jason said later when they'd been on the road for hours. Miles and miles of flat road, snaking through rich farmland, made a monotonous view that begged for a diversion. And Emerald had been quite diverting indeed, regaling him with Scottish tales all morning.

"Can we not stop for a while?" She flexed her shoulders. "Is it far still to Grantham?"

"Not too far. One more story." He tugged playfully on one of her braids. "In the sea fairy story you mentioned mermaids. Know you a mermaid's tale?"

"Aye. But 'tis a sad one."

"Tell me. We'll be there soon and we can have some dinner."

"Very well." She sighed and shifted on the saddle, a diversion in itself. "In the Land-under-Waves live the mermaids, which we call Maids-of-the-Wave. They are lovely to look at, and their voices are sweet and melodic. Their lower bodies are shaped like the fishes and glitter like salmon in the sun. They have long, coppery hair, and on beautiful days they sit on the rocks and comb it." She paused. "Unlike me, they have combs."

Jason laughed. "I will buy you a comb before the day is out, I promise. And a Chase promise is not given lightly."

"I will hold ye to that."

He didn't doubt it.

"On moonlit nights, the Maids-of-the-Wave sometimes take off their skin coverings and don pale blue gowns. They can walk on the land then, but they are fairer than any land-dweller woman."

"Not fairer than you," Jason protested.

She stilled, silent for a moment, then giggled. "If you're attempting to flatter me, I will warn ye 'twill get ye nowhere."

"You cannot fault me for trying."

"D'ye want to hear the story?" The words were stern, but her voice was warm.

"Did I interrupt?" Behind her back, he grinned. "Pray, continue."

She cleared her throat. "One moonlit night a young

farmer was walking by the cliffs when he heard the most beautiful voices raised in song. He looked down to see a company of fair women, all dressed in pale blue, dancing in a circle around one who was the fairest of the fair. Then he noticed nearby a pile of skin coverings, still wet and glistening in the moonlight. He crept down the rocks and took one, then ran home with it."

Absently, Jason ran a finger down the part in Emerald's hair.

She looked up and back, bumping her head on his chin in the process. "What d'ye think you're doing?"

"Did I do something?" Whatever had possessed him to do it, anyway? Irritated, he clenched his fist. "What happened next?"

Sending one more puzzled look over her shoulder, she faced forward. "When the mermaids saw the man stealing away, they screamed and ran for their skin coverings. Hurriedly they put them on and jumped into the sea. All except one, the fairest of the fair. Her skin covering was missing."

"This *is* sad," Jason remarked, not trying to hide the smile in his voice.

"Hold your tongue," she admonished. "Now, the farmer hid the skin covering in a box and put away the key. Afore long, a woman came to his door and knocked on it. He opened it to find the most beautiful woman in the land. Tears were pouring from her big blue eyes—" Interrupting herself, her head tilted up, and Jason followed her gaze. "Jings, that is the tallest spire I've ever seen." She sounded mesmerized.

"St. Wulfram's," he told her. A sight to see, the church seemed a combination of every period of Gothic architecture plus traces of Norman and possibly Saxon work. She remained transfixed as he started down the road that fed onto Grantham's busy High Street, a distinguished row of modern gray-stone buildings interspersed with some of half-timbered Tudor design. "Now to find a place to eat. In the meantime, please do continue your tale. You cannot just leave me hanging on the precipice of such tragedy."

"Very amusing. Now, where was I?" She fussed at her skirts. "Oooh, look at that angel." The angel she spoke of was fashioned of carved and gilded stone, perched over the gateway of an inn called—appropriately enough—The Angel. "Whose heads are those?"

Jason halted and squinted up at the corbel above the carved cherub. "King Edward the third," he decided. "So that must be his queen, Philippa of Hainault."

"I see ye are not totally uneducated," Emerald said. Before he could make comment on that thinly disguised insult, she added, "Edward was brutal to the Scots."

"Everyone was brutal in those days," he pointed out. "Edward only wanted revenge for Bannockburn."

"He got it," she said dryly.

"So this is what comes of educating women," Jason mused. He guided Chiron through the archway and into the courtyard at the rear, then helped her down and led her inside. The Angel's taproom had a fine timbered ceiling and an enormous stone fireplace, the hearth empty this summer day. The weather was warm, so Jason opted for a cold dinner of bread, cheese, and pickled onions and carried it to where Emerald had seated herself by a stone vaulted window.

"There are so many people," she marveled, watching them pass by on horses, in carriages, and on foot.

"Wait until you see London." He sliced the thick slab of cheddar. "So what happened after the woman showed up?"

"Pardon?" Dragging her gaze from the window, she looked at him.

He handed her a piece of bread topped with cheese. "The mermaid."

"Oh. The Maid-of-the-Wave." She took a bite. "Well,

she was standing there in her blue dress, greeting, ye ken. I mean crying."

"Greet means to cry?"

"Aye. And she said, 'Will ye not have pity and return my skin covering, so that I may go home to the Land-under-Waves?' "

"Let me guess." He popped a small onion into his mouth. "He couldn't stand to see the woman cry, so he gave her back her skin covering."

"Nay." Her eyes danced, looking turquoise today. "Mayhap that is what ye would do. But not this farmer. He thought she was so gentle and beautiful that he couldn't bear to let her go. So he said, 'What I have I will keep. But shed no tears, fairest of the fair, for ye may remain here and become my bride.' " She paused for a sip of The Angel's strong ale. "The mermaid walked away and returned to the sea, but without her skin covering she couldn't join her people. So in the morning she went back, and again the man asked her to be his bride. She knew she couldn't return to the Land-under-Waves, so she consented. She begged him to be kind and never tell anyone who she was or how she came to be there, and he agreed."

"And they lived happily ever after?"

"Nay. I told ye 'twas a sad story." A faraway look in her eyes, she touched her emerald. "All the people of the village loved the Maid-of-the-Wave, but the man kept his promise and didn't tell them where his wife came from. They believed she was a princess, brought to them by the fairies."

"Half-witted fools." He ate another onion.

A frown appeared on her forehead. "Ye dinna believe in fairies, either?"

"Hell, no."

"Well, then, that makes two of us."

When she grinned, he laughed. "So were they happy together?"

"Oh, aye. They lived in peace for seven years and had two bairns, a lad and a lassie. The Maid-of-the-Wave loved them dearly. Then came a time the farmer went to town to trade. It was a long journey, and he was gone several days. The mermaid was lonely without him, so she wandered the seashore. As she sang to her wee lass, she remembered her people who lived in the Land-under-Waves."

"Very sad. Are you going to finish that?"

With a roll of her eyes, she handed him the rest of her bread. "One evening her son found her on the rocks and said, 'I found a key. It opens Father's box, and I looked inside. There is a skin in there, a big, shiny, beautiful skin that looks like a salmon's.' She gasped with shock and excitement and asked for the key."

"And he gave it to her?"

"Of course. She was his mother. She took her children home, and put them to bed, and sang them to sleep. Then she opened the box and took out her skin covering. She sat by the fire for a long, long time, for she wanted so badly to go home to her people, but she didn't want to leave her bairns. Then she heard the sound of singing coming from the sea. Her sister mermaids were calling to her. She kissed her two children and wept—"

"Greeted."

She smiled, though her eyes were still sad. "—greeted over them until their precious faces were wet with her tears. And still she heard the songs from the sea. She put on her skin covering and hurried to the Land-under-Waves. When the farmer returned the next morning, he heard joy and laughter floating from the sea. In his cottage, his children were fast asleep. But the box was wide open, and the skin covering was missing. He sat down and wept, because he knew that the Maid-of-the-Wave had gone."

She paused and wiped a tear.

The action tore at his heart. Without thinking, he

leaned to cover her small hand with his. "You must miss your own children."

A puzzled look came over her face. "What d'ye mean?"

"Your children. Your . . . bairns. A lad and a lassie, is it not? Like the mermaid's."

"Ye think I have children?" She tugged back her hand. "Me? I've never even—"

"Never mind." He didn't like the feelings of doubt that had begun to plague him since overhearing the men in Newark this morning. But his gaze strayed to her amulet, glinting green in the sunshine that streamed through the window.

Of course she was Emerald. Emerald would deny this, like everything else. He drained the rest of his ale. "Did the mermaid ever come back?"

One finger traced her crisscrossing laces while she stared at him a moment, apparently nonplussed. "Nay." With a shake of her head, she drew a deep breath. "But it is told that she often returned in the night to peek through the cottage windows at her bairns as they slept. She left trout and salmon outside the door. The farmer told his children that their mother was far away but would never forget them. When her son grew up, he sailed the seas, and no harm ever came to him even in the fiercest storms, for the Maid-of-the-Wave followed his ship and protected him."

"That is not quite so sad, then."

She graced him with a wan smile. "Nay, I suppose it is not. She had to go back to her place, didn't she? Her home, where she belonged." Looking pale green all of a sudden, her eyes met his. "Even though they'd never see her again."

Like Emerald would go back to Scotland soon. Her home, where she belonged. "Yes, she had to go," he agreed, though damned if the thought of never seeing her again didn't seem somehow incomprehensible.

*   *   *

Hilly, with lots of trees and sheep, the road from Grantham was a welcome change after traveling through flat land all the day. At Stoke Rochford they took a wee bridge over a wee river—Jason didn't even hesitate—and rode up to the Church of St. Andrew and St. Mary, perched on high land with a spectacular view of rolling fields. There were no taverns or inns, though—no excuse for Cait to get off the horse and ease her aching legs and bottom. Her teeth were aching as well, from gritting them against the pain. But she'd say not a word to Jason.

Stretton had huge trees and a lovely field of yellow wildflowers, but nothing else of note. They plodded on. Casterton didn't present any reason to stop, either, being naught but a sleepy stone village, though it did boast a lovely Norman kirk. Jason didn't seem wont to look at it, however.

After hours in the saddle, Caithren thought she would scream if she didn't get some relief. The sun was on its downward slide when she spotted a jumble of stone and patted Jason's knee.

"D'ye think I might stretch my legs?"

"Your legs?" Jason cleared his throat, sounding amused. "Is something wrong with them?"

"Nay." She set her jaw. " 'Tis only that I've a mind to explore that ruin over there."

"Oh. I see." By his tone, she guessed he saw all too much. But thankfully he seemed willing to indulge her weakness. He steered Chiron off the road and up the grassy rise that led to the crumbling castle. "We've made excellent time today. And I could do with a bite."

She giggled. "I thought I heard your stomach rumbling. Are ye always hungry, then?"

"Seems so." He dismounted and spanned her waist with his big hands to swing her down. While he tethered Chiron to a tree, she flexed her knees, looking around. The remnants of walls meandered up and down gentle, grassy slopes, loosely connected by steps seemingly leading to nowhere. It felt both sad and terribly romantic. From one corner of the site rose a square tower, tall but open to the sky.

Rather than sharing her enchantment, Jason was digging in the portmanteau for the chicken, bread, and cheese he'd bought before they left Grantham.

"Come up the tower," she said. "I'd wager there's a lovely view."

"Go ahead." He pulled a napkin from one leather bag. "I'll arrange our supper."

With a shrug, she started up the winding stone steps. Though in better shape than the rest of the castle, the keep was far from habitable. The floors were half gone, and the walls were missing in places as well. The narrow stairs bore deep, concave depressions from centuries of feet, and there was no rail, but the steps themselves were solid and safe. She trudged up painfully, wondering if this were really a good idea after so many hours in the saddle, but when she finally reached the top she kent it was more than worth the long climb.

Puffing from exertion, she leaned on the crenelated wall and looked out over the countryside. "Oh, 'tis glorious!" The land rolled away in all directions, dotted with trees and houses, divided by glistening ribbons of rivers and streams. "Ye can see from here like a bird in the sky. Ye must come up!"

"Take your time," he called to her. "I'll wait for you here."

"Nay, come join me!" She rushed to the other side, saw the endless, brown swath of the road, steeples of churches, a working mill. "Ye can see a mill from up here, Jase! 'Tis running. The top of a mill—would that not be interesting?" He was a miller, after all.

His chuckle floated up the ancient stone walls. "I've no need to see a mill. I have one of my own."

"I knew that. But there's a big river too, and"—she

worked her way around the perimeter—"a town, Jase!
A bonnie large town!"

"Stamford," he told her. "We're almost there." From
her high perch, he looked small as he walked around to
her side. The sun glinted off his hair. "I can see the
town from here," he called up. "The keep is built on
a hill. They usually are, you know. A motte, the hill
is called."

"Ye cannot see it as well as I can," she argued. " 'Tis
a lovely town. With wee toy carriages going all over it."

He laughed. "Enjoy. Come down when you've seen
enough."

He sat below her on what was left of a crumbling
stone wall. "Please come up," she begged. She wanted
to share this with someone. The beauty, the wonder.
"Please."

He stared up at her for a minute, and she wished she
could see his expression better. "Has anyone ever told
you you're stubborn?" He stood and brushed off his
breeches, then disappeared around the other side of
the keep.

A few footsteps echoed up the stairwell, slow and
measured. Then . . . faltering? There was silence for a
minute before the footsteps resumed, then stopped once
more. Further silence, followed by the padding sounds
of walking across grass, and then the sun was glinting
off his hair again. He was standing below her, outside
the keep.

"I changed my mind," he called up.

Awareness slowly dawned. All those times he'd ridden
down the center of a bridge, she'd thought he'd been
superstitious. But that hadn't been it at all.

She turned and made her way down the tower. He
met her halfway around the building, with a shrug and
a self-deprecating grin.

"You've a fear of heights," she said softly. " 'Tis why
you'll not ride at the edge of a bridge, isn't it?"

Warm color flooded his cheeks. "Well, I did tell you I'm not superstitious."

'Twas just like a man not to come out and say it. "Ye should have told me the truth. I'd not have teased ye so."

"You, pass up that opportunity?" He rubbed the back of his neck. " 'Tis hardly a manly admission."

"But I understand. My mother was afeared of small spaces."

"Was she, now?" He raised a brow. "And I imagine she quoted you wisdom for this sort of problem?"

Caithren smiled. "A common blot is nae stain."

"Come again?" He started toward where he'd left Chiron and their food.

She trailed after him. "Dinna worry about small faults that are common to everyone."

"I see." Handing her a round of bread, he took the chicken and cheese and seated himself on a broken stone wall. "Well, I thank you for not laughing. I've never admitted this particular fault to a woman before."

An unexpected warmth spread out from her heart, that he would choose her in which to confide. Never mind that it was so obvious he'd have looked the fool for denying it—it was a rare man who would admit to such an affliction. She dropped to sit cross-legged on the grass, looking down and arranging her skirt about her.

"Miss your breeches, do you?" he asked, ripping a healthy portion from a chicken leg.

Composing herself, she tore off a hunk of the bread. "When I'm riding, aye. Mayhap ye should buy me a pair."

He only grinned, but it made her breath catch. Up here on this hill, she felt close to this man. Closer than she'd ever felt to any man not in her family. But it made no sense. He'd kept her off the coach. He refused to believe a word she said.

He was an Englishman.

She ate in silence for a while, watching the comings and goings of people passing under the medieval gateway to the town below.

" 'Tis a pretty town, all stone," she remarked.

"A rich town. The wool trade has made their fortune." He took a swig from his flask of water, then passed it to her. "They've a fine marketplace. There, see? And it looks as though they've a fair in full swing this eve."

She squinted into the distance. "Oh, just look how busy. So many booths!"

"Would you like to go?"

"Oh, aye!" But London was beckoning. Gothard was on the loose. Adam was waiting to be found. "We haven't the time," she sighed.

"We could not possibly make it to another sizable town by nightfall." He gestured toward the sun, low in the western sky. "We'll be staying the night in Stamford regardless."

She considered. "There will be things to buy at a fair, aye?"

One eyebrow arched. "What, have I not bought you enough?"

"One gown! One half a gown, truth be told." Her hand fluttered up to cover the top of her chest, although she was wearing her own laced bodice and modest shift.

Jason's laugh boomed over the hillside. "I was fooling, sweet." Her heart turned over at the careless endearment, even though she knew it meant naught. "I'll buy you a comb. And some clothes, if they've any ready made," he added before she could ask. "And we can eat."

"Are ye not eating already?" She aimed a pointed glance at the half-finished chicken in his hands.

"Fairgoing victuals," he explained, grinning as he took another bite. "One cannot attend a fair without eating. It counts not as real food."

It sounded too good to be true, an evening of frivolous entertainment in the midst of their urgent journey. But they had covered quite a distance today, and Jason was right that it would serve a purpose as well, in terms of replacing her belongings.

And she still hadn't quite recovered from him calling her a pet name, though for his part, he hadn't seemed to notice.

Confused, Cait stood and stepped over a pile of rubble, walked to the center of an enclosure. "When was this built, d'ye think?" She gestured at the remnants of walls that marked what used to be chambers, now carpeted with soft grass instead of rushes. "It looks to be very old."

"Norman, I believe." He nodded, the motion drawing her gaze to make a quick, involuntary appraisal of his arresting features.

My, but he really was a beautiful man. Sweet, he'd called her, and it had sounded entirely different from when Cameron called her sweet. Awareness flooded her being, and deliberately she looked away from him. "Can ye picture this castle all solid, with banners and tapestries? And knights battling. Over there, mayhap?" Feeling giddy, she whirled in a wide-armed circle. "Oh, I expect it was glorious!"

She stilled and turned to see his mouth curve in a crooked line. "I expect 'twas cold and rather crude."

"Ye see the world in black and white, dinna ye?" Compelled by some pull beyond her control, she moved toward him. His hair shone blue-black in the deepening shadows, and his chiseled features looked sculpted in stark relief. A curious quiver of wanting ran through her.

"D'ye not like castles?" she asked softly.

"I like them well enough." He made himself busy gathering the remains of their supper.

She went closer and knelt to help him. "I live in a castle."

He looked up sharply, assessingly. "Do you?"

"Aye, but 'tis not quite a real one, ye see. I mean, 'tis not ancient." Once again her nerves had her blethering, but she couldn't seem to stop herself. "Da built it for my mother on the land that she brought to their union. He always called her his queen. 'Tis fortified, but just a house for all that . . . fifteen rooms."

"The castle at home—Cainewood—has stood five hundred years. I believe it has a hundred rooms."

"A hundred rooms?" Looking up at him, she reached blindly, encountering his hand instead of the napkin she'd been aiming for. "Ye believe?"

His fingers gripped hers, and he grinned. "I'm not sure anyone has ever bothered to count." He swiped up the napkin and stood, pulling her to her feet with him.

"They've never counted?" Finding that hard to imagine, Caithren followed him back to Chiron. "Is that castle in ruins, then, like this one?"

"Oh, no. Though Cromwell did his best to flatten it, it still stands. I—people live in it."

"Is it very grand?"

He shrugged. " 'Tis home—a home, I mean."

"Have ye been inside?"

An enigmatic look passed over his face. "As a child, I used to play in the keep. That part is in ruins, though not as far gone as this." The sweep of his arm encompassed the half-walls that marched over the grassy knoll. "Of course, I never went up to the top." His lips curved in a wry smile.

"As a child," she mused. "I cannot picture ye as a child. What was your childhood like?"

"Happy. Until the War." He opened the portmanteau and started stuffing everything inside. "My parents were staunch Royalists. Father deposited us with friends and went off to defend the King, taking my mother with him. After that my childhood memories are naught but a blur." He was making a mess of packing the two bags, but she was afraid to interrupt to help. She sensed this was part of the puzzle. "When I was sixteen, my parents died in the Battle of Worcester. I was the eldest. I took over for my father."

"Ye did what ye thought he would have wanted ye to. Kept the family together."

He closed the first latch. "I was a man by then—"

"Ye were sixteen."

"He was a war hero." The second latch snapped into place. "Honorable, brave, self-sacrificing . . . I've never been able to live up to him."

"Ye make him sound like a god." She moved closer. "He couldn't have been."

"You knew him not." Her stomach felt odd, and she moved closer again. His eyes darkened, and he cleared his throat. "How is your shoulder?"

"My shoulder?"

"Where it was nicked by my sword. Would you mind if I looked?"

She blinked, feeling heat stain her cheeks. "All right." Slowly she loosened the laces of her bodice and pulled it and her shift off the shoulder, feeling terribly naked beneath his gaze. Nothing marked the skin but a tiny dark scab.

He bent close, nodding. "Looks good." His voice sounded husky by her ear, and her skin tingled at his nearness. Beneath the sleeves of her shift, the little hairs stood up on her arms.

"I-I thank ye for taking care of me." Her fingers fumbling, she shrugged back into her clothes, tightened her laces. "For caring . . ." Tying the bow, she swayed forward involuntarily, looking up at him.

He froze, his eyes locked on hers. Her heart skipped a beat. One hand came up, and his knuckles brushed her cheek. Her gaze dropped from his compelling green eyes to the lips that had touched hers last night.

He sucked in a breath. "The fair will be closing soon," he said, pulling back. "We'd best be moving."

Chapter Eleven

Caithren dodged a couple of dogs that were chasing one another 'round the entrance to the fair. " 'Tis delightful!"

Jason grinned. "It stinks," he countered.

"Aye, but 'tis exciting, dinna ye think?" She wrinkled her nose against the ripe smells of cattle and fish. But even that didn't dim her enthusiasm. "We've nothing like this near Leslie." She headed into the noisy crowd, straight toward the area where vendors displayed an amazing array of merchandise. Her gaze scanned stands piled with soap and candles, sugar and spices. Bright colors caught her eye, and she made a beeline for a table covered with a hodgepodge of gloves, ribbons, and lace.

"The blue suits you." Jason lifted a spool of ribbon and held it up to her hair. "Would you like a length?"

Her smile was quick, but she couldn't ask for luxuries—at least until Jason collected the reward he'd been blethering about. For now, she would rather he preserve whatever funds he had, lest his money run out before they reached London.

She opened her mouth to say nay, but he was already handing the ribbon to the vendor. "A yard, if you please. And some of the red, as well." He glanced at her skirt. "No, make that the green."

"Jason—"

"You'd prefer the red? I thought you would rather not wear that dress."

"Nay, 'tis only—"

"All three, then." He dug in his pouch for a coin. "Know you where we might find a comb for sale?"

The vendor pointed across the way and down the row, then handed over his change. Jason stuffed the coins and ribbons into his pouch. "Come along, Emerald." He took off in the direction the vendor had indicated, leaving her to follow.

Too excited to be irritated at the name, she found her attention pulled in all directions at once. A stall selling eggs, milk, and butter sat beside one offering fat brown sausages. The rich scent of coffee beans competed with those of tobacco and cocoa. She looked up, and Jason was gone. But his height was such that by craning her neck, she was able to spot his raven-topped head above the crowd. She hurried to join him.

"Do you fancy this one?" The comb he held was made of the finest ivory, like his own, polished to a high sheen.

"One of those will do." She indicated a comb of brown, mottled tortoiseshell. "Or this one." She picked up a plain wooden comb, but Jason plucked it from her hand and set it down. Experimentally he lifted one of her braids and ran the ivory comb through its tail, then dug once more in his pouch.

"We'll take it," he said, and that was that. Caithren blinked in astonishment. She had never seen anyone make such quick decisions. He exchanged coin for the comb and handed it to her. "Will this fit in your pocket?"

She nodded and slipped it inside, next to the weight of his pistol she still carried.

"Good. Now, for a gown . . ."

"I dinna think we will find a gown here, Jase. The fabric, aye, but—"

"Come along; we'll look."

He dragged her up one row and down another, past bolts of silks and muslin and calico. But she'd been right;

there were no ready-made garments for sale at all. She had a hard time keeping up with his purposeful strides and was relieved to have a chance to catch her breath when he paused before a cart offering rounds of gingerbread.

"I find myself hungry again." He grinned when she made a sound of disbelief. "Would you like some, as well?"

"Nay," she said. But she stood watching while the baker dusted a wooden board with ground ginger and cinnamon, then plopped on a hunk of hot, stiff brown dough he took from a pot over a fire. He rolled it out, and with a swift, practiced hand, cut it into small discs. Without further cooking, he piled several on a piece of paper.

When Jason paid the man and had a warm little circle of cake in his hand, the savory scent was too tempting. Her fingers crept toward the treat to break off a bit, and he laughed and handed it to her, taking another round gingerbread for himself.

'Twas spicy but not very sweet, and the doughy texture was unusual but not unpleasing.

A small hand tugged on Jason's breeches, and they both looked down to see a wee lad's grubby face.

"What, you too?" Laughing again, Jason handed him a piece, then sobered when the child stuffed it into his mouth and swallowed convulsively. "So that's the way of it, is it?" Jason turned back to the cart to purchase another serving. He handed it to the lad, along with the coins that were his change. "Run along, now, and buy yourself some milk."

The bairn's eyes opened wide in his filthy face. The coins disappeared into a fist gripped so tight the poor lad's knuckles turned white. He took off running without so much as a thank you.

Caithren lifted a turquoise plume from a nearby stand

and waved it through the air thoughtfully. "That was nice, Jase."

He shrugged and pinkened under his tan. " 'Twas nothing. Do you want that?"

"Nay!" She dropped it back to the table as if it had burned her fingers. Was he intent on buying her everything she so much as looked at? Mayhap 'twas a sign he was softening toward her, and that was a pleasing thought . . . or mayhap he was only feeling guilty she'd lost her belongings on his account. Either way, she didn't want him spending his money unnecessarily, so she'd best keep her hands to herself.

A wild burst of laughter drew her attention from the displays of merchandise. With Jason in tow this time, she fought her way into a crowd that circled a troupe of ropedancers.

"Look, Jase!" Indeed, she didn't know where to look first. One man was performing on a low rope, another on a slack rope that looked mighty dangerous, and a third was scaling a daunting slope. Another danced upon a rope with a wheelbarrow in front of him, two children and a dog perched inside. A duck on his head was singing to the crowd and causing much of the laughter. Caithren joined in at the absurd sight, laughing even harder when the man executed a silly little bow, almost tumbling from his rope in the process. The duck squawked in alarm, but of course it was all just a part of the show.

"I never thought to hear you laugh," Jason said wonderingly beside her. She turned to see an indefinable look in his eyes. A look that, if she'd not known better, she'd have interpreted to mean he liked her.

"I've had nothing to laugh at lately," she said gravely, the moment of light, unburdened hilarity lost.

"No, you've not," he agreed. "Let us see what else I can find to amuse you." With a light touch on the small of her back, he guided her through the crowd and across a trampled field. Another enthralled crowd loomed ahead. "Ah, a mountebank," he said.

"A what?"

"A man who calls himself a doctor."

"Calls himself? Is he a doctor, or nay?"

He looked down at her, flashing an enigmatic grin. "You decide." And he pulled her into the cluster of onlookers.

"Is that the mountebank?" She pointed to a rather dirty-looking fellow in a rumpled velvet suit that looked much too hot for the summer afternoon.

"Hush," Jason said. "Listen."

"Ladies and gentlemen," the man called out, "do ever you suffer from distempers and ails of the digestion? Why suffer when you can take Dr. Miracle's Universal Healing Potion? My tonic is made from a secret recipe sent down through the ages from the sages of Rome. Along with healing herbs, it contains miraculous powdered bones from the relics of the saints."

"Powdered bones will not cure anybody," Caithren scoffed under her breath.

"Rubbish!" bellowed a stout gentleman standing beside her.

"Ah! We've a disbeliever here, ladies and gentlemen. Well, sir, what must I do to prove my miracle cure?" The mountebank put one dirty finger to his chin, tapped it three times. Then his eyes lit up. "Aha! I shall poison someone, then cure him!" With a smarmy smile, he reached into a black bag at his feet and pulled out a squirming green creature that croaked. Cait jumped.

Chuckling, Jason put a reassuring hand on her shoulder.

Dr. Miracle raised the small, warty thing for all to see. "I have here a toad, the most poisonous creature known to mankind." His calculating eyes scanned the gathering. "If a fellow swallowed this animal, 'twould lead to almost certain death, would it not?"

The crowd murmured its agreement.

"But!" He raised a grimy hand. "I will have it be known that my Universal Healing Potion will cure even this toad's mighty poison. Now . . ." He paced in a slow circle. "Who will volunteer to swallow this creature? Who among you be brave enough?" Around and around the mountebank went, while the crowd pressed back, until suddenly he stopped right before the man who had shouted "Rubbish!" He strode forward and thrust the toad in the man's face, which was too close to her own for Cait's comfort. She leapt back, right into Jason's solid form.

His warm arms came around to steady her. "Watch," he whispered in her ear.

"Are you brave enough, my man?" the mountebank asked. "Will you swallow the toad and take the cure?" With a huff, the man turned and elbowed his way out through the crowd.

Dr. Miracle smirked as the mass of people parted, then closed in where the man had been. "Very well, then, I shall pay someone six pence if he will offer to swallow this poisonous toad, then be cured by my tonic." He walked slowly around the interior of the circle. "Will no one volunteer? Ten pence, anyone?" The toad sat docilely on his open palm, though Caithren could see its fat little sides heaving. "Hmm . . . I'll make that a whole shilling and include a free bottle of Dr. Miracle's Universal Healing Potion, worth another shilling. Now who will volunteer?"

"I'll swallow it for a shilling." A ragged young man stepped into the open. He looked like he could use a shilling.

The mountebank puffed out his chest. "Ladies and gentlemen, may we have a round of applause for this brave fellow?" Everyone clapped, and some hollered and whistled. More fair goers came to see what the commotion was about, pressing Cait closer to the center of the circle.

Dr. Miracle handed the young man the toad, then reached into his black bag and drew forth a dusty brown bottle. He tugged out the stopper. "Worry not," he assured the man. "My healing tonic will revive you—even should you be dead."

The volunteer looked alarmed at that pronouncement. He swallowed hard and gripped the toad harder. It croaked in protest.

"A whole shilling," the mountebank reminded the man. "Just for swallowing this fat little creature."

The young man scrunched up his face and squeezed tight his eyes before opening his mouth and stuffing the toad inside. With a gulp that could be heard to the back of the circle, he swallowed. Gasps and muttering ran through the crowd as they waited for something to happen.

After a tense minute, the man doubled over and let loose a pathetic moan. His head went back, and his eyes rolled up in his skull. "Cure me now!" He fell to his knees. "I'm dying!"

Dr. Miracle raised the brown bottle high into the air. He turned in an agonizingly slow circle, hampered by the suffering man who was clutching at his ankles.

"Shall I administer the cure?" he bellowed at the crowd.

"Save him!" a woman screamed.

"Let him die," a man yelled. "Serves him right for being such a gull."

"No, cure him!"

The young man collapsed on the ground and curled up in a ball.

"Give him the cure!" someone said.

Several joined in the chant. "Cure him! For God's sake, give him the cure!"

Caithren twisted to see Jason's face, but he didn't look

alarmed. His arms tightened around her. She turned back to the toad eater, now rolling on the grass in screaming agony.

"Cure him! Cure him! Cure him!"

The mountebank knelt slowly and cradled the young man's head in one dirty hand. He shoved the bottle between his lips, encouraging the man to drink. Two swallows later, the man's body relaxed and stilled on the ground.

In silence, the crowd waited. And waited.

The man drew a sudden breath, and his eyes popped open. His hands went to his stomach and felt around. He raised his head, then sat up, then stood up and did a little jig.

" 'Tis a miracle!" he cried. "The miracle cure works!" He skipped around the circle, snatched the bottle, and took another swig. "Give me no shilling," he told the doctor, "but an extra bottle of this Universal Healing Potion." When Dr. Miracle handed him a second bottle, he clutched them both to his chest as though they were of diamond, not glass.

The mountebank pulled more bottles from the bag. "Who else would like a bottle? Only one shilling for my miracle cure!"

As people jostled to buy, Jason pulled Caithren from the crowd. "What do you think?"

"Very entertaining," she declared with a smile.

"Entertaining?"

His look of confusion didn't fool her. "The toad is in the man's pocket," she said. "I wonder how much he makes for each bottle sold?"

"I wonder how else I've underestimated you," Jason returned. But he didn't look displeased. "What say you we buy tomorrow's breakfast and dinner now?" Low in the sky, the sun streaked the wispy clouds with shades of pink and red. " 'Tis getting late, and in order to outpace Gothard, we'd best make an early start."

And the fun was over, Caithren supposed with an inward sigh. She needed to find her brother and go home.

Before she could even nod her assent, Jason went into action. He purchased a burlap sack from one vendor, then wove through the market filling it with selections from others: bright yellow cheese, tart pickles wrapped in parchment, and small round loaves of bread. From a produce stand he carefully chose apples and costly oranges while Caithren amused herself watching two lambs in a pen, gamboling after their mother. She didn't like to think they might be someone's supper tonight.

Across from the fruits and vegetables sat a table laden with leather goods. Belts were laid out in neat rows, alongside coin pouches and scabbards and luggage. And by itself to the side sat one magnificent backgammon board.

'Twas a sight to behold. Black leather pips alternated with gray, the whole embellished with scrolling designs stamped in gold leaf. Two dice, fashioned of the blackest jet, lay as though just spilled from their matching leather cup. The markers were carved of jet and ivory.

Caithren smiled to herself, remembering hours on end spent playing with Cameron on the scarred wooden set that used to be Da's. Jason wandered to her side, his burlap sack laden with what she reckoned must be food enough to last for a week. "Know you the game?" he asked.

"I do." She squinted up at him. "I wager I could beat ye."

"Do you, now?" He stared down at her, his features schooled into serious lines. But his green eyes danced. "And what might you be willing to wager?"

She blushed furiously at the tone of his voice. "I haven't any money—"

"—thanks to me," he finished for her in a singsong manner. "Well, I expect we'll come up with something."

Once again, he spilled coins from his pouch and motioned the vendor over.

She'd meant to play him a game there and then, not for him to buy the board. She should have known better than to even look at it. She gasped at the price, but he didn't react. After closing the deal, he presented her with the set, picked up his sack, and announced he was thirsty.

She carried the board across her forearms, like it was a king's scepter.

Without asking if she wanted any, Jason bought white foamy drinks for them both. "Syllabub," he said, leading her to a bench.

She frowned into her goblet, then sipped. "Oooh," she breathed, sipping again. 'Twas the lightest, creamiest, sweetest thing she'd ever tasted. " 'Twould set the heather alight," she exclaimed. " 'Tis wonderful!"

Laughing, he reached to wipe a white mustache from atop her lip. Heat rushed to her face, and she turned away. Sipping their refreshments, they watched silently as other fair goers paraded past. Cait balanced the backgammon set on her lap, careful not to let any syllabub drip on the fine leather. She still couldn't believe he'd actually bought the game.

The sun was setting, casting the horizon in brilliant colors. As it sank below, a brief green flash lit the sky.

Part of her wishing the night would never end, Caithren sighed. "Tomorrow will be a clear day."

He sipped from his drink. "How come you to know this?"

"Did ye not see the green ray? They say it portends of fair weather." She rolled her goblet side to side between her hands. "Have ye never heard the verse?" She drank, then licked her lips. "Glimpse ye e'er the green ray," she quoted, "Count the morrow a fine day."

"Is that so?"

"Aye." She touched her amulet. "And it is said that

to see the green is to gain powers of seeing into the feelings of your heart, and thus not to be deceived in matters of love."

"Hmm. Sounds like yet another superstition."

She shrugged. "I didn't say I believed it."

He took a long swallow, then rubbed his bare upper lip with a finger. "I'm sorry there were no gowns here today."

"English gowns, pah! My own clothes will do if I wash them." She reached over the backgammon set to brush some dust off her forest green skirt, then toyed with an ivory marker, sliding it back and forth across the board. " 'Tis decent clothes I was wearing when ye . . ."

"Helped you off the coach?"

In the midst of a sip, she almost snorted syllabub out her nose. "Aye, ye might put it that way . . . if ye were a candidate for the asylum."

Jason let loose with a loud peal of laughter, his features splitting in the first genuine, unaffected grin she'd seen from him. It lit up his face, and a place in her heart.

She smiled in return, lifting her goblet to hide the blush that threatened to color her cheeks.

"Wait." He set his goblet on the bench between them. "Just wait right here."

At a loss, she sat and watched him take off, thread his lean form through the teeming crowd. Not a minute later he was walking toward her with his hands held behind his back. He stepped up before her, so close their knees almost touched, and leaned down to tuck a small bunch of violets behind her ear.

"Ah, lovely," he said. "Of a sudden, I thought that would complete the picture."

"Picture?" Now she really blushed. What was happening to them?

"When you smiled back then, 'twas like a . . . never mind." He looked away for a second, then back.

"Thank ye." She reached up to touch the soft, fragrant petals. "I do love violets."

Behind them, wives haggled over herrings, oysters, and mackerel. Across the way, feathers flew as a hundred chickens squawked their protest at being crammed in a wooden pen. But when Jason took the game off her lap and held her hands to pull her to stand before him, 'twas as though they were the only two beings there. Her breath caught, and she'd swear that her heart stopped for a moment, then pounded so hard she wondered if he could hear it.

His eyes burned into hers. Slowly he ran his hands up her arms to her shoulders, squeezed, then trailed back down to lace their fingers together. If he leaned any closer, she'd be tempted to take a bite out of him. When he lowered his head, her lips parted in anticipation.

But he only kissed her on the forehead. Her heart plummeted. 'Twas warm and sweet, but not what she'd been yearning for.

"We'd best be going," he said. " 'Tis almost dark, and with the fair in town, I expect the inns will fill up early around here."

Caithren popped an orange section into her mouth and licked her sticky fingers before rolling the dice. "Double sixes!" she crowed. She removed four white markers from the backgammon board and added them to her stack with a gleeful clink.

Jason shook the dice in their leather cup as he scanned the common room of the George of Stamford.

"What are ye looking for?" Cait peeled apart two more sections of the orange.

"Not what. Who." Men and women paraded past on their way upstairs, or into the taproom, or through double doors to the more formal dining room. The dice cup stilled in his hand. "The Gothard brothers."

"Ye think they're here in Stamford?" She glanced around as well, hoping he was wrong.

He rubbed the back of his neck. "Just a feeling, though they could easily be a town ahead or behind us."

"Well, they'd not afford a coaching inn as nice as this one. Or either of the other inns you've chosen along the way." The patrons in the common room looked well-heeled and groomed, not rumpled like she remembered the Gothards. She cocked her head. "Is that why you've been choosing as ye have? In order to avoid them?"

A distracted smile on his face, he rattled the dice. 'Twas obvious he wasn't going to answer. But she'd bet that he was attempting to steer clear of them. To keep her from getting the reward? She'd never understand him.

He rolled a one and a two. With an exaggerated groan, he advanced one of his black markers a paltry three pips. "Why did I buy this backgammon set?"

"Oh, but I'm glad ye did." She ran a caressing finger down one side of the board, then rolled again, a three and a five. Two more white markers came off her side. "Though Lord knows how we'll manage to carry it." She held out a piece of orange. "Would ye like some?"

He tossed the section into his mouth and rolled the dice. Double fours, and he was finally able to drop three black markers by his side of the board. But three rolls later the orange was finished and Caithren's side was empty. She celebrated her victory—she was two up on him now—with naught more than a yawn.

He glanced around as though something were out of place. "If you're wanting that bath I promised, you'd best take it now, Emerald."

Her head jerked up at the name. She didn't care for the look in his eyes. "Did ye see something?"

He held her stare. "No."

She made her own survey of the plush common room, but all she saw were people conversing in pairs and groups. Two men played cards in one corner. A couple made their their way up the stairs, laughing, their arms full of purchases from the fair. "What time is it?" she asked.

Her mouth dropped open at the sight of the watch he dug from his coat pocket. Gold, it was, with blue jewels stuck on the lid. "Eight o'clock," he said, and snapped it shut.

"May I see?"

"I know 'tis early." He plopped the pocket watch into her outstretched fingers. "But we must put in a long day tomorrow if we've a prayer of overtaking Geoffrey Gothard."

She stared at the watch, turned it gingerly in her hands, flipped it open. "Eight o'clock," she murmured. 'Twas not why she'd asked for the watch; she'd believed it was eight o'clock. She'd just wanted to feel it, to touch such a wonderfully beautiful thing. Mayhap she'd no cause for concern on Jason's behalf; mayhap he had more money than she'd imagined.

But he was a miller.

"Where did ye get this?" she asked.

He smiled as he took it from her and pocketed it. " 'Twas a gift. From a woman." He pushed back and stood up.

"Oh." A gift from a woman. Why should that matter to her? Three days from now they'd reach London, and then they'd part company. 'Twas what she'd been striving for all along, was it not?

"My sister-in-law," he added.

"Pardon?"

His grin widened. "The watch. A gift from my sister-in-law. Do you not know what a sister-in-law is? The woman who married my brother."

"I ken what a sister-in-law is, Jase." She rose and snatched up the backgammon set. "I simply cannot imagine ye having one, let alone her being fond enough of ye to gift ye with a watch like that. You're too ornery by half."

His laughter followed her up the stairs.

An hour later Jason knocked on the door and entered to find Emerald sitting by the fire, swishing her new comb through the long, silky tresses of her bath-damp hair. He'd never seen anything quite like Emerald's hair. The women in Cainewood's village always bound up their hair or hid it beneath a cap. And the court ladies of his acquaintance were always fussing with theirs, cutting it and curling it and crimping it and twisting it into all sorts of unnatural creations.

But Emerald's was straight and thick and shining. *Swish.* The ivory comb he'd bought her ran along its gleaming length. *Swish. Swish.* Her eyes were downcast, but he could still picture them lighting up at each of the small things he'd bought her. Sparkling with delight when she tasted the syllabub and laughed at the rope-dancers and tsked at the mountebank.

Swish. Jason didn't think he could stand it another moment. His fingers itched to bury themselves in that silk. Wrap the strands around his hands. Pull her head back and expose her creamy throat for his lips to plunder.

Bloody hell, he wanted to kiss her until she was breathless. In the dark hours of the night he'd dreamt of kissing her. The real experience couldn't possibly be as good as the dream, but damn if he wasn't tempted to prove it.

Stiffly he walked into the room and began loosening his cuffs. It helped not at all that Emerald wore nothing but Mrs. Twentyman's night rail; both her old clothes and the red gown were wet, hung carefully over the backs of two chairs to dry. Neither did it help that all the rooms available tonight had had naught but one bed.

At last she stood and set the comb on a bedside table,

beside the violets he'd given her, which she'd stuck into a pewter cup filled with water. The sight of them, bedraggled but saved, made his heart turn over.

He turned away and sat on the bed to pull off his boots, chucking them across the floor.

"Ye really should learn to be neater." Her hair waterfalled when she bent to retrieve them and set them side by side against the wall. He loosened his shirt and lay back, crossing his hands behind his head and staring up at the beamed ceiling.

Her head swam into view. "May I have one of the ribbons?"

"They're in my pouch."

She fetched the brown leather pouch and brought it over. God's blood, she looked beautiful standing above him, her thick hair bunched in one hand, the firelight revealing hints of her slender form beneath the white night rail. He could barely tear his gaze away long enough to fish in the pouch for the blue ribbon.

'Twas much too long to simply tie back her hair, but she used it anyway and let the ends dangle. He'd been right; the blue suited her perfectly.

He swallowed hard and closed his eyes, listening to the little sounds of Emerald readying herself for sleep.

When she crawled into bed beside him, he made no move to get under the covers. His blood was too hot; he didn't trust himself to keep his hands off her. The dream had done that to him. The dream and the woman next to him. Whenever she looked at him, whether outdoors by that ruined castle or over a backgammon board, it was with eyes that pleaded, a mouth that begged to be kissed. He wouldn't allow himself, couldn't.

Emerald MacCallum was not his type of woman. She was an outspoken, lying, Scottish—Scottish, of all things!—woman. No matter that she felt soft and smelled sweet. That was only part of the deception.

His eyes flew open when she turned to him and levered up on an elbow. A true hazel now, her gaze was riveted where his shirt lay open across his chest, revealing the angry puckered scar. "Does it still hurt?" she asked softly.

"Sometimes," he admitted. "But it's healing. 'Tis been more than three weeks."

"I should make a poultice for ye." She reached out, and his breath caught, but then her hand dropped away. "What happened?"

He couldn't tear his gaze from her concerned face. And that wide, pursed mouth. He was sure it was soft. It had been soft in his dream. "Geoffrey Gothard shot me."

"He shot ye?" She sat up in bed, shook her head violently. The dark blonde tail of her hair shimmered as it swished back and forth "Ye said he hurt, perhaps killed a wee lass. And almost raped—"

"That he did. And when I went after him to bring him in to the authorities, he shot me."

She twisted to face him, moved his shirt aside with gentle fingers, touched the pink, ridged tissue lightly. Something melted in his gut.

" 'Twas dangerously close to your heart," she said seriously.

A choked laugh escaped his lips. "No, 'tis naught but my shoulder. But I was already covered in another man's blood, so Gothard figured he hit his mark."

" 'Tis no wonder you're after killing him, then." Her fingers exploring, she leaned closer. Her hair fell forward, and the ends of the ribbon tickled his chest.

"No, I . . ." He couldn't seem to think. "I'm after him because he almost killed a little girl, and he'll kill others if he's not stopped." Absently he pulled one end of the blue ribbon until the bow came untied. Her eyes widened, but she didn't back away. "And—bloody hell, I know this is weak of me—but I cannot forgive him for causing me to kill a man. 'Tis a burden I'll carry the rest of my life. But that he shot me . . . no. That I blame on my own carelessness. I was not fast enough; I was stunned." His fingers combed through her hair as the words tumbled out. "And perhaps I should not have been taking the law into my own hands to start with. 'Tis not—'tis not the sort of man I am. Though you've seen no other, so I cannot fault you for believing so."

"Nay, I believe ye. I've seen the man ye are, Jason Chase." Her fingertips brushed his jaw. "I've seen a man of honor and compassion, and sometimes, when ye let it slip, even a wee bit of charm."

Reversing their positions, he came up on an elbow and hovered over her. She fell back to the pillow, and her lips curved into the sweetest smile, her eyes filled with blue light. Free of the customary braids, her hair was a mass of colors shimmering against the sheets. She trembled beneath him, and his name escaped her lips in a breathy murmur.

Of its own volition, it seemed, his hand moved to cup her face. "Emerald . . ."

The light in her eyes died, and she jerked her head away.

Not sure what had happened, he gazed at her a moment longer, then flipped onto his back and stared at the ceiling, saying nothing. There was nothing he could possibly say. He had no business kissing her in the first place; he certainly couldn't fault her for disallowing it.

Not that he was worried for her reputation. She was no simpering virgin, but a woman of . . . a woman of . . . what was she, exactly? A Scot, a mother, a daughter—a sister if he could believe her. A . . . businesswoman? What did one call a woman who made her living tracking outlaws? Well, whatever she was, she'd have no cause to blame him for ruining her. Most certainly she was beyond those social niceties.

But that didn't mean 'twas all right to kiss her. 'Twas

very much not all right. Her sensibilities aside, he had his own reasons for staying away.

He swore he could feel her heat penetrating the bed-clothes. With a muttered curse, he took the top quilt and slid off the bed. 'Twould not be the first time he'd slept on the floor.

Assuming he could sleep at all.

Chapter Twelve

"The birds are singing," Caithren said the next morning when they were back on the road. Since their almost-kiss last night, Jason had said hardly a word. She wasn't at all sure how she felt about him, but she didn't care for the awkward silence. "Is it not a beautiful day?"

"'Tis hot," he complained.

"'Tis warm and clear, just like the green flash portended. Will ye open your eyes? The clouds look like wool afore spinning."

She felt him shrug behind her. "They look like clouds to me."

"Is everything so black and white for ye, then?" One of her hands gripped his where it rested around her waist, while the other went into her pocket to feel Adam's miniature. For all his faults, Adam had an imagination. Too much of one, mayhap; he couldn't be less like Jason. "D'ye never see gray sometimes? Or purple?"

"Black is black, and white is white. I see no reason to call them otherwise."

"You're grumpy this morning." He was angry with her, even though last night's rejection had been an instinctive reaction. Well, he could be no more angry with her than she was angry with herself. She sighed and tried to put a note of compassion into her voice. "Did ye suffer the bad dream again last night?"

"No, I did not." With his free hand, he rooted in his

coat pocket for his water flask. " 'Twas rather impossible to dream given I wasn't asleep."

"Well, nobody said ye had to sleep on the floor. I shared a bed with ye the first night, and ye didn't hear me complaining."

"Did I not?" Awkwardly he brought the flask before her so he could use both hands to pull out the cork. "You didn't stay in it long, either—"

"Wheesht." She cupped an ear. "D'ye hear water?"

He shook the flask. "No. 'Tis empty." Disgruntled, he corked it and shoved it back into his pocket. "Are you thirsty?"

"Aye. And I hear a burn. Running water. There, to the right—I mean the left." Following where she pointed, he guided Chiron off the road, along a small path that had been trodden through the trees. She sighed in pleasure at the sight before her. "Oh, 'tis beautiful."

The stream ran babbling through a sparse emerald forest, its banks studded with multi-colored pebbles that looked like so many wet jewels. While Jason tethered Chiron, Caithren dismounted and sat upon a log to remove her shoes and stockings.

"What do you think you're doing?"

"I wish to walk in the water a bit. Does it bother ye, then?"

He shrugged. "I suppose not."

"Ye said it was hot. 'Twould cool ye off some." She shot him her best convincing smile. Jason didn't strike her as the type of man to doff his stockings and wade in a burn. Still, 'twas worth a try to get him out of his dour mood. "Come along," she cajoled. "Be . . . impulsive. Isn't that what ye called our excursion into the tunnel? And ye said it was fun."

His eyes locked with hers for a long moment, clear and unfathomable. "Very well," he said at last. "Get started." He waved her along the bank. "Let me fill the flask and check the map, and I'll follow along in a bit."

The stream felt lusciously cold when she dipped her bare toes. Raising her skirt, she inched in until the water lapped at her feet and then her ankles. She wandered along for a few minutes, keeping a hopeful eye out for the dark green notched leaves of water betony as she skipped stones across to the other bank. The burn smelled fresh and enticing. She bunched her skirt in one hand, then bent to cup the other and take a deep, refreshing drink.

When she looked up, it was into the beady black eyes of a wild boar.

Caithren's heart paused, skittered, started beating again. The beast stood a goodly distance away, perhaps twenty or thirty feet, eyeing her malevolently. She took a step back, pitched forward and had to catch herself from tumbling. The bottom of the stream wasn't the smooth slope she'd been expecting. It dropped off toward the center.

The boar took a step forward.

"J-Jason?" she stuttered ineffectively, afraid to yell and provoke the animal. She stepped back again, more gingerly this time. The hem of her skirt dipped into the water, and she hiked it higher and tucked it into her waistband. Her hand went up to grasp her amulet.

The smooth, polished emerald felt solid and reassuring in her clenched fingers. But the stone's protective powers didn't seem to be in force. Staring at her unblinkingly, the boar came two steps closer.

Her heart pounding, she reached her other hand into her pocket, and her fingers closed on the grip of Jason's little pistol. Slowly she pulled it out and cocked the flintlock.

At the distinctive click, the boar moved again. She would swear his eyes narrowed.

"Jason? Are ye nearby?" Her hand shook as she raised the barrel. "St-stay back," she ordered in the most convincing voice she could muster.

"Jason!" she wailed.

Her breath was coming in panicky gasps. The beast inched another step closer. "Stay back!" she screamed. "Keep away from me, ye mawkit beast!"

But it wouldn't listen. Jason wasn't coming to her rescue. When the boar took yet another step, she closed her eyes and squeezed the trigger.

The resulting *bang!* left her heart in her mouth. The pistol's kick sent her sprawling on her behind in the cold burn, and the boar charged splashing into the water, straight at her. She scrambled to get up, but her feet skidded on the muddy streambed, and the pistol slipped out of her grasp, plunging to the bottom.

Just as she was sure she was about to die, the animal collapsed. The silvery blade of a sword flashed in the sun, jammed between its shoulder blades.

Shuddering in both horror and relief, Caithren sat in the water, feeling a sudden warmth as the beast's blood spread in red ribbons beneath the surface. Her gaze was riveted to the motionless boar where its hairy back made a hump in the shallow stream.

Jason waded to her side and reached a hand to pull her up. She stood there, dripping, her hands clenching her crossed arms in a futile attempt to control the shaking.

"It would not have attacked you if you hadn't shot," he said calmly.

"B-but he wouldn't stop." Her teeth chattered, although the day was no less hot than before. "He was coming toward me."

"At a walk, no? He was only curious." He rubbed the back of his neck. "Boars won't attack people unless they're provoked."

"H-how was I supposed to ken that?" Her sodden skirt had come untucked and floated about her knees. Her bodice and shift were plastered to her skin. The pale ivory sleeves were streaked a sickening shade of pink.

She stared at the fallen animal until Jason took her by the hand and tugged her upstream. His fingers felt warm and reassuring.

"Submerge yourself," he urged. He waded back to the boar, lifting his boots high, heavy with water. "Go ahead," he called back. "The blood will wash out." Numbly she obeyed, watching him tug the sword free and rinse off the blade. He slid it back into his belt, then plunged his arm into the water and came up with his pistol.

For a long moment he held it dripping above the surface, looking from it to Caithren and back again. He cocked a brow. "I reckon 'tis best I keep this, no?" Tucking it into his boot top, he splashed his way back to her.

Trying to gather her wits, Caithren plucked her soaked bodice away from her body. " 'Tis sorry I am that your boots are ruined."

"They'll dry." He shrugged, then his forehead furrowed. "You're a lousy shot, Emerald."

"I'm not Emerald." Irritated, she waded out of the water at full speed. "I've never shot a gun afore. I didn't like it much."

He emerged from the burn and sat on a stump, shading his eyes with a hand as he gazed up at her. "You were carrying a pistol when I found you."

"Found me? Tricked me into staying with ye is more like it."

His hand dropped. "I can do without the wordplay." He tugged off a boot and spilled out a gush of water. "What were you doing carrying a pistol if you know not how to use it?" His stocking came off next, and he wrung it in his hands. Absurdly, Caithren thought he had nice toes. "Well?" he barked.

Her head jerked up. " 'Twas Da's. Cameron made me take it. To protect myself from Englishmen like ye."

A momentary look of doubt seemed to cross his face,

but he regained his normal implacable expression while he poured slowly from his second boot. "You're certainly one for the stories. Quick thinker, too." He peeled off his other stocking. " 'Tis a good thing the outlaws don't know you cannot shoot . . . 'twould put a damper on your business, I expect."

She glared at him in disbelief, then turned and stalked upriver, back to where she'd left her things. "You've an aggravating master," she informed Chiron. Plopping down upon a log, she spread her skirts around her, that they might dry a wee bit in the sun while she pulled on her stockings and shoes.

Her eyes were still trained downward when Jason's nice toes marched into her field of vision. She squinted up at him. "Where is the food ye bought yesterday? I'll be wanting a chitterin' bite."

"A what?"

"A chitterin' bite. D'ye not eat something after a swim, to keep from catching cold?"

"No." He stared at her as though she'd left her head in the water. "Is that another of your Scottish superstitions?"

" 'Tis not a superstition—'tis a health precaution. And I dinna care for the way ye say 'Scottish.' "

He raised a brow. "Will an orange do?"

"Aye. Sweet is preferable to savory."

"I will file that information." He fetched an orange from the portmanteau and handed it to her. "You will have to wear the red dress," he said, pulling it out as well. He draped it over the log, a jarring splash of crimson against the green of their forest surroundings.

"Nay." Ignoring it, she bit into the bitter skin of the orange and started peeling. "I'll not wear that dress again."

Ignoring her in turn, he shrugged out of his surcoat and took dry breeches from one of the leather bags.

"Michty me!" She jumped up, scattering orange peel

all over the ground. "You're not going to undress right here, are ye?"

"Nobody is around. What would you have me do?" In one single lithe motion, he pulled his shirt free from his waistband and off over his head. "I'd as soon not ride about the countryside soaking wet."

Cait knew how bairns were made. She was certainly familiar with breeding animals, and, as her best friend, Cameron had always answered her questions. She'd even seen Cam without his shirt. But never a stranger. Her gaze was riveted to Jason's chest. Lightly defined muscles rippled beneath a sprinkling of silky black hair.

When he started unlacing his breeches, she gave an outraged huff. "I'd rather not have to watch." Despite the calm words, her heart beat much too fast. "Indulge me in my false pretense of innocence," she said sarcastically, then whirled to walk away.

His laughter followed her. "Come back and take the red dress. I'll not have your skirt drenching my nice dry clothes as we ride."

The skirt in question was dripping on her nice dry shoes and stockings. In disgust she turned back and snatched the red gown from the log.

"Here," he said, digging in the portmanteau. "You'll be needing this as well." He held out the sheer chemise that had come with the dress.

Instead of arguing, she took it, though she had no intention of wearing it. Carefully she set the half-peeled orange on the log and made her way through the trees, far enough that she was sure he couldn't see her. She checked thoroughly for boars before unlacing her soggy bodice.

Goose bumps sprang up on her skin as she undressed. From cold, or confusion? This irritating and misguided man kept insisting on calling her Emerald . . . but he never hesitated to come to her rescue. He was exasperating and oddly compassionate, rigid yet honorable in his way. And though she'd truly never been as angry with anyone in her life—jings! He'd completely ruined all her plans!—his slightest touch sent her heart to racing.

That didn't bear thinking about. She didn't want to be with any man. She wanted to find Adam and get back to Leslie where she belonged.

He was right, blast it; her shift was entirely too soaked to wear beneath the dress this time. Disgusted, she dropped the chemise over her head and wiggled it into place. The gossamer fabric might as well be air for all the concealment it offered. She stepped into the gown, laced it up, attached the stomacher with fumbling fingers. Covering her exposed bosom with both hands, she made her way back to the stream bank. She was sure her face was as red as the gown.

Thankfully, Jason was decently clothed by now. His gaze trailed from her burning face to her hands splayed on her chest, and he burst out laughing.

He dug in his pocket and handed her a handkerchief. "Here," he said.

She cocked her head.

"To fill in the neckline."

"Oh. I thank ye." She shoved it down the front of the dress, tucking it in as best she could. She reached for the orange. "Ye should have a chitterin' bite as well," she told him.

"Why? So I'll not catch cold?"

"Aye." She sat on the log and divided the fruit, handing him half. "So you'll not catch cold."

He stuffed a section into his mouth and dug out some fresh stockings before joining her on the log. "I thank you for your concern," he said. "I was under the impression you'd just as soon I caught consumption and died."

Her mouth hung open. What a thing for him to say. Why had she ever thought she might like him?

"Not until ye get me to London," she snapped.

*   *   *

"A hat?" An hour later, Caithren dismounted at the Haycock Hotel and followed Jason into a charming courtyard with stone archways and mullioned windows.

"Yes, a hat. While you were provoking the boar, I checked on the map, and this is the only decent-sized village between here and Stilton." His gaze scanned the inn's patrons, mostly comprised this Sunday of well-off ladies and gentlemen sharing conversation or lingering over news sheets. "Should we ride all that way on a day like today, with only one hat between us, one of us will end up sunburned and suffering. I'd as soon it not be me, though common decency dictates it will be." He nodded at his hat, which was perched atop her braids.

She slowly drew it off. "Oh."

He took it from her and set it back on her head. "The shops are closed on a Sunday, but I'm hoping to convince someone here to part with a hat in exchange for a generous payment." With one finger, he tilted the brim up. "Perhaps a more feminine design would suit you?"

She'd been as nasty as she could to him since his comment by the burn, and now this thoughtfulness. Tucking his handkerchief more firmly into her neckline, she stared at him. "Sometimes you're too nice."

"I am not nice." He drew back his shoulders. "I'm doing what I have to do. No more, no less. I'm responsible for you, and for everything you lost on account of me."

"How many times do I have to tell ye that you're not responsible for me? I can take care of myself."

His mouth opened, closed, then he turned on his heel and strode into the cool, shadowed lobby to make inquiries at the desk.

Cait trailed behind him and stared at his back for a minute while he explained his problem to the innkeeper. Her legs were aching again, and her brain felt muddled. She went closer and tapped Jason on the shoulder.

"I'm away for a wee dander," she said.

He stopped mid-sentence and turned. "A wee what?"

"A walk." She gestured out the front door. "Down the street a bit, to stretch my legs."

"Stay on the High Street," he told her.

Wansford boasted *only* the High Street, so far as she could tell. She wandered down it, enjoying the sunshine and the solitude she'd lacked the past few days. Her irritation with Jason seemed to melt away as her feet put distance between them.

Charming stone cottages with tiny gardens lined the way, bees buzzing around the carefully tended flowers. There was one other inn, the small Cross Keys. Past a couple more houses and across the street sat a tiny kirk.

The door was open, and a service was in progress. Cait sidled closer to listen. The drone of the vicar's sermon sounded both peaceful and familiar. It was comforting to find that Sunday rituals, at least, were the same here as in Scotland. She slipped inside and into the back pew, feeling at home for the first time since she'd stepped onto the coach in Edinburgh.

It was there Jason found Emerald, dozing, after a frantic search.

Taking her by the arm, he pulled her up and out the door. "I was worried sick," he told her in hushed tones, dragging her farther away from the church. When they were out of earshot he turned her to face him. "I couldn't find you."

"Your face is red," she said, wrenching her arm from his grasp. "You're angry."

"Damn right I'm angry."

"But you're not yelling."

One of the two of them belonged in Bedlam. "What does that have to do with anything?"

"Ye should just show it. Why dinna ye show it?" She grasped her emerald necklace and hung on like it would save her from his expected wrath. "And you're angry because ye thought I'd gotten away and gone after Gothard on my own."

Amazing how she clung to that image of him. He took a calming breath. "Stay with me from now on, will you? I don't want you out of my sight." He swept his hat from her head and drew one with a white feather from behind his back, setting it atop her braids. "There. Now we'd best get back on the road."

"I've never owned a hat with a feather." Hurrying down the street beside him, Emerald pulled off the bonnet and turned it in her hands. " 'Tis bonnie. I thank ye."

He donned his own hat. "Don't lose it."

"Have I lost anything yet? Without your help?"

"No." He looked down at her and, despite himself, grinned. "I've been a great help in that area."

Her lips curved in a triumphant smile, she jammed the bonnet back on her head. "The Gothard brothers were sunburned," she said.

Baffled, he slanted her a glance. "Where did that comment come from?"

"Ye were talking about getting sunburned."

"An hour ago." He would never understand how women's minds worked.

"Well, they were both sunburned." They turned the corner and continued toward the stable yard. "D'ye think the Gothards cannot even afford a hat?"

"From what I understand of their circumstances, I'd not be surprised." Chiron was brought forward, and he took the reins and handed the groom a coin.

"Then they really wouldn't be able to change horses," she mused as he hoisted her up and mounted behind her. "And he's a blockhead."

"Who's a blockhead?"

"Geoffrey Gothard. We were talking about him, aye?"

"Were we?" He tapped her on the shoulder. "Gothard is not as stupid as you think. You'd best keep that in mind."

She giggled. "I didn't mean to say he was stupid. I meant he is *literally* a blockhead. He has a square head."

He squinted, trying to picture the man. She was right. Delighted, he laughed and squeezed her around the middle, then, without conscious thought, he tilted her hat up and pressed his lips to that enticing spot on the nape of her neck.

"What was that for?" she squeaked.

He asked himself the same question. She cried entirely too easily for a woman with her career, and she had no business carrying a pistol. Why, she wouldn't hit an outlaw from arm's length. She was superstitious. She believed in ghosts. And though she seemed educated, he couldn't understand half of what she said with her accent and all those unintelligible words.

A Royalist and a Cavalier born and bred, he couldn't imagine why he was drawn to someone so provincial and . . . well, Scottish.

"Just for being you," he said. "Though damned if I understand it myself."

Chapter Thirteen

After what seemed an interminable day, a black cat came up to rub against Caithren's legs when she wandered into the courtyard of the Bell Inn in Stilton. She knelt, petting him absently as she read the words engraved in stone above the arched entry. TO BUCKDEN 14 MILES, HUNTINGDON 12, LONDON . . . 74.

Still such a long way to go.

Spotting a well in the corner, she was careful to approach it from the east on the southern side, lest she bring bad luck on herself. In silence she drank three handfuls of water and closed her eyes to make a wish. *Please let me find Adam. And . . .* She squeezed her eyes shut tighter.

. . . let Jason kiss me again.

The shadows seemed longer when she opened her eyes, and she took a deep breath. Jings, that was an utterly improper wish. Never had she thought she'd ache for a man's kiss. She hadn't believed she had it in her.

She lifted the hem of the red gown and raised the chemise to her teeth to tear off a narrow strip, then turned to find Jason's gaze on her from where he stood just outside the open stable doors, seeing that Chiron was settled. Heat flooded her cheeks, but she shrugged and tied the strip to the branch of a nearby tree.

The inn was built around the courtyard, its walls enlivened by fragrant flowering plants and a vined trellis. Finished with the ritual, she seated herself on the lip of the well to wait for Jason. Even from a distance, he looked well-built and gut-wrenchingly handsome. His hair glinted in the waning sun, worn loose to his shoulders today. He kept glancing in her direction, a puzzled look in his eyes. A blackbird watched her from the tree, cocking its head as though it were puzzled as well. The cat meandered over and leapt up into her lap.

"Whatever were you doing?" Jason asked when he finally joined her. From the look on his face, she concluded he thought her a wee bit daft. Not that that was anything new.

"Is this not a clootie well?" The cat purred beneath her hand.

" 'Tis a Roman well, I believe." He placed his portmanteau and the backgammon set, which he'd carried in the burlap bag, atop the well's ledge. Leaning over, he looked inside. "What the hell is a clootie well?"

She smiled when his voice echoed back up. "A well where ye make a wish."

"And then tear your clothes?" He looked her up and down. "What was that about? Or is it only that you hate the dress?"

Her mouth twitched with humor. "When ye make a wish at a clootie well, your troubles are transferred to the cloth. Then ye tie it to a tree and leave the troubles there."

"You believe this?" he asked, clearly incredulous.

"Of course not. But it doesn't hurt to do it anyway. 'Tis a tradition."

"Ruining your clothes is a Scottish tradition?"

She shook her head. "Nay, we do not make a habit of destroying our clothes. Normally you'd tie a handkerchief or a rag." She couldn't resist a grin. "Ruining these clothes was a bonus."

A brief, amused smile curved his lips, then he tensed and shot a quick look over his shoulder.

"D'ye see something?" she asked.

"No. I just thought I did." He blinked and cocked his head, just like the blackbird. "What did you wish?"

If only he knew! She blushed to think of it. "I cannot tell. 'Twill not come true if I do." She held up a hand. "Nay, I dinna really believe that, either. But I'll hold to it all the same."

"Hush a moment." His gaze swept the grounds as he turned in a slow circle. "I have a strange feeling," he said low.

"What d'ye mean?" Relieved to be off the subject of her wish, she set down the cat and watched it scamper up an ivy-covered wall.

"I'm not sure." He grabbed the bags. "Perhaps I will feel different inside."

She'd given up hoping for her own room, but was pleased the one Jason took had two beds. Kisses were one thing; sharing a bed, quite another. Once upstairs and in the chamber, she unpacked their wet clothes and smoothed them on the bare wooden floor. Hopefully they would dry by morning.

Her task complete, she turned to Jason. "Let me guess. You're hungry."

"Actually, I'm not." His lips quirked in a half-smile. "I know you're shocked, but don't faint on me, now." To her complete surprise, he followed up the teasing words with a fake lunge to catch her in the imaginary faint.

She giggled, feeling overly warm where his hands gripped her upper arms. If he could loosen up and become more playful, she could as well. "Emerald MacCallum wouldn't faint," she declared.

His expression stilled. "No, she would not," he agreed slowly. His hands dropped from her arms, and he backed away toward the door, watching her.

" 'Twas a jest," she said weakly. When he didn't reply, her voice dropped to a whisper. "I'm not Emerald, but there's nothing I can say to convince ye." She squirmed under his gaze, and her hands moved to play with her laces but met the embroidered stomacher instead. Feeling a tightness in her chest that had nothing to do with its stiffness, she tucked his handkerchief more securely into her neckline.

"I'm going for a walk," he said abruptly.

"All right," she said with some relief. The time alone would be welcome. Time to think about how she was changing. How *they* were changing, together.

He turned, hesitated, turned back. "I think you must come along."

She groaned. "We only just arrived. I would rather stay here and rest."

Taking her by the hand, he pulled her toward the door. "I don't want to leave you alone."

"I'm not looking to escape ye." She tugged her hand from his.

"I'm not concerned you'll escape. I trust you." He paused and gave a slight shake to his head, as though he couldn't believe he'd said that. "But something has me uneasy." He ran a hand back through his hair. "We both go, or we both stay here."

The four walls of the small room seemed to be closing in on her. The thought of spending all evening in here, with him in his present mood, was daunting. With a sigh, she followed him.

A coach was departing as they went downstairs, its squeaky springs audible through the open front door. Another pulled up as they approached the innkeeper's desk for Jason to leave the key. Neither of them were Cait's coach, though—in truth, she'd given up looking. She knew by now it was days behind them.

"Busy place," Jason remarked to the clerk.

"A mail-posting station." The pale man shrugged. "The postmaster makes no wage—he paid forty pounds to obtain the position. Keeps the inn full." He nodded toward the door, where three more guests were straggling in.

In order to avoid all the activity in the front, they went out the back way and into the courtyard again. Once more Caithren's gaze was drawn to the engraved archway. LONDON 74.

"How many more days?" she asked.

Jason's gaze followed hers. "Two, I'm hoping." He stopped, propping one booted foot on a bench, and glanced around distractedly.

"And you're worried the Gothards'll get there afore ye?"

"Pardon?" He brought his attention back to her. "No, not really. I sent Scarborough a letter. Even should he not have gotten it, we should have ample time to warn him. The brothers might beat us there by half a day, but I seriously doubt they'll ride straight to his home and shoot him." He plucked a large leaf off the climbing vine overhead. "They'll want to plan first."

"It sounds like you're more concerned about saving Scarborough than killing Geoffrey."

"Scarborough's life is at immediate risk." As though he were uncomfortable, he rolled his shoulders, then winced and put a hand to where she knew the wound was hidden beneath his clothes. "The rest can wait. But not too long . . . these men have gone too far already. God alone knows what they'll plan next."

The courtyard's gravel crunched under Cait's feet as she shifted. "I'm thinking we should rise early tomorrow and try harder to outpace them."

"I'll not complain about leaving this place at first dawn." His fingers worried the leaf as he scanned the courtyard. "There's something eerie here."

She grinned, trying to lighten his mood. "Are ye sensing a ghost, Jase?"

With a thud, he brought his foot from the bench to the gravel. "How many times must I tell you—"

"—there is no such thing as ghosts," she finished for him and laughed. "Is this where ye wanted to walk?"

"No." He tossed the shredded leaf to the gravel. "We'll walk around to the High Street."

Jason led her out of the courtyard and around the corner. As they crossed the street, Cait glanced back at the Bell. It was a long range of stone-built bays and gables, with two massive chimney stacks and an impressive coach entrance. An ornate wrought-iron bracket supported a heavy copper-plate sign, painted with a large red bell.

There was nothing sinister about the place. But Cait's hand went to her amulet, just in case.

Another mail coach pulled away as they walked down the bustling street. There were fourteen public houses and inns along the High Street, and as they passed them, sounds of laughter and frivolity drifted out their doors. Beyond their candlelit windows, Caithren could see people eating, conversing, conducting business. Living their lives. Unlike her, none of them seemed to be questioning the very foundations of their plans. This night she hardly recognized herself, her feelings.

Jason's boots slapped the packed dirt road; her own shoes made a softer, shuffling sound. Had he really kissed her on the back of the neck? She couldn't be sure—it had all happened so fast.

Past the Talbot, the street became residential and quiet, a neat row of stone cottages with carefully tended gardens. Beyond that, nothing but the dusty Great North Road, stretching all the way to Scotland.

Caithren was so far from home. Her hand slipped into her pocket, feeling for Adam's portrait as she wondered what Cameron was doing right now. The long shadows of dusk paced her and Jason up the street; Cameron was probably having supper. He'd want to go to bed soon, to get an early start and take advantage of the long summer day. There would be a lot to do, with her not home to help him.

"What are you thinking?" Jason asked.

"Of home." The black cat from the inn came strolling up beside her; she reached down and picked it up.

"You sound melancholy." His tone was apologetic. "We shall get to London soon. Once I've—done away with Gothard"—he shrugged uncomfortably—"I'll . . . give you the reward. For all your assistance. I don't need it." He stopped walking and turned to her. " 'Tis why you're doing this, yes? For the money. I assume glory is not nearly as important?"

Her fingers tightened in the cat's fur, and it squealed and jumped out of her arms. "How much did ye say this reward is?"

"It said on the broadsides." He shot her a sharp glance. "A hundred pounds."

"And you're not needing that kind of money?"

He shook his head.

"Very prosperous mill ye have there, Jase."

Mill? Jason thought. What did his mill have to do with this? For the life of him, he couldn't think of a response.

They'd reached the end of the village now, and he took her arm to lead her across the road. In silence, they headed back toward the Bell. Another coach creaked by, this time from the north. The sun was setting, and he felt her shiver at a sudden chill in the air. Their footsteps sounded loud in this sparse end of the village. She crossed her arms, uncrossed them, reached up to twirl a braid.

The faint sound of plodding hoofbeats came after the coach. Two horses. Feeling the hair prickle on his neck, Jason turned and walked backward to have a look. Two men. Too distant to see their faces, but they were hatless, and damn if one of them didn't have a square head.

Although somehow he'd known all afternoon, he gaped in disbelief.

A cold knot formed in his stomach. His thoughts only of Emerald, he swivelled and grabbed her arm, dragging her between two houses.

"Wh-what are ye doing?"

"Hush," he whispered. "We're being followed." His hands went to her shoulders, and he backed her against the side of the nearer house. "Hold still."

As they waited, he felt her pulse speed under his fingers. One of his hands went to the hilt of his rapier, the other itched to reach for the pistol he'd hidden in his wide-topped boot.

But if he confronted Geoffrey Gothard here and now, what would become of Emerald? Torn in two directions, his thoughts raced incoherently. What would his father do? Protect the woman or stand up to the brothers like a man?

The hoofbeats were coming closer still.

Panic. Releasing his grip on the sword, he angled her away from the street, tilted her face up, and crushed his mouth to hers.

Startled, Caithren pushed weakly against his chest with both hands.

"Kiss me, will you?" His lips brushed hers as he spoke. "They mustn't see our faces."

"Who?" she asked, but the question was smothered against his mouth, and her thoughts whirled and skidded when he gathered her into his arms. Mayhap to shield them from view, but the truth was, she couldn't have cared less.

Improper or not, she was getting her wish, and she meant to make the most of it.

Her arms came up; her fingers wound themselves in his silky, blunt-cut hair. His mouth caressed hers, clever and persuasive. Heat sprinted along her veins. A little moan rose from her throat, and he coaxed her lips apart with his own.

Her bones seemed to melt when his tongue invaded

her mouth, soft and warm and more exciting than she ever could have imagined. She'd never tasted a man before, and this one tasted divine. This kiss wasn't like that bampot Duncan's, or like anyone else's at Leslie. As the laird's daughter, all the kisses she'd received had been chaste and respectful.

Jason's was anything but.

Just when she thought she could never get enough, he stilled. "I think they're gone," he whispered against her mouth.

She pressed closer. "Are ye sure?" Her lips strained for more of his touch.

"Mmmm." Another light kiss sent her heart to racing. "Pretty sure." He pulled back, and she slumped against the wall.

He stepped out into the street for a moment, then returned. "They are gone," he said.

"Who?" Her voice came out thin and reedy.

He drew a deep breath. "The Gothards."

"The Gothards?" She struggled to pull herself together. "Why did ye not just shoot them?"

"I . . . it . . . didn't feel like the right time." He looked into the street, down at his feet, everywhere but her eyes.

She gave a violent shake to her head, and it cleared with a rush of shock and outrage. "I heard no footsteps following us! Ye only . . . ye used that as an excuse to ravish me!"

"Ravish you?" He choked back laughter. "I think not. When I've ravished you, sweetheart, you'll know it." His hand went up to stroke his missing mustache, then fisted and dropped to his side. "Besides, I didn't hear you take exception. You kissed me back. I'm not the one who put your arms around my neck."

"Ye claimed we were being followed! I wanted to make it look good."

"Hmm, is that so?" He didn't look convinced.

He didn't look at all spooked anymore, either.

"Ye set this whole thing up," she accused him. "From the outset this eve, you've been telling me something was wrong. All so ye could kiss me."

Now he did laugh. "That hard up I'm not. I needn't make up stories to get women to kiss me. For example . . ."

He pulled her away from the wall, bent her backward, and ravished—there was no other word for it—*ravished* her mouth with his. Any protest died on her lips as tendrils of sensation stole along her nerves. His tongue traced the line where her lips met, and she opened her mouth, and he nibbled on her bottom lip. His spicy, warm scent flooded her senses. When he set her away, carefully standing her straight, she just stood there, trying to catch her breath. No words came to her stunned mind.

He had plenty of words for both of them, though. "So, you see, I've no reason to make excuses. If I'd wanted to have you, I've had ample opportunity. You'd not have stopped me, as our little demonstration has just proven."

"Oh," she breathed, shaken and embarrassed. Her knees trembling, she walked to the edge of the houses and looked out into the street. Although dark was encroaching, the little village was still busy. People drifted in and out of taverns, others rode the street on horseback. She didn't recognize anyone, but they were all far away and hard to see in the failing light.

She turned back, not quite sure if she believed him or not. While he was kissing her, a coach-and-eight could have thundered by and she'd not have heard it with the blood rushing in her ears. She glanced up at the hard line of his mouth. If she questioned his intentions again, he'd surely argue. She didn't want to argue with him.

She wanted him to kiss her again.

Her legs felt wobbly, and her heart was still racing as well.

He looked down at her. "As you saw for yourself, they're definitely gone." His voice was gentler—not that it had been terribly harsh in the first place. His innate calmness unnerved her; when a man was upset, he ought to show it.

He tucked a stray strand of hair behind her ear. "Don't be frightened."

She wasn't frightened; if she looked peaked, 'twas because she still hadn't recovered from his sensual assault. When she failed to respond, he took her hand. Even his fingers felt warm and exciting. Though she'd rather he held her hand because he wanted to, for him to do it out of gallantry was almost as good.

"Come along," he said. "We'll get you some supper, and you'll feel better."

That prompted a smile. "Is food your solution for everything, then?"

"Pretty much." He grinned, then led her back to the street. As they walked along, she shifted her fingers so they laced with his. That felt even better.

In tacit silence they made their way back to the Bell, their footsteps echoing in the dark. Jason seemed to be on the alert, leaving Caithren to her own thoughts.

After supper, Jason would leave her in their room for a while to give her privacy while she changed into Mrs. Twentyman's night rail. He would return, take off his surcoat, loosen his clothes. She would unbraid and comb her hair, then replait it into a single braid down her back. Then they'd climb into their separate beds. So it had gone almost every night.

But tonight felt different. Just thinking about sharing Jason's room tonight made her knees feel weak. Remembering the touch of his lips, feeling his hand in hers, her whole body seemed afire.

She wanted him to kiss her again.

"I'd like to go into the stables," he said, interrupting her thoughts.

"What d'ye mean?" As they turned off the High Street alongside the inn, her mind raced with possibilities—mostly ones that made her blush. Some stables had nice lofts. "Are ye worried for Chiron?"

"No. I want to make sure the Gothards aren't staying here."

"Oh." Disappointment flitted through her, but she told herself she was being ridiculous. Of course his mind wasn't on kissing her—he'd convinced himself they were being followed.

He drew her into the Bell's stables and quickly paced the length, looking into every stall. Pulled along by the hand, Caithren hurried to keep up.

"D'ye reckon the brothers are so poor they'll be sleeping in stables?"

"Not exactly." Reaching the end, he visibly relaxed and dropped her hand, leaning to take a fistful of carrots from an open wooden box. "I was looking for their horses. They're not here, though, so I have to assume they're staying somewhere else."

Happy he seemed no longer worried, Cait followed him back to where his own horse was stabled. Now mayhap she could turn his mind back to her. Chiron munched contentedly while Jason resettled the thin night blanket over his back. She moved closer and smoothed a corner of the cloth. "Ye would recognize their horses?" Brushing up against him, she tilted her face up, hoping for a kiss.

He stared down at her, his eyes dark and unfathomable. Her heart skittered.

Then steadied when he blinked. "I believe so." He drew her from the stall, guiding her from the stables with a warm hand at the small of her back. Their footsteps crunched on the gravel in the courtyard. When his fingers meshed with hers, she inhaled sharply at the contact.

She didn't ken what drew her to this man, but something did. She didn't want to ever marry, to share Leslie with anyone but Cameron. But the feelings Jason kindled in her were fascinating, particularly because she'd never thought much of the marriage bed or what she would miss. But surely, she couldn't want that with Jason. Just another kiss.

He wasn't immune to her charms—she was sure of it. There must be a way she could coax a kiss. One more kiss.

As they headed to the taproom for supper, she came up with a plan. That was, if she could find the nerve to carry it out.

"Nay, dinna leave."

The door to their room halfway open, Jason turned to look at Emerald. "Pardon?"

She finished unbraiding her hair, slowly dragging her fingers through the crimped, dark golden mass. "I . . . will ye remove this stomacher for me?" She licked her lips, fumbling with the tabs. "I've got it knotted. I'm not very good at it."

For a moment he could only stare. "You removed it yourself in Newark-on-Trent."

" 'Twas a struggle." She sighed prettily, her eyes turning a soft blue. "Ye should have been there."

He raised a brow. "Amusing, was it?"

"Nay. I mean ye *literally* should have been there." She came closer, reaching past him to shut the door. "Please?" With a coquettish flourish that made his breath catch, she whisked his handkerchief out of her neckline. "Ye said ye had a lot of experience taking these off." Tossing the handkerchief onto the nearest bed, she leaned into him.

What had gotten into her? She was hardly displaying her usual willful independence. "Very well. I'll help just this once." Easing her away to arm's length, he started detaching the tabs. "This really is quite simple, though. Watch."

She looked down, her warm breath fanning over his fingers. "I'm watching," she all but purred, sounding nothing like the Emerald he'd come to know. His fingers fumbled, then resumed. "Oooh, Jason, ye really are quite good at this."

He gave a nervous laugh and set the stomacher on the bed. "There."

"Thank ye." She leaned in again, looking for all the world like she was asking for a kiss, just like she had in the stables.

He couldn't, then or now. Though he had honestly begun kissing her to hide her from the Gothards, it hadn't ended that way. Bloody hell, the reality of kissing Emerald had been ten times better than the damned dream. And if he kissed her again, he'd be hard put to stop there.

But before he could turn away, her eyes seemed to spark with something akin to desperation, and her fingers went to the gown's laces, loosening them, spreading the bodice wide until he could see the rosy tips of her breasts beneath the sheer chemise that went with the dress.

He watched, stupefied. "What the devil are you about?"

She shot him an arch look, as though . . . she couldn't be *flirting*, could she? "G-getting comfortable," she stammered. "Like ye keep telling me to." She took a huge breath, and her breasts rose and fell with it. "Mrs. Twentyman's night rail, well, 'tis really too big and cumbersome."

'Twas a struggle to keep his face impassive. When she swayed closer, he stepped back.

Her eyes going hard with determination, she pulled out the lacing completely, tossed it on the bed, and began wiggling the dress down her body. Lit by naught but a few candles, the room was dim, but not so dim he couldn't tell she wore nothing beneath the thin chemise.

He swallowed hard. "Um . . . Emerald? Just how, um . . . *comfortable* are you planning to get?"

The gown dropped to the floor, puddling around her feet. She bit her lip and stepped shakily from the folds. "This ought to do it," she said in a soft, trembling voice.

It did it, all right. His gaze raked her all the way down to the torn hem of the chemise. He wondered if she knew that her entire form was silhouetted, from her slim torso to her shapely ankles, beneath the off-white cambric. Her nipples were hard points against the front of the filmy garment. And it wasn't cold.

Feeling overly warm himself, he removed his coat and loosened the laces on his shirt.

She walked up to him. *Right* up to him. Her scent surrounded her like a soft cloud. Flowers of Scotland.

Her hands came up to rest lightly on his shoulders. He stood, speechless, while she raised herself on tiptoe and pressed her lips to his.

Warm lips. His body responded immediately, and his arms went around her to press her close, no matter the painful wrench in his shoulder. He could feel the hard oval of her emerald pendant between them. Her lips parted, inviting him to explore the sweet cave of her mouth. Her almost-bare back felt small and vulnerable beneath his hands.

Vulnerable? Emerald MacCallum, vulnerable?

He pulled away. Of course she was vulnerable, or he wouldn't be bound on protecting her. He would have gone after Geoffrey Gothard tonight, instead of finding himself paralyzed at the thought of endangering her and deciding to wait until she was settled somewhere very, very safe.

But she was still Emerald MacCallum. A woman he had no interest in becoming entangled with. No interest whatsoever, at least in his mind.

He wished he could convince his body of that. She was staring at him, her eyes now darkened to a deep, hazy blue. Her tongue came out to moisten her lips, leaving a delicious sheen that he ached to kiss away. Deliberately he lifted her hands from his shoulders and moved to get into his bed.

She followed him, sat herself on the edge of the mattress and leaned close, silently begging him to kiss her again. Damn if some part of him didn't want to. The nonthinking part.

He forced a laugh instead. "Your bed is over there, Emerald."

She straightened. One hand went up to draw her thick hair over her shoulder and twirl it slowly. She looked innocent, nervous even. It must be his imagination—either that, or her acting skills were on display again. There wasn't a chance she could actually be innocent. Not a mother. Not an independent, free-thinking woman like Emerald MacCallum.

"Are ye sure?" she asked.

Forcing another laugh, he looked pointedly toward the second bed.

She winced, her eyes suddenly chagrined and embarrassed. "I ken there are two beds in this room, Jase." Her lower lip trembled. "Ye dinna have to laugh at me." Averting her gaze, she stood and walked slowly to her bed, lowering herself to it as if she might break. "So my seduction efforts are laughable, are they?" she whispered.

" 'Tis not that. 'Tis—" He would swear he'd heard tears in her voice, making him feel like a sorry excuse for a man. But he couldn't have her thinking he wanted her. No matter that he did. It was for the wrong reasons. Reasons no responsible, honorable man would act on.

"Go to sleep, Emerald," he said through clenched teeth.

Chapter Fourteen

Caithren set down the candle and shook Jason's shoulder. "Wake up."

"Wh-what?" He struggled to sit up, then fell back to the pillows. " 'Tis the middle of the night," he complained, blinking in the almost-darkness. "The birds haven't even started their chorus yet." He rubbed his eyes, then focused on her. "You're already dressed?"

"Ye agreed last night we should get an early start." She turned away, ostensibly to get her shoes, but really so she'd not have to look at him. She couldn't bear to see the rejection in his eyes after what had happened last night.

She could hardly live with herself, let alone what Jason must think of her. She wished to be outdoors, in front of him on his horse. Where he'd not be able to see her face, or she his. Too bad he'd refused to buy a second horse. Sitting so close to him would be almost as much torment as looking at him.

Cameron's teasing was right on the mark. Impulsive, that's what she was. Desperation last night had driven her to that and more . . . Jason must think she was a wanton. In her quest for a kiss, she had practically begged him to sleep with her—and the worst of it was that in the heat of that moment, she probably would have gone through with it if he'd given her the opportunity. She had to learn some self-control.

He was falling back asleep. She shook him again.

"Ye said this town made ye uneasy." Thank God she had a viable excuse to wake him and leave while it was still dark. "D'ye wish to overtake the Gothard brothers, or nay? We've no time to waste."

"All right. Give me a minute." With a groan, he rose from the bed and changed his shirt, tightened its laces and those of his breeches. Her eyes averted, she parted her hair and hurried it into two braids, tied the ends with the green ribbon he'd bought her at the fair. Thankful that her own clothes were dry, she folded the red dress and chemise and packed them away.

"Hurry up," she said.

"What is going on here?" he muttered, tugging on his second boot.

He would doubtlessly keep at her. Mayhap 'twould be better to face the problem straight on. Gathering herself together, she glanced over at him. "About last evening . . . d'ye reckon we can just forget it happened?"

"Nothing happened." He shoved yesterday's shirt into his portmanteau.

She pulled it back out to fold it. "Jase—"

"I've forgotten it already. I lack the sleep to think straight, in any case." Taking the shirt from her hands, he stuck it into one of the leather bags. " 'Tis a wonder I remember my name, let alone events from yesterday." Hefting the portmanteau, he ushered her out the door.

He peeked wistfully into the inn's dining room on the way out, but found it unattended and pitch-black. "The minute the sun comes up, we're stopping for food," he said.

No matter her mood, that prompted a tiny smile. "Far be it for me to deny your stomach."

The birds were singing by the time they reached Sawtry. A small, sleepy town, its few public buildings bordered one side of the village green, the other three sides lined with thatched-roof houses. There was naught but one tavern, a rectangular stone building called Greystones.

Jason chuckled when he saw the sign.

"What d'ye find so amusing?" Cait asked.

He cleared his throat. "My, brother—um, he . . . lives in a place called Greystone."

"So?"

"It just struck me as funny, is all." He took a deep breath. "We'll stop here for breakfast."

And sit across from him for a whole meal? She didn't think so. "Why dinna we eat it on the road? I'll wait here with Chiron while ye go inside and get something."

"The Gothard brothers were in Stilton," he said, "and that means they are not making better time than we are. I'm certain they're fast asleep," he added. "We have time to stop and eat."

"I'd rather not, if ye wouldn't mind."

He hesitated, then took her elbow to help her dismount. She took his horse by the reins. "I'll just walk Chiron over there"—she indicated the village green and a post with a sign in its center—"and wait for ye."

"I'd rather you come inside. After yesterday—"

"Ye said the brothers are still sleeping. How unsafe could it be? Ye can watch me from the window."

He fixed her with a penetrating gaze that had her looking away. "Very well," he said at last. "But stay in sight."

The grass was soft and springy, and it felt good to walk after more than an hour in the saddle, although she realized all of a sudden that she wasn't really sore anymore. After four days on horseback, her body was finally adjusting.

She tethered Chiron to the signpost, which was topped by a fancy wrought-iron affair with letters spelling not only Sawtry but the village's name from Roman times as well, Saltreiam. Doffing her shoes and stockings, she wiggled her toes in the grass and tried to relax. She wondered what Jason was thinking of her after last night. He was acting normal. Probably because he didn't want her, so her behavior hadn't mattered to him. A depressing thought.

In an effort to dispel the feelings, she rolled her shoulders, reached for the sky, then bent to touch her feet, coming face to face with a fresh, white daisy.

She plucked it from the grass, bringing it to her nose and smiling at the sweet, familiar scent. Sprinkled liberally throughout the green, the flowers reminded her of a childhood pastime, and she picked a handful, tucking up her skirt to collect them.

Jason found her sitting cross-legged and working industriously. "Is that what I think it is?" he asked, amusement lacing his voice. "A daisy chain?"

She slit another stem and slipped the last daisy through it, then looked up into his smiling eyes, finding it easier than she would have thought. "For ye," she said, rising. "A peace offering." Standing on tiptoe, she crowned him with it. "A daisy chain is supposed to protect ye from the fairies."

Instead of teasing her about another superstition, he turned pink beneath his tan, revealing freckles she'd never noticed before. "We've already found peace between us," he said. "Have we not?" With a sheepish smile, he removed it and put it on her own, smaller head.

The daisy chain slipped right down and around her neck. He leaned closer, settling it into a gentle curve atop the swell of her bodice. His fingers lingered there, longer than was necessary.

A frisson of confusion ran through her, and she licked her lips and looked down, then reached to grasp the amulet that lay framed within the flowers. Something solid and familiar to cling to in the midst of all this foreignness.

When she glanced up, he was smiling down at her

bare feet. He bent to pluck another daisy and tucked it into the braid behind one ear. Stepping back, he grinned.

"You look very Scottish," he said.

"Do I now?" She gazed straight into his eyes, surprised to find she was able to do so and smile. "Well, *ye* look very English."

"Hmm . . ." he said, looking contemplative. "Both of us managed to say that without sounding insulting." He turned to untie Chiron. "Imagine that."

"Imagine that," she echoed. Imagine that, indeed.

White and yellow wildflowers dotted the gently rolling land on either side of the narrow road leaving Sawtry. Jason could see Emerald lazily fingering the daisy chain around her neck as they rode along, silent as the peaceful landscape. But not an adversarial silence, for once, merely the silence borne of exhaustion, the comfortable silence that ensues when two people coexist without the need to fill it with senseless chatter.

Indeed, the only sounds were those of Chiron's hooves on the rutted road and the occasional travelers who passed. Until there came a wild yell, and three young bareback riders came racing down the road right at them, almost forcing Chiron into the stream that ran alongside.

"Gypsy lads!" Emerald came alive. "They pass through Leslie every year, and oh, they play the most lovely music." She cocked her head. "Can ye hear a lute?"

"Easy, boy." Jason reined in. "I can hear nothing except—damn, here they come again."

From the other direction, they thundered past.

"Follow them," she urged. "They must be encamped nearby."

Sure enough, over the next hill came the delicate notes of the lute she had heard. The lively tune became more distinct as they turned off the road, following the trail of clumps kicked up by the racing horses. In the distance, the Gypsy boys stopped and slid from their mounts beside a makeshift community of people milling among tents, carts, and pack animals. Smoke rose up, hanging in the air over the encampment. The lads bent over in laughter, pointing at Jason and Emerald.

An old woman motioned them closer, flashing a gap-toothed grin.

Emerald turned and tilted her head back, one hand on her hat to secure it. "Have we time to stop? Just for a minute?"

He'd never seen her so excited—he couldn't deny those dancing turquoise eyes. "Ten minutes." A few minutes couldn't make much difference.

Emerald was already waving to the short, round-faced woman. "Hallo!" she called as they pulled close.

"Hallo, me lady," the Gypsy woman returned. She wore a long, many-layered skirt in a myriad of bright colors and a head scarf of another color altogether. Thick gold loops hung from her ears. "Will you buy?"

"I could have told you that's what she wanted," Jason muttered.

"Wheesht!" Emerald admonished. She slid from Chiron. "What have ye to offer?"

The woman patted Chiron's flank. "A beauty." She pulled an apple from her pocket and held it out for the horse to munch. "How much?"

"He's not for sale." Jason dismounted and held the reins possessively.

"Pity." She sighed. "Trade?" With an expansive gesture, she offered several horses grazing nearby. "Two for one?"

Jason laughed. "No trade, either."

"Pity." Giving a dismissive wave, the woman turned and walked into the tent village.

Emerald shrugged. "Come, let us find the music. They dinna usually mind visitors."

He lifted Chiron's reins. "Is it safe to leave him here?" It felt deucedly strange to be asking Emerald for advice, but the truth was, he felt completely out of his element among these people.

"They'll not be stealing him, if that's what ye mean."

He tethered the horse, then followed her into the encampment. He'd lived all over the Continent as a young man in exile, but he'd never felt at such odds with his environment as he did in this little pocket of foreignness here in his native land.

They wove between tents made from fresh-cut hazel pushed into the ground and bent over, forming a resilient frame covered by colorful blankets. Delicious smells came from a huge iron kettle suspended from a prop over a stick fire. Women sat on stools around it, weaving lace and chattering in the Romani language, guarded by soft-eyed lurcher dogs. A woman rose to stir the soup as they walked by, and when she set down the wooden spoon, a dog came up to lick it.

"Bah!" she said, and threw the spoon into the fire.

At Jason's sound of surprise, Emerald turned to face him, walking backward. " 'Tis *mockadi*," she explained. His face must have registered his confusion, because her laugh rang out over the lute's music. "Dogs and cats are unclean," she clarified. "Ye really are a *gaujo*, aye?" She laughed again. "A house-dweller."

"The woman fed Chiron by hand," he said. "Horses are not mock"—he frowned as he searched unsuccessfully for the word—"unclean?"

"Nay. Horses are revered. And they're not *mockadi* because—" She stopped walking backward, and when he almost ran into her, she put a hand to his chest and raised on tiptoe to whisper in his ear. "They cannot lick their own backsides."

He laughed so loud they attracted several blatant stares. A tall, gaunt man with a wide mustache ducked out of a tent, dressed in ordinary breeches and a shirt topped by a colorful vest. His black eyes fastened on the sword that hung by Jason's side. "Sharpen it, milord?"

"N—" Jason started.

"Oh, for certain it should be razor sharp, *my lord*." The sparkling of Emerald's eyes made clear her amusement at the thought of him bearing such a title.

If only she knew.

"Ye must let him do it." Impulsively, she reached for the hilt and pulled the rapier from his belt. "Since ye'll be wanting to"—she cleared her throat—"take care of Gothard with it."

When she handed the sword to the fellow, Jason didn't argue, although 'twas plain she still thought he was out to kill. He had no intention of killing anyone with that blade, ever again. One innocent man was more than enough life lost at his hands.

The man sat at a portable whetstone and began grinding. Over the sound of the wheel, the delicate notes of the lute were joined by a guitar, violin, drums, and cymbalom. The music rose, becoming even livelier. After Jason retrieved his sword and handed the man a coin, Emerald took off in search of the musicians, leaving him to follow.

In a small clearing, dancers swirled, a wild mass of colors. Emerald turned to him, an avid look transforming her features. "Shall we dance?" She took both his hands, held them up between them, pulled him toward the clearing.

He took several tentative steps then stopped altogether. "This is not the minuet, nor even a country dance."

She giggled up into his face. "Nay, 'tis not. Can ye feel the music?" Indeed, it seemed to vibrate from the grass beneath their feet. "Cameron and I dance with them every year. Does the music not make ye want to move like they do?"

"They" were whirling in circles, stomping their feet,

clapping their hands, snapping their fingers. "No, it does not," he said honestly.

"Come, try it!" She tugged his hands harder, until he stumbled into the midst of the dancers. But his feet refused to move like theirs, no matter how hard he tried. After a few halting steps, he pulled his hands from hers and backed away with a small bow and a sheepish smile of apology.

And he watched. Watched her swirling and dipping, swaying to the music that obviously spoke to her soul. Others watched as well, their feet slowing as they watched hers fly. Her hat flew off, and he ducked into the fray to retrieve it, then hurried back out. Her braids whipped around, shimmering in the summer sunshine. The daisy chain about her neck whirled in her breeze, swooping up and down and around with her.

Murmured conversations sprang up all around him. Though he understood not a word of Romani, he knew admiration when he heard it. She was a—*gaujo*, had she called the house-dwellers?—becoming one with their Gypsy music.

He shifted on his feet, his eyes riveted to her lithe body, a blur against the backdrop of colorful clothing, tents, and trees. She'd come alive, an effervescence he'd been unaware of spilling out . . . lodging somewhere in his heart. Here was a small piece of England where she was more comfortable than he. What a difference it made. And, in contrast, how difficult it apparently was for her to operate in his world.

When the music ended and she stopped, the Gypsies burst into wild applause. Her cheeks reddened, and she made her way over to him, stumbling and laughing at her dizziness. Another tune took up where the last one had left off, and she swayed to the beat.

" 'Tis like a fair, is it not?" she said, breathless while he resettled the daisy chain around her neck. "Except we are the only ones in attendance." The ring of flowers flew again when she twirled in a circle, her arms wide. She stopped, her eyes sparkling to rival the sunshine. "Imagine living like this every day."

" 'Twould be exhausting."

A frown flitted across her features. "There ye go again, seeing the world in black and white."

"Right here I see it as most colorful." He tugged on one of her braids, then set the hat back on her head. "And quite lovely."

She blushed prettily. Why had he never noticed before how very pretty Emerald was? The milkmaid had bloomed before his eyes.

"I've never seen anyone dance quite like that," he said, struggling for the words to describe it. To describe her. "So . . . free."

"The dancing brings the freedom, ye ken? While I'm dancing, I dinna care."

"About what?"

"About anything."

Their eyes locked, and a moment of silence stretched between them, the Gypsy music pumping in the background. Slowly he nodded, and she smiled, then sighed. "I suppose we must get back on the road. 'Tis been more than ten minutes."

"Wait, me lady." The old woman came out of nowhere and plucked Emerald on the sleeve. "You buy, first."

"I have no money," Emerald said firmly.

Jason put a hand on her arm. "I have money."

The woman's lips curved up in her gap-toothed grin. She led them to an area between the tents, where carts were piled with goods. "Basket, me lady?"

"We cannot carry that," Emerald told her. "We're on horseback the next few days."

The woman frowned. "Livin' like you are, you got no need for a broom or a rake, then."

Emerald smiled. "Nay."

"Cooking utensils?" the woman asked hopefully. "Nails? Tools?"

Now Emerald laughed. "No nails or tools, either."

A foot tapped the grass beneath the woman's colorful skirt. Her hand went up to one of the heavy loops in her ears. "Me lady like gold?"

Emerald's own hand went to her gold-framed amulet. "Nay."

Not for a moment did Jason believe her. "Show me what you have," he told the Gypsy.

The woman ducked into a tent and came out with a handful of black velvet. She pulled up a stool and sat, opening the fabric in her lap to reveal a heap of gold trinkets.

Leaning over, Jason stirred the pile with a fingertip. The jewelry gleamed in the sunshine, every piece embossed or engraved with elaborate designs, some of them set with gemstones besides. "They are lovely, madam."

"You buy one?"

He selected a flat engraved band embedded with tiny, bright green emeralds. Turning to Emerald, he took one of her hands and slipped it over the fourth finger. It fit perfectly.

Her pretty mouth hung slack for a moment. Her eyes turned a cloudy blue, and a frown appeared between them. "I cannot take this."

"Of course you can. Keep it as a memory of this day."

"I will remember without it."

"Then as a token of thanks. From me. I enjoyed watching you dance."

Her cheeks flamed red. She twisted the band around her finger. Another Gypsy tune played in the background, but she didn't move to the music. "I . . . I cannot take it," she said again.

"Go away, then," he said with a wave of his hand.

"Pardon?"

"Over there." He pointed to the next tent.

Looking bewildered, she solemnly backed away until he nodded.

"How much?" he whispered to the Gypsy woman. When she told him, he dug out his pouch and paid her, then beckoned Emerald back over.

"You're supposed to dicker," she informed him. She tugged off the ring and took one of his hands in hers, turning it palm up as she leaned close to whisper in his ear. "She thinks you're an easy mark." She deposited the ring in his hand and folded his fingers over it firmly.

He shrugged and put it in his pouch. He would give it back to her later.

"Come, me lady." The Gypsy woman stood. "I tell your future."

"I think not," Emerald said, but somewhat wistfully, he thought.

The woman held up one of Jason's coins. "No charge." The gap-toothed smile appeared again.

"Go ahead," Jason urged.

"Have we the time? The Gothards—"

"The Gothards ought to be rolling out of bed right about now," he said dryly. He could tell Emerald was intrigued. As he was himself— he'd never been to a fortune-telling. It ought to be entertaining. And if the brothers were already on the road, 'twould not be such a bad thing if they got ahead. A good thing, in all likelihood. He felt more comfortable as the pursuer than he did as the pursued.

"Are ye sure?" she asked, and when he nodded, she added, "Come with me, then."

He grinned. "You couldn't keep me away if you tried."

The Gypsy woman motioned for them to follow her to the edge of the encampment, where Chiron was grazing lazily. "Milord does not believe in dukkerin'?"

"My lord," Emerald said, almost stumbling over the

two words if his ears didn't deceive him, "is a confirmed skeptic."

He swept off his hat and ducked his head to enter the woman's tent. Inside, he couldn't stand straight, but the Gypsy motioned him into a beautifully carved gilt chair. Two lamps set on a low table threw glimmering light into the small space, which, in contrast to the clutter outside, was immaculate. Waterproofed canvas lined the ground, and a fringed cloth, patterned with costly metallic thread, covered the table. His hat in his lap, he leaned back and stretched his legs, content to watch the show.

The woman settled Emerald on a low stool, then sat herself on the other side of the table. Emerald swept off her hat and set it on the floor.

The Gypsy reached across, took Emerald's hands, and just held them for a minute, smiling into her eyes. Then she leaned close, her gaze darting from one palm to the other. "Ah . . . a long life you will see." Her voice sounded different than it had outside—low and soothing. Emerald smiled, slightly swaying to the music that drifted in from the clearing.

"And children. *Many* children."

Emerald stilled and shook her head. "Ye cannot tell that from my hands."

"The hands tell all." The woman's tone left no room for argument. She measured Emerald's white fingers against her own brown ones. "Middling," she declared. "Life is balanced."

"You." She swung on Jason, pointing a craggy finger with a curved, lacquered nail. "Your fingers long. Very responsible. Too responsible. You plan too much."

"Hmm." Emerald raised a brow.

He fisted his fingers to hide them, crossing his arms. He hadn't come in here to be analyzed. He'd come in here to be entertained. He'd kiss a ghost before he'd believe such nonsense.

He crossed his ankles, almost regretting the stop, except for seeing Emerald dance. The fortune-teller hitched her stool forward and made a humming sound deep in her throat. Laying Emerald's hands palm up on the table, she traced the lines with one crooked finger. "One of a kind. You go your own way." She looked closer. "Fate line is broken. A great life change."

"My father recently died." Jason strained to hear Emerald's whisper over the lively beat of the music.

"We all lose our folks." The fortune-teller shook her head. "Something more than that."

Outside, the musicians slid into something slower and faintly sensual, the violin rising above the other instruments in long, poignant notes. With a light touch, the Gypsy indicated a spot on Emerald's hand. "A grille, like bars." Her voice shifted, too, matching the rich tempo. "The bars of a gaol, where your heart hides, locked away. You must open the bars and trust." She stole a glance at Jason. Uncomfortable, he leaned to part the tent's opening and looked outside. A whir of life bustled past the narrow slit; a woman sauntered by with a basket of laundry; a child chased a dog in the bright sunshine.

It seemed darker inside when he allowed the tent to close. "Ah." The woman nodded, and her bobbing earrings gleamed in the lamplight. She touched another place on Emerald's palm. "A cross. A happy marriage in this lifetime." Pausing, she looked up. "Far from home."

Emerald blinked. "Aye, I'm far from home. I live in Scotland."

An enigmatic smile creased the fortune-teller's face. She turned Emerald's hands, skimmed her nails lightly over the backs. Emerald visibly shivered. "Sensitive. Your body begs to be touched."

Jason swallowed hard as the woman turned Emerald's hands again.

"Mount of the Moon, high and full . . . A lover bold, creative, beguiling."

Though Emerald turned red, Jason thought that was the most accurate thing the woman had said yet. Bold—last night flashed into his mind—and beguiling. Alarmingly so.

Black Gypsy eyes fastened on his and held steady while the music pulsed in the background. "A man in love with you," she said to Emerald, but still commanding his gaze, "must respect your independence. If he wishes to hold your heart."

"I'm not—" Jason started.

"Shush!" The harsh word vibrated in contrast to the sensuous violin. The woman swung back to Emerald and pointed a finger at her chest. "That green talisman . . ." Emerald's hand went to her amulet, and the woman nodded. "When it changes hands, a change of heart."

Emerald's fingers clenched around it. "It will never change hands, not while I live."

The Gypsy shrugged, a movement so expressive it spoke volumes without words. The music stopped.

A hush of silence enveloped the tent, then Emerald rose, breaking the spell. "I thank ye."

"My pleasure, me lady."

"I think we should leave," she said to Jason. Her voice was very quiet. "It was time to go almost afore we stopped."

He tried to rise, but bumped his head on the low ceiling. The woman stood as well. "I come see your pretty horse." She followed them out and watched them mount.

"My bonnet!" Emerald clapped a hand to her head.

"I get it, me lady." The Gypsy disappeared into her tent and returned with the feathered hat. Moving closer, she rose to her toes and set it on Emerald's bent head, then put a gnarled hand on her arm. "You not like your fortune?"

" 'Twas very . . . interesting." Jason could hear the

catch in Emerald's voice. "I'm afraid, though, I found it a wee bit confusing."

" 'Twill come clear in time," the woman predicted. "Wait, me lady." She hurried off toward the fire, returning with one of the lace handkerchiefs the women were working on there.

" 'Tis lovely," Emerald said sincerely. "But I have no money."

"We've been paid." Black eyes sparkled up at Jason. "You keep, to remember."

Emerald tucked the intricate hanky into her sleeve. "I will not forget."

"You come back?"

"Not here, I'm afraid. But I will dance with your people again. At home."

The woman reached to grasp Emerald by the hand. "Farewell, me lady." She nodded at Jason and ducked back into her tent.

Jason waited until they were out of earshot before he spoke. "So . . . you mentioned that you've danced with the Gypsies before."

"Aye, many times."

"You've camped with them, then. During your travels." It made perfect sense.

"My travels?" Her laughter floated back on the breeze. "Until now, I've never been farther from Leslie than Edinburgh. Twice. I told ye, Jase—a group of them camps by Leslie each year."

Damn if she wasn't convincing. He almost believed her.

Chapter Fifteen

"I dinna believe it," Caithren said later when they'd stopped in Buckden for dinner.

"Am I to understand you're not a believer?" Jason spooned soup into his mouth, following it with a gigantic bite of bread. He rolled the dice and took two markers off the backgammon board they'd set on the table between them. "You believe in ghosts but not fortune-telling?"

"Dukkering," she corrected. Despite her cross mood and the fact that he was winning, she felt her lips quirk in a faint smile. "They say what ye want to hear." Taking a deep breath, she poked at her Dutch pudding, using her spoon to flake off bits of the minced beef. "Or rather, what they *think* ye want to hear. The Gypsy woman misjudged me."

"Did she, now?" His gorgeous eyes looked speculative over the rim of his tankard.

"Aye." Avoiding his gaze, she tossed the dice and made her move. "I dinna intend to have children at all, let alone many."

He stuck the dice back in their cup and rattled it a bit, his gaze straying to the window by which they were seated. "Do you not like children?"

"I like them fine. 'Tis the necessary husband I'd as soon do without."

He set down the dice cup, raising a brow. "So much for the happy marriage she predicted."

"Are ye going to take your turn?"

Slowly he reached across the small table, traced a fingertip across the back of her hand. A shiver ran through her. "But are you not sensitive to physical touch?" he drawled in a voice low and lazy.

She was sensitive, all right. 'Twas all she could do not to leap across the table and kiss him. "Aye," she breathed, struggling for control, forcing herself to remember last night. "Why today should ye want to touch me?"

"Perhaps I've had a change of heart." He chucked her under the chin. "Like you will when your precious amulet changes hands."

She took the dice cup and firmly wrapped his fingers back around it. "The amulet will not change hands. The Gypsy was wrong."

Even with the noises of conversations and dishes rattling around them, the dice sounded loud as Jason shook them, then spilled them onto the leather board. Two more of his pieces came off and into his haphazard pile. "Someday—"

"Nay. I will never take it off." She bit her lip, then decided to come out with it. The terrible words she'd thought to herself, but never said aloud. "My mother took it off only once. To wear a pretty necklace my father had brought for her from Edinburgh. She died that day. She was thrown from her horse."

"You blame your father for her death," Jason said flatly.

"I do not."

He was silent for a minute while she dropped the dice back into their cup, one by one. "You blame her," he said.

"Nay." Mayhap she'd thought it, but she didn't believe it. "Though I'll not tempt fate by making the same mistake."

" 'Tis naught but metal and stone," he said gently.

" 'Tis more than metal and stone," she disagreed. "It has been in my family for centuries."

"Has it?" He dipped a piece of bread into his soup. "Know you a story behind it?"

"Of course." As he glanced out the window again, she touched the amulet, then rolled the dice, smiling when they came up double fives. "We Scots have a story for everything." She moved her last two markers into home court and stacked another two neatly by the board. "I was made to memorize it word for word afore the necklace could be mine."

He grinned. "Tell me."

She handed him the cup. "In 1330, Sir Simon Leslie set out to accompany James, Lord Douglas, who was charged with returning the heart of King Robert the Bruce to the Holy Land. On their way through Spain, they fought with the Moors, and Douglas was killed." She paused for a sip of ale. "Leslie went on to Palestine, and there he fought the Saracens and captured one of their chiefs. When his mother came to beg for his release, she dropped an emerald from her purse and hurried to scoop it up. Leslie realized it was of great importance to her, and he demanded it as part of the deal for the release of her son."

She stopped, because Jason was staring out the window again. "Go on," he said, looking back to her.

"That is it, really." Gazing down at the amulet, she traced its setting with a finger. "He had it set in this bezel, and brought it home, claiming it had miraculous powers for seeing him through the journey. It has been handed down through the generations. People used to come from far and wide to obtain water it had been dipped in. They would put a bottle of this water by their door, or hang it overhead, for protection against the evil eye."

His bowl empty, he set down his spoon and rolled the

dice. "But not anymore?" His final two pieces clicked as he dropped them onto his pile.

She shook her head. "The old ways and beliefs are dying."

"Yet you won't take it off."

"Mayhap it is naught more than unwarranted superstition." She wrapped her fingers around the emerald. "But there will be no change of hands." Nor would there be the change of heart the Gypsy woman had predicted.

"Ye won," she said, and he nodded, his gaze turning to the window yet again. Idly she started making his pile of markers into two tall stacks. "Are ye seeing something?"

"Not exactly." He lifted his tankard of ale. "I'm just getting that feeling like last night . . ."

One of the stacks toppled over. "Ye mean that strange feeling that gives ye an excuse to kiss me?"

The tankard hit the table with a thud. "The feeling that we might be followed."

Cait looked out the window at the red-brick walls of the George Inn across Buckden's busy High Street. People rode or strolled by, but no one suspicious or familiar. "I see nothing."

He shrugged.

"Here," she said, pushing the rest of her Dutch pudding toward him. "I am not finding myself very hungry."

"Still worried about your fortune and future?" He dug into the remains of her dinner.

"Of course not. 'Twas naught but a lark. I've forgotten it already." But she hadn't, not really. For a moment she stared unblinking at the creamy plastered walls of the Lion's common room, then began packing up their game.

Nay, she was more intrigued than anything, and not by the woman's meaningless predictions. More by the fact that the Gypsy had assumed she and Jason were a pair. And his attitude had changed in the encampment as well. When she'd told the story of her amulet, he hadn't interrupted her to insist the fellow was a MacCallum, not a Leslie. Gypsy magic? Would it wear off? Or might he be beginning to feel more kindly toward her?

"Ready?" He shot another glance out the window, then stood. "We should be going."

She slipped the set into its burlap bag, then rose to follow him toward the back door to the courtyard and stables. "My hat." Feeling her head, she stopped Jason with a hand on his arm. "I've forgotten it."

"There it is," he said. Sitting on the wide window ledge, right where she'd left it. "I'll get it," he volunteered.

She pushed through the door and into the sunshine, taking a deep breath of fresh air. Turning to see if Jason was following, she was startled when someone lunged at her.

She saw a flash of silver, heard the shout of a stable boy before she screamed. The man jerked back, but she felt a sharp sting on her upper arm. The backgammon set fell with a bang, and markers rolled out of the bag, bumping across the cobblestones as she drew back her other hand, curled it into a fist, and propelled it into the short man's face. He yowled and grabbed his jaw, dropping his sword. A metallic twang rang out as it clattered to the stones.

Wat Gothard.

"Ye murdering cur!" She planted her feet, aiming to come after him with a deadly knee.

"Dunderhead!" a man shouted, thundering into the courtyard on a horse. He scooped up Wat before she had the chance to damage him further, wheeled around, and rode out the gateway and into the busy street.

The stable boy rushed forward as Jason burst out the door, rapier at the ready.

"Go!" Caithren yelled, gesturing out the gateway. The stable boy took off running. She turned on Jason. "Go! 'Twas the Gothards, and he'll never catch them on foot. Get Chiron and go!"

He turned to her, his eyes frantically searching her body. "You're bleeding." He dropped his sword and reached out to make a ginger exploration.

"I'm fine!" She bent and swept his sword off the ground, shoved it into his hands. "Just go, will ye?"

A torn look in his eyes, he backed away a few stumbling steps, then turned and raced for the stables. Moments later, he galloped bareback out of the courtyard.

Reeling with both relief and disbelief, Cait sank to the cobblestones. She gripped her upper arm. It didn't hurt too badly, considering.

The stable boy limped back into the courtyard, puffing from exertion. "They're gone," he said. "No one out front saw what happened, so they got away unscathed." He knelt to collect all the backgammon pieces, then looked up at her, shoving blond hair from his face. "Are you quite all right, milady?"

She waved aside his concern. "My . . . friend"—how was she to describe Jason, anyway?—"went after them on a horse. Mayhap he will catch them." She hoped so. If they got away, he'd likely blame her once again.

Her heart sank at the sound of hooves on the cobblestones. "They disappeared," Jason said. "Just disappeared." He slid off Chiron, and Cait scrambled to her feet as he came close. "Besides this"—one finger skimmed her upper arm, and she winced—"are you hurt?"

"Go back!" Sharply she gestured with her good arm. "Ye cannot have looked well enough."

"What I cannot do is leave you bleeding while I play hide-and-seek. I never did make a very good 'it.'" He tugged at the neckline of her bodice, swore when it wouldn't budge, then his fingers went to loosen the laces. "What the hell happened?"

"Wat," she said. "He sliced me, but I think he was going for ye. He pulled back when he saw who I was." Frantically she pushed at his hands. "Oh, will ye not just leave? Go after them! I can tell ye the story later!"

Stuffing the backgammon pieces into the bag, the stable boy glanced up. "She punched the bastard but good," he told Jason.

"You what?" Jason's gaze shot from her arm to her face. "You hit him?"

"Ye want I should stand there and let him kill me?"

Tossing the hair from his eyes, the boy stood straight and snorted in approval. "She was fixing to unman him as well, I believe."

Jason stared at her a moment, then reached for her laces again.

"Jason!" Her gaze flickered toward the stable boy.

Jason's green eyes flashed with impatience. "Come inside, then." He leaned to retrieve Wat's sword. The stable boy thrust the burlap sack into his hands and moved to take Chiron.

The innkeeper stood gaping in the doorway.

"If I may see to the lady's wound," Jason prompted him.

"Of course." He ushered them inside, alternately gasping with horror and clucking with sympathy. "Buckden is a quiet town."

"I will require a room for the lady."

The lady? Since when did Jason refer to her so? And his voice was even more authoritative than before, if that were possible.

The man showed them up a flight of wooden stairs to a small chamber. "Shall I bring water and cloths?"

"Please do."

"As you wish, my lord." The innkeeper bowed and backed away.

My lord. Jason didn't seem wont to correct the mistaken form of address. Instead, as the man's heavy footfalls descended the stairs, he shut the door, turned, and stared into her eyes.

Her head swam. From the pain, the shock, the intenseness of Jason's gaze locked on her own? She couldn't tell. It all seemed muddled in her brain.

She stood silent and limp while his fingers went to work on the laces of her bodice. He eased it off and dropped it to the bed. She shivered in only her shift. Like last night, except this time, instead of turning away, he reached to loosen the neckline. As he drew it down to expose the cut on her arm, his breath hissed in, then fanned warm over her bare shoulder.

"Sliced you good, didn't he?"

Her heart racing, she held the shift to her chest and glanced down. "Not too bad, I'm hoping."

A knock came at the door, and Jason went to answer, coming back with a bowl of warm water and some bandages, which he set on the bedside table. With a quiet snick the door closed, and they were alone again. Shaking his head dolefully, he sat her on the bed, dipped a cloth in the bowl of water, and dabbed at the bloody wound. " 'Tis clean, but deep."

She hadn't kent a man's hands could be so gentle. "I'll make a poultice for it when we stop tonight."

He dabbed some more, for all the world looking helpless. "Would it be better to do it now?"

"My herbs are outside, in the portmanteau." She swallowed hard. "I'll be fine."

Nodding, he wound a clean cloth around her upper arm. Used to blood she was, but not necessarily her own. She felt dizzy, from that or Jason's proximity, she wasn't sure. He looked very businesslike as he tied the bandage. Apparently he didn't notice she was about to expire from wishing he would kiss her.

"Why did ye not go after the Gothards?" she asked.

"Geoffrey Gothard will get his due." His eyes bore into hers. "But I'll not see you hurt in the interim. Never that. Never again."

His voice wasn't loud, but she detected a tremble beneath the control. She was finding it hard to breathe. His hand went to the neckline of her shift, and she released her hold on it, watching his long fingers draw it up to cover her shoulder.

Michty me, her nipples stood out dark against the sheer fabric. Her breath hitched in shock. She stood and grabbed her bodice, sending a surge of fresh pain through her arm.

"Hush," Jason soothed and helped her ease into the bodice. She stared at his chest as he slowly threaded the laces and tied a crooked bow. Then his fingers trailed up her neck, leaving shivers in their wake, until his hands came to rest, cradling her face.

He tilted it up, moving closer. He was going to kiss her again. For real, this time, with no excuse of being followed. Caithren's heart pounded in anticipation. She was certain he could hear it in the still, dim room as he lowered his mouth to hers.

His lips were soft, gentle, tender. Her blood sluiced through her veins, and she pressed closer, wanting more, needing more. With a sudden clarity she realized she wanted Jason more than she'd wanted anything in her life. His mouth . . . all of him. Just this once, to know what it was to be in a man's arms . . . to give herself to a man. To this man. Her lips opened under his, her tongue traced his bottom lip. And his kiss turned wild and demanding.

He eased her onto the bed, and she felt no pain in her arm as the weight of his body settled on hers. She felt nothing but his warmth, his strength. As his mouth plundered hers, his fingers caressed her cheeks, then inched around to the back of her neck to pull her closer and deepen the kiss.

Another knock came at the door, and he bolted upright.

"Is the lady all right?" the innkeeper called. "Will you be needing aught else?"

As Cait sat up more slowly, Jason ran a ragged hand through his hair. He rose and went to open the door. "She is fine," he said. "We were just leaving."

When the man's footsteps faded once more, Jason turned to her. "We have to leave," he said, his voice husky and . . . apologetic? She couldn't be sure. "Are you all right to ride?"

The door was still open. She stood and took a steadying breath. "I'll survive." Her arm throbbed, but she wouldn't have admitted to the pain were she like to faint from it. She'd not be a burden on his journey, and she needed to get to London herself. There would be time to tend to the injury later. When she wasn't reeling from his kiss. And its abrupt ending.

"Let me know if you start hurting. Emerald—"

She wouldn't answer to that name. Not after what had just happened between them.

"I'm sorry," he said, looking like he meant it. "For . . . for letting things get out of hand." Somehow she was sure he'd intended to say something else, but he barreled on. " 'Twas wrong of me to—"

"I've forgotten it. Like ye forgot last night. We're even now." She pushed past him out the door. "And my name is Caithren, whether ye believe it or not."

He did believe it. Now.

And he cursed himself for not believing it sooner.

She cried far too easily; she couldn't shoot; she didn't know north from south or right from left. She was shorter than Emerald was rumored to be. None of that had convinced him. Neither had her ongoing protests.

But seeing her reaction to the Gothard brothers had. She'd defended herself, but she'd urged him to go after them. Emerald MacCallum would have been after them herself, bleeding or no.

She was Caithren, as she'd said all along. He didn't like that at times like this his father came to mind. A father who had never made mistakes. Certainly not a mistake like this one.

He swore at himself for two solid miles.

If he wasn't already certain he was ill-suited for this quest of justice, he had the proof riding in front of him. First he'd ended the life of an innocent man, then he'd endangered that of an innocent woman by mistakenly dragging her into this mess. If only he could turn back time and leave her on that public coach. He would, honestly he would, even though it would mean he would never have held her in his arms. Would never hold her in his arms again. An almost unthinkable thought, and his arms tightened around her waist at the mere notion.

Yet 'twas naught but wishful thinking. The hard truth was, now that the Gothards had seen them together, it was more important than ever he protect her. Their wild attraction only complicated matters.

He needed a clear head to see this through. Distance, both emotional and physical. He'd proven that to himself back at the Lion in Buckden. Only by thinking of her as Emerald had he been able to check his emotions.

Only by continuing to call her Emerald aloud could he make sure she kept her distance as well.

They rode through Southoe, a sleepy village with three moated manor houses and a single old brick inn. "Are ye hungry?" Caithren asked as they passed it, jarring him out of his thoughts.

"Hardly." He pushed back his hat. "I've been thinking . . ."

"I cannot say I am surprised. Ye seem to do that a lot. Did the Gypsy not say ye plan too much?"

"Hush." He tugged on one of her braids. "And listen to what I have to say. We've no need to rush anymore.

We do not have to worry about the brothers getting to London ahead of us."

"Why think ye so?"

"They've been following me. They tried today to kill me."

"Not a very good attempt," she said doubtfully.

"Walter isn't known for his sharp head. Still, they obviously had a plan, with Walter doing the deed and Geoffrey then spiriting him away. Geoffrey wouldn't want another death on his hands, and Walter is a malleable sort."

"So . . ."

"They won't be racing off to London, the way they planned when they thought I was dead. It seems that they intend to do away with me first. Alive, I can bear witness to their deeds, and well they know it. They're desperate. If ever they had a decent bone in their bodies, it's disappeared now that they're backed into a corner."

She was silent as she took that in.

He drew a deep breath. "Another change in appearance would be prudent. And they'll recognize Chiron as well. I will have to board him and buy another horse." Another thought occurred to him. "Two. They'll not expect us to be riding two."

"I will not try to escape ye," she said, reading his mind.

"I didn't think that you would." He would miss holding her before him, though. The feel of her warm body, the scent of her hair beneath his nose. He pulled her closer, until he reminded himself he needed to maintain distance. "We'll stop overnight in the next town. You can rest and tend to your wound while I gather what I need. For the both of us."

"For me?"

"For your own protection. They've seen you with me now. You could bear witness as well." His voice dropped. "I'm sorry. 'Tis for your own good."

"Whatever ye say, Jase," she said softly. Her hands tightened on his where they met at her waist. He squeezed back.

He felt a maddening concern and tenderness for this infuriating woman, a feeling that slowly penetrated his anger. But the soft, nurturing emotions did nothing to calm the shakes that assaulted him at the thought of Gothard following them. Christ, Caithren had been hurt and might have been killed. And it would have been his fault for dragging her into this.

He was caught in a trap of his own making, and he felt the jaws closing—teeth of steel that he'd sharpened himself.

"How is your arm?" Jason asked the next morning as he tied back his hair. He swept something long and shaggy off a table and took it over to the mirror.

Caithren sat up in bed and flexed her arm, perusing the breakfast tray he'd just brought her. "Not too bad. I used up everything I collected in the woods, though. I hope to find more today." She watched him shake out the shaggy thing and hold it high in the air. "What *is* that?"

"A periwig," he said, settling it on his head. "What do you think?"

Popping a radish into her mouth, she stared at the reddish wig. Crimped and curly, it draped far down his chest, longer even than his own hair had been before she cut it. She chewed and swallowed before answering him. "Ye look different," she said diplomatically.

He smiled as he dug through his portmanteau, scattering clothing all over the other bed as he worked his way to the bottom. A dark blue velvet suit with gold braid trim came out, then a fine lawn shirt with lace at the cuffs, and finally a snowy cravat. None of it was at all similar to any of the other garments he'd worn. Had the clothes been there all along? Or had he brought them last night? She'd fallen asleep hours before he returned.

"You don't like it, then." Turning back to the mirror, he adjusted the wig's crown and flipped a hank of curls over his shoulder.

Giggling, she hid her face in her cup of chocolate.

"Many men wear periwigs, you know." His eyes met hers in the mirror.

"But not such long ones." She chewed slowly on a bite of bread, studying him. " 'Tis as though you're trying to look like a nobleman."

He raised a brow at that.

"And—'tis red!"

"You're hurting my feelings." He pouted, but the eyes in the looking glass were a sparkling green. "Does it look so out of place, then? My sister is a redhead, and my mother was as well. Myself, I was a skinny, freckled lad—I expect red hair would have been more fitting than the black."

She reconsidered. "The red is not too bad. But I cannot picture ye skinny and freckled."

" 'Tis no lie. I was awkward, too. Gangly." As he fussed with the wig, Cait watched the muscles move beneath his shirt. He wasn't gangly now. "Took me years to grow into my looks."

"Ah." She grinned. "And here I thought 'twas the mustache that transformed ye."

"That as well." He leaned closer to the mirror and stroked his bare upper lip. "I'm getting used to its loss, I think." Turning, he reached to steal a cube of cheese off her tray.

"I thought ye had breakfast downstairs."

"That was an hour ago." He filched another cube. "Do you like me better with or without?" He chewed thoughtfully.

"Without. Both the mustache and the wig." She set the tray aside. "Supposing I like ye at all, that is."

"Supposing." Moving to the other bed, he lifted the velvet surcoat and shook out the creases. "Your clothing is waiting behind the screen."

"Is it?" Curious, she climbed from the bed and made her way over to have a look.

She blinked and looked again.

"By all the saints," she breathed. " 'Tis worse than the red dress."

A bright turquoise brocade gown lay draped across a chair, with a purple underskirt and stomacher tossed on top. All was trimmed with a gaudy wide edging of embroidered silver ribbon. Even without trying it on, she could tell the scooped neckline would reveal a lot more skin than she was comfortable displaying. She couldn't believe it, after she'd made such a fuss over the red dress. She stepped out into the room to give Jason a piece of her mind, then dashed back behind the screen.

"Michty me! You're in the scud!"

"Translate?" he called.

"Ye . . . you're naked!"

"One does have to undress to change clothes." He sounded amused, not angry. "Are you putting on the gown?"

Touching her hands to her cheeks in an effort to cool them, she dragged her mind from its vivid picture of him without clothing. "Ye expect me to wear this?"

"Hell, yes. I spent a fortune for it."

"Just who am I supposed to be posing as in this monstrosity?" She grabbed the gown and held it up to her body, looking down at herself in horror. "Queen Catharine?" She kicked at the hem.

"No." He laughed. "My mistress."

The gown slipped from her fingers. "Your *what*?"

"My mistress. Are you undressed?"

"Nay. Not yet." Self-conscious, she fluffed Mrs. Twentyman's night rail. "Are ye?"

"Not anymore. Come out and have a look."

Cautiously she stepped from behind the screen—and burst out laughing.

He glanced in the mirror critically, then back at her. "What is so funny?"

"Ye—as a nobleman." Tears ran from the corners of her eyes. "Y-ye expect people to f-fall for that disguise?"

A small smile quirked at his lips. "Yes, as a matter of fact, I do."

"Just because one innkeeper called ye 'my lord' yesterday—"

"And don't forget the Gypsy."

She laughed even harder. "O-oh, aye. The Gypsy called ye milord as well!"

He took her gently by the shoulders and turned her toward the screen, patted her on the behind to get her moving in that direction. She yelped, then looked back over her shoulder at him and giggled again.

He pulled on her single nighttime braid. "Go get changed," he said with mock sternness.

"Very well." She hiccuped and went behind the screen.

She was thankful the long puffed sleeves didn't rub her injured arm, but the gown hugged her upper body like a second skin. Small though they might be, her breasts welled over the top. The stomacher was stiff and uncomfortable. No surprise there.

"Don't forget the shoes," Jason called.

The shoes. Embroidered silver brocade with pointed toes. And high heels. The only positive thing she could find to say about them was that they fit.

Too bad. She'd have liked an excuse not to wear them.

"Very practical for riding around the countryside," she said sarcastically. She took a deep breath. "I'm coming out."

"Thank you for the warning."

His smile died and a low whistle sounded as she

stepped from behind the screen. His eyes widened. "Whoa."

She teetered to the mirror and pulled her braid forward to unplait it, stilling when he came up behind her and slowly ran his hands down her sides. His palms felt hot, even through the fabric, skimming a tingling path on her skin beneath the turquoise brocade.

Cait swallowed hard. "Could I not be cast as your servant instead?"

"Hmmm." He blinked and jerked his hands away, as though they had just been burned. "I think not."

She took the Gypsy-lace handkerchief and started stuffing it into her neckline.

"Uh-uh." He reached over her shoulder to pluck it out of her hands. "My mistress wouldn't wear that."

Her exposed bosom broke out in goose bumps. "Mayhap I could pose as your little sister, then?"

A choked laugh was his reaction to that idea. "Wouldn't help. Kendra doesn't dress all that differently from this, sweetheart."

Sweetheart. Her gaze met his in the looking glass.

"And you don't look like my little sister," he added huskily.

"I dinna feel like your little sister, either."

He flexed his hands. "No, you most certainly do not."

Her fingers fumbled with the ribbon on her braid, but she managed to untie it while he backed away to sit on one of the beds and watch her.

She'd never imagined it could be so difficult to unravel one thick braid. 'Twould help if her hands would stop shaking. She took up her ivory comb, reaching to part her hair in the back.

"No." Jason's voice came from behind her. Confused, she met his eyes in the mirror. "Leave it loose. My mistress doesn't wear braids."

Slowly she ran the comb through her hair. Crimped from the plaiting, it hung in shimmering waves to her waist. "Wouldn't a nobleman's mistress wear her hair in curls?" Her stomach fluttered. "And pulled up on the sides, with a bun at the back, like I've seen—"

"Not *my* mistress." He got up and began stuffing clothes into the portmanteau.

She turned from the mirror and pulled a shirt back out to fold it. "Clearly you're used to having someone look after ye," she said softly. "D'ye have a mistress, my lord?"

Beneath the blue velvet, his shoulders stiffened. "I do now."

For a long minute, neither of them said anything. Then he looked away.

It meant naught, she decided. Nobleman and mistress. A game, nothing more. She finished folding his clothes and tucked them into the portmanteau, then went to fetch the night rail, wavering on the unaccustomed heels. "I cannot walk in these."

"You'll learn," he said, tossing the comb into one of the leather bags. As he took the folded night rail from her hands, his gaze swept her again from head to toe, and she felt her cheeks heat. Turning to face the mirror, she put her hands back under her hair and fanned it forward to cover her chest.

His eyes locked on hers in the mirror, holding her captive. Then she saw his jaw tighten, as if he were angry. At her? His expression became a mask of stone while he slowly backed away. "I've arranged for two horses," he said. "We'd best go, Emerald."

Chapter Sixteen

As they rode side by side in brooding silence, Caithren snuck glances at Jason, enjoying the novelty of riding beside him. Wind whipped the long red hair around the planes of his clean-shaven face. Encased in the dark velvet suit, his lean, hard body moved with the big, black horse as though they were one. She had to admit she might have thought he was a nobleman if she didn't know him. Her stomach felt fluttery just looking at him. It might have been fun to playact lord and mistress under different circumstances.

But there were no other circumstances. Always she would want him, and always he would come temptingly close and then back off.

'Twas better this way, Cait decided firmly. She needed to find her brother. Jason wanted to find the Gothards. Pursuing their attraction would only get in the way. And ultimately lead nowhere, since she lived in Scotland and he lived here in England.

But her stomach didn't feel fluttery anymore, just sick.

With a sigh, she tried to turn her mind to more pleasant thoughts. "I miss Chiron," she finally said conversationally as Jason waited to cross another bridge.

"I, too." He seemed distracted. "And I hope he's well taken care of. I paid enough, he should be." He nodded at a man coming from the other direction, then guided his mount down the center of the bridge.

Caithren followed, reaching to pat her horse's red-

chestnut neck as they came into the small town of Biggleswade. "This mare is a bonnie lass. What is she
called by?"

"I didn't think to ask."

"Nay? Then I will have to name her myself."

"You do that." He twisted in the saddle, scanning the
street. "Mind if we stop? There's a baker next to the
Coach & Horses. We'll just run in and get some bread."

"I'll wait here."

"No." His gaze shifted to her injured arm. "I want
you to come with me."

She'd lost this argument before, so she slid off her
horse—whatever the creature's name might be—and
tethered her beside Jason's. Though the sun wasn't high
in the sky yet, it seemed a long time since breakfast.
Delicious smells of fresh bread came through the bake
shop's door.

Jason tugged it open and hurried to pull her inside.
Unused to the heels, she almost stumbled. "Jase—"

"Hush." Baskets tacked on the wall were brimming
with crusty loaves. With a rigid hand on her elbow, he
guided her over and turned to her expectantly. "Grain
or manchet?"

"Um . . . manchet."

He shot a glance over her shoulder, out the window,
then suddenly grasped her around the waist and swung
her to face the baker. "What did you say, sweetheart?"

"M-manchet," she stuttered out. She leaned closer to
whisper. "What d'ye think you're doing?"

"Two loaves of manchet," he told the baker loudly.

"Two pence, my lord." The flush-faced baker took
two small loaves and wrapped them in paper.

Jason threw a quick glance out the window as he
pulled out his pouch. "Geoffrey Gothard," he muttered
under his breath.

Cait's spine stiffened.

One eye on the window, he took his time paying the

man. Finally she saw the tension in his shoulders ease. He put the two breads under one arm and curled the other around her waist. Casually, he drew her through the door and outside.

His fingers tightened just before he whirled her around and urged her back against the building. "Pretend you're flirting with me," he said, the words coming stilted through a wide, devastating smile. He leaned into her suggestively as one arm stole around her.

The hot bread was pinned between their two bodies. It was broad daylight. All morning he'd been acting like he wanted nothing to do with her.

Her breath caught when he pressed his forehead to hers, hot and close. *"Now,"* he demanded in a harsh whisper. "Geoffrey Gothard is walking this way—he won't look twice at a couple in a passionate embrace."

She tried to lean and see for herself, but his free hand came up to hold her face. "Put your arms around me." When she shakily did so, his voice came warm in her ear. "That's right." His tongue flicked out, his teeth nipped her lobe.

He'd been staring at her oddly since she'd donned the turquoise gown. Mayhap he just wanted to kiss her. She tried once more to see Gothard, but Jason's fingers tensed on her chin. His gaze bore into hers, so intense her knees almost buckled.

"You're m-making this up as an excuse to kiss me."

"If you value your life, you'll play along." His mouth brushed her cheek and trailed down her neck, leaving a sweet, quivery path of dampness. "You're my mistress," he murmured into the sensitive hollow under her chin. "Try to look like you're enjoying this, will you?"

Aye, she was enjoying it. When she arched against him, he claimed her lips in a soul-searing kiss. The heat from the bread seemed to seep into her stomach and spread. Her head felt woozy. Her entire body felt limp, but the wall and Jason's arms were supporting her.

His tongue traced her lips, then swept inside, kindling a hot rush of excitement that changed everything.

Her fingers tangled in the coarse hair of the wig. The now-familiar pleasure stole through her, and she wondered vaguely how she could have thought she was better off without this. She clung to his lips, molding herself against his body, wishing she could flow right into him.

Were they really being watched? Regardless, she felt safe with him here, just as she always had, though it made no more sense now than it had in the beginning. The melting intimacy felt real, not staged, and despite herself—despite the danger—she found herself savoring every second.

She couldn't let him deny these feelings again.

Finally he raised his head and looked both ways. "He's gone," he said.

She held him captive, with one hand behind his neck and the other splayed against his back. "What else can ye tell me about your mistress?" Her voice shook, betraying her emotions. "I–if I'm to act the part, then—"

He groaned, a heart-wrenching sound of capitulation. "My mistress . . . she kisses like a dream." The green of his eyes turned dark and unfathomable, and his hands ran down the back of the brocade gown, fitted themselves around her waist, skimmed up her sides, and around again to clasp her against him. His mouth brushed hers, first caressing her lips more than kissing them, then devouring them with an urgent hunger. She was stunned at the possessiveness of his embrace. He wanted her, she was sure of it . . . now that she was dressed like an Englishwoman.

But it wasn't right. She'd wanted him all along, mustached or no, long hair or short, dressed like a peasant or a nobleman. 'Twas the man she wanted, not the package he was presented in.

She pulled away, trying to regain her senses. "Now ye look at me differently," she accused. "Since I put on these clothes."

"No." He captured her eyes with his. "Since I saw you dance."

Since then? Her heart leapt. She'd been herself then, Caithren Leslie, more than at any other time since she'd stepped foot in England.

He backed away, catching the bread from between them before it fell to the ground.

Cait blinked and put her palms to her cheeks. She focused on the loaves in his hands. "They're squished," she said stupidly.

"Gothard is gone." He handed her a loaf. "I think we fooled him."

"I hope so," she said. But mayhap not. Mayhap she'd like to try to fool him again.

Although she wasn't altogether convinced this was the only way to keep from being seen. It could, however, be the only way Jason would allow himself the pleasure of kissing her. That sort of bloody-mindedness she was determined to change.

The bread didn't feel as hot as it had between their bodies. Though she wasn't hungry, she unwrapped the loaf, tore off a warm hunk, and stuck it in her mouth. Before she could say something else stupid.

"Shall we go?" he asked her.

"Aye." She swallowed, wrapped her bread back up. "Of course."

They untied their horses and headed out. The road from Biggleswade was narrow, with a few small houses scattered alongside. As scattered as her thoughts.

Jason was the most confusing man she'd ever met. Exasperating. Authoritative. Protective. And michty me, could he kiss.

'Twas clouding up and cooling off, but the brocade

gown was heavy enough to keep her warm for now. The gown and the hot blood pumping through her veins.

What would she have done without Jason? It felt like a lifetime since he'd kept her off the coach. She'd still be on it, wouldn't she, slowly making her way toward London, listening to Mrs. Dochart, day in and day out.

She'd have her money and her clothes. Clothes that didn't leave half her chest exposed for the world to leer at. But she wouldn't have gone to a country fair, tasted syllabub, or danced with the Gypsies.

Or learned what it felt like to really be kissed.

He'd swept her plans out from under her. And, she was afraid, he'd swept her heart out from under her as well.

My dearest Malcolm and Alison,

I did not have to travel all the way South, as evidence proves the Gothards to be following the Great North Road toward London. They are not good at covering their tracks. So I hope to be home sooner than planned, which is a very happy thing, because I miss you both more than words can say. All the day, as I ride the road, I think about my two bairns and what you might be doing. Every day that passes without you is a day I've missed forever, and I cannot wait to see your two bonnie faces and hold you in my arms again.

From what I have learned, these men are very, very bad people. I ken I will be doing the world a good deed to see them gone. All the same, I would rather be with you, and I count the days until it will be so. I cannot wait to hug and kiss you, and my dearest prayer is that when I come home to you this time, it will be forever.

Your very loving Mama

During the ten long miles from Biggleswade to Baldock, the weather did not cooperate. As the long blowing grasses gave way to Baldock's neat clipped gardens, the clouds grew darker and the wind picked up, whipping under Caithren's heavy skirts. They rode past the Church of St. Mary, a pleasing amalgam of several centuries of architecture, and Jason slowed before the Old White Horse.

"You hungry?"

She held up her half-eaten loaf of bread. "I can wait if ye can."

With a glance at the menacing clouds, he nodded. And so they continued on toward Stevenage, with Cait trying her best to keep the conversation flowing over the hours, so as not to think too much. Because truly, she didn't ken what to think anymore.

When the temperature dropped, they donned their hats even though they didn't really match their disguises. Jason dug in the portmanteau and jostled his horse near to settle his cloak over her shoulders.

"Thank ye." She snuggled into the woolen warmth, fastening the clasp beneath her chin. "Maid-of-the-Wave," she said.

"Pardon?"

"I am naming my horse Maid-of-the-Wave. Her coat is glittery like a mermaid, dinna ye think? And sort of reddish, like a salmon?"

He shrugged. "If you say so."

"What will ye be naming yours?"

"Nothing." He shot a glance over his shoulder. "I'll only be riding him through tomorrow. He won't have time to learn a name."

She shook her head mournfully. "All creatures need a name. If you'll not name him, then I shall have to. Hmm . . ." Shivering a bit, she gathered the edges of the cloak more closely around her. "Hamish," she decided.

"Hamish?" Jason slanted her a puzzled glance. "After who?"

"The farmer who married the Maid-of-the-Wave."

His lips quirked. "You never said that his name was Hamish."

"Well, I dinna know his name, actually. But it seems to me that about one out of four men in Scotland is named Hamish, so I figure 'tis a bonnie good bet." Since he looked like he was about to laugh, she studiously looked away. She was blethering again. Catching sight of a flutter in the sky, she sought to change the subject. "Magpies," she said, watching over her shoulder as one of the black-and-white birds flitted to a tree. "D'ye see their dome-shaped nest? I hope there are at least two in it."

Frowning, he looked back again. "Why?"

"Less than two are unlucky, ye ken? And doubly so if ye see one alone afore breakfast." He was still looking back. "Are ye counting them?

"Pardon? No."

"I dinna believe it, ye ken, but I do know a verse." She started quoting. "One for sorrow, two for luck, three for a wedding —"

"Bloody hell." Her heart lurched when he reached across and grabbed her reins. His hat flew off as he kicked his horse into a gallop and drove them both off the side of the road.

"What are ye doing?" she yelled, holding on for dear life, one hand on her head to keep her own hat from flying away.

"Just hold on!" His jaw set, he pressed on, and Cait wondered wildly what they could be running from. There were six strange little round hills off the road a wee distance, and he drew close before reining in and dragging both horses to a halt. He was down in a flash, reaching up both hands to help her dismount. Impatiently he tugged her toward one of the hills.

"Will they stay?" she asked. "Maid-of-the-Wave and Hamish?"

He shrugged, hurrying her along. " 'Tis the least of our worries."

"Dinna tell me ye think those brothers are after us again."

"All right, I won't tell you." He shot a glance around the little hill, back toward the road. She followed his gaze.

Her heart seized when she spotted Walter and Geoffrey Gothard astride two horses.

"Damnation." With a hand on the scruff of the neck, he pulled her to her knees. She gasped, and her hand went to her hurt arm. "Sorry," he hissed, and her hat fell off as together they scrambled behind the hill and out of sight.

But there was no way to hide the beasts they'd been riding on. And in the name of the saints, Jason was right. She'd seen the brothers with her own eyes this time. Their faces brought a vivid memory of standing outside Scarborough's house and overhearing their wicked plans. As then, she shivered. But her heart was pounding a good deal harder than that day, knowing the Gothards were out to do them harm.

"Cooperate this time, will you?" Jason's eyes burned with an intense green fire. "There's nothing for it. Hopefully they will stay on the road, but if they come over that hill and get a good look at our faces—"

He broke off, and once more, his mouth covered hers.

This time his body covered hers as well, heavy and warm, pinning her to the cushiony grass. Her blood raced in both fear and passion, and she felt boneless and aflame, all at once.

Was it hoofbeats she heard drawing nearer, muted by the grass, or her own heartbeat in her ears? Whichever, stark panic overcame the softer feelings, and her heart pumped even faster as she imagined Gothard spearing

Jason in the back as she lay under him, or shooting him, or—

"Pardon my impudence," he murmured, "but I've got to make this look good." The next thing she knew, his hand was venturing under her skirt—

And the hoofbeats came even closer—

"Damn me, Caroline," a man's voice drawled. "Someone's found our favorite spot."

Jason opened one eye to peek at the speaker, then sat up, muttering a curse. Caithren just lay in the grass, trying to calm her heart while he adjusted the tangled cloak and tugged down on her skirts. She stared up at a young man and woman, both on horseback. Country folk, stealing away to court on the sly, from the looks of it.

"Come away!" Horror widened the woman's round gray eyes. "Can you not see they're quality?" Her cheeks staining red, she dug in her heels and took off.

"Caroline!" the man called, riding after her.

Releasing a long, slow breath, Jason crawled to look around the mound, then came back. "The Gothards . . . I guess they rode past." He raked a hand through his hair. "We scared off those lovers but good." He offered a hand to help Caithren sit.

"We did, didn't we?" Struck by the absurdness of it all, she burst into hysterical, relieved laughter, hugging her sides until she'd gathered her wits enough to speak. "My mam always said, 'guid claes and keys let ye in.'"

"Good what?"

"Clothes. Dressing well can open doors for ye the same as a key, ye ken. We've dressed the part, and they believed it, just like that." She snapped her fingers and stood up, not an easy task in the silver shoes. Her legs felt shaky. "What are these strange hills?"

"Roman barrows." Jason rose as well, brushing off his velvet breeches. "Burial mounds."

"Oh," she said, making a face. "Faugh."

"Faugh? That's it?" He bent to pick up her hat. "No quote of your mother's for this one?"

"I'll tell ye, Jase. I dinna think Mam ever kissed anyone while layin' on top o' dead Romans."

He threw back his head and laughed.

"I wouldn't mind trying it again, though," she added.

The laughter abruptly ceased. "What?"

"The kissing, ye ken." Still struggling to compose herself, she shook out her skirts, pulled up on the dratted stomacher. "Ye seem to enjoy the kissing enough, but ye need to have an excuse." She squared her shoulders and faced him boldly. "You're attracted to me, aye?"

"Yes." He'd be lying to deny it. "But God knows why." Maybe because she made him laugh. He'd been far too serious the past weeks—the past years, come to think of it. Ever since his parents had died and left him with all the responsibilities. "And God also knows I've no business acting on that attraction."

She moved toward him. "Why not, I ask ye? I wouldn't tell a soul, and I wouldn't try to trap ye, either. I have every intention of going home to Scotland, and I'll not be expecting ye to come with me. Afore I leave, though, I'd just like to know . . ."

"Know what?" Both her proximity and her earnestness made him uncomfortable. Turning her hat in his hands, he started walking back to the horses.

She hurried after him, stumbling in the new shoes. "What it would feel like, is all. To—"

When she broke off, he risked looking back at her. Her cheeks had turned an attractive shade of pink. "Ye know," she said.

He halted mid-step. A Scottish woman propositioning him. He needed a moment to digest that. 'Twas absurd, no matter how much his hands burned to run themselves over her body. And 'twas wrong, as well. More so now that he knew she was a provincial baronet's daughter, not some bold reward hunter.

He'd already compromised her just by traveling with her alone. There was nothing he could do about that now, but he sure as hell wasn't going to take it any further.

He leaned and stuck the hat on her head.

"With ye," she added in a whisper. "I've never been tempted afore. Afore I met ye, I mean." Her hand went to her amulet. "But ye will not do anything about it, will ye?"

"No, I won't be doing anything about it." Her lower lip trembled, and her eyes were a gorgeous hazy blue. Christ. "You should be grateful for that. 'Tis wrong to take a woman and—just leave her."

He strode to the horses, and she called after him, teetering in his wake, "If ye believe that, have ye never, then? With a woman, since you've said you're not wanting to marry. I mean . . ." She jumped in front of him and stood blocking his way, looking up at him. "Are ye a virgin, Jason Chase?"

Her words seemed to echo across the open fields. He was horrified for a second, and then he laughed. "No, I'm no virgin. But 'tis different in my circle of acquaintances." King Charles' court was licentious as hell. Barring his sister— he hoped—he doubted there was anyone over the age of fourteen that could call him or herself virgin. "Different expectations. With you, there is a matter of responsibility."

"I have no expectations." Her eyes were guileless, but he couldn't believe her. "For once, could ye forget about responsibilities, and just let yourself feel?"

"I think not." He felt all too much, and that was the problem. If he thought he could honestly just love her and leave her, he might consider it. He'd not been tempted so in a long time. In all his life, maybe. But with Caithren it would be all or nothing—he knew that in his bones. "Look, we've been tied at the hip for days now. All you really want from me is to get to London.

And I'll get you there, I promise. A Chase promise is not given lightly."

Her eyes cleared and turned a disappointed, indistinct color. "Ye have no idea what I want from ye, Jason. And I dinna believe ye ever will." She wrapped her arms around herself and shivered.

"You're cold," he said. "Come along. We're almost to Stevenage. With the way the weather is kicking up, I'll need to buy you a cloak of your own."

The clouds had grown dark and menacing, and Jason found the interior of The Grange even darker. Brushing off the drizzle that had beaded on his cloak, he stepped into the taproom and blinked in the dimness.

Caithren was not at the table where he'd left her.

Panic sprinted along his nerves, but he got himself under control. He tossed the new wool cloak he'd bought over her chair and walked around the tavern, looking into every corner of the oddly shaped room. Then back to the table, his heart beginning to beat unevenly. He'd left her with his portmanteau and the burlap bag with the backgammon set. All was gone.

Geoffrey's and Walter's faces flashed in his mind. But none of the other patrons in the taproom looked at all concerned. It was inconceivable that a woman like Caithren would go with the brothers without a fight. True she couldn't shoot, but he'd seen her in action, punching, kicking, wielding a knife. And there was no sign of a confrontation.

Still, his pulse raced, his head felt woozy. What if they had managed to take her? How would he find them? What would he do? He couldn't think clearly when he kept seeing her standing in that courtyard with blood running down her arm. Blood from a Gothard's blade.

If anything more happened to her, he would never forgive himself.

He paced around the tavern, stopping at tables.

"There was a woman sitting there," he queried one patron after another. "Did anyone come and take her?"

No one had seen a thing.

When she came down the stairs, gingerly on the heeled shoes, he spun around. His long legs ate up the distance between them.

"Where the hell were you?"

"Hold your tongue. Everyone is looking at us." She walked to their table, set down the burlap bag, shrugged the portmanteau off her shoulder. "I took everything with me so nothing would go missing. I was gone but a minute."

"Where? Damn it, how dare you disappear on me. I thought the Gothards had—"

"I had to . . . ye know. Use the privy." Frowning, she peered into his eyes, and then, unbelievably, her lips turned up in a hint of a smile. "I've never really seen ye angry afore. I didn't think ye had it in ye."

"I've never thought you were missing before," he snapped out.

She crossed her arms and leveled him with a stare. "How about when I tried to escape ye? Or when I fell asleep in the kirk?"

" 'Twas different then. Then I didn't—oh, bloody hell."

"Then ye didn't *care*?" she supplied. "Ye cannot say it, can ye? That ye care." Her eyes looked pale green and unbearably sad.

"I care," he said. "I care about making things right. I care about replacing what you lost on my account. I care that you get to London in one piece, not carved up by a Gothard's blade."

The sound of raucous laughter came from another table. Pewter tankards clanked on wood. "I dinna want anything to happen to ye, either," Caithren said softly.

"Why?" he asked, though he wasn't sure he wanted to hear the answer.

"Because *I* care." Her gaze dropped to her crossed arms. "And I dinna mean about getting to London or the money ye owe me."

With a finger he lifted her chin. "Emerald—"

"And no matter what ye call me, I care because of this—" She went up on her toes and pressed her mouth to his.

With a groan of surrender, he closed his eyes to return her kiss. Apparently, calling her Emerald wasn't working. His arms went around her, and the sounds of the tavern receded as she arched herself close until he felt her damned amulet between them. Her lips were warm velvet; her flowery scent assaulted his senses. How could such an exasperating woman be so sweet?

A whistle came from behind them, and he pulled away to the sound of applause. "We see you found her," someone yelled. Caithren's cheeks went from the pink of passion to the red of embarrassment.

"Shall we go?" he asked with a laugh. He drew the new cloak from her chair and settled it over her shoulders. " 'Tis seven miles to Welwyn and starting to rain already."

Chapter Seventeen

"We're not going to make it, Jase." Caithren didn't know it was possible to feel so wet. In this sort of storm, the cloak was all but useless. "If this gown soaks up any more water, poor Maid-of-the-Wave will be driven to her knees."

Just then a huge crash of thunder made both horses shy, and the sky opened up, pouring twice as much water, if that were possible. It came down in blinding sheets. Cait couldn't see ahead as much as two feet.

She felt Jason's leg bump up against hers, and his hand came through the downpour to grab her reins. "Shelter!" he yelled over the next crack of lightning. "Come with me!"

How he found the place she would never know. He led them off the road, along a trail she could barely make out. Set back in the trees was an old thatched cottage.

Caithren held both the horses while Jason pounded on the door. No one came to answer. The shutters were all latched from the interior and the door was locked. Water streaming into her eyes, Cait waited while he walked all the way around the one-room building.

"Closed up!" he called through the pounding rain.

She wanted to cry.

He stood stock-still for a few moments, then disappeared again behind the cottage and came back with a hefty log in his hands. Bracing it against his good shoulder, he stepped back, then ran at the door.

It didn't give, and she winced at his anguished yell. "You're going to kill yourself," she called. "You're in no shape for this!"

But he tried it twice more, until the door crashed in. He almost fell on his face after it, and, miserable as she was, Cait had to bite her lip to keep from laughing.

He tethered the horses under some trees, then took their things and led her inside, propping the door into its space behind them.

They stood there, dripping, for a long minute. Rain pounded on the roof. The cottage looked clean enough, and there was a bed with a thick quilt, a small table, two wooden chairs, and a brick fireplace. No wood, no candles, no oil lamps. The warped shutters let in a little light and a lot of rain that puddled near the glassless windows.

But it was shelter, and Caithren couldn't remember being more grateful in her life.

"Thank ye," she whispered.

Jason gestured helplessly. " 'Twill be cold come night. And dark. All the wood outside is soaking wet." He looked at the table and chairs.

Her gaze followed his. "You're not thinking of burning them?" When he shrugged, she giggled. "They're not yours to burn. Besides, where would we continue our backgammon tournament?"

"That's right. I'm ahead." Grinning, he pulled off his hat, pouring water from the wide brim.

"Ye are not." She set her own hat on the table. "We're dead even. Seventeen games each."

He dragged off the wet wig. His own hair underneath was just as soaked, sleekly black and plastered to his head. "Ye look like a selkie," Cait said.

"A what?" He unfastened his cloak, and it dropped to the floor in a sodden heap.

"A selkie. A mythical creature that takes on the form of a seal in the sea and a man on the land."

"How flattering." Amusement lit his eyes as they raked her bedraggled self from head to toe. "You on the other hand, look the picture of perfection."

"Aye?" Laughing, she shrugged out of her cloak. "I wouldn't be surprised if this gown weighs more than I do." Bending at the waist, she gathered her hair and twisted it. Water streamed out onto the wooden floor.

As she straightened, her hair still bunched in one hand, Jason's arms came around her from behind. She hadn't even heard him walk up. He pressed his lips, warm and soft, to the nape of her neck.

Her breath caught, and she stood stone still. "Wh-what was that for?"

"I've been wanting to do that since the day I met you," he said huskily.

She turned to face him, quite unsure about this side of Jason Chase and where it had come from. "Well, I wouldn't have stopped ye." She hadn't imagined it the first time, she realized—a little thrill ran through her at the thought—and she hadn't stopped him then, either.

"I don't expect you would have." His penetrating gaze was entrancing. He took a deep breath and looked away. "Let me fetch some dry clothes."

Still stunned, she stood and shivered while he went through the portmanteau, the Jason she knew back in place. One after another, items came out, her clothes and his all soaking wet. Groaning, she draped the garments on the floor around the room, hoping they would dry. Finally, from the very bottom, he unearthed a pair of buff breeches and one of his shirts and held them up triumphantly.

"Dry. Almost. Which do you want?" He waved the breeches, a distinct leer in his eye.

Surprised and a bit unnerved by his playfulness, she

snatched the shirt from his other hand. "This will do, thank ye. Turn around."

Though he obeyed, one foot impatiently tapped on the wooden floor, the wet boot leather squeaking with each motion. "No peeking," she admonished. Quite adept at removing stomachers now, she did so in all haste.

"Are you finished yet?"

"Nay. Stay put." The foot kept tapping while she wiggled the gown and chemise to her waist and slipped his shirt over her head. Unexpectedly soft, it smelled like he did, warm and spicy. Reaching underneath it, she pushed everything down and off, leaving her shoes in the wet pile when she stepped out of it.

"Now your turn." She faced away to wait.

A hand came down on her shoulder and slowly swung her around. His gaze traced a lazy path down her body. She blushed, aware that the shirt only reached to her knees.

He raised a brow. "Much better than Mrs. Twentyman's night rail. I think we ought to burn that thing."

"Ye haven't got a fire," she said crisply. "Are ye going to change or not?"

"In due time."

Mindful of his eyes on her, she yanked up on the sleeves, which fell well past her hands, and tightened the shirt's laces. "Are ye not freezing?"

"Are you?"

Her skin erupted in goose bumps, though it really wasn't too cold now that she was out of the wet gown. "Not since I changed. I'll just take these clothes"—she bent to retrieve them—"and lay them out while ye dress." She turned her back and started spreading the garments over what little floor space was left. "Dinna worry—I promise not to look."

" 'Twould not bother me if you did, sweetheart," he drawled.

If past experience was any indicator, she had no cause
to doubt him. Blushing furiously, she made long work
of squeezing the water from the brocade gown and
wringing out its chemise. Her shoes were alarmingly
soggy, but she sat them on the floor and hoped for the
best. The stomacher was soaked, yet still just as stiff.
Apparently Jason hadn't been fooling when he said
there was bone inside.

"Ready," he called.

She turned around, then whirled back away. "You're
still half-naked!"

"If you'll hand over my only dry shirt, I can finish
dressing," he said drolly.

She hugged the shirt in question around her middle.
"Oh, never mind." Averting her eyes from his bare
chest, she fetched the backgammon set and removed it
from the burlap bag. "Sit," she said, plopping the
drenched board onto the table. "'Tis wet, but I reckon
it'll survive, seein' as it's made from a cow that likely
got wet in its day." She lined up the markers on their
respective pips.

"I reckon it will," he said, his voice tinged with unmis-
takable amusement. He took the dice cup and rolled
two sixes.

She sat across from him, trying not to stare at his
chest—the way the muscles rippled when he leaned
across the board to make his moves. Though still a livid
pink, his wound looked all but healed. Rain beat down
on the roof, and thunder and lightning disturbed her
concentration. Damn if she didn't lose three games in
a row.

"I'm hungry," Jason complained as she set up the
game once more.

"There's some bread left in the pocket of my cloak."

He rose to fetch it, treating her to a view of his broad
shoulders and back, then returned with a handful of

soggy white mush. "I don't think so," he groaned and tossed it into the empty fireplace.

"Mayhap it will stop raining soon, and we can continue on to Welwyn before ye waste away of starvation."

He snorted. But the weather didn't let up. By the time Cait had lost two more games, the rumbling was right overhead and almost constant. 'Twas getting dark, and although brilliant flashes of lightning lit the room through the ill-fitting shutters, it was not really adequate to play by.

Caithren squinted at the dice, but it was too hard to see what numbers she had rolled. With a sigh, she rose and picked her way around the clothes littering the floor to get to the door. She pried it free from where Jason had propped it within its frame, just enough to see outside.

The rain pounded down in what looked like solid sheets, assaulting her ears. "I dinna think we'll be going anywhere," she yelled over the noise.

"I expect not," Jason said softly, right beside her. She jumped, but one of his arms came around to steady her. The other hand reached to shove the door back into place, blocking some of the sound.

She could still hear the rain on the roof and through the shutters, but the room seemed suddenly and immeasurably quieter. It seemed she could hear her own heartbeat, and the soft sigh of Jason's breath by her ear. Surely that wasn't possible.

Just as it wasn't possible that he was sweeping aside her hair and kissing that spot on the nape of her neck again. She shivered.

"Are you cold?" he whispered.

She wasn't sure whether she were cold or just unbearably aware of his lips on her body. But she nodded anyway.

"Come to bed, then, and I'll keep you warm."

Hope blossoming, she spun in his arms. A flash of

lightning illuminated his eyes, and she could see they were guileless. "I'll just keep you warm," he repeated. "I promise. A Chase promise is—"

"—not given lightly. I ken." She sighed. She wanted more than to be kept warm—much more. But she couldn't face yet another rejection.

She wouldn't ask with words, ever again.

Asking with her body instead, she pressed against him, ran her hands over the hard planes of his bare shoulders, pulled the tie out of his hair, meshed her fingers in its silky softness as it fanned out to graze his collarbones. She was rewarded with hearing his sharp intake of breath.

"To bed. To keep warm," he said firmly and turned her around, leading her across the darkened room with a hand clamped on her shoulder.

She clenched her teeth, but a groan slipped out anyway.

"Have I hurt you?" he asked. "Oh, damn, 'tis your arm, is it not?"

She nodded; then, realizing he couldn't see her, moved to face him, flattening her hands against his chest. "Aye," she whispered. "I never found time to gather plants today." Her palms tingled.

"Is it getting any better?"

"Nay." She wouldn't lie. But she didn't want to alarm him, either. She didn't want to be thinking about her arm now—she wanted to be thinking about his body, warm and tucked next to hers. " 'Tis been but a day. These things take time."

"I wish I could have a look."

"Well, 'tis dark. Ye can look in the morning, if it pleases ye. For now . . ." She snuggled close and felt him hesitate, but she also felt his heart pounding beneath her hands. With a muttered oath, he swung her into his arms and carried her to the bed, no doubt messing up all their carefully laid out clothes as he went.

Not that she cared. She kent she had won. The bed ropes creaked as he set her down, and another flash of lightning brought out his features in stark relief. Enough so she could raise herself and find his lips with hers by the time the responding thunder rumbled through the sky, shaking the bed.

Or mayhap she was shaking. Nay, she kent she was shaking for sure. His hands crept to cup her face, and he eased her back, coming down on top of her. His shirt rode up her thighs, and it was scandalous, but she didn't care. Though his lips were gentle and giving, she could feel his hesitation, a sweet hesitation that teased her. She grabbed at his hair and fitted her mouth to his, reveling in his groan, the tensing of his shoulders above her as he shifted his weight to his elbows, pressing against her, his bare chest feeling warm through the thin cambric shirt.

Her world was reduced to his hands and his mouth and his body, the heat and the glory, the pure pleasure of him touching her at last.

His fingers worked at the shirt's laces while his mouth trailed down, lingering in the hollow of her neck while she arched in shivery delight. Then the lacing was gone, dropped to the floor, and his mouth teased in the vee of the shirt's placket, licking, biting, kissing. And lower, until his lips played over the tops of her aching breasts and grazed her sensitive nipples. Michty me, she had never felt anything so wickedly marvelous.

He moved to take her amulet and draw it over her head.

"Nay," she whispered, wedging a hand between them to settle it back into place.

"Nay," he repeated, the word sounding foreign coming from him. His knuckles brushed her face, then he closed his eyes and pulled away. He sat up, his breath coming in slow, loud puffs. "I said I'd not do this," he ground out. " 'Tis not responsible, and—"

She reached up to grasp his shoulders. "In the name o' the wee man, would ye forget about being responsible, for once in your life? I want ye, Jason."

Another flash of lightning, and his answer was in his eyes. *No.*

Despite her resolve, she had asked with words again, and, no, he'd not have the likes of her. With a sob borne of frustration, embarrassment, endless rejection, and unfulfilled passion, she leapt up and made for the door, clawing at it with frantic fingers, throwing it to the floor behind her. A mighty crash resounded from the cottage as she raced out into the storm.

He was behind her within seconds, but she kept running, darting around the shadows of the trees, until finally he caught her by the hem of the shirt and pulled her to her knees in the wet grass. She threw herself forward, shutting her eyes tight against the sight of him, though she couldn't really have seen him anyway in the darkness and the driving rain.

"Leave me alone," she screamed over the deluge. Never had she realized water could be so loud. But 'twas good— it drowned out her harsh breathing and the staccato beat of her heart. It pounded on her skin, cold needles that drove away all her anguished thoughts as she concentrated on the chilled wetness. It caressed her body with the icy fingers she needed to cool her ardor and bring her back to her senses.

Then warmer fingers were on her, rolling her onto her back. "What the hell are you doing?" Jason demanded over a rumble of thunder. "You'll catch your death out here."

"Leave me alone!" Angrily she pushed at his hands and struggled to her feet. "Always, since I met ye, ye will never leave me alone," she screamed as he came up after her.

A bolt of lightning illuminated his face, just for a second. But long enough for Cait to see his tortured face, his eyes. And that the rejection she'd seen in the cottage had been a mistake. She'd seen what she'd expected to see, not what truly was. The naked hunger.

"I don't want to leave you alone," he bellowed over the wind and the rain and another hard crack of thunder. "Damn it to bloody hell—I never wanted to leave you alone!" And he was on her in an instant, his bare torso hot on her chilled, wet body, his mouth searching for hers.

Their lips met, and a jolt of aching desire shot straight through to her heart. The kiss was not gentle, but devouring, demanding a response she was only too ready to give. His tongue swept her mouth as his hands swept down to the hem of the shirt, dragging it up her body until he broke contact to pull it over her head.

Lightning flashed as he crushed her to him, skin against skin, and fused his mouth to hers again. Rain pounded down around them, but they were so close not a drop could have shimmied between their straining bodies. His lips traveled her cheeks, her nose, her hairline, leaving a burning path that no cold water could erase. Unshaven roughness grazed her skin, a man's texture that gave rise to a thrill as wild as the storm.

He eased her to the grass, his hands roaming her body, leaving a riot of sensation in their wake. Her own hands skimmed his back, his shoulders, wherever she could reach. Thunder rumbled—in the distance, then closer— matching the uneven beat of her pulse. The rain smelled chilly and fresh, but Jason smelled warm and male, unbearably exciting.

When his hand raced down her side and his fingers explored between her legs, she cried out, feeling herself wetter than the rain somehow, straining for more. More of his body, more of his mouth, more of his fingers where they teased. More, more. She pressed her lips where his neck met his shoulder, then tasted him, her teeth nipping his heated skin.

He reared up, and all four of their hands were fumbling on the laces to his breeches. In moments he had peeled them off, and his mouth closed over hers as he plunged into her.

A wee bit surprised at the intrusion, Cait stiffened and gasped. He hesitated above her, but she couldn't see his face through the dark and the rain. She only knew that he couldn't stop now. She wouldn't let him. Like the rain and the thunder and the lightning, nothing would stop them, and she pushed up against him, taking him deeper, her heart soaring when she felt him respond. Her hands clawed at his back as he rocked against her, the water sluicing over them in a relentless rhythm that matched their own.

Relentless, like the feeling building inside her, a feeling so urgent and wondrous it could only come from nature. Relentless. A jagged bolt ripped from the sky as Caithren hurtled to a point of no return, then did return, only to feel Jason pull out of her as the answering thunder rumbled the earth beneath them. Shuddering, he buried his face in her shoulder.

"Caithren," he choked out.

She'd thought she couldn't feel any more wonderful, but hearing him utter her name—her real name—made her heart constrict with an unbearable pleasure. Her feelings weren't entirely unreciprocated . . . and, even more significant, he finally believed she wasn't Emerald.

Finally.

He struggled to his elbows, hovering above her. "Caithren, sweet Cait." The words came in ragged pants. "I'm—Christ, I'm sorry."

She moved under him, feeling entirely too drained to respond to his distress. "I told ye I was Cait—"

"Not about that." He rolled off her, onto his back, putting a hand over his eyes. One knee was raised, and her greedy gaze roamed his body as another flash of lightning revealed it. "Bloody hell," he said, "I lost my head, and I've—ruined you. Let you down, your family, myself . . . I'm so damned sorry."

"Dinna ye dare be sorry," Cait yelled over the crack of thunder. "Be sorry ye didn't believe me, if ye will— ye haven't believed a word I've said since day one. But dinna ye dare be sorry for this. I am not ruined. A man's contrivance, that." By the saints, he looked anguished enough to do himself damage. "It was good, was it not?" She sat up and hovered over him, shoved his hand from his eyes. "Was it not?" she demanded.

"It was." He sat too and clutched her close, covering her mouth with little kisses, with all the tenderness they'd abandoned during their heated encounter. "It was good." Another kiss, and his tongue flicked out to trace her lips. "But 'twas wrong, and for your first time—"

"It was good," she said. It had been more than good— it had been unbelievable. The sheer force and power of it, of them together. "Michty me, I would never have known how good it could be, and I can only be better for the knowing of it. I didn't have a clue. Not a glimmer—"

He groaned. "All right. It was good. My sweet, independent Cait. What is it the Gypsy said? You go your own way." He kissed the dripping rain off her nose. "Sweet Jesus, have you ever in your life been so damned wet?"

She was still laughing when they made it back to the cottage and he shoved the door back into place. Except for when lightning lit the sky and seeped through the shutters, the room was pitch-black, but he managed to find some of the less wet clothes and rub her down with them, then tuck her into the bed before seeing to himself.

Thankful that she couldn't see him in the darkness, he scrubbed mercilessly at his skin, as though he could scour away the guilt. Oh, she was right—it had been good. Damned good. Better than he'd ever had; better than he'd imagined. Even now, his blood ran hot wanting her again . . . wanting to give it to her nice and slow, the way a virgin should be treated. God damn him for being so weak and irresponsible, letting his body rule his head. He shouldn't have taken her in the first place—it had been selfish and wrong. Like everything else, he would make this up to her. Somehow.

After this was all over. Now, he would have to work hard to put the distance back between them. The distance they both needed in order to make sure Gothard was dealt with and no harm came to Caithren. His precious Cait.

When he crawled into the bed, she reached for him, her lips searching blindly for his in the darkness, fumbling, then finding their target. A sweet, sleepy kiss.

He wrapped his arms around her, settled himself against her welcoming body, and listened to the patter of rain on the roof. Distance, he thought as he felt her drifting into sleep. He had meant to put distance between them, yet here they were, almost as close as two bodies could be. But she felt too good against him to be thinking of distance now.

The morning would be soon enough.

Chapter Eighteen

Michty me, she was in the scud.

Sunlight streamed through open shutters to where Caithren lay alone in bed, naked beneath the quilt. Last night came rushing back, mad images of rain and passion she knew must have really happened because she couldn't possibly have imagined anything so perfectly glorious. Heat rushed to her cheeks just thinking of it.

She rubbed her aching arm. The wound felt hot beneath the bandage. She should have taken it off last night and allowed it some air, instead of keeping it swathed in damp cloth. But she hadn't been thinking of anything practical then—she'd thought about nothing but how Jason was making her feel.

How, in the name of the saints, would she live the rest of her life without a man?

Nay, not without any man—without Jason.

Every fiber in her body reacted to that thought. She sat abruptly, pulling the quilt about her shoulders as she tried to talk sense into herself. Jason had said they'd be in London by tonight. Friday—two days from now—she would find Adam at Lord Darnley's wedding. Then she'd go home to Scotland, where she belonged.

Even should she spend the rest of her life with Jason—an idea so absurd it didn't bear considering—she would never again experience a night like the one they'd shared, the depth of feeling brought on by that wild combination of attraction, frustration, and weather. Mayhap it *was* her imagination. Could touching him, loving him, really feel that all-encompassing?

She had two more days with him, and she would use them to find out.

The door lay flat on the floor, and their clothes, except for her mistress outfit, were all gone. Crammed unfolded into the portmanteau, no doubt. A smile tugged at her lips as she wrapped the quilt around her body and walked to the gaping hole where the door belonged. The sky was cloudless, and the last remnants of the rain glittered like diamonds in the sun's rays. Songbirds chirped in the trees. A beautiful, lovely morning.

The best morning of her life.

Jason was outside by the horses, already dressed in his nobleman disguise, securing their belongings. Her gaze skimmed his gleaming black hair and the masculine planes of his face. He had shaved while she slept, and her fingers itched to feel the smooth skin and compare it to the roughness of last night. Oooh, the very thought of that roughness brought a rush of urgent heat that weakened her knees and made her stomach flutter. She drank in his muscular physique, imagining what was underneath the fancy blue velvet suit. Nay, not imagining . . . remembering.

She blushed. "Good morn," she called.

He looked up, favoring her with one of those white grins that made her heart turn over. But as she watched, it faded. His eyes looked hooded, uncomfortable. Like last night had been a mistake. "Good morn," he returned, then glanced away.

Her heart floundered in confusion. The pleasant flutter in her stomach turned to an uneasy jumble of nerves. After what they'd shared, still he was holding back.

Her face must have betrayed her disappointment, because he came toward her with concern in his eyes. She turned her back, leaning against the empty door frame.

Traitorous, her body responded immediately when he laid his hands on her shoulders, and she felt a hot stab of desire. He tried to swivel her to face him, but she stayed stubbornly facing away. She wouldn't let him see the tears that glazed her eyes.

She pulled from his grasp, and he followed her back into the cottage.

"The horses did fine," he said from behind in a matter-of-fact tone. "Get dressed, and we'll make for Welwyn. I'm starving."

Then he wasn't even going to mention last night. Wasn't going to reassure her. Nothing.

When she heard the clink of coins hitting the table, she turned. "For the damage," he explained, indicating the door and the mess of congealed bread in the fireplace. "The owners will have to pay someone to fix it up, wash the bedclothes and all."

Pay someone? What kind of a man hired people to do his work for him? When something needed doing at Leslie, she or Da or Cameron did it themselves.

Still, leaving the money was so like Jason. He was a good man. Despite her uncertain feelings, she felt compelled to try to reach him one more time.

"I want to thank ye," she started.

"For what?"

"Last night." She clutched the quilt tighter. "I will never forget it."

"I won't forget it, either," he said. "But that doesn't make it right. It shouldn't have happened."

Robbed of breath, she turned toward her still-damp clothes, feeling his gaze on her bare back, revealed by the drape of the quilt. A back she'd never thought a man would see. But she'd exposed more than that to him—more her back and her breasts and the rest of her body. She'd exposed her entire soul. And he'd wrenched it right out of her.

He regretted last night.

* * *

Hours later, somewhere between Highgate and Hampstead, Jason admitted to himself what he'd known for days and hadn't wanted to face.

He had fallen in love with Caithren Leslie.

He was not ready for this. He'd tried so hard to resist. Because Caithren Leslie was no promiscuous courtier. He'd known all along that, with Cait, it would be all or nothing.

He'd wanted distance, to keep his head clear and do what needed to be done. He had responsibilities. Urgent ones, like little Mary, her mother, the innocent dead man. Gothard. Less urgent but nonetheless important responsibilities, like seeing his sister settled.

Distance. Until last night—until he'd lost his head—he'd maintained it. This morning he'd attempted to recover it. A disastrous attempt. But how could he share his feelings when so many responsibilities stood between him and the woman he wanted?

He wasn't ready.

But he knew he'd hurt her. His heart sinking, he took refuge beneath the shady cover of the trees overhead, thankful Cait couldn't see his face. Silent, they rode past small houses with their shutters closed against the wind, like his mind had been closed to the truth. Cows and sheep in the fields turned as they passed, pinning him with liquid, accusing eyes. Two magpies mocked him from a tree.

He snuck a glance in Caithren's direction. She looked pale, tired, on the edge of tears, her fingers white-knuckled on the reins. His fault. Tonight he would leave her safe at his London town house while he took care of Geoffrey and Walter Gothard. Another responsibility—keeping Cait safe. When the Gothards were behind bars, he would help her find her brother. Tell her he believed everything she'd told him.

Ask her to marry him.

The mere thought pulled the breath from his body, and suddenly he knew that nothing else would do but to keep her by his side forever. Never had he met anyone who could make him laugh and live like she did. His life before her seemed bleak in comparison. Leslie was a baronetcy—Scottish or no, the match would be considered suitable. Not that he really cared; the Chases didn't go out of their way to placate society. His own brother had, with his blessing, married a commoner.

Another glance at her tore at his heart. He didn't deserve Caithren. He'd put her very life in danger, then compounded his sins by taking her, callously, with no thought to her pleasure or the words of commitment she had every right to expect from him. 'Twas no wonder she was mired in gloom.

Soon he would give her everything she wanted, if only she'd give him the chance. He'd spend the rest of his life making it up to her. Making her happy.

The road was disastrous in the aftermath of the storm, and the day's progress had been slow and aggravating. It seemed a lifetime before they made it to the tollhouse. A lifetime of torture. He would rather have submitted to the rack.

"We're in Hampstead," he told Caithren, hoping to cheer her up. "London is in reach."

" 'Tis good." Her voice sounded weak. He handed a coin to the tollkeeper and motioned her down the hill toward the heath.

"Soon I'll be able to warn Scarborough," he said. "That will be a weight off both our minds, will it not?"

Though she nodded and forced a smile, he could see her jaw was tight.

The heath, wild land punctuated by weedy ponds, was slower going even than the Great North Road. Narrow trodden paths led through sprawling acres of wooded dells and fields of heather. Jason took the lead, since they couldn't ride side by side.

"Could that be a real tree?" Wonder in her voice, Caithren uttered her first unsolicited words since they'd left the cottage that morning. "An elm, is it not?" A gigantic elm, perhaps ten yards around, with steps inside leading to a wooden platform that rose above the topmost leaves. " 'Tis amazing."

He turned to see a smile on her face—a smile he'd been afraid he might never see again. His heart warmed. "Would you like to go up?"

She looked like she was seriously considering saying no, then her eyes lit with determination. "Aye. I would like that very much. Will ye come with me?"

He eyed the platform. It looked sturdy, and the steps didn't look too daunting, housed as they were in the trunk of the tree.

" 'Tis not so very far up," she coaxed. "Nothing like that tower outside Stamford."

There was nothing he wouldn't do at this point to make her resent him a little less.

"Very well," he said. "I'll be up in a moment." At her doubtful look, he added, "I mean it this time. Just let me secure the horses."

He tethered the animals to a nearby tree that was dwarfed by the elm, then gritted his teeth and started up, mentally groaning when he saw the stairs were slatted instead of solid. The first few steps weren't too bad, but then the staircase started spiraling up inside the trunk, getting more and more narrow. *Look up,* he told himself, *look up.* Eyes on the goal, not the drop. His pulse skittered, his head whirled, the blood roared in his ears. Halfway up, he paused to lean against the hollowed interior and close his eyes.

When he opened them, his vision was blurry, and he shook his head to clear it. One foot in front of the other, one step at a time, and if he felt as though his dinner might come up, well, he'd just have to ignore it.

He was shocked when he caught up to her, given her head start. She seemed to be expending quite an effort in the climb. Last night must have taken its toll on her. Another blade of guilt stabbed at his heart. What kind of man took a woman in a thunderstorm?

She glanced back at him. "Ye look pale."

He blew out a breath and shrugged. His eyes on her back, he ordered his legs to stop shaking, and finally they made it to the top.

"Forty-two steps," she announced. "Michty me, will ye look at that view." She rushed to the rail, her gaze scanning from right to left and back again.

"Beautiful, is it not?" The platform looked as though it might hold about twenty people. Wiping sweaty palms on his breeches, he stayed in the exact center. "We're lucky to have a clear day. London is often mired in fog." His stomach did a flip-flop when she leaned over the rail. "Keep back, will you?"

"London is incredible. So huge! I've never seen so many buildings in one place."

The view stretched for miles and miles. From his spot behind her, he pointed out the ruins of St. Paul's Cathedral, destroyed in last year's Great Fire, and the hills of Kent south of the Thames.

"And what could that be?" Cait asked, staring at something much closer, in the shrubby area just at the bottom of the heath. She turned to him. "A reservoir? With horses and carriages driving right through it?"

"Whitestone Pond." Jason nodded at a large marker that sat near it. "Named for that old white milestone. King Henry the Eighth designed it to keep the City free of the countryside's mud. All horses and wheels pass through it on the way in from Hampstead." He laughed at her expression of disbelief. "We'll be doing so ourselves in a few minutes."

"It still looks a long way to London," she said quietly.

He frowned at her tight features. "Naught but an hour or so."

"I-I'm hurting, Jason." She dropped her gaze, plainly uncomfortable at the admission. "My arm," she explained. "I thought I could make it all the day, but . . ."

"Damn, and I didn't take you foraging for plants." Forgetting his dizziness, he moved closer, drawing her near to sling an arm around her shoulders, remembering her clenched hands and the stoic set of her jaw as they rode. "Was that why you were so quiet?"

She nodded miserably, and he felt another stab of guilt, this time for being happy she wasn't so resentful of him after all, even though she was clearly distressed. "You cannot make it another hour?"

Clouded with pain, her eyes went to his. "I dinna know," she whispered. "All the day I've been—"

"London can wait," he decided, alarmed. Caithren was nothing if not strong and steady. "We'll ride back up the hill, to Spaniards Inn. You saw it, by the tollgate?"

She nodded.

" 'Tis not far at all. You're going to be fine." He swung her up into his arms, as one would carry a small child.

"Jason!" Despite her distress, she giggled, and his heart lifted a bit. "Put me down!"

"I'll hear none of it," he told her with mock sternness, starting down the steps and forcing himself to ignore the rush of vertigo. "We will have you in a room in no time. Can you sit your own horse?"

"Of course I can. I rode all the day, did I not?" Warm laughter rang through the hollowed trunk, bringing him waves of relief. But the feeling was short-lived once he looked down the steep, winding stairs. One step after another, he ordered his feet to comply, his breath coming in short pants, even worse going down than up and with no hand free to balance against the wall.

The arms that cradled Cait were shaking, but she didn't comment on that, or on his lack of speed. "I'm not an invalid, Jason. I only wish to rest."

At the bottom, he had not the luxury to let his knees buckle, or to sit a spell and recover his composure. Silently congratulating himself, he perched her on her reddish mare and mounted his own black steed.

Afraid to jar her, he led her slowly back over the heath and up the hill to the white, weatherboarded inn. Securing a room seemed a process that took forever. And forever to him must have been even worse for her.

Finally he closed the door of their oak-paneled room behind them, and she dropped into a chair, white faced.

"That bad?" he asked.

She put on a brave smile. "It hurts. But mostly because I'm so tired, I'm thinking. I didn't sleep much last night." Color sprang to her cheeks as she doubtlessly remembered why. "We should have gone on to London. 'Tis sorry I am that I made ye stop."

He wasn't falling for her false bravado. "Let me have a look." Without waiting for her agreement, he crouched before her and detached the tabs of her stomacher. A flush came to her skin as he loosened the gown's laces, and her heart sped up beneath his fingers, as clear an indicator of her desire as if she had told him outright.

Despite his worry, answering need rushed through him. Clenching his teeth, he carefully lowered her bodice and the chemise underneath, helping her pull her arms from the sleeves. With one hand she pressed the gown to her chest, holding out the injured limb.

All lust fled when he pulled at the edges of the linen bandage and glimpsed what lay beneath. A soft moan escaped her lips.

"I'm sorry." Jason unwound the fabric as gently as he could.

" 'Tis all right," Cait whispered. "I ken ye dinna mean to hurt me."

He smiled a little, then grimaced as the wound was revealed. Not long, but deep. Deeper than he remembered and surrounded by angry, pinkened flesh. A drop of dark red blood seeped out when the bandage fell away, and he could see a sickening taint of white deep inside.

"I should have been checking on this." Yet another failure on his part.

"Ye wanted to last night—"

" 'Tis getting infected."

She looked down, then averted her gaze. "It looks very bad." He watched her jaw tighten with determination. "I will be fine, Jason. Dinna worry for me. 'Twill heal. I will make a poultice." Her face brightened. "So close to London, there might even be a shop. I can tell ye what I need—"

"I imagine it hurts like hell." He rose and paced away, then turned back. "I'd best fetch a surgeon. I believe it should be stitched."

"Stitched?" Her pretty forehead wrinkled, making his gut twist with sympathy.

" 'Tis getting worse rather than better." He stared at her colorless face. "The surgeon will know for sure. Bloody hell, I'm sorry."

Cursing himself for messing up yet again, he took himself downstairs to send a man to find a surgeon.

Jason came back a few minutes later with a goblet that he handed to Caithren. She sniffed at the contents suspiciously. "What is it?"

"Whiskey."

"I kent as much." She handed it back. "Nay, but I thank ye for the thought."

He frowned. "You don't like whiskey?"

"Have ye seen me drink whiskey afore now?"

"No, but . . . you're Scottish."

"And . . . ?"

" 'Tis whiskey, which the Scots invented if my—"

Caithren burst out laughing, then stopped when the movement pained her arm. "We dinna all fancy whiskey, Jase. 'Tis not a law. And here ye accuse me of painting all the English with one brush." She watched as his face slowly turned red. "Some ale wouldn't be amiss—"

A sharp knock came at the door, and Jason went to answer it.

Cait felt the blood drain from her face as the surgeon marched in, a burly man with one beefy hand clutching a bag of implements. But she told herself to be brave. She didn't want to embarrass herself before Jason. He thought little enough of her as it was.

"I'm told of an injury," the surgeon said. "A slash wound, is it?"

"Aye." She clutched her bodice to her chest and proffered her bare arm.

The surgeon came closer, yet gave it but a cursory glance. "What've you got there?" he asked Jason, indicating the goblet in his hand.

"Whiskey." Jason's voice sounded weak to Cait's ears. Or mayhap the blood pounding in her head was muffling the sound. "Here," he said more clearly. He offered the goblet.

The surgeon took it and downed a healthy gulp. "Decent stuff," he declared, then poured a thick stream over Caithren's wound.

Her breath hissed in, but she would not cry. She'd shed the last tears she would in front of Jason. "Wh-what did ye do that for?" she managed to stutter.

"To cleanse it. Stop infection."

"What?" It stung like blazes. "My cousin Cam would skin ye alive if he saw ye wasting good whiskey like that. Give it here." She snatched the goblet from the surgeon's hand and gulped greedily, feeling the liquor burn a hot path down her gullet and into her empty stomach.

When Jason looked like he was about to laugh, she

quelled his humor with a dark glare and sipped again. The stuff was not nearly as nasty as she'd thought. At least under the present circumstances.

"I have always practiced gentle healing," she told Jason. "I cannot believe he did that."

" 'Tis not unheard of, sweet. Ford did the same for my bullet wound, and he's no surgeon, though he does fancy himself a scientist."

"Ford?" She drank again. The warmth in her stomach was spreading, and her arm seemed to hurt less. Her head was beginning to feel like it might detach itself and float away.

"My brother, Ford." Jason stooped down and gazed into her eyes, and a tiny smile tilted the corners of his mouth. "Never mind." He stood and motioned the surgeon closer.

She sipped once more, then set her jaw and angled her arm out. "Have at it," she declared.

The man rummaged in his bag and came out with a needle and some black thread.

Caithren winced and looked up at Jason. "Are ye sure he has to do this?"

"I'm sure. Drink." He shoved the goblet closer to her lips, and she complied. He ran a hand through her hair, raking it back from her forehead. " 'Twill not take long."

She nodded and steeled herself for the pain. When it came, a sharp prick and a scraping sting as the raw edges of flesh were bound together, 'twas not as bad as she'd thought it would be. Not nearly as hurtful as when the surgeon had doused her arm with the whiskey. Or mayhap the whiskey had numbed it some.

Jason put a hand on her good shoulder, and she jumped at the contact, momentarily dropping the top of the gown and exposing the tops of her breasts. The surgeon seemed not to notice, but hot blood rushed to her cheeks. She wasn't sure if 'twere from embarrassment or the burning feelings that raced through her at Jason's touch.

"You're doing fine." His voice sounded proud, impressed. It made the whiskey curl warmer in her belly. It seemed all she wanted was his trust, his approval.

Nay, not all, not if she were to be honest with herself. She also craved his arms around her, his lips on hers.

His love.

Everything—her whole life—seemed so confused. When had her goals changed; when had she started yearning for the love of a man? She didn't know. She knew only that 'twas wrong—wrong for her, for her plans, for her life. She belonged home with Cameron, tending their land, their heritage. Not with this exasperating man, far away in England.

Yet her thoughts turned to Jason more every day . . . her thoughts and her heart. 'Twas impossible. Even if Jason wanted her, 'twould be impossible.

And he didn't want her, which should have made it easier. But it didn't make it easier; it made it worse. Much, much worse.

The hated tears flooded her eyes, and one rolled warm down her cheek. She dashed it away with her good hand.

"Hush," Jason soothed. "He's almost finished." Again he stroked her hair. She felt another jab and tug on her arm, and the tears flowed faster. Not from the pain, though . . .

Oh, aye, from the pain. The pain that weighed heavy as a brick in her chest. The pain in her heart.

'Twas not long at all before the surgeon knotted the thread and cut it with a knife. He tied a bandage around her arm to protect his handiwork. Then, mindful of his patient's distress, he put his things away quietly and went to Jason. "Go to Hampstead Wells and ask to see Dorothy Pippen. She sells medicinal water."

"My thanks." Jason pressed a few coins into the surgeon's hand and followed him to the door, softly closing it behind him. Cait put her arms back in her sleeves and tightened her laces.

"There." Jason came close and patted her shoulder. " 'Twas not so bad, after all, was it? And now it's done."

She shook off his hand. She couldn't bear his touch. Not when she kent they'd gain London on the morrow and go their separate ways, with no regret on his part. Only pride, she imagined, that he'd kept her where he wanted her, ensuring his successful, unimpeded capture and murder of Geoffrey Gothard.

Oh, 'twas not to be borne! Despite a heroic effort to rein in her emotions, she wandered away in tears. Her hand went into her pocket; her fingers caressed the hard metal frame that cradled the miniature of her brother.

She pulled it out and stared at it, drifting to the window where she could see it better in the failing light. Her thumb ran lovingly over the glass that protected Adam's familiar face.

Adam. Where was he? Mayhap she would find him in London tomorrow, and when she saw him, her world would be set to rights. Her plans would be back on track, and she wouldn't feel as though her life were so out of control.

Adam. Dear, familiar Adam. She gazed at his oval face, his wheaten hair, his hazel eyes. All just like hers. The foppish outfit he'd posed in, all velvet and ribbons and snowy linen, brought a smile through the tears. So unlike herself and Da, but typical Adam.

"Adam," she whispered under her breath.

"Who is that?" Soft behind her, Jason's voice took her by surprise.

"Adam," she said louder, feeling better just saying her brother's name. She had a goal—a worthy goal—and finally it was within reach. So close. "Adam. My brother."

When she turned to look at Jason, his face was whiter than the lace on Adam's cravat.

"Wh-what is it, Jason?" She'd never known a man to faint, but he looked as though he might keel over at any second. "Is something amiss?"

"Yes." He blinked and shook his head. "No." She saw his face go pink, the hidden freckles appear, like they did when he was upset.

"Have I said something, done something—"

"No." He drew a long breath, and his lips turned up in a forced smile. "You're tired. Let me go downstairs and bring up some supper. Then I'll go to Dorothy Pippen and get you the water."

Cait's hand went to her amulet. "I dinna need special water. And I'm not hungry. Can ye just stay with me here?"

His gaze skittered away. "I must at least make some inquiries and see if I can find out where we need to go tomorrow. Where Scarborough lives, I mean." He made as though to reach for her, then pulled back. "Sleep well. I'll be up later." With a distracted kiss to her forehead, he left her to go to bed.

Alone and reeling.

Gasping, he checked his momentum, but not in time. His silver blade flashed, sliced in, sending a shiver up his arm. The man before him crumpled to the ground, his lifeblood pumping into the dirt. His eyes stared unseeing at Jason . . . hazel eyes . . . Emerald's hazel eyes . . . Caithren's hazel eyes . . .

Caithren's brother's hazel eyes.

His heart racing, Jason let out an anguished yell as he awakened. He curled up on the bed. His breath heaved. He couldn't recall what he had eaten for supper, but it felt like it were about to come back up.

"Jason?" Caithren leaned over him, patting his shoulder uncertainly.

He moaned. His head pounded from overdrinking last night—something he *never* did—and a frustrated dampness squeezed from beneath his clenched eyelids. Dear God in heaven, he'd killed her brother.

He'd killed the brother of the woman he loved. Bloody hell, she would never accept him. Not a tainted man like he was, a man who had killed . . .

A man who had killed her brother, no less.

With all his might, he wished that she were Emerald, instead. He would still love every stubborn inch of her, but if she were Emerald he might have a chance with her. Emerald would understand this driving need for justice. She would understand the way killing, even unintentional killing, changes a man.

But Caithren . . . sweet, unspoiled Caithren never would.

How could he expect her to forgive him, when he couldn't even forgive himself?

He couldn't tell her the truth.

He *had* to tell her the truth.

"Jason?" Her hand jiggled his shoulder, spiking the pain in his head. Not that he didn't deserve it. Slowly he rolled over and gazed up at her.

"Was it the nightmare again?"

He nodded.

Her lovely eyes filled with compassion. "It will go away when ye ken who he was."

"I . . ." When words failed him, she leaned closer. Her breath was heavenly, coming warm through concerned, parted lips. She leaned closer still. Her mouth was close, so close. Resolve melted, and he closed the distance and covered her lips with his.

She flung herself against him, a low moan vibrating in her throat as she deepened the kiss.

Sweet Mary, she wanted him. He could feel the need, pumping from her center into his own body. His arms moved to enclose her, then his hands fisted.

If he was going to take the comfort of her body, the least he could do was slow down, show her the tenderness he'd failed to the first time. Keep his head. Protect her injured arm.

Protect his injured heart.

That heart pounding, he pulled back.

He needed to tell her. He couldn't tell her. Not telling her was a lie.

Though he knew he'd be damned to hell for the lie, not to mention for taking her—again, when he knew the truth—he couldn't seem to help himself. Just this once, before she discovered what he had done—what kind of man he was—he would worship her. With his hands, his lips, his body . . . he would make her his, make her happy, if only for one night.

Chapter Nineteen

She knew the moment he gave in.

His hands relaxed and pulled her close. His mouth searched out hers, but when he found her lips, the kiss wasn't angry or hesitant, but sweetly desperate. 'Twas as though the whole of his attention was focused on that kiss, and nothing else existed in his world for that moment.

The sheer intensity frightened her. She had wanted the chance to see if the feelings of that stormy night were repeatable. Now she was afraid to learn the answer. If it were yes . . . how would she ever find it in herself to leave him?

Not that he would ask her to stay.

The truth brought a pang to her heart, but all thought fled when he eased her onto her back and she felt his welcome weight press her to the bed. She wrapped her arms around him, and he coaxed apart her lips, and his tongue swept into her mouth. Cait found herself a melting mass of sensation, a puddle on the mattress for him to do with as he would. But still he only kissed her, a kiss that drugged, a kiss that precluded all thought.

When he came up for air, she regained her senses and the fear returned. She wasn't having second thoughts—never that—but intentionally loving him in a bed in the morning was so different than impulsively on a rainswept night. A surrender of sorts, and a huge leap of trust, but she was willing to take it. She could only hope the cliff didn't prove to be too high.

Jason's hands went to the tie at her neck, trying to loosen the high ruffle. He only succeeded in knotting the bow. "I thought we were going to burn this," he complained, the words tainted with frustration.

"Here, let me do it." Her heart pounded while her fingers worked at the tangle. "I thought ye were practiced in removing women's clothes."

"Not night rails. I don't believe I've ever removed a night rail. Off-putting garments, night rails. Mrs. Twentyman's in particular." Impatient, he moved to help, but she pushed away his hand.

"Wait." She laughed. "You'll only make it harder."

"Harder." Early morning light filtered through the curtains, and in the gray shadows she saw his jaw tense. " 'Tis absolutely harder." His voice sounded husky and breathless.

"Nay, 'tis easy now." Her own voice shook, betraying her anxiety. " 'Tis almost undone."

"That is not what I meant, Caithren."

She froze when he took her hand and moved it down to the bulge in his breeches. "Oh." She didn't seem able to breathe properly. "Oh, michty me. It *is* hard. How very interesting." Exploring, she forgot she'd managed to untie the night rail's ruffle until she heard his moan and felt his lips nibble her throat. "Oooh, Jase." Her hand tightened.

"I think . . ." His muffled words tickled the hollow of her neck. "Not that it doesn't feel good, but I think . . . I think you'd best touch me elsewhere now." When she didn't comply, he reached for her hand. *"Now."*

His eyes looked rather frantic, and she reluctantly released him, arching in delight when his lips went back to her throat. This sweet, melting seduction wasn't anything like last time, nor was it—or Jason—anything like the animals she'd seen. "Well, now, I've seen a horse's, ye ken, but I've never felt—"

"A horse's?" On a choked laugh, Jason's head came up. "I've never been compared to a horse, but I thank you for the compliment. I think. Then you've seen horses, ah . . . ?" His busy mouth went back to work, making a shiver run through her.

"Oh, aye. But the first time, well . . . it didn't work exactly the same way, did it?" Her hands played restlessly in his hair. "Of course I kent it wouldn't, because Cam told me people do it face to face. I can see why. The kissing is nice."

"Mmmm. Nice, yes." Settling his mouth on hers again, he kissed her long and deep, as though to prove it. At the same time, one hand wandered down her body, leaving a fiery trail in its wake.

"H-have I told ye that Cameron and I are breeding horses? Highland ponies, actually." She paused for a much-needed breath. "This past year we've been crossing them with some Spanish stock, in an effort to—"

"Are you nervous, Cait?" He spread the night rail's neckline wider and skimmed the tops of her sensitive breasts.

"Mayhap." An understatement. "A wee bit." A bigger understatement.

His head came up again. "Has anyone ever told you that you babble when you're nervous?"

"Cameron." Through the night rail, his fingers lazily traced the line where her legs met, inciting a tingling current of desire. Her own hands trailed up and down the back of his shirt, then found the bottom edge and worked their way beneath it. The skin on his back felt hot. "But I dinna think I've ever been quite this, um . . . nervous with Cam."

"I'm glad to hear it," he said dryly. "Let us get rid of this, shall we?"

He sat and reached for the hem of the night rail, but

the yards and yards of fabric only got hopelessly tangled. Giggling, she rose to her knees to help him struggle her out of it.

"You're supposed to take this seriously," he said.

"Am I?" She gasped when cold air hit her middle, but she couldn't see him—her face was swathed in white wool. "This entire act is rather absurd, if ye think on it."

"Then don't think."

As if she could. Her breasts were uncovered now, and she still couldn't see.

But she heard his sharp intake of breath. "Sweet Jesus. You're perfect."

She shoved the night rail off her head, blinking in the brightening morning light. Blushing at the hunger she saw in his eyes, she tugged up the quilt to cover her body. "Am I not scrawny? Ye said I dinna eat enough."

"You're perfect," he repeated. "I was wrong. Besides, I so enjoy your leftovers." She gasped when he swept the blanket off the bed. While she was still speechless, his hands reached out and fitted themselves to her breasts, which she'd always thought were too small. "Perfect," he breathed, closing his eyes momentarily.

She fell back to the pillows, weak with shock. Or something. "This is not fair."

"No?" His eyes opened and ravenously roamed her body.

She blushed and folded her arms across her breasts. "Ye should be in the scud, too."

"In due time."

"Now."

"Has anyone ever told you you're demanding?"

"Aye." He leaned close, and her hands went to loosen the laces on his shirt. "I'm demanding, and I babble when I'm nervous, and I'm impulsive."

"And you talk too much." He kissed her, and her fingers faltered in their task.

"But I'm perfect," she reminded him.

He nodded solemnly. "Yes, you're perfect."

With a single lithe movement, he stood and pulled the shirt over his head, then made short work of divesting himself of his breeches. Michty me, he was perfect, too. Like the drawing she'd seen of Michelangelo's *David* in one of Adam's schoolbooks. She'd spent hours studying that picture, but she never thought she'd see it come to life.

When he came down on top of her, skin to skin, she sighed loudly in contentment. Supporting himself on his elbows, he hovered over her. "Now, will you just hush up?"

"Oh, aye," she breathed, and his mouth closed over hers. Slow and deep, the kiss made her senses spin. This was different than last time, but no less glorious. Just different.

His dark head bent, and his clever mouth moved over a breast, wet and warm and tingling. "Oooh, Jase. I never kent—do all men do this?"

She felt his chuckle. "I cannot speak for all men."

"This is t-taking much longer than with a horse." She sucked in a breath. "Generally, the male horse bites the female on the neck—"

"Like this?" His mouth trailed up and demonstrated.

She arched in shock and pleasure. "Aye. But . . . go back to the other."

A low laugh riffled through the dim room as he lightly bit a nipple. "You like this, do you?"

"Aye, very much." Excitement surged through her when he started suckling away the bite. "But horses accomplish this much faster, ye ken. It is all over in a matter of minutes. Like the first time we—"

When his mouth left her, she wanted to smack herself for blethering. "We are not horses," he pointed out in a low voice. "And this is not the first time." A hand skimmed down her body, tracing a sensuous path. " 'Tis another time, another place."

"I see what ye mean." She squirmed and bit her lip to keep from crying out her pleasure. "I-I have never been in this place afore."

"Did I not ask you to be quiet?" he murmured. His mouth started following his hand, trailing little wet kisses down her torso. When his tongue swept into her navel, a stab of hot desire arced from there to deep inside. She clenched her teeth, her hands fisting in his hair. She wouldn't say anything more, not even if—

His lips traced her hipbones and down to her thighs. "Oooh, Jase." Warm, oh so warm and teasingly tender, making shivers ripple through her. "I dinna think a horse has ever done this."

Apparently he was finished dignifying her inane comments with responses. His fingers and mouth roamed her body for long, intimate minutes, while her pulse quickened and her fingers clutched at his hair, his shoulders, the sheets. Then he coaxed her legs apart and cupped her with a hand, and stilled.

Matched by her own, his breath sounded harsh in the suddenly quiet room.

She felt an incredible urgency under his fingers.

When at last they started moving, she almost jumped off the bed. Slowly he stroked, ever so slowly, for ever so long. Her heart raced faster and faster, and when she thought she would explode from the pleasure, he slipped a finger inside her body.

"By. All. The. Saints." Incredibly, she felt herself pulsing around it. "I—I dinna think," she whispered, "I . . . dinna think a horse has ever done this, either."

His finger retreated, a slide of exquisite sensation, then plunged deep. Again. Another finger joined the first, and the pleasure built, the explosion imminent. She called out his name and reached to pull at his shoulders, begging him to move up, craving his lips on hers, wanting him inside her.

He hesitated, and then with a tiny shake of his head,

his mouth closed over her, impossibly hot and soft. "Oooh, Jase!" Her eyes drifted closed, and she grasped her emerald and hung on tight, trembling all over. If she'd thought she might explode before, she knew it now. Her words came out in short, hard pants. "I'm— quite—certain . . . a horse—has never—done *this*." She meant also to ask what made him think of such a thing, but then she did explode, into a million wee pieces.

Somehow they all came back together. She found herself shuddering, gasping for breath.

He crawled up to meet her, his mouth curved in an erotic, heart-wrenching smile of masculine pride, and put his fingers to her lips. "Hush now, sweet Cait." And she did, not only because his mouth claimed hers. She didn't think she could force another word out even if she wanted to. There was no breath left in her lungs.

Tenderly his hands stroked her skin, calming her . . .

Except it wasn't calming—the excitement was building all over again.

His kiss was devastatingly cherishing, and there wasn't a spot on her body he didn't touch and tease into awareness. Her own hands wandered his warm skin, feeling the hardness of his muscles beneath. The spicy maleness of his scent was intoxicating. His low groans echoed her own mews of pleasure, but his movements were controlled, agonizingly slow, designed to bring her to a fever pitch of passion.

She reached down, thinking there must be a way to give him some of the same pleasure, but he stilled her hand. "Hush, sweet Cait," he whispered. "This time is for you."

"Nay—"

"Hush." The kiss he hushed her with was so exquisite, it brought tears to her eyes. The wanting built and built, until she quivered and cried out, and finally he moved over her and slid inside. She arched up, taking him deep . . . deeper, as though she could hold him captive.

"Sweet Cait," he murmured, and then he rocked against her, slowly at first, and then faster. She met his movements in a blissful harmony that proved almost unbearable, clutching him with her hands and legs, her entire body pulsing with an overpowering desire.

She had never thought to feel so close to another, as though they were one and the same. Emotions peaked along with the physical sensations, pushing her up, up . . .

"Nay." 'Twas too much—she couldn't stand it. "Not again."

He lifted his head. "Again. Fall for me, sweet Cait." His rhythm below punctuated his words, and she plunged over the edge, falling faster when she felt him go with her.

The cliff was high, but her landing was soft, cushioned by his arms. They lay still for a long, satisfying minute, then he rolled to his side, taking her with him, and she cuddled close as she fought to catch her breath.

Like the last time, he'd pulled out at the critical moment. Responsible Jason. It made her a wee bit sad, although she kent she should be grateful. Being impulsive and independent was one thing, going home with a bairn in her womb quite another.

But she didn't want to think about going home.

He kissed her on the forehead. "Your arm?"

" 'Tis fine. I forgot all about it." She drew back enough to smile into his clear green eyes. "Ye made me lose my head."

"Not only that, I almost got you to stop talking." He raised a brow and grinned, then groaned as his gaze wandered to the now-bright window. "We'd best grab some breakfast and get to London to warn Scarborough."

"Aye," she sighed. "I hope I can walk. I feel weak as a day-old bairn."

"Before you try to stand, say it again." Smoothing the hair off her face, he kissed her softly. "My name."

She frowned. "Jason?"

"The other."

"Oh." Feeling her heart swell, she raised herself to meet his lips. "Jase."

"It sounds right from you, sweet Cait," he said before his mouth covered hers.

"Number twelve. Is that it?" Two hours later Caithren indicated a brand new, impressive three-story house that bordered on St. James's Fields. "Jings, but Scarborough lives well. No wonder Adam aims to be his friend."

Adam. The man's name made Jason's gut twist. He led her up the gravel drive. Mindful of her arm, he helped her down and tethered their horses.

"Someone else is here," she said. "Or rather, leaving." A fat-bellied gentleman sporting an unfashionable brown beard turned from the door and headed down the steps. Jason nodded at him as they passed, but the man didn't make eye contact. Frowning at his back, Jason watched him hurry away, his feet kicking up gravel in his haste to depart.

Cait plucked his sleeve. "What are ye staring at?"

"I know not." He blinked and turned to her. Scarborough's red-brick town house loomed behind her, reminding him that he'd be bringing her to his own town house soon, and then she'd discover the truth. He couldn't bear the thought. When she started up the steps, he reached to snag her back and gathered her into his arms, pressing his lips to hers.

A strange little sound escaped her throat, and her mouth opened under his, encouraging him to explore her velvet warmth. They kissed for a long, melting minute. A kiss of desperation, a kiss of unguarded lust. A kiss so sweet it made him ache, knowing it might be the last kiss of hers he'd ever receive. Even worse, knowing he had to tell her the news of her beloved brother and his own part in the man's death—shattering all her new and tentative feelings for him. Breaking her heart.

Breaking them both.

One more night. Desperate, he grasped at the thought—he could shield her heart for one more night. 'Twas a day yet, a night yet, before she expected her brother in town. 'Twould be the most bittersweet night of his life, but for her, it would be the most magical night of her life. He would make it so, no matter the cost to his soul. Before he confessed the truth and broke her heart, he would give her one night to remember him by.

He drew away and took her by the hand. "Cait, I . . . let us warn Scarborough."

Sputtering, she accompanied him up to the imposing door. Their knock brought an aging, curly-haired maid-servant to answer. She bobbed a curtsy, her gray curls bouncing along with her beneath a small, white lace cap. "My lord?"

"I've a matter to discuss with Lord Scarborough. Of some urgency."

"Cuds bobs, you're the second in as many minutes. As I told the other gentleman, Lord Scarborough has left town. He is expected back just in time to attend Lord Darnley's wedding."

"That is where Adam will be!" Caithren said excitely.

Frowning, Jason waved her off. "Who was the other man?"

"I don't rightly know. He didn't say."

Something niggled at the back of Jason's brain. "Could he have been Geoffrey Gothard?"

Caithren made a sound suspiciously like a snort, and the maidservant let out a short bark of a laugh, then composed herself. "Not hardly. You wouldn't be asking that if you'd seen him." She brushed at her apron. "Mr. Gothard will not be showing his face around here, in any case. Not if Lord Scarborough has any say in the matter."

"Not showing his face," Jason repeated under his breath. The man had not looked him in the face, either. "Have you an address to reach Lord Scarborough?"

"No, my lord, we do not. He will be here tomorrow. That is all I have to tell you."

"I sent him a very important letter last week." His arm stole around Cait's waist. Had it been but a week since he'd met her? Eight or nine days, maybe, but it felt like a lifetime. "Might you know if he received it?"

The older woman's expression was implacable. "I am not privy to Lord Scarborough's personal matters. And his secretary went with him."

He sighed, knowing he'd get no more out of her. "I thank you."

"My lord." She curtsied again and shut the door in their faces.

Doubtless the other man had gotten more information. He could hardly have gotten less. But who would have been enquiring about Scarborough if not Gothard? "Jason?"

He chided himself; it could have been anyone. He knew none of Scarborough's acquaintances. With not a little relief, he dismissed the problem and looked down at Cait. "What is it, sweet?"

A small blush stained her cheeks at the endearment. "D'ye think Scarborough is safe then, for today?"

"We can hope." He rubbed the back of his neck, then smiled. "Yes, I imagine he is safe. Gothard won't be getting any more information than we did—less, judging from that maidservant's attitude. So he'll not know where to find Scarborough today, any more than we have a clue where to find Gothard. But in case Scarborough failed to get my letter, I will stop by here again tomorrow."

"We can both stop, on the way to the wedding. If

you're willing to take me, that is? I could go on my own, but . . ."

A wave of guilt washed over him. She had no reason to attend the wedding, and he had to tell her that. His moment of reckoning could not be postponed much longer. But first he would give her one perfect night. After all he had put her through, she deserved one perfect night.

The time had arrived to come clean with it all. Part of the truth she would learn today . . . and the rest, the painful part, in the morning.

Tenderly he searched her eyes. What shone from their depths was such loving trust, it caused a weight to settle in his chest. Shoving aside his guilt for her sake, he mustered a grin. "I am willing to take you anywhere, sweet. For tonight . . . would you like to go to a ball?"

"A ball? A London ball?" A spark of excitement brightened her features. "I never thought . . . How is it ye know there is a ball this night?"

"There is always a ball in London," he said dryly.

"And ye can gain entrance?" She looked at him skeptically.

He raised a brow. "I think I can manage to get us in."

"Aye," she said slowly, and he could almost see the gears turning in her head. Her gaze swept over what she undoubtedly considered his nobleman's "costume." "You're a master of disguises." Her eyes sparkled turquoise, the shade he'd decided meant she was happy.

If only he could keep her so.

" 'Twould be a grand adventure," she said. "An *impulsive*, grand adventure. Am I making ye impulsive, Jase?" She grinned. "And mayhap I could find Adam at a ball. He must be in town already." Looking down at her now-bedraggled gown, her expression suddenly fell. "I've nothing clean enough to wear."

"My sister keeps gowns at our town house." His gaze

flicked over her, assessing. "One of them should fit you well enough."

"Ye have a town house?" Her hand came up to grip her amulet as her eyes clouded with confusion. "But—"

He distracted her with a big, smacking kiss. "Yes, I have a house here in town." He took her by the hand. "Come along, and I will show you."

Chapter Twenty

"There are so many people!" As Caithren and Jason jostled their horses through the teeming streets, she found herself astonished at the city called London. It seemed to sprawl forever, building after building, crammed between with animals, vehicles, and pedestrians. Huge gaudy signboards hung on heavy wrought-iron brackets, so far into the narrow streets that they appeared to block the air and sun. "London stinks," she added. "And 'tis very, very noisy."

Street vendors cried their wares from every corner and in between, calling colorful descriptions of mundane goods like matches, rat poison, and razors. Eatables and drinkables of every sort were offered as well, customers clustering to purchase from the criers' laden barrows. In a span of less than a minute, Cait's ears were assaulted with competing invitations to buy hot eels, pickled whelks, a singing bird, and asses' milk, resulting in an almost deafening hubbub. Performers danced on stilts to the beat of tambourines.

Above it all, she heard a man singing lustily to a gathered crowd. Dazed, she stopped to listen. "What is he doing?" she asked when Jason noticed she was missing and rode back to her.

"Teaching them new tunes. He's a ballad seller." A carriage squeezed by, edging his horse up against hers. "When he's finished, they'll buy sheets with the words for half a pence."

Caithren was amazed. Songs were old, passed down through the generations. She couldn't remember ever hearing a "new" song. "What if they cannot read?"

"Then they'll memorize the words. Running patterers sing news ballads, to pass on reports of murders and executions. But this fellow is selling the latest popular songs."

A flower girl strolled by with a basket, reciting a list of her posies in singsong rhyme. Bewildered, Cait shook her head. "How can anyone think in this city, with this din? Does anyone get anything done?"

Jason smiled as they turned a corner and rode onto a street bordering a busy parkland. She fully expected that his "town house" would turn out to be a garret in a questionable neighborhood. When he stopped before a four-story brick house with columns dividing a facade studded with large, crowned rectangular windows, she was confused.

"Is he tired?"

"Who?"

"Hamish. Your horse. Why are we stopping?" Turning, she glimpsed a vendor hawking fat brown sausages in the large square across the street. "Oh, of course. You're hungry."

Jason laughed. "We had breakfast not two hours ago." He slid off his horse and lifted his arms to help Caithren down from hers. "No, I'm not hungry." His hands still resting lightly at her waist, he took a deep breath. "I . . . have something to explain to you."

She stared up at him. "Aye?"

Releasing her, he swept the red wig off his head and finger-combed his hair. "I've been less than completely honest with you, and—"

At the same time a liveried stableman rounded the corner to take their horses, one of the home's double front doors swung open, and a tall, thin butler poked his nose out. "Lord Cainewood—what a surprise."

He couldn't possibly be as surprised as Caithren was when Jason answered to the name. "Yes, Goodwin, I've found myself in town for a few days. I apologize for failing to send word."

"No problem a'tall, my lord." The butler eyed Cait with interest. "And the lady—"

"The lady will be lodging here as well."

"Jason?" she whispered. Jason was . . . a *lord*? And this was his house? Her mind reeled. Goodwin held the door open wide, and Jason ushered her inside. She stopped dead on the threshold, staring at the home's interior. The huge windows made it lighter inside than any house she'd ever seen. Carved flowers and ribbons decorated the pale-painted plaster walls. A wide staircase curved gracefully up to the next floor.

She turned to Jason. "Michty me, what kind of a lord are ye? A prince?"

"Nothing so exalted." He offered her an apologetic smile. "A marquess."

She blinked, trying to absorb it all. Her legs felt shaky. "You'll excuse me if I need to sit for a moment." Spotting a pair of brocade chairs in the entry, she made her way over and lowered herself into one of them. A marquess. Her head spun at the mere thought. In the name o' the wee man, she certainly couldn't picture her very-Scottish self the object of an English marquess's love. Not that Jason—Lord Whoever—would ever really love her. The blasted man didn't believe a word she said.

She looked over at him, trying to focus her eyes. The room seemed too bright. "Who are ye? The Marquess of What?"

"Cainewood. A castle and lands down south." He set the wig on a small gilt and marble table. "I told you about it, remember?"

The butler discreetly disappeared while Caithren digested the information. And here she'd made fun of him "pretending" to be a nobleman. Well, he'd deserved it then, didn't he? "I live in a castle as well," she said, lifting her chin. "And my father was a baronet."

"I know. You've told me."

"Ye believe me, then?" He shrugged, the telltale red starting to stain his face. But she wasn't going to feel sympathy for his predicament. To the contrary, she felt like lashing out with her claws bared. "Well, I've always told ye the truth. Which is more than I can say for ye."

"I never told you anything that wasn't true." He moved close and put a hand on her shoulder. His green eyes begged her to understand. "I just—left out some details."

"Details?" She pinned him with her best disdainful look. "That is the most glaring understatement I've ever heard." She closed her eyes, put her fingers to her forehead, opened them again, and looked up. "My mam always said that credit lost is akin to broken glass."

"Pardon?" His jaw tensed, and he stared at the toes of his black boots. "I understand the words, for once, but the meaning eludes—"

"Broken trust can never be restored."

"Cait . . ." He went down on a knee before her, and she almost—almost—felt sorry for him.

But she felt too betrayed. "With all the deception that's passed between us—"

Glimpsing something over her shoulder, he stood and pulled away. She looked up and back to see a man and a woman trooping down the stairs.

"Jason!" the female exclaimed. She ran down the last few steps and threw herself into his arms, hugging and kissing him enthusiastically. "Are you healing well, then? Any news on the Gothards? My God"—she reached out and touched his face—"what happened to your hair and your mustache?"

"Let me guess," Caithren said sarcastically, rising from the chair. "Your wife." She wouldn't put it past him at this point, no matter he'd taken her to his bed.

The woman was petite and prettier than she was, with dark red hair and a fine complexion.

"No," Jason said. "This is my sister, Kendra. And my brother Ford," he added as the gentleman, a tall man with long, wavy brown hair and the bluest eyes she had ever seen, made it down the stairs. "Ford, Kendra, this is Caithren Leslie."

"Caithren, is it?" Kendra said with a wide smile. "Familiar, aren't we?"

Cait curtsied, but Kendra rushed forward and kissed her on both cheeks. "She's lovely, Jason. Where did you find her?"

"Kendra—"

"Ye misunderstand, Lady Kendra. I am only traveling with your brother due to some . . . unforseen circumstances."

"You're Scots," Kendra said. "I can hear it in your voice."

"Aye, and—"

"Scots?" Ford interrupted. He looked her up and down with keen interest, his gaze settling on her amulet. "Might you go by the nickname of Emerald?"

"No," Cait said firmly. "My name is Caithren. Not Emerald." She sent Jason a glare, half expecting him to protest.

"Emerald?" Kendra scoffed. "As in Emerald MacCallum? Look at her, will you?" She put a hand on Cait's arm. "Men can be so thickheaded at times. I apologize for my twin. He is more thickheaded than most."

Cait's lips thinned. "No more than Jase."

"Jase?" Kendra turned to him. "You allow her to call you Jase? Now I *know* you're in love."

Cait blushed so wildly, she could only hope the color would wear off by evening. But Jason ignored Kendra's cheeky comment. "What are you doing here?" he asked his siblings.

Ford sighed. "I'm sorry to say I've been unable to discover the name of the man you . . . er—"

"Killed," Jason supplied succinctly.

"Um, yes. But I turned Chichester upside down, found a tavern the man had frequented along with two friends. A serving maid there remembered overhearing the men saying they were going to Lord Darnley's wedding. Tomorrow, is it not? So we ought to be able to talk to them then and find out who the man—say, are you all right?"

"I'm fine," Jason said woodenly, though nothing could be further from the truth. Tomorrow Cait would learn he'd killed her brother, whether he told her or not. He should have confessed the minute he'd realized the truth; surely his soul would be the better for it now . . .

But he'd promised her a night to remember, and he'd not ruin it for her just to ease his own anguish. She'd have her one night of happiness, before their world collapsed on them both.

"I thank you for making the inquires," he told Ford. "Excellent work."

"And what of Gothard?" Ford asked.

"Still unresolved. 'Tis a long tale, best discussed over dinner." He turned to his sister. "How fares Mary? Is she—"

"Dead? No." Kendra grinned. " 'Tis a miracle, the doctor says, but she's getting better."

"Better?" A rush of hope coursed through him. "She awakened?"

"Yes. Her speech is slow, and she couldn't walk at first; she has trouble walking still. But she improves a little every day. We know not if she'll ever—"

"She's alive." Jason made his way to the chair that Cait had vacated and dropped into it. "That is all that matters."

Kendra walked over and took his limp hands from his lap. "You feel a responsibility for her, I know. But it wasn't your fault."

"He feels a responsibility for everything." Cait crossed her arms. "I've been trying to cure him of that, to no avail."

"A worthy project." Kendra dropped Jason's hands and went to Cait, a conspiratorial gleam in her eye. "Have you managed to get him to do anything just for the hell of it? Not to accomplish some specific goal?"

"Well, we did chase a ghost. And—"

"Cait," Jason groaned.

"We went to a fair, but that was to accomplish something—to buy me some things. And—oh!" She grinned. "He danced with the Gypsies. But only for a few seconds."

"He danced with the Gypsies?" A flash of curiosity crossed Kendra's face. "I will need to hear more of this."

Jason rose. "Cait does not have time to gossip with you. We have plans. Kendra, have you knowledge of a ball this evening?"

"Lady Carson is hosting one." She regarded him with puzzled light green eyes. "But why?"

"Lady Carson's balls are boring," Ford put in.

"They are not," Kendra argued. "And I've heard Charles will be in attendance this eve. But why?" she repeated.

"I've promised Caithren an evening of London entertainment. She's not been here before. And no," he added, forestalling her question, "you may not come along." He frowned at her pout, then realized 'twould be hours until evening and the ball. Too many hours—too much time for his sister to question Cait. "What is playing at Lincoln's Inn Fields Theatre?" he asked.

"Dryden's *The Feign'd Innocence*." Kendra brightened. " 'Tis hilarious. Ford and I saw it yesterday, but I'd love to see it again."

He smiled benignly, deliberately misunderstanding her. "Maybe Ford will take you again tomorrow."

"I've nothing to wear," Caithren reminded him.

"Oh!" Kendra's eyes sparkled with intrigue that almost made Jason regret his plans. "I can take care of that."

"Choose quickly," he said. "We need time for dinner, too."

" 'Tis not even noon yet." His sister's smile was all too knowing. "We'll eat first, and there will be plenty of time to dress when we're finished."

Kendra's chamber upstairs was a confection of mint green decor. She strode to her carved-oak clothes press, threw the doors open wide, and perused the gowns hung on pegs inside. "Green, blue, purple?" She turned to Caithren. "Which do you fancy?"

"I-I dinna ken," Cait stuttered. "I've never been to a ball."

"No?" Kendra riffled through a few more, then pulled out a gown in a deep, rich rose and held it up to Caithren's cheek. "Lovely," she declared, dragging Cait over to a gilt-framed pier glass. "Look."

Caithren had to admit it flattered her complexion, but 'twas the most elaborate gown she had ever seen. Gold threads were woven into the fabric, making a diamond pattern, and the underskirt was of shimmering gold tissue. "I couldn't possibly wear this," she breathed, wishing all the while that she could. Even though it was English.

"Don't be a goose." Kendra tossed the gown on the curtained four-poster bed. "Not only can you wear it, you can keep it as well. It looks hideous on me with this red hair. I cannot imagine what possessed me to order it." Her hand reached to lift a hank of Caithren's straight mane. "What beautiful colors. I'd wager you could wear anything with this."

She let go, and Cait watched in the mirror as the wheaten strands cascaded back to her shoulders. Mayhap her hair *was* pretty, out of braids. She'd never paid it much attention other than to bind it out of the way.

"I will have Jane in to curl it," Kendra decided.

"Jane?" Caithren's voice sounded feeble to her own ears. Too much had happened in the past two hours— too much had changed. Her world was off-kilter.

"Jane is my maidservant." Kendra led Cait to a marble-topped dressing table and sat her down. "But I'll not call her in until after we've finished with the cosmetics," she said, pulling open a drawer filled with little boxes and bottles.

"Cosmetics?" Cait felt as though she'd been spirited to a country more foreign than England, even. France, perchance.

"Do you not wear cosmetics in Scotland?"

"Michty me, nay. I've got nowhere to wear any *to*."

"What a shame." Kendra clucked her tongue. "I think you'll be happier here with Jason."

"With Jason?" Caithren jumped from the chair. "Whyever would ye think I would be with Jason—I mean, Lord Cainewood?"

"Caithren . . ." Kendra pushed her back onto the embroidered velvet seatcover. "You are called Caithren, are you not?"

"Aye," she said weakly. "Or Cait."

"Cait, then. I like that better. Jason calls you Cait, does he not?" She sifted through the drawer and came out with a small box. "Anyway, as I was about to say, you can protest all you wish, but the fact is I've got two good eyes in my head."

"Two eyes?" Cait's own eyes bugged out in the mirror as she watched Kendra fluff white powder onto her face. She couldn't believe she was allowing this, but she was still too shocked and overwhelmed to protest.

Jason was a marquess.

"Two eyes," Kendra said firmly. "And I'd only need one to see the two of you belong together." She set down the powder and took up a stick of kohl. "Why, I've not seen Jason squire a woman to a ball since—since forever. Or at least since we were exiled on the Continent." She leaned closer. "Look up."

"So he doesn't have a . . ." Cait couldn't think how to put it, and besides, 'twas difficult to concentrate when someone was drawing under your eye. It tickled. "What I mean is—"

"Heavens, no." Kendra laughed and stood up straight. "Of course he's been known to go home with women—he's a man, after all—but he never bothers to take a special one anywhere. Most especially not to a ball. I have to beg him on my knees to chaperone me as it is. He hates the things."

Now this was interesting information. But Cait found her hopes rising, and she kent that wasn't a good idea. Not with all the half-truths and deceit. She didn't know what to think of Jason anymore. "He just feels sorry for all he put me through," she said.

"And what was that? Do tell." Kendra smudged some color onto Cait's cheeks.

Caithren had never had a female friend close to her age, and though she barely knew her, she reckoned Kendra could be a good one. "He saw me confronting the Gothard brothers," she found herself explaining, "and decided I was some woman named Emerald MacCallum."

"Him, too?" Kendra opened a wee pot. "Is he daft?"

"Exactly what I said. Then, under this preposterous misconception, he tricked me into missing the public coach, to keep me from getting to Gothard first and ruining his chance at revenge."

"Revenge?" Kendra bit her lip and swirled her finger in the pot. "He wants to see Gothard put to trial; he has no intention of murdering the man."

Caithren shook her head. "Ye are wrong about that. He wants the reward."

Her fingertip coated with shiny balm, Kendra paused. "Cait, he *posted* the reward."

"Oh." Of course. She ought to have been bright enough to put two and two together upon learning his identity, but her brain was still reeling. "Nevertheless," she said, "he intends to see the cur dead."

"Jason? Nary a chance." With a decisive finger, Kendra slicked the gloss onto Cait's slack lips. "Jason would do anything to avoid murder. 'Tis not in his nature to do harm." She capped the pot. "He's out for justice, no more. And to see that no one else suffers at the man's hands . . ." A small smile emerged on her expressive face. "Like you."

"Like me?" Caithren glimpsed herself in the mirror, then quickly looked away. She looked a stranger. A mysterious stranger. At this moment, her feelings were as strange as her appearance. "I'll admit he claimed as much, but d'ye truly think Jason took me along to *protect* me?"

"I'd bet my life on it. 'Tis a very Jason thing to do. You don't know him like I do, Cait." She rummaged in the drawer again and came out with a burnt cork. "Sit still. I'm going to use this to darken your lashes. It might feel funny."

Nothing could feel as funny as Cait's stomach did now. Could Kendra possibly be right? That would mean she'd been wrong, all along. About more than just his identity. Those qualities she'd glimpsed shining through—

"Look," Kendra said, pressing a hand mirror into Caithren's limp fingers.

She raised it to her face. "By all the saints," she whispered. She hardly recognized herself. Or rather, she did, but she never thought she'd look so . . .

"Beautiful," Kendra said, though Cait had been thinking *English.* Kendra flicked through a small box with a fingertip. "Hold still." While Caithren watched in the mirror, Kendra stuck a tiny black heart on her cheek. "There," she said. "You're perfect."

"What is it?" Cait lowered the mirror and felt for the little heart.

With an indulgent smile, Kendra pulled away Cait's hand. "Careful, or you'll dislodge it. 'Tis a beauty patch." She shook the patch box. "Would you like another?"

Cait felt foreign enough as it was. English. "Nay, though I thank ye." Her hand went to her amulet.

Kendra's gaze followed. "My, that looks old."

"It is."

"It won't match the gown. Would you like to borrow some rubies?" She lifted the lid to a lovely enameled box on the dressing table. Jewels flashed as she delved inside.

Cait reached to shut it. "I appreciate the offer, but nay. This belonged to my mother, and I never take it off."

"Are you certain?" A frown creased Kendra's forehead, then she smiled. "I can see that you are. I'll just get Jane, then. I've no talent with hair." She walked from the room, leaving Cait alone.

Again she took up the mirror. English. She looked very, very English. She put a hand to her quaking stomach.

Jason was a marquess. Jason had been trying to protect her.

Kendra rushed back in with a plain-faced woman at her heels that Caithren assumed was Jane. " 'Tis past two o'clock already. The play will start in less than an hour, and we must dress you before Jane does your hair." She swept the gown off the bed while Jane put curling tongs to heat at the edge of the banked fire on Kendra's hearth.

Cait's fingers shook as she detached her purple stomacher and loosened the laces beneath. What was she doing in London, dressing in English clothes, planning an evening out with an English marquess? Who would have thought, less than a month ago in Da's study—

Her thoughts were interrupted by Kendra's impatient hands drawing the turquoise gown down and off. She touched Cait's bandage with a fingertip. "What happened here?"

"I was cut. And then I failed to care for it properly, so it festered and had to be stitched."

"Ouch." Kendra's face scrunched up in sympathy, then turned speculative. "And I've a feeling there's more to the story. But it will have to wait until tomorrow. You'll not want to be late."

Jane came to help, and together they lifted the rose gown and dropped it over Cait's head, settling it carefully to avoid damaging the artfully applied cosmetics. The top was a wee bit loose, but the cloth-of-gold stomacher took care of that, pushing her breasts up to fill it. She could only wonder what Kendra's more generous chest looked like in the low, square neckline. Scandalous, she imagined.

The gown was stiff and heavy. Very English.

By the time Jane was done with the curling iron, Caithren's hair looked English as well. Long curls draped to her shoulders in front and gathered in back, entwined with rose-colored ribbons. With Kendra standing behind her, she stared at herself in the pier glass.

"I look English," she whispered, watching her glossed lips form the words.

"Is that bad?" In the mirror, Kendra looked worried.

"I dinna ken," Caithren said. "Last month I would have thought so, but now . . . I am only confused."

Kendra took her by the shoulders and turned her to face her. Familiar eyes, the same shape as Jason's but lighter, searched Cait's. "We're not evil," she said. "The English."

"Not all of ye, anyway." Cait looked down and

straightened her overskirt until Kendra, with one strong finger, lifted her chin. A gesture that smacked of Jason.

"Not most of us," she said. "And certainly not my brother." She pulled Cait into a hard embrace that took her by surprise. "Give him a chance," she whispered in her ear. "He needs you."

Chapter Twenty-one

"You look stunning, Cait. I expect you'll be the talk of the ball." As she and Jason walked catercorner through the square toward the Lincoln's Inn Fields Theatre, Cait saw him shoot her a sidewise glance, probably the hundreth since she'd come down the stairs wearing Kendra's clothes and cosmetics. When she finally met his gaze, his gorgeous green eyes smoldered. "Though I must say," he added, "I think I prefer you barefoot with your hair loose and a daisy chain about your neck."

She almost tripped, even though Kendra's gown was a couple inches too short, and she'd thought she was becoming rather competent walking in the absurd English high heels.

He took her arm to escort her across the busy street. "You're quiet," he said, his gaze safely fastened on the traffic. "If it's because I deceived you, I'm very sorry. But I had my reasons. Though damned if I can remember what they were."

"My head is awhirl," she admitted as they dodged a sedan chair. "I never thought to find myself in London at all, let alone attending a play and a ball. I mean to enjoy it. Though I fully intend to be angry with ye. Tomorrow."

"I don't doubt it," he said dryly. He led her up to a flat-fronted brick building with the same tall rectangular windows as most of the others around the square.

"The windows are enormous." Cait looked up in awe. "The building must hold a thousand people."

"About right," he said, although she had been fooling. A *thousand* people. 'Twas mind-boggling. "I don't suppose you see Palladian windows in Scotland. As for the size of the theater, it used to be a tennis court."

"A tennis court?" A wooden sign leaned against the wall near the entrance, advertising the day's performance. Caithren read aloud. " 'Sir William D'Avenant presents The Duke's Company in *Sir Martin Mar-All, or The Feign'd Innocence*, by John Dryden, adapted from Molière's *L'étourdi*, as translated by William Cavendish, Duke of Newcastle.' Whew. I am suitably impressed."

"Nothing like London pretension." Jason laughed as he ushered her toward the entrance. "People are saying the play was conceived by Newcastle, but *corrected* by Dryden." He counted out eight shillings and handed them to the doorkeeper, "A side box, please."

Inside, the large windows allowed plenty of afternoon light to illuminate both the stage and the patrons. "We must make haste." Jason sought out their box. "The play will be starting momentarily. It must finish before dark."

A symphony played onstage, but Cait could hardly hear the tune over the theater's noisy assemblage. People in the middle gallery were seated for the most part, but those in the pit were milling around, talking and laughing, some of them even fighting. Scantily dressed orange girls circulated among the crowd, offering their sweet, juicy treats in a singsong chant. Caithren suspected some of the young bucks were buying more than fruit.

The upper tier had no seats—'twas crammed with people leaning over the rails. Jason led her up a flight of stairs and into a quite-civilized private box that sat off to one side, equipped with four chairs. No one else was seated there yet, so they took the two in front.

"Never did I think to see so many people in one

place," Cait said as she adjusted her skirts. "And so
many sorts of people as well. I imagined only the
wealthy would attend the theater in London."

"At the price of one shilling"—Jason gestured up to
the top—"many can afford to be entertained. Footmen
and coachmen are admitted free near the end."

"Who would want to come at the end?" she wondered. "Ye wouldn't ken what was happening."

He took her hand. "Most folk don't seem to pay attention anyway." And he was right. Despite a lot of
hush-hushing that rippled through the crowd when the
curtains opened, no one seemed to quiet down much
when the play began. The patrons in the pit scrambled
to take seats on the backless benches, and Cait was distracted by more than one brawl before everyone was
settled.

The play was a piece of humor, a complete farce from
one end to the other. Caithren found herself laughing
not only at the actors, but also at the comments and
suggestions shouted to them from the audience. "Look
behind you!" someone yelled, and she dissolved in mirth
when the performer did just that. The spectators' robust
criticism was entertaining as well.

A few minutes into the performance, a couple entered
their box and sat behind them. Jason and Cait both
turned around and smiled, and Cait's eyes widened at
the haughty lady's gown. Fashioned of screaming yellow
satin, the gown's train was so long it trailed into the
corridor, and the neckline was so low, Cait wouldn't have
been surprised if the woman's ample bosom popped out.
Jason took a look at her face and started to laugh, but
she squeezed his hand until he settled down. Before long
she was engrossed in the story and forgot about the
woman altogether.

The stage was unlike any she'd ever seen. There was
a painted background, and the first time it moved, she

gasped. "I take it there is no moving scenery back home," Jason whispered.

"There is no scenery at all. Traveling players come to Insch sometimes and perform in whatever place is handy. I've never been in a real theater." She watched, fascinated, while the stagehands manipulated the scene. The curtains weren't closed for this, and actresses sang and danced at the front of the stage, to entertain the audience during the change. Many people whistled and cheered, apparently enjoying the between-scenes acts more than the play itself.

Though she laughed at all the buffoonery, Caithren's attention wandered between the play and Jason's hand in hers. After a while, he moved his chair closer, and the press of his thigh against her skirts was distracting. She could feel his warmth. When he draped his arm across the back of her chair, she laid her head on his shoulder and sighed, wondering if ever she'd see him again. Tomorrow she'd find Adam, and it would be time to head back home. Adam might even attend the ball tonight. A tiny part of her almost hoped he wouldn't be there after all.

All too soon it was over, and they rose to depart. "I have never laughed so much in all my life," she told Jason. "I thank ye for bringing me."

He gave her a smile that sent her pulses to racing. "Nothing could make me happier than seeing you enjoy yourself."

A throat cleared behind them, and he swung her around and introduced her to their box companions, Lord and Lady Martindale, who it turned out were going to the ball as well. Lady Martindale leaned close, her sausagelike fingers reaching for Caithren's amulet. "A lovely, large emerald," she sniffed, "but my heavens, the mounting looks like it's been around since the Crusades."

Cait snatched it from her hand and held it posses-sively. "It has."

The woman's blonde curls seemed to shudder with her as she pulled back in surprise. "Fashionable people have their jewels reset every few years, dear."

"I'm not fashionable. I'm Scottish."

Jason stifled a laugh while Lord Martindale took his wife by the arm. "That will do, my dear," he said, mak-ing Cait a small bow. Lady Martindale looked at her curiously as they said their good-byes and took leave.

Jason took Cait's hand again and led her to the stairs. "Lady Martindale is wondering what you're doing with a provincial Scot," she commented.

"Bosh." He paused to let his gaze wander her figure-hugging gown. "You look damned English tonight."

"Not when I open my mouth."

He grinned at that and kissed her smack on the lips. He was acting mighty strange this eve, as though he were determined to show her a good time even if it killed him. She wondered what was responsible for this sudden change in attitude, even as she laughed and pulled him out of the theater.

"Hmm." Jason glanced around at the many inquiring faces that swung toward the doorway as a footman ush-ered them through it. "I suspect Lady Martindale has arrived before us."

Before Caithren could comment, their hostess, Lady Carson, rushed up to greet them. "Lord Cainewood? Why, I hardly recognized you without the mustache. You look like your brother." She smoothed her lavender lace skirt. "Do come in."

Cait could only gawk as the tall, elegant woman led them through an enormous entry hall and past a few other large, well-lit chambers, one set aside for card playing, another for the ladies to freshen up. In yet an-other room, long tables groaned with food and drink. If

Cait had thought Jason's house was impressive, she was positively bowled over by Lady Carson's abode. It could only be described as a mansion.

They were ushered into a chamber that Caithren thought looked out of a fairy tale, where the ball was in full swing. Under the light of hundreds of candles in chandeliers overhead, masses of glittering guests danced, ate, and conversed. The ballroom opened onto a vast garden that she was shocked to find in the middle of London.

Lady Carson's thin lips curved in a polite smile as she turned to Jason. "Your attendance is a delightful surprise. And this is Lady . . . ?"

Jason blinked, and Cait saw his freckles appearing. He was definitely put on the spot. "Caithren Leslie," she piped up for herself. "Of Leslie Manor, by Insch in Scotland." She'd made up the "manor" part, but her father *was* a baronet.

"Lady Leslie," Lady Carson gushed. " 'Tis a pleasure to make your acquaintance."

"Lady Caithren." Jason corrected the name, but not, Cait noticed, the unwarranted title. "My companion is yet unmarried."

"Ah, I see."

Cait thought Lady Carson saw all too much. "I'm glad of your acquaintance," she told her, her gaze wandering the room. Many faces were turned their way, and ladies were obviously gossiping behind fancy upheld fans. She wondered if they were discussing Jason's new look. Or her, his mysterious companion.

She was certain she'd find Adam here. He must be in London by now, and he would never miss a social occasion like this.

"Lady Carson," she ventured. "I am wondering if my brother is on your guest list. Sir Adam Leslie?"

"Adam Leslie? Not that I'm aware of. Though my balls are often attended by many uninvited." She looked as if she were proud of that fact. And apparently, she was thrilled to have a new face at her party, because she was already looking around for someone to introduce Cait to. "Ah, Lady Haversham." She snagged a pale, elfin woman by the arm. "May I present a guest of Lord Cainewood's, Lady Caithren. From Scotland," she added in a conspiratorial voice, as though that fact alone should be of significant interest.

"I am glad of your acquaintance," Cait said again with a little curtsy. "I am wondering if you've seen my brother, Adam—"

"If you'll excuse us," Jason interjected smoothly, "I've someone I need to talk to. Ladies." He nodded politely and took Caithren's arm, dragging her back to the entry hall, which was mostly deserted now that the most-anticipated guests—Jason and Caithren, apparently— had arrived. He pulled her into the shadows behind a large post and gathered her into his arms. Before she could voice a protest, his mouth came down on hers, and anything she might have said was smothered by his lips.

Caithren's heart raced as his tongue plundered her mouth. She kissed him back with wild abandon. He truly was a changed man tonight, but she wasn't sure she wanted to know why. She'd rather just enjoy it for now.

When he finally drew back, she stared at him, dumb-founded. Her knees felt like pudding, but his strong arms held her up when she would have slumped against the tapestried wall. "I've been wanting to do that since we got to London," he said.

"Oh, aye?" She blinked at him, confused. "Ye had ample opportunity in your carriage on the way across town. It took forever to negotiate the traffic."

He frowned. "I'd other things on my mind." His fingers traced her jaw, then he tapped the little black heart on her cheek and leaned to kiss her forehead. "Come, let us dance."

As quickly as he'd dragged her out of the ballroom,

he pulled her back in. The musicians were playing a sedate tune, the melody accompanied by scrapes and taps of the dancers' shoes and the soft swish of the ladies' gowns as they traversed the polished-wood floor in an elegant configuration.

Caithren licked her lips and cast a worried glance at Jason. "I-I cannot dance."

He smiled down at her, prodding her closer to the dance floor with a hand at her back. "I seem to remember you dancing with the Gypsies."

"But not like this!" she exclaimed, tripping over the blasted high heels.

He caught her. " 'Tis a simple pattern. I'll give you two minutes to watch. Two," he warned with mock severity.

The music was eight beats, and the dancers balanced on their toes. Short gliding steps, a change of balance, a pause every third and seventh beat. Cait thought she had it figured out, until suddenly the women ran 'round the men and they all did a little hop. "I cannot tell what they're doing," she complained. Just then the dancers bowed and curtsied "Anyway, 'tis over," she said with not a little relief.

"Ah, but there will be another."

Following some discordant re-tuning, the musicians launched into a country dance, not so different from what Cait was used to at her village dances in Leslie. "This one I can do," she declared and let Jason swirl her into the crowd.

All her reservations melted away. 'Twas heaven being in his arms, and it didn't even seem to bother him in front of all society. Though the dance was energetic, she couldn't keep her eyes from his clean-shaven face. "Ye dinna look like Ford."

"Ford?" They crossed arms and switched sides. "You have the most disconcerting habit of starting a conversation midstream. Where did that come from?"

"Lady Carson. She said ye look like your brother."

"Ah." He twirled her around. "She referred to my other brother, Colin. And yes, I expect with my hair cut and without my mustache, we do look somewhat alike. Green eyes and black hair. He's always kept his shorter. Prefers convenience over fashion, in all things."

"I like him already." The music came to a close, and she curtsied. "What other siblings are ye hiding?"

"Only a sister-in-law. Colin is married." He led her from the dance floor. "Her name is Amethyst, but we call her Amy."

"The woman who gave ye the watch."

"That's right." Another country dance followed the first, and he swept her back out and into the double line, leaving her with the women while he stood across from her with the men. "Amy used to be a jeweler. Or rather, she still is a jeweler, but without a shop. Colin is building her a workshop at Greystone, their home."

"Greystone," she murmured, clapping her hands and then touching them to the women's on either side of her. She remembered him chuckling at seeing that name on an inn. "Your brother married a commoner?"

He smiled down at her. "We Chases don't play by the rules."

"I've noticed." The dance separated them for a moment, then they came back together. "Ye certainly dinna play backgammon by the rules."

"I am not a cheater. If I'm ahead five games, 'tis naught but proof of my skill."

"Ha!" Linking arms, they skipped in a circle. "Ye distracted me with your bare chest. That is hardly playing fair."

She was getting breathless by the time a portly gentleman tapped Jason on the shoulder. "May I claim the pleasure?" he asked.

Jason didn't look very happy. But he pulled Caithren

from the dance and introduced her to the man, a Lord Berkeley.

" 'Tis glad I am to make your acquaintance," Cait said. "And by any chance, have ye seen my bro—"

"Beg pardon," Jason interrupted. "We must be off." And he propelled Caithren back to the entry and the shadow of the post.

"Wait." With two hands on his chest, she stopped him when he would have kissed her again. "Why dinna ye want me to ask after my brother?"

"I only want to kiss you," he protested, drawing her close. His warm breath washed over her face, and she felt dizzy. "I . . . I know not what's come over me, but I cannot keep my hands off you." To demonstrate, he ran them down her back, all the way to her bottom. Her pulse sped up, but she wasn't going to fall for this seduction.

"D'ye think my head laces up the back?"

His hands froze in their motion. "Pardon?"

"Dinna take me for a fool. You're trying to keep me from my brother, and I want to know why."

He caught her gaze with his. "I want only to be with you tonight. Besides, do you really think you'd fail to notice your brother were he here?"

He had a point. And when his lips captured hers, she was afraid he made that point completely. So much so that she was tempted to drag him down to the floor and make him follow through. One more time before she found Adam and headed back home.

The footman opened and closed the front door, admitting a new guest, but Caithren hardly noticed the footsteps or low murmur of the servants' awed acknowledgments. Jason's tongue was tracing her mouth, his teeth were nibbling her lower lip. She wound her arms around his neck and twined her fingers in his thick hair.

"Cainewood, is that you?" The voice was deep, the

words drawled and amused. " 'Od's fish, I cannot wait to see the lady who has taken your fancy."

Caithren pulled away and stared up at a tall, dark stranger. Heat flooded her cheeks and arousal and embarrassment made her feel weak as a newborn bairn.

Jason turned her to face the man square on.

"Egads," the man said. "What happened to your hair and face?"

"A long story, best told another time. Sire, this is Caithren Leslie." The fact that he hadn't called her by the invented "Lady" title was not lost on Cait, even in her confused state. "Caithren, King Charles."

King Charles? She felt the blood drain from her face. Jason supported her with one steady arm. " 'T-tis pleased I am to make your acquaintance," she said by rote. She caught herself before reciting the "have ye seen my brother" part. "Y-your Majesty," she added instead with a tremulous smile.

The King reached down to take her hand and raise it to his lips for a kiss. His eyes burned into hers, a sensual, compelling black. "A pleasure to meet you, my dear. The woman who captures Cainewood's heart is a special one, indeed."

He was still holding her hand. Her heart was beating like it wished to escape her chest. She wanted to drop into the intricate parquet floor. Which was ridiculous. He was but a man.

"Love's wan e'e and ower deef," she blethered.

The King dropped her hand. "Pardon?"

"Caithren likes to quote her mother's favorite sayings," Jason explained. "Scottish wisdom."

"I'm of Scottish descent, but sorely lacking in wisdom." In a gesture that reminded her of Jason, Charles stroked his thin mustache. "And this saying means . . . ?"

"Love is almost blind and a bit deaf," Cait interpreted.

With that, he threw back his head and laughed, a great roar that rattled the enormous chandelier overhead.

"She's a gem," he told Jason. He peered over their shoulders and frowned. " 'Od's fish, Barbara and Frances are at it again. I'd best be off." And he made his way toward the ballroom, a commanding figure in dark red velvet trimmed with some sort of fur instead of ribbons.

Cait practically collapsed against Jason's chest. "Barbara and Frances?" she asked weakly.

"His two mistresses of the moment." When she looked up at him in shock, he just laughed. "Come along, I think you could do with some wine." He guided her down the hall toward the refreshment room.

"I didn't mean to imply there was love—I mean, that ye— that line just popped into my head, and—"

"Think nothing of it."

She halted in her tracks and turned to confront him. "And why did ye not tell me the *King* might be here? He must've thought I was sodie-heid"—at the look on his face, she translated—"feather-brained, ye ken?"

"Kendra did say Charles would be in attendance." He led her to a table and picked up a cup. "If you'll remember."

Caithren wracked her brain while he handed her the cup and lifted a gigantic, solid-silver ladle that must have weighed ten pounds if it were an ounce. "Aye, that is exactly what she said. *Charles* would be in attendance. As though he were a personal friend of the family or some such—"

"He is."

She dropped the cup, then jumped back as it splashed and rolled under the table.

"We spent years together with him in exile, after the Civil War. In abject poverty, I might add. The Restoration restored more than Charles's throne—he saw our property restored as well. And he settled titles on my two younger brothers, who otherwise would have—"

"How was I supposed to ken such a thing, ye daftie? In the name o' the wee man, the longer I'm around ye, the more confused I get." She looked down. "And now I've gone and ruined Lady Kendra's fancy gold shoes."

Jason only smiled. "So I'll buy her another pair or three." He filled a second cup and curled her fingers around it. "Here. Drink."

Served from an enormous silver punch bowl shaped like a swan, the wine was spiced and delicious. She drank two cups of it, danced with Jason, then drank another. Her eyes never strayed too far from King Charles, so amazed was she that he was in the ballroom. But he didn't stay long. When he left, she sagged against Jason in something akin to relief, tempered with a healthy dose of awe. She had actually attended the same ball as King Charles. Cameron wasn't going to believe it.

Jason introduced her to Lady Castlemaine and Lord Arlington and the Duke of Buckingham. Everyone she'd ever heard of seemed to be here. Everyone but Adam.

She couldn't bring herself to be too sorry, though. Much as she wanted to see Adam and accomplish her goal, this night was too magical for her to really want such mundane matters to intrude.

Jason followed her when she staggered off the dance floor and over to a wall, leaning against the mantel of one of the immense fireplaces that flanked either end of the ballroom. They weren't lit tonight, which was a good thing, because the chamber was overly warm as it was.

A giddy little giggle bubbled out as she looked up at Jason. Surely no one in the room was as handsome as he, dressed in a dark green velvet suit that brought out his eyes, his own glossy black hair skimming his shoulders. The hair that she'd cut. She'd cut the hair of a marquess.

She giggled again at the memory. "Will ye fetch me another cup of wine?"

He grinned. "I think you're tipsy enough as it is."

Now that he mentioned it, her head reeled a wee bit, but she wouldn't admit it. " 'Tis only this glorious night. I will remember it forever, my lord."

"I'll not have you start 'my lording' me now. Not after what we've shared between us."

She blushed and giggled once more. "The wine? Please?"

"As you wish. Come along, though. We will get you some supper as well."

He guided her back to the refreshment room and handed her a knot biscuit. She nibbled on the braided, anise-flavored bread while he wandered down the buffet table, loading a plate with light fare: asparagus, cubed cheese, and an assortment of luscious fruits. He handed her the plate and filled two more cups with the heady spiced wine.

Cait looked around for two open seats. "Come along," Jason said, inclining his head toward the door. "I've another idea." Munching a cube of cheese, he led her back through the ballroom and out into the formal garden.

Burning torches were set about. Cait breathed deep of the night air, refreshingly cool compared to inside. Here and there a couple strolled the garden paths, but 'twas mostly quiet and serene. She followed him out beyond the bright light of the torches, where he sat himself on a low brick wall, handed her a cup, took the plate from her, and set it down.

"We cannot see out here," she complained, seating herself on the other side of the plate.

"Ah, but we cannot be seen, either." He plucked a raspberry from a small pile and popped it into his mouth. "Your eyes will adjust."

"They're adjusting already," she said, suddenly

lightheaded. The hand holding her cup was trembling a little, but she raised it and took a sip.

He selected another raspberry and brought it to her lips, running it back and forth across her mouth before he slipped it inside. Sweetness burst on her tongue as she bit into it, and he watched her swallow, then leaned across the plate to take her lips in a gentle kiss.

He pulled away an inch. "Shall we move back near the torches?"

"N-nay." She leaned closer, bringing her mouth to his again. With a satisfied chuckle, he brushed her lips, and his tongue flicked out to taste them. He sat back and sipped from his cup.

An asparagus spear made its way toward her mouth. She opened, and he fed it to her slowly. "Lovely night, is it not?"

"Mmmm." Anything more intelligible was beyond her at the moment.

"Are you sure you'd rather not go back inside?"

She shook her head. "Mmm-mmm." When the asparagus was gone, he leaned to kiss her again, taking her chin in one hand, plundering her mouth 'til she was breathless. He tasted of fruit and spiced wine, lust and man. A most heady combination.

"I cannot go back inside," she whispered. "I dinna think my legs would carry me."

"Are you cold?"

"Nay." But she was shivering. "Aye. I dinna ken."

"Come here, then." He took her hand, drew her off the wall. "I'll keep you warm." And spreading his knees, he eased her to stand between them.

With him still seated, their mouths were on a level. 'Twas not surprising when they met, hot and urgent. His hands wandered to her back, pressing her closer between his legs. She could feel the hardness of him beneath his breeches and her layers of skirts. There was an ache, a throbbing, low in her belly.

"I'm not cold now," she murmured against his mouth.

"No?" He drew back, sipped from his cup, tilted it to her lips so she could sip, too. Reaching for the plate, he selected a ripe strawberry, bit into it, and fed her the rest. Then another one, but this time he bit off a piece and covered her mouth with his, transferring it to her with a flick of his supple tongue.

Never had a strawberry tasted so delicious.

"Hmm . . ." He watched her, holding up the half-eaten berry. His eyes looked gray in the half-light, but she didn't miss the speculative gleam. He set down the berry, and his fingers moved to her stomacher, detaching the tabs at the top.

She licked her lips, tasting strawberry and Jason. "Wh-what—"

"Hush." He bent down on the stiff stomacher and something snapped.

"Jase!" It hung drunkenly away from her chest, folded in half and dangling.

He worked to loosen the laces beneath. "Kendra's seamstress can make another." His mouth warm and damp, he bent to kiss the swell of her breasts, and her heart lurched—she was certain he could feel it pounding. Her hands tangled in his hair, but he pulled away, carefully lowering the delicate chemise that shielded her breasts from his view.

"Christ," he bit out, watching her chest heave. Then he lifted the half-eaten berry and rubbed it over one taut nipple. Immediately his mouth moved to cover it, suckling off the sticky sweetness with a low groan that made the heat curl in Caithren's middle.

Lest her other nipple feel neglected, he doused it and fed off it, too, his teeth nipping the hard bud until a little moan escaped her lips. Then his mouth was on hers, wild and demanding, and his arms went around her, tugging her against his hard body. The blood rushed through her veins and straight to her head, and she was dizzy, but he was holding her up. One hand groped back to find the berry, and it was in their mouths, first hers, then his, until the pulp was gone and only a tart-sweetness was left on their fencing tongues.

A woman's high-pitched laugh startled Cait as a couple meandered close. She jerked away and held the stomacher up to her chest, panting.

Jason sat straight and calmly fed her another spear of asparagus. She didn't think she could chew and swallow, but somehow she managed, and he handed her a cup of wine to wash it down. Hers, his . . . it didn't matter. He drained the other cup himself.

Music tinkled from a distance then abruptly ceased, telling them a door had opened and closed, and the couple had reentered the ballroom. Jason unbuttoned his surcoat and spread the sides to envelop her, and Caithren dropped the stomacher and leaned in, pressing her breasts against his chest. She wedged her hands between them to loosen his cravat and work at the laces it hid, frantic to get to the warm skin beneath.

The slap and scrape of shoes told them more people were approaching.

"Bloody hell." Jason pulled away and hopped down from the wall. Straightening his disheveled clothing, he took the plate in one hand and Caithren's hand in the other. She held the stomacher up to cover her bosom, teetering on Kendra's high shoes while he led her through two small formal gardens and into a long, arched arbor, the lattice entwined with flowers and climbing vines.

Halfway through, he stopped and fed her a raspberry. And another. Laughing, still holding the dress up with both hands, she chewed and swallowed. Some juice ran down her chin, and he leaned to lick it off. A warm shiver rippled through her body. The plate between them, he nuzzled her neck, ran his tongue up to her ear. "You're delicious," he whispered there.

"You're very sleekit," she returned.

"I'm what?" His lips grazed her forehead.

"Very . . . charming."

He pulled back and fed her another raspberry. "I thought I was exasperating and unimaginative. Black and white."

"Exasperating, aye. But unimaginative . . ." She leaned forward to tongue another raspberry from his hand. "Ye are causing me to reevaluate. Ye seem to be changing. Or I may have been wrong."

"You? Wrong?" His laughter rang through the fragrant tunnel. He selected a few raspberries for himself and tossed them into his mouth. "Besides," he said around them, "the Gypsy woman said that *you* were supposed to be the creative lover. And beguiling, if I recall aright." He waggled his eyebrows at her.

" 'Twas my lover she was talking of, not me. And will ye never let that go? I told ye, she misjudged me."

"I think not." He pushed the last raspberry between her lips before she could disagree. "You're beguiling as hell, Caithren Leslie."

Her hands and the plate were all caught between them when he yanked her against him and sealed his mouth to hers. He was a new man tonight, she thought blissfully. Something had changed him. And if that something was her . . . could he love her? Because she knew in her heart that she loved him, no matter that he'd deceived her, and although she'd been unable to admit it, even to herself, until just now.

Her senses spun at the thought, and his kiss, and the intoxicating fragrance of the flowers overhead combined with Jason's distinctive scent. Just when she thought her knees would give out, yet another couple came sauntering down the arbor.

Jason pulled back with a muttered oath. "What are all these people doing out here?"

"I imagine they're wondering the same thing." Clutching the stomacher with one hand, Cait rubbed with the other at where the plate had pushed into her abdomen. "Why dinna ye put that down?"

"This?" An astonished look on his face, he held up the plate. "Whilst there are still three strawberries left?"

"Ye can get more inside."

"Ah, but I want them outside." His eyes glittered suggestively, while one fingertip lightly traced her lips.

"Please, Jase." She shivered, but not from the cold. "I dinna think I can stand up any longer. Not . . . not when ye do that."

"Hmm." Looking over her head, he craned his neck to see the back of the garden. "I spy a solution. Come along." And once more she found herself hurrying after him, holding both his hand and the top of her disheveled dress.

Through the arbor, a white gazebo shone in the moonlight. The only opening was in the back, so he walked her around, pulled her inside, and they were alone. Crickets chirped beyond the latticed walls, but other than that, the only sound they heard was each other's harsh breathing.

"Sit," Jason said, waving her to the bench that ran along the circular structure's walls. "Better?"

"Much. I was . . . feeling weak there, for a minute."

"Good." He set the plate aside and sat close by her. "I hope to have you feeling weaker still in a minute more." And he lifted her and sat her straddling his legs, facing him.

She gave a little start of surprise, then looked around, although she kent they were alone. "This feels wicked."

"Mmmm." He gave her one slow kiss. "That's the idea."

'Twas wicked but good. It gave her access to his face, which she covered with little kisses. And her hands were free to roam his body, although he was entirely too clothed to make her happy.

He laughed at her frustration, then tilted her head back. His mouth played in the sensitive hollows beneath her chin and along her throat. She reached under his surcoat to pull the shirt from his breeches. His skin beneath felt warm and taut, his back smooth and muscled.

When his hand snuck below her skirts and played along one thigh, her own hands froze on his body. "Is something wrong?" he asked, bending his head to draw the tip of his tongue along her bared breasts.

"I—not here—ye cannot . . . oooh," she said when he lifted her skirts and rearranged them, drawing her closer so she could feel him straining against his breeches. "This is very wicked."

"You think so?" He eased his hand from beneath her skirts and started loosening the laces of his breeches.

"Jason, ye cannot—"

"Watch me." His hands moved to her waist, lifted her, brought her back down slowly, slowly . . . and she felt him sliding into her.

He pierced her with his eyes at the same time he pierced her with his body. With a groan she couldn't quite believe came from her own throat, she felt herself opening, welcoming his warmth into hers. She licked her lips, closed her eyes, threw back her head.

"Oooh, this is very, very wicked."

He laughed low and licked a shivery line up her throat to her mouth, then settled a soft kiss on her lips. Pulling away, she looked down. He'd arranged her skirts quite carefully around them.

"No one can see," he whispered. "Even should they stumble upon us. Can you move?"

She did, slowly, feeling him slip out and back in. "Oh, michty me." Had anything ever felt so good?

"Excellent. Now stop." He held her hips in place with his hands. "I've a craving for a strawberry."

"Wh-what?" She tried to wiggle, but he wouldn't permit it.

"Hold still."

"I cannot!"

"Yes, you can." He lifted a berry, licked it slowly, bit off half. He held out the other half, but she shook her head. With a shrug, he finished it, then brought his mouth to hers, kissing her long and deep until all the strawberry flavor was gone and her whole world tasted like Jason.

Involuntarily she shifted her hips, but he stopped her and deprived her of his mouth.

"Not yet. Two left."

Feeling an incredible urgency where his body met hers, she let out a wee bleat of frustration. He took up the second strawberry.

She lurched forward and took it in one bite.

"Tsk, sweet." He eased her back down on him, grinning when she moaned at the forbidden friction—a grin so lethal, she wondered it wasn't illegal. "Now we'll have to make the final one last that much longer."

He drew the scratchy tip of the berry over her cheeks, her chin. Down into the valley of her cleavage. Around her bared shoulders to her back, where he traced a tickly pattern.

"What am I writing?" When she whimpered her impatience, his face hardened in a mock frown. "Concentrate."

Around, up, down . . . "Caithren!" she breathed with relief.

"Um-hmm."

A curve, up, down, a squiggle . . . "Jason?"

"Excellent. Now . . ."

A big, swooping line that enclosed all he'd written. Could it be . . . "A heart?"

"Brilliant. I shall have to reward you."

But their names in a heart were reward enough. Could it mean—

He bit into the berry then and smeared its juice across her chest and up her neck, his tongue following the sweet path all the way to her mouth. "Now," he murmured against her lips. His hands tightened on her hips and lifted—

And another couple stumbled into the gazebo, mouth to mouth, locked in a torrid embrace.

With a groan Caithren's head dropped to Jason's shoulder, and 'twas all she could do to keep tears from springing to her eyes. Jason stifled a strangled laugh. The couple didn't notice. They fell to the grass in the center and started tearing at one another's clothing.

"How could they?" Cait whispered. "Dinna they see us?"

"I suspect they are in no condition to care." A pained look came over his face. "I expect you do not feel the same?"

Her shocked look told him all he needed to know. "I was afraid of that," he whispered dryly, lifting her with a mighty heave and setting her on her feet. She smoothed down her skirts and spread them wide, doing her best to hide his efforts to lace his breeches, though the other couple was half undressed now and completely oblivious. Their panting moans filled the air, striking Caithren as sounding rather comical. Surely she and Jason didn't sound like that when they made love.

Did they?

Giggling, she followed him out of the gazebo. "This is not funny," he muttered, buttoning his surcoat in an only partially effective attempt to hide the bulge in his breeches. She giggled again, and he looked up, then grabbed her by the shoulders and hushed her with his lips.

That move, at least, was very effective.

"Shall we make for home?" he asked against her mouth, the words teasingly warm. "I believe I've had quite enough of this ball for tonight." With a mastery that made her pulse pound, his tongue swooped inside. "I've a bed at home. And . . ." He looked up and raised a brow. "Privacy."

Chapter Twenty-two

They ran through the gardens, laughing all the way, Caithren struggling to keep her clothes on as they went. A few feet from the door, Jason pulled her behind a hedge and turned her to face him. Together they got her chemise into place, her bodice laced, the stomacher attached—although it had an odd crease in the middle. She crossed her arms over it.

"There." Jason adjusted the curls on her shoulders and kissed her on the lips. "You look perfect."

"So do ye." Her gaze wandered down his body and back up. He pulled the surcoat tighter around his middle. "Almost." She giggled.

He loved the way she could go from hot passion to laughter in a split second. Though she could be as quick to anger as well, 'twas worth it. 'Twas what made her Caithren. 'Twas what made him want her. If only she could still love him after this night.

He knew he was asking for the impossible.

"But that other couple," she said, "they will have grass in their hair. They're not nearly as creative as ye are—as the Gypsy foretold ye would be." Her teasing grin caught at his heart. "That other couple will not look perfect."

"And Charles's courtiers will think nothing of it. So long as they are not man and wife." He drew her from behind the hedge, toward the glittering ballroom. "In these circles, men expect only their mistresses to be faithful."

"Is that so?" Her eyes held a challenge, and somehow, he thought she wouldn't put up with that sort of marriage.

If only it mattered.

He could but make the rest of this evening as perfect as it had been so far, and then hope against hope . . .

He took a deep breath and opened the door to the music and the dancing and all the people who'd done their best—albeit innocently—to keep him from loving Caithren this night.

Grabbing her hand, he strolled through the crowd, one purpose in mind. To get her into his arms again and finish what they'd started.

"Cainewood! I've not seen you in ages! Will you introduce me—"

"Later."

Later. Later. Later. Always one more interruption, one more excuse. It seemed an hour before they escaped out the front door and stood waiting for the coachman to bring around the carriage.

Jason drew Cait near and enclosed her in his arms.

She snuggled closer. "Mighty me, 'twas hot in there."

"Hot?" He took her lips in a deep kiss, his hands wandering down to squeeze her bottom. "I'll show you hot."

She giggled. A sweet, sweet—bittersweet for him—giggle.

When the carriage arrived, they hurried inside, and he pulled her to straddle his lap. "Can we do it in a carriage?" she asked as the door slammed shut.

"I mean to find out." His hand went under her skirt and wandered up her shapely legs to find her slick and ready. With a little gasp, she moved to unlace his breeches, a seductive, impatient gesture that made him bite his lip. The carriage started with a lurch, hampering her fumbling efforts. When he finally burst free, he couldn't remember ever being so relieved.

She wiggled close, wound her arms around his neck, fastened her lips on his, her tongue a warm promise in his greedy mouth. Then—*bump!*—the wheels hit a rut, and their noses mashed together. "Sorry," he whispered, adjusting her on his lap.

"Mmmm," she murmured, going again for his lips, but missing and grazing his cheek instead. " 'Tis all right. I think." A little giggle sounded by his ear.

Steadying her head in his hands, he tried once more, managing naught but a couple of fleeting baby kisses. The carriage bucked over the cobblestones as though it had no springs, never mind how much he'd paid to outfit the damned contraption.

"I dinna think this will work," she whimpered when they jounced in and out of a pothole with a bone-rattling jolt that brought their mouths colliding together with enough force to nearly crack their teeth.

Ruefully he rubbed at his lips. "I will make it work." Nuzzling her neck, he concentrated below instead, moving his hands down to her hips in a feverish effort to guide their two bodies together. But the bench seat was hellishly narrow, and she shifted and swayed on his lap. No matter how hard they tried, they couldn't connect. Rounding a corner, Cait bounced right to the floor and stayed there, convulsed in laughter.

" 'Tis not going to work." She came up on her knees and steadied herself with her hands on his shoulders. Her skirts were twisted around her legs, the bent stomacher was skewed, and her tangled curls bounced on her shoulders in the same uneven rhythm as the carriage. "How long to your house?"

This late, traffic was negligible. With the exception of aristocratic carousers, Londoners kept inside at night. "Five more minutes."

"Five minutes." She sighed as though it were hours

and hours. Then she reached to lace him back up, weaving on her knees while she tried to keep her balance. He pushed away her hands, knowing he couldn't take her fingers on him at present. Quickly he did it himself, loosely, then pulled her up and across his lap.

" 'Tis sorry I am, Jase." She burrowed into his neck, her breath warm there, her mouth moist. "D'ye think ye can wait?"

"I reckon I'll have to."

Her only response was another sweet sigh.

"You know," he said with a self-deprecating chuckle, "my brother brought a woman to this house last year and took her to his bed. And I was terribly righteous and told him he'd have to marry her."

She sat upright, steadied herself with an arm across the seatback. "Ye mean Colin and Amy?"

"Yes." He grunted when she bounced in his lap. "Last month they had a beautiful baby daughter."

"That's very nice. But ye dinna have to marry me, Jason. In fact, I wouldn't hear of it." Her voice dropped until he could hardly hear it over the wheels rattling on the cobblestones. "My home is in Scotland."

With a hand on her chin, he brought her gaze to his. "Caithren?"

"Hmmm?" In the soft glow from the sidelight, her eyes looked hazy blue.

"Are you enjoying yourself this night?"

She nodded seriously. "More than I ever thought possible."

"Even though you're in England?"

"Even though." Managing to guide her lips to his, she kissed him softly. "Maybe especially so." Her words were almost shy, surprising him. Caithren was never shy. "Because you're here. In England."

A heaviness settled in his chest. "Will you remember that tomorrow? No matter what happens?"

Her gaze was steadfast—and perhaps a bit curious. "I will remember it forever."

"Good. I am counting on it." He was praying for it as the carriage drew to a halt. Because when the sun rose in the morning, what he had to tell her would surely break her heart.

The house was dark and still. He eased the door shut and found her lips with his once more as he felt for the candle that was on the nearby table. Pulling away, he went to light it, fumbling when her hands streaked under his surcoat. He cursed softly, and Caithren giggled.

"Hush," he whispered. "We cannot wake Kendra. I am half-surprised she didn't wait up to hear all the juicy details." With a soft hiss, the flame came to life, and she snuggled against him, her eyes a deep blue in the sudden light. Beneath the coat, her arms tightened around him. A choked sound escaped his throat, and he fused his mouth to hers. His breath quickened at her indescribable flavor, the way her soft curves molded themselves to his harder body.

She angled her head, deepening the kiss, then suddenly broke contact. "Where is your room?" Her eyes blazed, full of impatient promise. "Hurry."

The candle in one hand, he slung an arm around her, and they scrambled up the stairs, both of them stumbling in the mad rush.

The minute his bedchamber door closed behind them, Caithren was on him, her mouth pressed to his. "Now," she demanded. "No food. No teasing. Here. Now."

He reached blindly to set the candle on a table, teasing the furthest thing from his mind. 'Twas all he could do not to rip her clothes or his in their haste.

They tumbled onto the bed, all arms and legs and hot, wet mouths. "Now," she said again, and he drove into her, groaning at the sheer perfection of her body taking his. She climaxed with a sharp cry that met his own deep moan. He felt her tighten around him, and gusts of pleasure overcame him, stunning his senses. In seconds it was over. This time. There would be more time before the morning, time to be slow and caring, time to taste and touch. Time to savor the last hours before the truth destroyed everything between them.

At the thought, an ache overwhelmed him. He nuzzled her ear, then words spilled out in a whisper. "I love you, Cait."

Beneath him, she seemed to stop breathing. "I—"

"Hush." He didn't want to hear it, not from her. Not when she wouldn't be able to say it again on the morrow. "I love you, and I want you to remember that. No matter what happens tomorrow."

"Why d'ye keep bringing up tomorrow?" she asked in a voice soft and sated. "What is happening tomorrow? Besides the wedding and finding Adam? And hopefully apprehending Gothard?"

He pulled back and captured her gaze with his. "We will wake to the morning sun, wrapped in each other's arms. I will bring you breakfast in bed." The candlelight seemed to flicker in her passionate, hazel eyes. "And then—then I have something to tell you. And I want your promise that you'll remember I love you."

She struggled up on an elbow. "That is something," she whispered, "that I will never, ever forget."

"Then show me," he said, and she melted into his arms once again.

In the gray light of dawn, Jason jerked awake.

He'd forgotten his head last night.

Bloody hell, what if he'd gotten Cait with child? He lay stone still, a fist pressed to his heart. A few hours of mindless passion, and he might have ruined both their lives.

What would she do? What would *he* do? He wasn't a man to force a woman to the altar, nor was he one to want his child raised in a foreign country, far from his love and influence. But the decision was not his, he knew. If she carried his babe, Caithren would not even find out until after she returned home. She wouldn't have to tell him. He might never know.

How would she cope, a never-married woman with a child? Here she would be shunned. He was admittedly ignorant of the social pressures where she lived, but he'd wager it was the same. For the rest of her life, she might suffer for his lack of responsibility.

He could only pray his seed hadn't taken. And though he was not a religious man, he did pray, fervently.

Beside him, Caithren slept, looking happy and peaceful. He could barely resist reaching to touch her beloved face, but he'd not risk startling her awake. She would waken soon enough, and then it would be over . . . because then he would tell her the truth. Any feelings she had for him would die. And now she might be carrying his child—the child of their precious, fleeting love. Could things get any worse?

Beneath his window, Jason heard the bellman call the hour of six, followed by muffled conversation. His skin prickled with a sudden, foreboding awareness. He slid from the bed and over to the window, parting the drapes just enough to see between.

Through the morning fog, he could barely make out the bellman, his lamp held high, casting a yellowish glow. Beside him, talking to him, sat a man on a horse.

A man with a squarish head.

Apparently things *could* get worse.

Letting the drapes drop closed, he dashed for the stables, pulling on his clothes as he ran.

We will wake to the morning sun, wrapped in each other's arms. I will bring you breakfast in bed . . .

Caithren woke to the morning sun, but Jason was not wrapped in her arms.

Her heart plummeted. Then she decided he must be off getting her breakfast in bed.

Until three hours later, when he still had not materialized with it.

Tears stinging her eyes, she finally gave up and rose to get dressed. Everything in Jason's chamber reminded her of him. His personal style was evident in the solid, masculine furnishings. His scent clung to the bedclothes, the very walls. She cleaned up at his washstand, rinsing away the traces of his body on hers. But not the impression he'd made on her heart.

After a night of blissful loving, she'd fallen peacefully to sleep, sure he was going to ask her to wed him this morning. She'd been certain that was what he'd meant—that she should remember he loved her when he asked her to be his wife. And he hoped that his declaration of love would prompt her to agree, even though she'd already told him she belonged home in Scotland. She had yet to decide what her answer would be. But she'd been sure of the question.

And now she realized she'd been wrong. He'd only meant she should remember he loved her when he told her they couldn't stay together. That he loved her, but it wasn't enough. There were too many obstacles, too many differences. Her family was too low-ranked. Something.

She could live with that, if she had to—'twas not as though she hadn't been expecting it. But after promising the morning together to straighten things out, he'd gone off somewhere and left her alone to wrestle with all her wrenching doubts. So much for his promises not being given lightly.

The pain and uncertainty were crushing. But Caithren Leslie could bear it.

She should have known not to take an Englishman at his word.

*   *   *

Jason held his nose as he rode past a ditch that had been used as a communal grave for over a thousand bodies during London's last great plague. Though the remains had been covered over with dirt, after two years it still seemed to reek, although surely that was his imagination.

Damnation, he'd lost Geoffrey Gothard's trail. As he turned the corner into the used-clothes market on Houndsditch, Jason found himself wishing again that Caithren really were Emerald. Emerald MacCallum knew how to track a man. Emerald MacCallum would have gotten close enough to capture her quarry. It had cost him precious minutes to get a horse and take off, but Gothard hadn't ridden away until he glimpsed Jason rounding the corner of the town house. Yet he'd never managed to catch up, and now the man had seemingly disappeared into the maze that was known as London.

Once again they were playing hide-and-seek, but Jason couldn't figure out the rules of the game. Gothard had chased him all the way to London—why did he not come after him now instead of running off? It couldn't be that Gothard were afraid of shooting him on a public street, because Jason had followed him halfway across town. The man had had ample opportunity to lead him somewhere more private.

Cursing his ineptitude, he kept one hand on his pocket watch as he jostled his mount between two unkempt riders. If Cait were Emerald instead, he wouldn't have panicked and left her, terrified for her safety. Not to mention he might have done a better job of following the man if he'd not been swamped with guilt. Guilt that muddled his mind. For more than thirty-six hours he'd known the truth, known that Caithren was searching for a brother she'd never find. Every one of those hours had taken its toll on his soul.

Piles of clothing cluttered the street, guarded by watchful owners. Barking madly, a dog skirted around the mounds and darted under Jason's horse, making him shy. A wagon splashed mud as it careened on by, its driver ignoring several vendors who angrily brushed off their soiled goods, yelling obscenities after him.

Once again Jason had proven himself a failure, unworthy of his father's name.

He had failed to catch Gothard. He had failed to tell Caithren the truth yesterday, he had failed to keep her safe from pregnancy, and now again he had failed her this morning. She had no reason to attend the wedding, yet by now she was probably getting ready, excited to see her brother. He pictured her choosing a gown from Kendra's clothes press, carefully painting her face, sticking on another adorable heart-shaped patch. All for nothing.

He craned his neck. Was that Gothard's sandy head he glimpsed through the mass of haggling customers? Thinking it just might be, his hopes lifted. He dug in his heels, racing after the man, then caught up to find himself disappointed once again.

'Twas not Gothard after all. But the man had to be nearby . . . somewhere.

He would give it one more hour. Then, if he were unsuccessful, he would go home. And, no matter that it would be the hardest thing he'd ever done in his life . . . he would tell Caithren the truth.

"He will be back, Cait."

Caithren looked up from her feet, which were trodding a path through Lincoln's Inn Fields, and over to her new friend Kendra. "I ken he will be back. He lives here." With a sigh, she made her way over to a stone bench. "Ye just dinna understand. He *promised* me we would be together this morning. H-he said he had something to tell me."

Kendra sat beside her, her features lit with intrigue. "Any idea what?"

Slowly Cait drew off her bonnet and set it on the bench. Raking the long hair from her face, she watched a dove flutter from the sky and peck around in the grass, foraging for food. A fresh scent in the air hinted at coming rain, reminding her of home, but the thought did nothing to raise her spirits.

"You're hiding something," Kendra insisted. "I can tell."

"Are ye always so observant?"

"Always," Kendra said smugly. "So what is it?"

"This is going to sound daft." Cait licked her lips and smoothed the skirts of the blue day dress she'd borrowed from Kendra. Until the Gothards were caught, she felt safer disguised as an Englishwoman. "I know we've kent each other less than ten days, your brother and I, but I thought . . . well, I thought mayhap he would be asking me to marry him."

Kendra clapped her hands. "I knew it!"

"Nay, ye dinna understand." Tears sprang to Caithren's eyes—michty me, she hated that. She brushed at them angrily. "He made such a point of saying we'd talk in the morning. Then he disappeared." She turned on the bench, took Kendra's hands in hers. "I was wrong. He only wanted to tell me we cannot be together. But he lost his nerve, or just decided something else was more important."

"Maybe you misunderstood about this morning."

Cait shook her head. "Impossible."

"Then something unexpected came up." Kendra's fingers squeezed tight. "I'm sure of it. Did you not say you needed some papers for your brother? I'll wager he wanted to take care of that before he talked to you. And when he does, 'twill not be to say you cannot be together."

"It doesn't matter what he went to do or what he's going to say." Caithren took her hands from Kendra's and hugged herself. "I hadn't made up my mind, anyway."

Jason's sister fixed her with a penetrating stare. "Oh, yes, you had." She smoothed her own apple-green skirts. "Whether you know it or not."

Uncomfortable under that gaze, Caithren rose and resumed walking. Kendra jumped up to follow. "How is your arm today?"

" 'Tis healing." Cait shook her head in disbelief. "After English doctoring. I never would have thought it."

"They say never trust an English surgeon. Quacks, one and all." Kendra grinned. "How was it cut? You said you would tell me today."

A small smile threatened to burst through her melancholy. "I never said anything of the sort. Ye said ye would ask." She took a deep breath. "Wat Gothard nicked me with his sword. We think he was going after your brother."

"He was?" Kendra stopped dead on the path, her face a mask of concern. "Maybe Jason went after Gothard. What if he's not here because he's hurt?"

"Hurt?" Cait echoed numbly. "He was going to warn Scarborough today, but he said naught about chasing down Gothard. He knows not where to find him. We dinna ken if he even made it to London." She couldn't bear to think of Jason hurt—she couldn't live with that. He didn't want her, and he didn't want to tell her, either. That was all there was to it. He would have said something were he planning to go after Gothard.

Kendra was still watching her, as though waiting to be reassured. Suppressing her own unease, Cait touched her friend's arm. "Your brother didn't go chasing after Gothard this morning." When Kendra still looked wary, Cait forced a smile. "I'm certain of it."

Surely there was nothing to be worried about.

Kendra nodded, apparently placated. "Still, I cannot

believe you were injured. It sounds so romantic, being saved by the man you love." She leaned against the rail that edged the path, her eyes lit with envy. "What sort of adventures have you two been up to? My life is so boring."

So much had happened, Cait didn't know where to begin. And she couldn't bear retelling all the events that had brought her to admire and love Jason in such a short time. It hurt too much. "Your brother brought me from up north to here. A long, tiring journey. Things happened."

"Things." Kendra's voice sounded speculative, but she let the matter drop for now. "At least tell me what you meant last night, when you said you hadn't cared properly for your cut. What could you have done that the doctor didn't?"

"There are healing plants, but—"

"You've knowledge of healing?" When Cait nodded, she looked excited. "Could you teach me, then? I visit the sick at Cainewood, but sometimes I know not what to do for them, and—"

"It takes years to learn." Cait reached up to pluck a leaf off a low-hanging branch overhead. "I cannot teach ye in an afternoon."

"When you come to live at Cainewood—"

"I dinna think that will be happening." Walking again, she shredded the leaf between her fingers and avoided her friend's eyes. "Your brother doesn't love me, Kendra. Or at least not enough. I am naught but an annoyance to him." She kent that wasn't precisely true, but she didn't know how to put it. She only knew that if Jason wanted her, he would have been there this morning as he'd promised.

A Chase promise is not given lightly. If he had ever considered marrying her—which she disbelieved—he must have had serious second thoughts. Now, even should he return and ask her to wed him, she couldn't say aye, knowing he had doubts.

Mayhap this "adventure" had changed her mind about what she wanted from life. But for her, 'twas all or nothing. She kent he bore guilt for taking her outside of marriage, but that was no reason to wed. A half-commitment would never do. Even if she were pregnant—a possibility after last night—she'd not marry him if she were less than sure of his love. She adored children, and she'd feel blessed to have one, even out of wedlock. Cameron could stand in as a father figure—people would whisper, but she'd never been conventional, anyway.

'Twas a gray day, to match her mood, even darker along the paths where the trees met overhead and cast their shadows. She walked beside Kendra, listening to her own thoughts and snatches of conversation from passersby. When they scooted to the side to let a wizened old vendor pass with his barrow, he nodded to them and recited a little verse.

> "Buy marking stones, marking stones buy,
> Much profit in their use doth lie;
> I've marking stones of color red,
> Passing good, or else black lead."

"Thank you, no." Kendra smiled, and the aged peddler went on. "Marking stones," she mused. "That man will be scrambling for business soon, if Jason has his way."

"Aye?" Caithren could barely muster interest, but she couldn't be rude.

"He's set some cottagers at Cainewood to making pencils from the graphite mined on the property."

"What is a pencil?"

"A long strip of graphite encased in wood. Like a quill, but you don't have to dip it. Just sharpen it, instead. Jason heard they were being made in Cumberland

and traveled there to see. There is nothing he won't do to make Cainewood profitable. The Roundheads ran it into the ground while it was in their hands—when Charles restored the title and lands, Jason had to start from scratch." Her heels clicked on the hard dirt path. "My brother is an admirable sort, do you not think?"

"All this new knowledge of Jason is a wee bit too much," Cait admitted. "I spent our whole journey trying to puzzle him out, and then when I finally reckoned I understood him . . . yesterday I discovered he's a completely different man than I thought."

"No, he's not." As they walked, Kendra ran a hand along the low fence beside her. "You may be surprised to find him titled and a man of means, but inside, he's exactly the man you saw. Or what you've made him to be." She stopped and leaned against the rail. "You've changed him, Cait, in good ways."

"I dinna ken . . ."

"Come, they sell lemonade on the other side of the square. I'll treat you." Kendra linked her arm through Cait's. "With or without brandy?"

"Definitely with," Cait said dryly.

The lemonade was cool and bracing. They walked around the fields for a spell, drinking and chatting, and after a while Cait started to feel better. Children ran circles around them, their harried mothers not far behind. Street balladers were there to entertain, as well as violinists and one lone bagpiper that made Caithren's heart swell. She touched her amulet, rubbing her fingers over the smooth oval emerald. Tonight was the wedding. She'd best head back to the house to ready herself.

"May I borrow another gown for this night?"

"Of course." Kendra eyed her assessingly. "I've a lovely one in yellow that I think will just fit."

"I'm sure 'twill do. Whether Jason comes back or nay, I must go to the wedding to meet up with Adam." By force of habit her hand went into her pocket, to feel for his portrait and pull it out.

"Ford and I can take you. We were planning to go anyway, in order to find out who Jason killed." She squinted at the miniature. "What is that?"

"Adam's picture." When Kendra reached, Caithren handed it over. "D'ye see a resemblance?"

"Oh, yes." Kendra grinned, looking from the painting back to Cait. "You've the same eyes and chin and hair."

"That is all we share," Cait said. "We could not be more different." She sighed. "I'd best get back and prepare to leave." One more night dressed as an Englishwoman to find Adam, then she would head back home where she belonged. Her hair would go back into braids, and she would be herself again. Hopefully without these devastating pangs of unrequited love.

Her hand went up to stroke the foreign English curls, and she felt something missing. "My hat! I forgot my hat! I must've left it on that bench." She started running.

"Wait!" She turned back at Kendra's shout. "Have you no sense of direction?"

"Nay." Cait laughed at herself. "Where was it, then?"

"There. Behind that big tree, and back along the path a bit."

"Aye. Bide a wee. I mean, wait here. I shall be right back." She hurried along the shady path, relieved when she finally spotted the bench and saw that no one had taken her bonnet.

Just as she jammed it on her head, a horse came thundering through the park, and someone scooped her off her feet. Her heart hammering, she found herself face down across a man's lap, his hand tangled in the chain around her neck in an effort to wrestle her upright.

She kicked and twisted, trying to find freedom, but his grasp tightened and the chain bit into her throat. Finally it snapped, and her amulet fell to the grass, her heart plummeting along with it. Her protection, gone. Her hope, gone.

"Let me go!" she wailed, her eyes filling. The emerald looked smaller and smaller as they rode away, her last glimpse of it blurry through her tears.

Something cold and thin pressed into the back of her neck.

" 'Tis the dull edge of a knife," Geoffrey Gothard growled, "but one more move, and it'll be the sharp side instead."

Chapter Twenty-three

"What do you mean, she never came back?" Jason paced the drawing room, then came to stand beside Kendra, staring down at her. "Where could she have gone?"

"I looked all over, then I figured she must have come back here." Her gaze kept straying to the window, as though she expected to see Cait emerge from the park across the street. "Lincoln's Inn Fields is not that big. How could anyone possibly disappear in it?"

"You don't know Caithren." He tried to steady his erratic pulse, reminding himself how easily she tended to get lost. "She has a terrible sense of direction."

"So she told me. But I thought she was fooling." At Jason's glare, she flinched. "I looked, Jason. Everywhere. I'm sorry. 'Tis not as though I lost her on purpose. Come, I'll show you where we were. Perhaps she's waiting there now."

Calm. As he followed Kendra out the door, he struggled for calm. Geoffrey Gothard couldn't have gotten her. He'd spotted him less than an hour ago.

He hoped. Suddenly he wasn't sure. He pulled out his watch, but his hand was shaking, so he shoved it back into his pocket. Dodging the traffic that always surrounded the square, he trailed his sister across the street and into the park, hurrying with her along a path.

The gray day was his enemy, its shadows tricking him

into thinking he saw Cait everywhere. "What color is she wearing?"

"Blue. The gown with the puffy sleeves that I wore to Lady Stanhope's house party."

"I haven't memorized your wardrobe, Kendra."

Wisely saying nothing, she slanted him a glance. "Here." She stopped before a stone bench. "She left her hat here. 'Tis gone. So she must have found it."

"I've eyes in my head," he snapped.

"Your face is turning red. You never get upset. Or you never used to, until this whole thing with Gothard started. Even then, you were not this short-tempered."

Until he'd fallen in love. "You two should not have been walking here alone."

"Everyone walks here alone." The sweep of her arm encompassed plenty of unescorted women.

"Not everyone has a deviant after them." Her pale green eyes filled, and he drew a deep breath. Patience. "Show me the path you were on when she left you."

Once again he followed her, scanning the square while he tried to reassure himself it wasn't possible that Gothard had Cait. Or could he have his timing skewed? How long had he wandered the streets of London, berating himself for not coming clean with Caithren yesterday or the night before? He pulled out his pocket watch again, flipped it open, but for the life of him he couldn't remember what time it was when last he saw the man.

"Wait." When Kendra stopped, he snapped the watch closed and whirled to face her. Her brow knitted, she motioned off the path. "Is that Cait's?"

A white feather fluttered from behind a tree. He ran closer, saw it was attached to the hat he'd bought in Wansford. "God. Yes." He plucked it up and clutched it to his chest.

"Look, there was a horse here." Hampered by her high heels, Kendra came along more slowly. "The grass is torn up. By hooves, I think." She bent down and scooped up a glint of gold. "And what is this?" She handed it to him. " 'Tis Cait's as well, is it not?"

His heart plunged to somewhere in the vicinity of his knees as his fist closed around the emerald pendant. "I've lost her," he whispered, staring at his clenched hand.

"She's lost, yes. But that doesn't mean you've lost her."

"You don't understand. This amulet is ancient—it's been in her family for centuries. She believed something bad would befall her if ever she was without it."

A sudden wind whipped Kendra's skirts. "Tell me not that *you* believe that nonsense."

Stricken, he slowly looked up at his sister. "I know not what to believe anymore."

"I'll explain this one more time, numbskull. Now, pay attention." Listening to the Gothard brothers argue, Caithren nervously wandered the small chamber, the back portion of a two-room suite. A table, bed, and two plain chairs were the only furniture. The brothers must be as short of funds as Jason had guessed. "Thanks to Cainewood doing just as I expected of him, things are right on schedule."

"What *things*, Geoffrey?"

Geoffrey's gaze flickered to Cait. A lascivious gaze. Swallowing bile in her throat, she moved around the other side of the table and feigned unconcern, running a finger across the bare wood.

"Things." Geoffrey blew out a perturbed puff of air. "I'll be going to the wedding alone." As he talked, he donned padding to bulk up his body. The same as he'd worn to inquire at Scarborough's house, Cait realized. Jings, Jason had been right. "You will wait here and guard the chit." He jerked his squarish head in her direction.

In reflex she backed up and sat on the bed. The ropes creaked, and a musty smell wafted from the mattress.

Geoffrey glared at his brother. "Think you can handle that?"

Wat shrugged.

A heavy sigh escaped Geoffrey's whitish lips. "I will lock the two of you in, then. She'll not be going anywhere, unless Cainewood breaks down the door. If that should happen, you know what to do?"

Wat just looked at him questioningly. With a huff, Geoffrey marched over to Cait and pulled her off the bed.

"Ouch!" She yanked free. "I will thank ye to keep your hands off my arm. It hurts where your brother cut me."

Without answering her, he prodded her in the middle of the back and sent her sailing into the small anteroom, shutting the door behind her. She stumbled over to sit on an unpadded wooden settle. This room was even more austere than the first. Fuming, she got back up and pressed her ear to the door, but try as she might, all she heard was unintelligible murmurs.

What was he saying? What was he planning? Her mind raced with possibilities. Was he telling Wat to detain Jason? Kill him? Kill them both? No, somehow she thought not. The way Geoffrey had been looking at her, she suspected he had plans for her of his own before doing away with her. She shuddered.

At the sound of footsteps approaching, she raced back to the settle. Geoffrey opened the door between the rooms, and she watched through the frame. He went back to the table and pulled a cracked mirror from a bag, along with a fake beard and some adhesive, then set to work, turning himself into the man she'd seen yesterday morn.

Rising again, she positioned herself on the threshold and frowned. "Why would Cainewood be breaking down the door?" Her words came out a challenge, mayhap not the smartest thing to do. But she never had been good at controlling her emotions.

A nasty grin appeared in the bushy brown beard. "He'll be receiving a note explaining your whereabouts. Any minute now, I expect."

"What makes ye think he cares for me?" she asked snidely, almost hoping Jason didn't care, so he wouldn't walk into a trap.

He settled the wig on his head. "Cainewood's not let you out of his sight. Nor far from his lips, I might add." Had he seen them, then, those times they'd kissed to hide their faces? As though reading her mind, Geoffrey let loose a sinister chuckle. "He'll be coming after you. Conveniently keeping him from the wedding, where I'll be."

"I wouldn't be so sure." She wished she could put more conviction into that statement. Jason had said over and over he felt responsible for her, and he'd charged in on his silver horse to save her more than once. Just because that particular horse was stabled miles away didn't mean he wouldn't be arriving this time.

Still, she couldn't count on it. She walked to the window. Four stories down. Her first thought had been to open it and jump. But even when Geoffrey left and she had only to deal with thickheaded Wat, 'twas still four stories down. She wouldn't be jumping.

Pressing her forehead to the cold pane, she strained to see the wall below. Vines. Old, gnarled vines, the stalks as thick as her forearm. She could climb down the vines.

But only if she incapacitated Wat somehow. Her gaze darted around the room and into the next one. There must be something here that could help her.

Whatever it took, she had to get to the wedding. 'Twas her best—maybe her only—chance to find Adam.

And if she could save Jason from risking his life as well, so much the better.

Somehow Jason managed to dress for the wedding, though he knew not how it happened. His heart pounded so hard that his fingers shook. He was torn in three directions at once.

One, find Cait—absolutely his first priority, but at the same time the least likely to be successful. She could be anywhere. *Anywhere.*

Two, get to Scarborough's house and warn him. Three, go to the wedding and hopefully capture Gothard once and for all. Since Scarborough was expected there, he had a strong hunch that Gothard would be there, too. For the bride and groom and wedding guests, he hoped he was wrong, but at least it would be done.

Scarborough and Gothard. Those last two he could handle. He hoped. He frowned at himself as he tied his cravat in the mirror, messing the knot for the fourth time.

He couldn't think about past failures. He had to pull himself together and do what needed to be done. Save Scarborough and apprehend Gothard. Or go after Cait—

A knock came at the door. Giving the cravat a final yank, he went to open it.

"A letter, my lord." Goodwin proffered a neatly folded square.

The note was obviously scribbled in haste. Eleven words that made up his mind. *Your woman can be found at the Bull Inn on Bishopsgate.*

A clue. A direction. Relief coursed through him, though he knew it was premature. He nodded at Goodwin. "Have the carriage brought around immediately." He hoped Scarborough had received the warning letter; if not, the man would have to fend for himself. Or—

"Ford!" Grabbing his velvet surcoat—black, to match his mood—he bolted from the room and down the stairs.

*   *   *

Wat sat slumped in a chair in the back room, his shifty brown eyes watching Caithren pace back and forth as she did her best to ignore him.

She was envisioning Lord Darnley's wedding. There they were, walking down the aisle, Lord Darnley and whomever he was marrying. The kirk, of course, was huge, this being London. Her mind conjured up a bonnie image of a man in a dove-gray velvet suit and a woman in a lovely pink gown. Very English. Guests filled row after row of pews, dressed in every color of the rainbow. On one end sat a man wearing bright blue satin bedecked with gaudy ribbons.

Adam.

She had to get to Adam. She'd come all this way, and 'twas her one and only chance—

"Sit down, wench. You're making me barmy."

She sat. Geoffrey had given Wat a pistol.

Congealed food sat on a pewter plate before her, making her stomach roil. There was a spoon, but no knife. No weapons at her disposal.

She closed her eyes, and a vision of Jason's smile seemed to hover behind the lids. What was it about him that made her miss him so fiercely all this day, the first day she'd spent without him since he'd kept her off the coach? Certainly not his blanket judgments, his innate stubbornness, his overdeveloped sense of responsibility. But whatever it was, he had changed her life. Changed an essential part of what was Caithren Leslie. She could no longer imagine living all her life without a man . . . without Jason in particular. But somehow she would have to.

She knew what her answer to his proposal would have been—but he wouldn't be asking. The minute he captured Geoffrey Gothard, he'd be leaving for his home in the country. She'd been telling him to leave her all along, after all.

'Twas painful, knowing he cared but not enough. If she could even believe he'd been telling the truth when he said he loved her. Wishing the three words had never passed his lips, she reached to touch her amulet and splayed her hand across the bareness there instead. So much ill luck had befallen her lately.

She had to get to Adam. Everything had gone wrong, but this one thing . . . this one thing must go right. With her emerald or without.

"What does Scarborough look like?" Kendra whispered as she and Ford quietly entered the church.

"How the hell should I know?" Scarborough had already left his house when they'd arrived there to alert him of his brothers' plans. "We will have to ask around after the service. Surely there will be time to warn him." The ceremony hadn't started yet, but everyone was seated, and at the far end, a harpsichordist played a gentle tune. Ford drew Kendra along one wall, so they could view the assemblage. "Jason thinks Gothard won't show up until the reception—"

"Look! There's Cait's brother, Adam!"

"Silence!" a matron warned, turning in her seat to give them a cold gray glare.

Kendra ignored her, reaching into her drawstring bag for the miniature that Caithren had left in her hands in the park, when she'd run off to find her hat. She thrust the little painting at Ford. " 'Tis him, is it not?"

He frowned at the picture. "This fellow looks oddly familiar."

"Because he's Cait's brother and looks like Cait."

"Makes sense." Ford looked back and forth between the man and the small oval portrait. Though his clothing was less flamboyant, the gentleman in question did indeed share the same wheaten hair and hazel eyes as the man in the painting. "Could be," he mused. The features were not exactly the same, but close. Perhaps the painter was not very talented.

"Go back outside—I'll bring him."

"Kendra, 'tis about to start—"

The music had changed to a sedate march, and the groom was taking his place, but Ford's protest was futile. Kendra was already down the aisle and tapping the man on the shoulder. He looked up, startled, and she bent down to whisper. "May I speak with you a moment?" He seemed confused, but he nodded and rose to follow the twins outside.

They'd barely reached the steps when Kendra turned to him and started babbling. "I realize you know not who we are, but your sister is—"

"I dinna have a sister," the man interrupted.

Kendra and Ford looked at each other. Ford handed him the miniature. "Are you not Adam Leslie?"

"Nay." The man stared at it, then looked up. "Where did ye get this? Adam is dead."

Kendra gasped. "Adam is *dead*?"

"I'm his cousin, Cameron Leslie. And ye are . . . ?"

Cameron stuck out a hand, and Ford shook it. "Ford and Kendra Chase. We got the portrait from Adam's sister, Caithren. Our brother has gone after her. She meant to come here to find Adam, but she was—"

"—delayed," Kendra finished for him. No sense alarming the man right off.

"I received word of Adam's death and came to fetch my cousin back home." Cameron's hazel eyes filled with concern. "Wore out four horses getting here, because she said he would be at this wedding today, and 'tis the only place in England I kent for certain I could find her."

"If she doesn't make it here for the ceremony, she'll be at the reception." Kendra reached to touch him on the arm. "My brother will make sure of it."

*   *   *

Caithren rose again and walked slowly around the chamber, pacing off her nervous energy. How could she get to Adam?

"Sit down, wench," Wat growled from the front room.

She sat back at the table. Jason hadn't arrived. Mayhap he'd never gone home to get the note Gothard sent—assuming Gothard had told her the truth about that.

Or mayhap she'd been wrong about Jason altogether. He'd ridden halfway across the country chasing after Gothard, and he was determined to find him. And saving Scarborough's life figured into the equation. Mayhap those goals were more important to him than she was. She wouldn't have thought so, but she knew not what to think anymore.

At least she didn't have to worry about him showing up and being detained—or worse, shot—by Wat. Although her stomach gave a little leap at the thought that he might show up after all, she decided Jason could defend himself. Especially against Wat. Geoffrey's attitude toward his brother might be exaggerated, but it had base in fact. Wat was definitely missing something upstairs.

That weakness of Wat's should be a boon to her as well. He was still in the other room, not even really watching. Slowly she stood, sliding the plate off the table as silently as possible.

Hiding it in her skirts, she drifted to the window, reached out and turned the latch, pushed—

"What the hell do you think you're doing?" In a flash of fury, Wat came up behind her. She whirled and raised the heavy pewter plate, smashing him atop the head with all the strength she could dredge from her body. The spoon went flying, along with putrid bits of dried meat and gravy that rained down on them both.

Wat yowled, but he didn't go down. Evidently he was stupid *and* hard-headed.

Red with rage, he came after her. She scooped the

spoon from the floor and aimed its handle for his face, hoping to get him in the eye. She missed, grazing his sunburned cheek. Bright blood beaded up in a ragged line. With a growl, he wrested the pistol from his waistband.

Dim-witted or not, he could kill her. She was already braced to bring up her knee when she heard the click of the flintlock being cocked. Icy fear took a grip on her heart. She shifted, thrusting both hands to force Wat's arm toward the ceiling.

As she tried to wrestle the gun from him and bring it butt-down on top of his hard skull, a blast tore through the air. Her ears ringing, she felt his body go lax and slump to the floor.

Panic rose in her throat as she stood there, the pistol in her hands, watching blood well from a neat round hole in Walter Gothard's head.

"They've got to be here," Ford said. "Hell, there are just too damn many people."

The wedding celebration was in full swing. Lord Darnley's house was lit with hundreds of candles. Wine and other spirits flowed freely, and the resulting raucous laughter rang through the halls, the ballroom, and into his garden beyond.

"Who are ye looking for?" Cameron asked. "I thought we came here to find Cait."

"We also need to find the Earl of Scarborough." Kendra's gaze scanned the glittering room, then she turned back to Cameron and frowned. "But we know not what he looks like."

"Also two other men," Ford added, his words directed into the milling throng. "My brother accidentally killed someone, but we've been unable to discover his identity. These other men were witnesses. I have seen them and think I remember what they look like, but I've yet to spot them here. A serving maid in a tavern told me one of them might be named Balmforth."

"Balmforth?" The blood drained from Cameron's face.

"Yes." Ford craned his neck, still looking, but Kendra's gaze was riveted to Caithren's cousin.

"Whatever is wrong?" she asked.

He took a deep breath. "Balmforth—"

"There they are!" Ford took off, threading his way through the crowd of revelers.

"Are you all right?" Kendra stared at Cameron. "You look like you've seen a ghost."

"Nay. 'Tis only—" His mouth opened, but no more words came out.

"Would you like to sit down?" She took his arm, intending to draw him to one of the silk-upholstered chairs that were lined up against the tapestried wall.

"Nay." He shook his head as though to clear it. "Lady Kendra, I dinna ken how to . . ." He blew out a breath. "Here they come."

The three men walked up, Ford's face as white as Cameron's. Whiter, even. Kendra clutched his arm. "What is it?"

Her whispered words failed to carry through the din that surrounded them, but it mattered not. Ford knew what she was asking. "The man Jason killed . . ." he started, then just looked helplessly at the other men.

"He was Adam Leslie," Cameron said. "Cait's brother."

Caithren heard the door latch rattle in the other room. Geoffrey was back. Somehow he realized his brother was dead.

While she waited for him to burst in and murder her, she knelt for the tenth time in as many minutes to feel Wat's neck for a pulse. Nothing. The rattling stopped, but she felt little relief. Tears flooded her eyes. Shaking, she sat back on the floor and hugged her knees to her chest. For long minutes she stayed that way, rocking herself, a human ball of misery.

Her head jerked up when the window moved, a disembodied hand shoving it open the rest of the way. Through a blur of tears, she watched a second hand clench the ledge. A head and shoulders appeared—wide shoulders and frizzy red hair beneath a man's hat. A woman hoisted herself up and through the window, landing on the floor with the grace of a cat.

Her heart pounding in fear and confusion, Caithren rose. The woman topped her height by a good foot—she was taller than Jason, even. A sword hung from her belt, and a pistol peeked from the top of one boot. She was dressed like a man, but no one would have taken her for one. Ever.

Cait dashed her tears away and blinked. She heard another rattle of the door latch, but was too stunned to even react. "You're . . ."

"Emerald MacCallum." The woman stared pointedly at Wat. "I take it he's dead?"

"I-I reckon so."

Emerald reached to touch Cait's hand. "Dinna fash yourself, dear. I dinna normally hold wi' killin' my quarry, but these brothers . . . well, the world is better off wi'out 'em."

"B-but I've never killed a man! And I didn't mean to, even though he was such a bad one. I swear on"—she reached for her missing amulet, then let out a sob—"on my mam's grave." She searched Emerald's golden eyes. "Will ever I get over it?"

"Nay." The single word was blunt, yet kind. Emerald patted her on the back. "But others will thank ye for it, and some day, you'll realize it wasn't really wrong. Nay, you'll never get over it completely, but ye will learn to live with it." She turned and headed for the window. "It will, however, change ye, mayhap even for the better."

Her hand on the sill, Emerald turned back. "A wee keek back keeps ye on the right path," she said. For a moment, Caithren could only stare. One of Mam's sayings. *Let life's experiences guide you forward.*

"Ye came for the reward," Cait said softly, remembering Jason accusing her of the same.

The other woman nodded, then shrugged and went to duck out. Their gazes both flew to the ledge when another hand appeared beside hers, larger and squarer, with a light sprinkling of black hair across the back. Caithren gasped. A second hand settled next to it, then a face rose into the frame.

Jason's face, though so colorless that Cait feared for his life.

Emerald reached down a hand and pulled him up and into the room.

He stood there, visibly shaking, looking back and forth between Caithren and the woman he had once thought her to be. Before he could say anything, Emerald climbed out the window and was gone.

He looked back to Cait, his face still pale, his eyes wide. "That was Emerald MacCallum?"

"Aye."

He shook his head, then pierced her with an intense green gaze. "Are you all right?"

Tears threatened, and she bit her lip, nodding.

"Caithren." Her name was a harsh whisper in the air. He held out his arms, and Cait rushed into them, fresh tears flowing at the feel of him crushed against her. She drew deep of his familiar, comforting scent, underlaid with a trace of the sharp smell of fear. He was warm and solid in her arms, his body still shuddering with residual tremors.

With a long sniff, she pulled back. "I . . . I cannot believe ye climbed up the wall."

"What do you take me for?" For a split second he looked angry or hurt, she wasn't sure which. Then his eyes softened. "I love you, Cait. I would move heaven and earth to see to your safety. Climbing that wall was nothing." At her look of disbelief, he released a shaky laugh. "Well, not nothing, but I would do it again. For you. But give me a few days first, will you? I need some time to recover."

She laughed through her tears, reaching forward to clutch his hands in hers. "Geoffrey went to the wedding, to deal with Scarborough. Ye were right, Jase—he was wearing the fat man disguise, with the beard —"

She broke off at his gasp. His gaze was riveted over her shoulder.

" 'Tis Wat." Her lids slid closed, but the tears leaked through them anyway. "I didn't mean to kill him, I swear it." She opened her eyes, willing Jason to believe that she'd not done such a terrible thing deliberately. "I hit him over the head, but he didn't fall, and then he pulled a pistol, and it went off, but it was pointing up in the air. I dinna know what happened!"

Jason looked up at the ceiling. The molded Elizabethan pattern was damaged. "It ricocheted, Cait."

She followed his gaze. "I only meant to knock him out so that I could go find Adam—" At her brother's name she froze, and with a mighty effort she pulled herself together. She'd no time to feel this wrenching regret; not right now. She'd allow herself that luxury later. "Adam. I have to find Adam. I must get to the wedding. 'Tis sorry I am to leave ye now, but I've come all this way, and—well, you'll be wanting to go, too, will ye not? Gothard is there."

"Cait. There is something I need to tell you. I meant to this morning, but Gothard—"

"I know. There are reasons ye dinna want to stay with me. We'll talk of it on the way."

He took her by the shoulders. "That is not it, Cait." His eyes and voice were frantic. "Not at all. You mustn't think such a thing—"

He had scaled the wall for her. She'd been wrong, and he loved her enough after all. Her heart sang with joy, but she pressed her mouth to his, to silence his proposal. She'd no time for such things now. She put her answer into her kiss, a caress of such fiery possession that he had to know how she felt. Regretfully she pulled away, her lips clinging to his for a last moment, savoring the sweetness of his love. A love she would be sure of the rest of her life. He'd climbed four stories for her. The equivalent of a mountain for other men.

"I love ye, Jase. We'll talk of it later. I must get to the wedding."

"You don't understand—"

At the sound of pounding she tore her gaze from his and hurried into the front room, Jason at her heels. He yanked her back just as the door slammed in, barely staying on its hinges.

Beyond its frame, Kendra and Ford stood in the half-dark of the hallway. And behind them, rubbing the shoulder he must have used to break down the door—

"Cameron?" Confused, she stared at him in disbelief. He looked pale. As Jason moved behind her to shut the door to the bedroom, she took a wooden step forward.

"Cait." Her cousin pushed his way between the twins and wrapped her into a hug. Smelling of home, he rubbed her back in a familiar, comforting rhythm. "Cait—I'm . . ." Laced with sympathy, his voice faltered. "I'm so sorry."

"Wh-what?" Her gaze flickered to the door shielding the other room. Could the news of Wat's death be spreading already? " 'Twas an accident, Cam."

He pulled away, searching her eyes with his. "Ye kent it afore now, then?"

She only looked at him, baffled.

Jason peeled away Cameron's arms and took her by the shoulders. "Caithren. The thing I've been trying to tell you . . ." He looked down at his boots, then back up and straight into her eyes. His own eyes held such pain, she was taken aback. A cold knot formed in her stomach.

He drew a strangled breath. "Adam is dead. At my hands."

She was speechless. Adam was dead? It didn't seem possible.

His green gaze implored her, but she couldn't get past the shocking news to figure out what he was asking of her. "There was a duel. Geoffrey Gothard pulled your brother from the crowd and used him as a shield. I wasn't fast enough—or skilled enough—to control my blade. And Adam died for it."

"Adam is dead?" Her words were barely a whisper. "And ye kent it and didn't tell me?"

Jason stared at her for a long, silent moment. Then he turned and walked out through the empty doorway, into the emptier world beyond.

Chapter Twenty-four

Ford chased Jason down the corridor. "You cannot just leave!" He plucked him by the sleeve. "How long have you known?"

"Almost two days. And every minute I didn't tell her was agony. But I knew it would be like this." He wrenched from Ford's grasp and continued walking down the hall.

Ford ran after him. "You knew it would be like what?"

"Did you not see the love die in her eyes?" It had been worse even than he'd thought it would be. Much, much worse. "I cannot stay and watch that. I love her. God damn it, Gothard's ruined my life." He started down a narrow flight of stairs.

"You never would have met her without Gothard." Ford's voice came from behind him; they could only fit single file. "She's in shock, Jason. She might need some time to absorb it all, but if she loved you before, she still will. 'Twas an accident."

Jason whirled at the bottom of the steps. "I killed her brother. Her *brother*. Do you reckon I'd find forgiveness for the man who killed you, or Kendra, or Colin? 'Twas bad enough when the man was nameless. This is not easy to live with, Ford." The pain was excruciating, but he had to put it aside for now. He had other responsibilities. "Just leave me alone. Go back to Kendra and Cait. And—her cousin, is he?" Ford nodded. "She loves him—he will comfort her much better than I could. She killed Wat, you know."

"What?"

"He's in the back room. You'll need to send for the authorities. I take it you warned Scarborough?"

"Bloody hell." Ford's eyes widened. "No. We ran into Cameron and learned the truth and—damn, I forgot. We came straight here to tell Cait what we'd learned, and—"

Jason was already running for the exit.

He strode through Lord Darnley's front door, past the gaping footman and into a swarm of glittering guests. Scarborough. Where was Scarborough? What the hell did the man look like? He'd seen him once or twice at Court, but damn it, he'd never paid much attention, and—

With a jolt of relief he spotted him. Sandy-haired, like Gothard, but taller and sporting a broad mustache. Dressed in deep blue velvet and apparently unconcerned about his half brother, Scarborough was discussing with his friends the shocking news that Clarendon, the Lord Chancellor, had resigned earlier in the day.

"Barbara was leaning from her window, cheering at his departure," Scarborough said as Jason walked up, unsurprised to hear that. Barbara, Countess of Castlemaine and the King's longtime mistress, had always hated Clarendon. "So do you know what he said to her?"

The men leaned closer into the circle. "What?"

" 'Pray remember, my lady, that if you live, you will grow old.' "

Amid their laughter, Jason touched him on the arm. "I apologize for interrupting, but there's a matter of some urgency."

Scarborough turned, a look of confusion on his face. "Yes?"

Just as Jason was about to respond, a flash of silver caught his eye. He spun around, shoving Scarborough from harm's way as he drew his rapier from its scabbard. "I arrest you in the name of the King," he said in a booming voice, startled to hear how it carried. "You will put down your weapons and wait here for the magistrate."

The music stopped, and as one, the wedding guests turned to watch. Jason's grip tightened on the hilt of his sword. "Now, Gothard."

The disguised man's gaze held hard and unwavering. "We meet again," he drawled through the bushy brown beard. "My nearest and dearest enemy."

Words familiar to Jason. Familiar and enraging. "Once and for all, what mean you that I am your enemy?"

Geoffrey Gothard's sunburned features went tight with resentment, and his blue eyes narrowed. "You've taken what should rightfully be mine."

"Rightfully yours?" Again Jason knew the feeling that he'd seen those eyes. Befuddled, his head swam. "I have nothing that is yours. And because of this misconception, you've been chasing me, trying to kill me?"

"I never wanted to kill you," Gothard said with a smile—a cold smile. "Only to enjoy some of your riches. They should have been mine. Including your woman." The familiar eyes turned as cold as the smile. "I'd have had her long before now if you'd ever left her alone."

Jason ignored the threat to Cait. She was safe. He swiped at his missing mustache, infuriated. All those disguises and hiding, and Gothard had never been out to kill them. Just playing hide-and-seek. "And Scarborough?" He nodded in the man's direction.

"Him I want dead." The wild sheen in Gothard's eyes said he wasn't sane. "With him dead, Wat inherits and I get what I deserve."

What he deserved was questionable at the moment.

He was well and truly mad. "What about what I deserve, Gothard? What do I owe you and why?"

"Damn you to bloody hell." Gothard moved forward, then pulled back when Jason brandished his sword. "Both you and the father we share."

Pain and confusion sliced through him. "We share nothing!" Jason advanced a step closer, slowly circled the tip of his rapier, then sliced it hissing through the air in a swift move that brought a collective gasp from the wedding guests. The blade's thin shadow flickered across the candlelit parquet floor. His mind whirled with thoughts of Mary, Cait, Adam . . . all the blood, the irrational violence.

With a roar, Gothard lunged, and the first clash of steel rang through the ballroom.

"I was born first," Gothard yelled. "It should be mine, all mine!" He slashed wildly, catching Jason's sword across the middle. The vibrations shimmied up Jason's arm. Muscles tense, he swung and thrust, and again steel bashed against steel. His heart pounded; blood pumped furiously through his veins. What Gothard was saying couldn't be true. No way in hell was he this evil man's half brother.

They scrambled onto the dance floor, and the crowd scurried back. Gothard was cornered, but Jason was incensed. He would never believe it, *never*. He edged Gothard back against the wall. Gothard took sudden advantage, and Jason found himself retreating as their blades tangled, slid, broke free with a metallic twang.

His arm ached to the very bone. Perspiration dripped slick from his forehead, stinging his eyes. But the other man's breath came hard and ragged.

Measuring his foe, Jason put his all into one determined swipe of his sword, and Gothard's went clanging to the floor and skittered into the crowd of gaping spectators.

"I came not to kill today, Gothard, but merely to see

justice done." Jason sucked in air, smelled the other man's desperation. "There are those here who will see to it you'll not escape." An affirming murmur came from the crowd, and men jostled forward.

He waved them back. "Tell me what you said isn't true."

"As God is my witness, it *is* true. And you'll not live to enjoy what should have been mine!" Gothard went into an all-too-familiar crouch, coming up with a pistol in his hand.

In a flash of blue velvet, Scarborough leapt forward and knocked the gun from his brother's grasp. It went flying, barely missing a matron's head as it sailed though the window with a startling crash. "You'll not live to kill again, *brother*." Scarborough nodded at Jason, who moved closer, his sword still outstretched.

An unearthly sound escaped Gothard's throat before he shoved past Scarborough and ran through the crowd. Rainbow shades of satin and silk swirled in a colorful kaleidoscope as wedding guests darted to avoid him. He burst through the doors that lead to the garden, broken glass crunching beneath his feet as he disappeared into the inky blackness.

Within a heartbeat Jason was after him, chasing him along a graveled path. Footsteps pounded behind him; he assumed they were Scarborough's and ran faster. He'd not prove himself less than a man this time. Gothard would not get away, even should he have to do the unthinkable. But first he needed answers.

His lungs burned with the effort to catch up. Damn, Gothard was fast. But not fast enough. He might be running for his life, but Jason was fueled by fury and a resolve borne of weeks of frustration. His muscles pumped with determination; his jaw gritted with iron will. His quarry was almost within reach.

He pulled up short when Gothard staggered to the ground.

He'd not even registered the sharp report of the bullet. But he turned to see the pistol from where it had come. And the woman on the other end of it.

Emerald MacCallum. It had not even occurred to him that she was after the reward when he saw her at the inn. He'd thought of nothing but Cait.

Now he looked to the ground. Gothard's still, lifeless form. He dropped to his knees and felt for a pulse.

Dead. Gothard was dead. He frantically searched the limp body, for a letter, a miniature, anything. Anything that would prove or disprove what the man had claimed.

"He was telling the truth," Scarborough said quietly from behind him.

Jason sat back on his heels, felt an unmanly sting of tears in his eyes. A crowd was gathering again, people pouring through the doors and out into the garden. Scarborough turned and conducted a hasty, whispered conversation with Lord Darnley. Together they hustled the guests back inside. It took some minutes, and by the time Scarborough returned, Jason had composed himself.

The gray day had finally delivered on its promise, and a light drizzle fell from the sky. Silently Scarborough walked Jason down the garden path, away from the sight of the body. Their brother. Jason dropped onto a stone bench, his hands dangling limply between his spread knees, his eyes blindly perusing the wet gravel beneath his feet.

Scarborough sat beside him. "My mother had an affair with your father before either married." His voice was low, his words matter-of-fact. "When he fell in love with your mother, he left mine pregnant. Eventually she was offered to my father as a widow with a young son. She was beautiful, and her family had land that bordered his. Her dowry. He knew not the truth at the time, but when he learned it later, he forgave her. Their marriage wasn't bad, all things considered."

His father—the valiant war hero—had had an illicit affair. Had left a pregnant woman.

"Geoffrey was the oldest," Scarborough continued, "but he would never inherit. He resented it. He made my life a living hell."

"I'm sorry," Jason muttered, feeling somehow as though he were to blame.

"He never knew who his own father was until our parents died. While going through their things, we found—a letter. From your father to my mother. From that moment, Geoffrey . . ." Scarborough seemed at a loss for words. His fingers curled into fists. "He lost his mind. 'Tis the only way I can put it. 'Twas as though he finally had somewhere to channel all that hatred. I am sorry I threw him out, though. If I'd known he would come after you, I'd have coped with him somehow. I feel a substantial burden of responsibility here, and for that I apologize."

" 'Tis not your fault." Jason shoved the damp hair from his eyes. 'Twas his father's fault. His not-so-perfect father. A human man after all, selfish enough to act in his own interests, a man who had made mistakes. Mistakes that Jason had paid for. And little Mary and her mother. And Adam and Caithren, and who knew how many others?

"I thank you for being so candid." He rose and held out a hand.

Scarborough stood and grasped it tightly. "I'm sorry."

"And for jumping in to save me from Gothard's pistol."

"I was only evening the score. You saved me from his sword. I would never have recognized him in that disguise." Their eyes met, man to man. Two men who both did what needed to be done. "I'll leave you to your thoughts." With a nod, Scarborough backed away, then turned and walked toward the house.

"Pardon me, but are ye the Marquess of Cainewood?"

The voice was light and musical, and Jason swivelled to see Emerald MacCallum. By God, she topped him in height. How had he ever insisted that Cait was Emerald? Taken aback, he blinked. "Where is your emerald amulet?"

Her eyes looked puzzled. "My what?"

"Your . . ." He shook his head to clear it. "How did you get your name?"

She grinned. "My birth name is Flora. The first time I went tracking, I recovered a large cache of stolen emeralds. The news sheets called me 'Emerald' MacCallum, and the name stuck."

Of course. It made perfect sense. Another misconception that had stubbornly lodged in his head.

"Lord Cainewood . . ." She swept off her man's hat, and the drizzle beaded on her bright red curls. "I believe ye had offered a reward . . . ?"

He measured her, unblinking. He sensed she was a good woman, drawn to desperate measures. Something he understood now more than ever before. And he remembered a man saying she was a mother. "You have children?"

"Aye." Her eyes saddened, and he knew what to do.

The pouch in his surcoat was heavy. He drew it out and handed it to her.

Frowning, she spilled the contents into her hand and slowly counted a hundred pounds, then put the rest back.

"Keep it," Jason said. "All of it."

"But . . . there is more than two hundred pounds here! The reward was a hundred." She looked at him like he'd lost his mind.

Perhaps he had. "Keep it," he repeated. "I didn't exactly want to see justice done this way, but perhaps it is for the best." He shrugged. "As for the money . . . I would just as soon not picture you chasing men all over England. Go home to your children."

She smiled, her face transforming. Her eyes brimmed with tears. And once he'd thought that a woman like her would never cry. Another thing he'd been wrong about. "Take it and make a life for yourself," he said. "And your children."

"I will," she breathed. "God bless ye, Lord Cainewood."

Caithren could barely lift her feet to mount the steps to the town house. Her father was gone, and now her brother. And, dear God, she'd killed a man. And Jason was gone from her life. 'Twas all too much to absorb.

"Why is it that anything the authorities are involved in seems to take forever?" Ford shoved open the door.

A sound of derision came from her throat. "I expect they've nothing better to do than be bothersome."

"Hush, sweet Cait." Cameron took her by the elbow. "Ford's question was rhetorical. 'Tis been a long night, but ye can rest now." He stopped short on the threshold, then turned to Kendra and Ford. "Good Lord. Ye people actually live here?" Clearly aghast, he stared into the plush interior.

Kendra beckoned him inside. "Father bought it in the pre-War days, before the family's capital was depleted in defense of the King. Jason is cash poor, but he has . . . things."

"Jason seems to have plenty of money," Cait disagreed.

" 'Tis all relative." With a shrug, Kendra started down the corridor. "Come, we'll sit in the drawing room and talk."

"I dinna want to talk," Cait said to her back.

Cam lifted a brow. "She wants to wallow."

Kendra turned and sent her a sympathetic look. "Go on in. I'll stop by the kitchen and ask for some refreshments."

Cait set her jaw, but followed the men into the drawing room and plopped onto the burgundy brocade couch. Cameron sat beside her, and Ford settled into one of two matching carved-walnut chairs.

Kendra took the other chair moments later. "Cait. Are you all right?"

"I'm fine." Her hands tried to find her amulet, then her laces, and finally fell into her lap. " 'Twas an accident. I didn't mean to kill him."

"I'm not speaking of Wat Gothard." Kendra's green eyes mirrored everyone's concern. "I am asking how ye feel about your brother. And . . . about Jason."

"I'll miss my brother. We weren't close, and, truth be told, I didn't hold him in high regard. We hadn't seen much of each other in years. But he was my brother, my blood, and I loved him." She struggled to swallow the lump that had been lodged in her throat since the moment Jason told her the truth "As for your brother, he kept Adam was dead, and he didn't care enough to tell me."

Ford rose. "That isn't so." As he paced the Oriental carpet, the butler walked in with a large silver tray. "I talked to him outside the door. He'd known for but two days, Cait, and he failed to tell you because . . ." He turned, and his blue eyes sought hers. ". . . not because he didn't care, but because he cared too much. He was afraid you would hate him once you knew."

"Hate him?" She accepted a cup of warm chocolate from the butler, but shook her head at the plate of proffered cakes. "Whyever would I hate him?"

Ford's brow knitted. "For killing your brother."

"That is the most unbelievable thing I've ever heard." Stunned, she sipped from the cup, grateful for something to do with her hands and mouth. Other than throttling Jason and yelling. "Jason kent I didn't think the killing intentional. We discussed it, days ago. Afore either of us knew it was . . . Adam." At her brother's name, her vision blurred, but she took a deep breath.

"He thought that wouldn't matter to you. Whether it was intentional or not." Ford took a cake, but just held it, as though he wasn't sure what it was for. The butler set down the plate and left. "It was your brother, Cait."

" 'Twas an accident." She sat a while, open-mouthed. "Now I do hate him." But the thought that Ford could be right brought a thread of hope. She held to it like a lifeline.

"If not for killing your brother, why hate him, then?" Kendra frowned into her cup. "Because he left you there after telling you?"

"No. Never that." The chocolate was not sitting well in her stomach. "Gothard and Scarborough were both at that wedding. He had to go." Setting her cup on a low table, she drew an embroidered throw off the back of the couch and wrapped it around her shoulders. "He had no choice."

"Then why?" Rising, Kendra came close and knelt at Cait's feet. "I want to understand. If not because he left you, why do you hate him?"

"I dinna hate him." Tears flooded her eyes. Tears she wouldn't shed for Adam—not in so public a place—flowed freely when she thought of Jason's betrayal. "I love him, and he doesn't trust me to forgive him. That hurts."

Beside her, Cam took her hand. "D'ye really love him, Cait? A man you've kent for but days? An . . . Englishman?"

She nodded, afraid what he must think, yet unable to deny it.

But he surprised her. "Then ye must forgive him for thinking such of ye." His hand squeezed hers. "It goes two ways, ye ken. Remember what your mam used to say? Gae it oot and get it back."

"Pardon?" Ford said. Kendra shot him a lowering glance.

"What we give, we have," Cait translated softly. She

took a deep breath. "Forgiveness. And trust. Jason and I . . . we've not seen a lot of either between us, but mayhap it must come from me first."

Kendra reached for a cake and turned it in her hands. "Make him suffer, Cait. God knows he deserves it." She looked up, and they shared a wan smile. "But then you'll marry him, will you not? Because—"

"Nay." Fresh tears leaked out. "I love your brother, but I cannot marry him."

"Why?" Kendra breathed. "I thought—"

Cait shivered, but not from the cold. "Upon marriage my property would be Jason's. The land that goes with the title is worth nothing without the larger portion, the property that came through my mother. To me, now that Adam is gone." Swallowing against the sadness, she tightened the wrap around her. "Cameron deserves it, and I love him too much to see him lose it."

With a gasp, Cam pulled his hand from hers. " 'Twas never meant to be mine, Cait! Any of it!"

"Aye, it was and it is." She blinked back the tears. "Ye were next in line. Eldest son of my father's brother. Sir Cameron Leslie, now that Da and Adam are gone. Ye kent that, surely?"

"Nay." He looked stunned. "I mean . . . Good Lord. Of course I kent I was next in line, but I never thought about it. I thought only of ye, Cait. Not an hour after I heard the news, I was on my way here to fetch ye back home. Knowing ye wouldn't find Adam."

"See? Ye thought of me first. It has always been that way between us, Cam, and 'twill not be changing now."

After telling his story to the authorities, Jason walked the streets for hours, far past the time it was safe to be outside without linkboys to light the way. 'Twas past midnight before he mounted the steps to the town house and threw open the door.

"Jason! Where have you been?" Kendra must have

been watching by the window, because she flung herself at him, then pulled back. "You're soaking wet."

He hadn't noticed. "I need to talk to you and Ford. In the drawing room. Now."

"Should you not dry off first?" She stared at him, then down to the marble floor, where a small puddle was collecting at his feet. "About Cait . . ."

Concern etched her wholesome features, but he couldn't muster the energy to comfort her. "Now."

"All right. I'll—I'll go get Ford."

He strode to the drawing room, lit a fire, wrapped himself in the costly embroidered throw that was wadded in the corner of the brocade couch. And waited, pacing the dark red and blue carpet.

"Sit down," he said when the twins came in.

Obediently Kendra perched on one of the chairs, but Ford strode to a small inlaid cabinet. "I could do with a brandy. And you?"

Jason nodded his assent and took the goblet when Ford had poured. He waved him into another chair. "How is Caithren?"

"Fine," Kendra said carefully. "Disappointed and grieving, but fine. Jason, she—"

"Good." Cait was important—the most important thing of all. But his world had turned upside down tonight, and he had to work that out. He sipped the brandy, felt it burn a path to his empty stomach. "Geoffrey Gothard was our brother."

"He was *what*?" the twins said in unison.

"Our brother." He tugged the throw more tightly around his shoulders. "Our half brother, to be more precise. As well as Scarborough's. Our father impregnated their mother before he wed ours," he said, almost mechanically. He was still having trouble wrapping his mind around that fact. "And he left her, pregnant, knowing she was pregnant. Our father."

An uneasy silence settled over the room. Jason could

hear the clock ticking on the mantel. Ford blew out a slow breath. "You said he *was* our brother."

"He's dead." Kendra rose as if to come to him, but he waved her back. "At Emerald MacCallum's hands. But I do believe I was almost pushed to the point where I would have done it myself."

Ford nodded knowingly. "He threatened the woman you love."

"No. I mean, yes. That would have been enough. But it was more than that." Shivering, Jason moved to put his back to the fire. "All these years—"

The words wouldn't come out, wouldn't align themselves in his head.

"All these years," Kendra repeated gently, "you've tried to live up to the legend of our father—the brave, honorable, self-sacrificing man who gave up his own family to fight for his King. To fight in a losing war, die in a losing war, taking our mother along with him."

He drew a deep breath. "That vision of him was wrong."

"Yes, it was. But you weren't ready to see it." Kendra reached for Ford's brandy and took a fortifying sip. "They left you the head of the family at too tender an age. Too many responsibilities. But they did it out of love for each other and the monarchy, not lack of love for us."

"I know that." Jason's voice came out rough, and he cleared his throat. "I agree with that. Unlike Colin, I never took it as a personal affront. But . . . responsibilities." He took another sip of his brandy—a gulp, truth be told—and stared into the goblet. "It seems I've always had responsibilities. And I resented those meaningless deaths, and I think I avoided any violence that reminded me of it." He looked up. "And I hated myself for it."

Kendra rose and walked over to him, and he didn't stop her this time. Her light green eyes burned into his darker ones. "Our father hadn't been so brave and honorable, had he? Or responsible. He'd been a man. Human."

'Twas the same conclusion he'd come to while walking in the rain. It was time he give himself permission to be human as well. Free of the overwhelming shackles of his father's expectations. Free to live his life with his own set of values. In his own way. With Caithren—if only she'd have him.

If only she'd forgive him. At long last, he had the peace that he'd been craving—but not the woman he loved.

"Cait and we . . ." His voice cracked. "We all lost brothers this day."

"But ours was not worth claiming." Ford stood up. "Go to her, Jason. She's hurting."

Kendra's mouth gaped open at her twin. "When did you get to be so sensitive?"

He shot her a scathing glare, then turned back to their brother. "Go to her. She's in your chamber." His lips turned up in a hint of a smile. "Just hope Cameron doesn't have it in his mind to protect her."

Jason couldn't smile, not now. And just let her cousin try to stand in his way. His heart ached as he climbed the stairs to his chamber. He eased open the door, his knees going weak just at the sight of her lying on his bed, Cameron in a chair nearby, murmuring soft words of comfort.

She rolled over to face him, her eyes brimming with tears. Cameron stood and walked to the door. "Remember what I told ye, Cait, I beg ye. Your happiness comes afore—"

"Leave us, Cam." Her voice sounded breathless, uneven, no doubt from hours of crying. "Please." Wordlessly, Cameron slipped through the door, and it clicked shut behind him.

Jason's hands loosened their hold on the embroidered

throw, and it slid from his shoulders to the floor. "You hate me, don't you?" he whispered.

She sat up. "You're wet. Ye should dry off."

He took a hesitant step closer. "Cait—"

"Ye hurt me," she said.

He'd go to his knees if he thought it would make a difference, but he stood frozen in place. "I'm so sorry. If I'd known earlier 'twas your brother I'd killed, I would have told you immediately, I swear. But I loved you by then, Cait—I couldn't bear to bring you the news that would make you so unhappy. That would forever tear you from my side. I wanted that last night with you more than I wanted to live."

Her eyes widened a bit through the tears, but she hugged herself as if to shut him out. "Ye didn't trust me." She swiped miserably at the wetness on her cheeks. "And ye dinna trust me still. How can ye say in one breath that ye love me, and in the next that I would be so shallow as to hold an accidental death against ye?"

"But—"

"I ken that Adam's killing wasn't intentional, any more than my own killing of Wat."

A sudden trickle of relief sang through his blood. Guilt slowly began to fade away, replaced by a tremulous hope for the future. "But would you feel the same way if you hadn't killed Wat?" he wondered. "Would you still have understood?"

She shook her head as if disgusted, but bold determination lit her hazel eyes. "See, there ye go again." She bit back the tears and drew a calming breath. "I am devastated that ye dinna think better of me. D'ye remember that night in Newark, when ye had the bad dream?"

He remembered. A gruesome nightmare, and an angel that soothed him. Wearing a ridiculous white night rail. "You said you didn't fault me. You understood."

"And just what d'ye think would ever change that?"

He was afraid to believe, but deep down he knew she harbored no anger, no resentment. 'Twas not in her.

"I will expect more respect from ye from here on out, Jason Chase."

He blinked, and his breath caught in hope. "Does that mean—"

"You've left me alone all night, with little to do but think. And I think I will marry ye, Lord Cainewood. Never mind that ye haven't asked. But only on two conditions."

His heart soared. "Anything."

She stood, and he reached to pull her into an embrace. But she wrenched away. "Ye will hear me out."

"Very well." Though his arms ached to hold her, he crossed them instead. "I'm listening."

"One. Ye will not underestimate me again."

"You can wager on that." He risked a small, hopeful smile. "And two?"

She blew out a breath and locked her gaze on his. "Cameron must have Leslie. The part that came through my mother, I mean. With Adam's death, he's already come into the title and small entailed lands. But those lands alone cannot support a man."

"Cait—"

"Nay. Ye will hear me out. Cameron hasn't asked for this, and he would likely strangle me if he kent I was asking for him. But he deserves Leslie, Jase—it should have been his in the first place. He was a better son to Da than Adam ever was. And even though Kendra told me ye need money, I'll not see Cam go without his due—I'll not take my happiness at his expense. 'Twould not be fair."

"And Caithren Leslie is always fair," he said softly. "Now, you will hear me out."

She sat on the bed, apparently reserving judgment.

"I was only going to say, back when you interrupted me, that Cameron can have the property—the only part of Leslie I need is you. And I *do* need you, Caithren. More than I ever thought possible."

"Oh." She looked properly chagrined, but a tiny smile tugged at her lips.

"And I have something for you." He reached into his pocket. "Hold out your hand." She did, and he gazed into her eyes as he folded her fingers around a flash of green. "When it changes hands, a change of heart," he quoted solemnly.

"My amulet?" She looked at it, then back at him. "Where—how did ye get this?"

"I found it in the square. When I went looking for you. I knotted the broken chain so you can wear it until I have time to get it repaired properly."

She stared down at it for a moment, fingering the neat, wee knot, then slowly held it out to him. "Keep it."

"Pardon?" He didn't reach for it, just gaped at her in disbelief.

"I thought that if I wore it I would be safe. But it brought me more luck when ye had it. Then I found the strength to save myself from the Gothards. All by myself, without the emerald to depend on. And it brought me your offer of love and marriage. At least I think it did—ye haven't asked me yet, and I've been waiting nigh on two days already."

He dropped to one knee and took both her hands in his, the emerald trapped between their fingers. "Will you marry me, Caithren Leslie?"

"Lick your right thumb." She pulled away her hands. He was speechless for a moment. "Pardon?"

" 'Tis a Scottish custom. Lick it."

"I cannot believe—"

"*Lick it.*" For emphasis, she licked her own. Shaking his head, he did the same, and she took his hand and pressed their wet thumbs tightly together. " 'Tis a bond. Now ask me again."

He captured her eyes with his. "Caithren Leslie—"

His voice broke, and he sucked in a long, audible breath. "Will you marry me?"

With a look so intimate it tugged at his heart, she pulled him up and slipped the necklace over his head. He touched it, almost as reverently as she always had, and she smiled.

"Jason Chase, I thought ye would never ask." And her lips gave him his answer.

Chapter Twenty-five

"**H**urry," Kendra urged. " 'Tis about to begin."

Her sister-in-law, Amy, giggled. "They'll not be starting the ceremony without the bride."

Caithren turned from the window, where she'd been staring at the small cluster of people gathering in the bright sun that flooded Cainewood Castle's quadrangle. Blinking in the chamber's relative dimness, she walked to Kendra's four-poster bed and slid the gold brocade robe from her shoulders.

Amy held up a sheer chemise. "Dressing for your wedding should be a calm, soothing experience." She shot Kendra a warning glance as she slipped the garment over Cait's head.

"Like yours was?" Kendra returned with a lift of one expressive brow. "I seem to remember you shaking in your—excuse me, *my*—red-heeled shoes."

Amy's eyes sparkled. "That was different. I was terrified. A shopkeeper's daughter marrying an earl. It seemed wrong." She smiled, tossing one long black ringlet behind her plum, velvet-clad shoulder. "But it was right."

Kendra smoothed her mint satin skirts. "Cait has nothing to be nervous about."

"Nay." Caithren rolled her eyes. "Daughters of provincial Scottish baronets wed English marquesses every day of the week." The other women laughed. "But I'm not nervous," she told them. "This is right, too." She believed it, with all her heart and soul.

Still, 'twas no small step to be taking. Cait took a deep breath and drew her wedding gown off the bed—the first English gown that had been specifically made for her. Fashioned of sky blue silk, it had a silver tissue underskirt and real silver lace around the scooped neckline. The sleeves were double-puffed with a spill of silver lace at the wrists, the stomacher embroidered with scrolling silver designs.

She held it up. "Marry in blue, love ever true."

"Is that what they say?" Kendra helped her wiggle into it, watching appreciatively as it settled into place. "Oh, 'tis lovely! If ever I fall in love, I want a dress just like this, but in green."

"Oh, ye wouldn't want to wear green." Cait glanced up from tightening the laces. " 'Tis unlucky. The choice of the fairies."

Amy handed her the stomacher. "You believe in fairies?"

"Well, nay." Cait grinned. "But 'tis not worth taking a chance now, is it? Not on your wedding day. Besides," she added, looking at Kendra, "Jason says ye dinna want to marry."

"Not any of the men he chooses," Kendra scoffed, helping her attach the tabs. "Stodgy old dukes, ancient rich earls, widowed marquesses with children." When they finished, Cait sat to draw on her stockings. Kendra tossed her red ringlets. "I will not marry a boring, acceptable man. I am looking for peerless passion." She handed Cait two blue ribbon garters decorated with silver lace. "And not," she added, her eyes narrowing, "a duke. I'll not be 'Your Graced' for the rest of my life." She held out a sky blue satin shoe.

"I need the right shoe first." The shoes were straight, not made for one foot or the other, but Cait had worn them yesterday to break them in. No sense getting blisters at her wedding.

"For luck?" Kendra frowned at both shoes, then handed her the other.

"Aye. And that silver coin I left on your dressing table goes in the left one."

"I'll get it," Amy volunteered.

"D'ye hear that?" Cait froze. Haunting notes floated up through the open window. "Could it be bagpipes?"

"Jason's surprise. Tell him not that you heard." Kendra moved to shut the window.

"Leave it open, please. I'll not tell him." Her heart swelled as she slipped the coin into her shoe. "Though how he thinks anyone within ten miles could fail to hear a bagpiper is beyond me."

"I have something for you." Gold gleamed when Amy pulled her hand from her pocket. "The first thing I made in my new workshop. May I pin it on you?"

Cait nodded and stood, her gaze riveted to the gorgeous oval emerald stomacher brooch in Amy's hand. Surrounded by diamonds and pearls in a delicate filigree bezel, it glittered through the sudden tears that filmed her eyes. "Jason told me you gave him your own emerald," Amy said as she pinned it to the middle of Cait's neckline. "So I thought it would make a perfect wedding present."

Cait's fingers moved to caress it. " 'T-tis the most beautiful thing I've ever owned," she whispered. "I will never be able to thank ye."

"Marry come up!" Amy laughed. "You have just thanked me already." She stepped back to view her handiwork, then her gaze swept Cait from head to toe. "God in heaven," she breathed. "You look beautiful. Come to the mirror and see."

"Nay. I cannot see myself fully dressed for my wedding." Self-conscious, Caithren played with the ends of her long, straight hair, which Jason had requested be left free and uncurled, then fanned it over her exposed bosom. She touched the little heart patch on her cheek and sent both women a tremulous smile.

"Another sister." When Kendra gathered them all into a group hug and they bumped foreheads, Cait giggled through her tears.

A knock came at the door. "Are ye ready?" Cameron's voice came through the sturdy oak. "Colin said you're taking so long ye must be eating in here."

"Quick," Kendra said loudly. "Hide the food." They all laughed as Cait went to open the door.

"Cait?" Dressed in a borrowed, deep blue velvet suit, Cameron looked almost as English as she did. "Good Lord," he said. "Cait, ye look lovely."

"Thank ye." She blushed, looking down to see big cornflower eyes and a head of bright blonde curls. "And who is this?"

"Her name is Mary, and she and her mother are special guests." Cam lifted his hand, and Mary's little hand came up with it. "She, uh, attached herself to me." He gave a sheepish shrug, but Cait didn't miss the pleased glow in his eyes. "She may be walking down the aisle with us."

So this was the Mary that Jason had run off to avenge. Caithren knelt, her silk skirts pooling around her. "Good day," she said.

"Good day," Mary returned in a small, polite voice. "I am pleased to meet you, my lady."

"I'm not—" Cait started.

"You'll be a lady within the hour," Cam said with a teasing smile. "Ye may as well get used to it." He blew out a breath, ruffling his straight, wheaten hair. "I, on the other hand, will never get used to being a sir."

"Aye, ye will." Cait stood and linked her arm though his. "Shall we go?"

Luckily the three of them fit side by side down the corridor and wide stone staircase, because Mary still clung to Cam with an iron grip. The only remaining evidence of the lassie's ordeal seemed to be a slight catch in her gait and a wee slur in her speech. Cait had taken Kendra foraging around Cainewood yesterday, showing her which plants were useful, and tomorrow she would teach her how to make an infusion to help Mary regain her strength.

The bagpipe music swelled when they reached the double front doors and stepped out into the sunshine. Kendra wandered off to find her twin. Colin was waiting outside for Amy, their infant daughter Jewel cooing in his arms. The bairn between them, he bent to give his wife a sweet, lingering kiss, and Caithren smiled at the three of them together.

A family. Although she now knew she wasn't yet pregnant, she smiled at the thought that she and Jason might have a family soon.

'Twas a glorious day to be wed, the quadrangle redolent with the scent of newly cut grass, the sky blue as her gown and dotted with wee puffy white clouds. Cait's gaze swept the castle's crenelated walls and the ancient keep built on a motte—reminding her of the one outside Stamford. Beyond it was an area where the grass grew high and untamed.

"Gudeman's croft," she murmured.

"What is that?" Mary asked.

Cameron knelt down to her. "A place allowed to grow free as a shelter for the fairies and brownies."

"Oh." Mary's eyes opened wide. "Know you stories of fairies and brownies?"

"Many." With his free hand, Cam ruffled her unruly curls. "But they'll have to wait for later." He stood and faced Cait. " 'Tis really the old tilting yard," he said. "Colin told me they dinna groom it since 'tis long been in disuse."

"I kent that." Her lips curved in a soft smile as she

scanned her new home. "Can ye believe this place, Cam?"

His hazel eyes met hers. "Ye always were meant to live in a castle, sweet Cait."

"Aye," she said, thinking of Da's tiny castle at home—Cameron's castle now. "But who'd have ever guessed it would be such a huge, historic one . . . and in England?" Her head reeled with the impossibility of it. Nothing Jason had told her could have prepared her for the sheer size and grandeur of Cainewood Castle. She could scarcely believe she would be living within its four-foot-thick stone walls. As the Marchioness of Cainewood, no less.

"You'll do fine." Cam leaned to kiss her forehead, then looked up. "There's your man now."

Her gaze flew to Jason, and suddenly what had seemed impossible was gloriously real. She was going to live here, in this castle, with the man she loved.

Clearly comfortable in this place, he walked beside the gray-haired parson, deep in conversation. He wore a forest-green velvet suit that brought out his eyes, trimmed in gold braid that matched the stiff ribbon bows on his formal heeled shoes. When he looked over at her and smiled, her heart did a slow roll in her chest.

A pretty woman in a clean but simple pink dress came up to take Mary by the hand. " 'Tis time," she said gently, and reluctantly the wee lass released her grip on Cameron. The girl looked over her shoulder, her blue eyes lingering on him as the woman led her away.

"Her mother?" Cait guessed.

"Aye. Her name is Clarice Bradford." Cameron's own gaze followed the two as they walked toward the gatehouse on their way to the family's private chapel, the woman's rich brown hair gleaming beneath a pink-ribboned straw hat. "You'll like her." He turned to take Cait by both hands. "Are ye ready?" he asked.

"More ready than I ever thought possible." Smiling

at him, she squeezed his fingers. "Ye ken, Mam always said it is better to marry over the midden than over the muir."

"I've heard that said, that 'tis wise to stick within your own circle." Did she only imagine it, or did his gaze flick over to Clarice? "But I'm not sure I believe it."

"I dinna believe it, either." Her own gaze trailed to Jason, waiting for her by the barbican. She was sure she'd never glimpsed so romantic a vision as her husband-to-be standing with the soaring castle behind him, his blue-black hair ruffled by the slight breeze, his clear green eyes locked on hers. "I reckon even mothers are wrong sometimes."

The parson cleared his throat. "Caithren Leslie, wilt thou have this man to thy wedded husband, to live together after God's ordinance in the holy estate of matrimony? Wilt thou love him, comfort him, honor, obey, and serve him, and keep him in sickness and in health; and, forsaking all others, keep thee only unto him so long as ye both shall live?"

Jason's hand squeezed Caithren's. She looked around her at all the people gathered beneath the hammerbeam roof of Cainewood's ancient chapel, in the multicolored light that filtered through the stained, arched windows. Cameron, who'd insisted on coming here for her wedding before going home to his new life in Scotland. Kendra and Ford, who'd stood by her side that wrenching night in London. Colin—like Jason, but different—and Amy and their beautiful bairn. Mary and Clarice, whose tragedy had set Jason on the path that led him to her.

They were all looking toward her, so expectantly.

"I will," she said. "All except the obey and serve part."

Cameron snickered. Kendra smiled. The parson just looked like he was going to choke.

"I accept those conditions," Jason said loud and clear.

The parson still looked confused. "Go on, will you?" Jason prompted. "Before she changes her mind."

Most of the wedding party sat around the dining room table, waiting for Colin, who had gone to settle the baby in her cradle, and Ford, who had told them he wanted to fetch something. A stack of marzipaned wedding cakes sat in the middle of the long mahogany table, which was set with fine china and crystal that Caithren had only read about in books. She kept looking down at the wedding ring that Jason had slipped onto her finger as a surprise.

"Do you like it?" he murmured from his seat beside her. "Father sold off most of the family jewels to help finance the War, but I could have found something, or had Amy make—"

" 'Tis perfect." She smiled at the gold band studded with emeralds, remembering when he bought it from the Gypsy woman without dickering. "There is no other ring in this world I would rather have."

"Whenever I see it, I'll remember your dance," he said low. "And the moment you stole my heart."

Her own heart melting, they shared a smile.

"I'm starving," Kendra announced. She reached for a cake, then froze. "Did you hear something?" She sat up straighter, twisting her head toward the high, arched windows. Cait turned to look, too. But the dancing flames in the fireplace reflected off the beveled glass, making it difficult to see anything.

"Hear something like what?" Cameron asked.

Kendra frowned. "Like . . . scratching."

"I was sipping." Jason rolled his eyes and drained his crystal goblet with a prolonged slurp. "There. Was that the sound?"

"No . . . wait! Listen . . ."

"I hear it too," Amy breathed. " 'Tis—"

Kendra's eyes widened. "The ghost! The Parkinson ghost!"

"What is this about a ghost?" Clearly unshaken, Cameron took a sip of his wine, swirling it in his goblet appreciatively.

"There is no such thing as ghosts," Jason declared.

"Now . . ." Cam paused for another swallow. "You'll not be finding a Scot admitting to that."

Kendra glared at her brother. "Just because you cannot explain ghosts does not mean they don't exist. The Parkinson ghost is hardly a new legend. And have you not heard of all the sightings in the week since we've been back?" She turned to Caithren, apparently looking for support. "Did you know this room was once a private chapel, built by Henry II when the castle was in the hands of the Crown?"

Cait's gaze swept the stone arches overhead, fit between with a centuries-old oak barrel–section ceiling. "Tonight it feels like it still belongs to the spirits, aye?"

Cameron's goblet hit the table with a little *clink*. "Tell us about this ghost." Little Mary climbed up and plastered herself against his side, one arm around his neck, her other thumb stuck into her mouth. He shifted to hold her close. "What are these stories?"

Kendra sat forward on her lattice-backed chair. "Just this week Cook saw him twice, once in the quadrangle and once walking across the drawbridge, and Haversham saw him on the drive, and Sally saw him on the roof—"

"—and Carrington saw him under the barbican," Jason interrupted, "and Mrs. Potts saw him on the wall walk. Our servants have very impressionable imaginations." He reached for the wine decanter. "Let us suppose there were such a thing as ghosts—just for argument's sake, you understand. Why would this Parkinson fellow show up *now*, after all this time?"

"Could it be *my* fault?" Cait wondered.

"No." Kendra shook her head. "He died exactly

twenty years ago this month. And he was killed by a Royalist—not that he didn't deserve it, the Roundhead cur, presuming to live in *our* castle—"

"Wheesht!" Cait whispered. "There it is again!"

Kendra moved to Colin's empty chair and grabbed Amy's hand. " 'Tis him, I know it," she whispered. Caithren took Jason's hand as well.

"It is *not* him." Unlike his sister's whisper, Jason's voice was loud and sure. "She is famous for jumping to conclusions," he said to no one in particular. " 'Tis a bush being blown against the window."

" 'Tis not windy," Clarice murmured, her cheeks turning red at having said something aloud. Her daughter let out a little whine, burrowing into Cameron's shirtfront.

"Not to mention," Kendra whispered more fiercely, "there are no bushes under those windows."

Caithren turned to see out the windows and gasped. Something white was . . . floating beyond the leaded panes. Like the monk she'd seen in the tunnel beneath Newark.

Jason turned too, and despite himself, drew in a sharp breath.

"What? What is it?" Kendra whispered frantically, her eyes shut tight.

" 'Tis . . . I'm not sure." Calmly Cameron took a sip of his wine. "But a ghost isn't necessarily something to be afraid of, ye ken?"

A sudden clatter from the chimney echoed in the high, arched chamber. Cait gripped Jason's hand harder, and Clarice grabbed for her daughter and somehow ended on Cameron's lap. They all swung around, their gazes riveted to the rattling fireplace.

"Oh, my God!" Kendra breathed. "He's up on the roof, just like Sally said! Oh, my God! Oh, my God!"

They all flinched when the dining room door swung open and a rush of wind made the tapestries flutter against the stone walls. Apparently forgetting he was supposed to look fearless, Jason clutched Cait, and she let out a high-pitched squeak. When Kendra screamed, the rest of the females joined her.

With an unnerving suddenness, mad laughter burst forth to accompany the rattling. Colin rushed in, whipping off a white sheet with a grand gesture.

They all stared at him, dumbstruck, as he strode over to the fireplace and bent down to shout up the chimney. "Ford! Come on down!"

"Bloody hell." Jason disentangled himself from Cait and sat back.

Amy unclenched her fingers from Kendra's and flexed her hand, shaking her head at her husband. "I cannot credit that I fell for that."

Colin grinned wickedly, raising one black eyebrow.

"Fell for what?" Caithren asked.

"Colin," Kendra said ruefully, "is famous—or I should say infamous—for his practical jokes."

"Oh." Cait's gaze flickered to Jason. "Well," she told Amy, "if it makes ye feel any better, Jase fell for it, too."

"I did not."

"Then it was someone else's heart I felt pounding beneath my hand?" She giggled when he sputtered.

Red-faced, Clarice slid off Cam's lap and onto her chair. "Then there's no ghost?"

"None." Colin's green eyes sparkled with mischief. "The staff was quite obliging with the mysterious sightings and all. I would not be surprised if they're about now, waiting to see how it all turned out."

The door opened, and they all looked out into the corridor expectantly, but 'twas only Ford returning from his chain-rattling responsibilities. He took one look at Cait's good-natured pout and burst into peals of laughter.

"On our wedding night!" she chided, but she couldn't help laughing along with him.

Cam rose and, settling Mary on her own chair, walked

over to shake Colin's hand. "Well done, I must say. This is my kind of family."

"Then welcome to it." Colin turned to Caithren. "You, too." He went to the door and signaled, whereby more servants than were necessary paraded in carrying the many dishes that comprised the wedding supper. They smiled conspiratorially as they set down platter after platter, slanting sidewise glances at Colin and each other before parading back out. Steaming dishes of chicken cullis, fricandeau of beef, and artichoke pie wafted their scents toward Caithren's nose.

She *did* feel like part of this family. Jason's hand squeezed hers under the table. One foot moved to tangle with hers, and his leg pressed against her thigh, making her face heat with thoughts of their wedding night to come. When she looked over at him, she felt so warm and happy, she couldn't quite believe it.

There was a grand sallet on the table, a bed of young greens with mandarin oranges, eggs, and long sprigs of rosemary standing tall, stuck into lemon halves and hung with cherries. But Kendra went for a cake.

"She always eats dessert first," Ford said at the look on Cait's face.

Kendra only smiled, licking marzipan off her lips. "I might not have room for it later." She took another bite. "Would you like some?"

Cait shook her head and reached for some chicken. Toasts were drunk and good-natured teasing abounded. An hour later, when the meal was finished and everyone still sat around talking, she pushed back her chair and rose. They all turned to look at her.

"A Scots funeral is merrier than an English wedding," she declared. "Whatever happened to that bagpiper?"

Jason shrugged. "I think he's eating in the kitchen."

"Well, would somebody fetch him already?" She moved from the table and shook out her skirts. "I'll be wanting to dance."

While Ford went off to do her bidding, she gave the others instructions. "Hold hands in a circle, lads and lassies alternating. That's it. Now, who has a hankie?" Colin produced one, and she handed it to her cousin. "Cameron, ye take the middle since ye ken what to do."

When the piper arrived, Caithren surprised everyone by kicking off her shoes, then running to scoop up her lucky silver coin when it rolled across the floor. Laughing, Kendra and Amy doffed their shoes as well, and although they couldn't convince Clarice to dance in stockinged feet, at least her shoes were sensible and flat. Wee Mary was wearing flat shoes, too, but she was only too happy to get rid of them and her stockings, besides.

"Very well." Cait turned to the piper as Ford took his place in the circle. "We'll have a reel, if ye please."

Around and around they went in time to the rousing tune, until Cameron came from the center to Cait. The circling stopped, and he laid the lace-edged hankie in a neat square at her feet. They knelt on either side, and she bestowed him with a kiss on the lips. This met with mixed laughter and startled gasps, then Cait snatched up the handkerchief and took her place in the middle. Around they went again, dancing until she chose Jason. Their kiss was long and deep, causing much throat-clearing and finally applause. Then Jason went into the center, and the circling resumed.

Jason chose Amy, and Amy chose Colin, and Colin chose Kendra, and Kendra chose Ford, and Ford chose Mary . . . and no one was surprised when Mary chose Cameron. By the time Cam chose Clarice they were all worn out, and Cait signaled the piper to take a rest before Clarice had to go to her knees. Just in time— Clarice's cheeks had gone as pink as her dress.

"A kissing dance!" Kendra said, breathlessly making her way to a chair. "I've never heard of such a thing!"

"There is much kissing at Scottish weddings." Cait winked at Cameron, still hovering close by Clarice. "A kiss can be claimed at the beginning and end of each and every dance. Now, get up, all ye lazybones. We'll have a strathspey, and a hornpipe after that."

The piper played those and more, and some English tunes as well, and if the familiar notes sounded a bit odd wafting from the pipes, nobody cared. 'Twas past midnight before Cait let the poor musician go and the wedding party began stumbling off to bed with a lot of final kisses and good nights. Jason fetched a footman to see Clarice and Mary home, and Cameron closed the door behind them, then turned to kiss Cait on the cheek.

"Lang may yer lum reek—an' may he huv the coal tae fill it."

Jason's brow creased. "What is that, Gaelic?"

"Nay." Cait laughed. "We dinna ken the Gaelic. After all this time with me, ye still cannot understand plain English when ye hear it, aye?" She smiled. "He was wishing we live long and well."

"I thank you, then. I think." Jason clapped Cameron on the shoulder. "And I wish you a good night."

"He wants me to leave ye," Cam said to Cait.

"Aye, and I second the request." Minutes ago she'd felt exhausted, but her body came alive at the thought of what was ahead. "I'd thank ye to take to your bed now."

"Good night to ye, then, sweet Cait." A little drunkenly, she thought, her cousin nodded and went up the stairs.

Cait's heart thumped in anticipation as she turned to Jason. Locking his gaze on hers in a way that set the pit of her stomach to fluttering, he waited until Cam's footsteps had faded, then swung her into his arms and took the steps two at a time.

When he set her down before his bedchamber door, she wound her arms around his neck and pressed her mouth to his. "Ye must carry me over the threshold," she whispered against his lips. " 'Tis bad luck if I trip."

"I'd not want to start with bad luck." Her eyes slid

closed as his tongue swept into her mouth, hot and exciting. His lips still sealed to hers, he caught her up and brought her inside. When her feet hit the plush carpet she reluctantly opened her eyes, then blinked when he took her by the shoulders and turned her around.

The chamber was lit by candles, seemingly hundreds of them. They marched across the dressing table and along the windowsill, their flames reflecting off the leaded, beveled diamond panes. They graced the bedside tables and the massive headboard beneath the cobalt blue canopy. They sat on stands, on the floor, atop the tall, carved clothes press. But the brightest concentration flanked both ends of a wee table with a chair on either side . . . and their backgammon board in the center.

He swept the hair off the back of her neck and planted his lips there, warm and caressing. "You've pulled even," he murmured, the vibrations on her nape making her arch in pleasure, "but not for long. I intend to win this eve."

"Y-ye want to play backgammon?" With a gasp of disbelief, she turned to him. "On our wedding night?"

"Um-hmm." He nodded solemnly. "I remembered this morning that when I bought the set, we agreed to come up with something to wager. Then we never did. So I've settled on a forfeit."

Warily she backed up, not sure she liked the look in his eyes. "And what might that be?"

His smile made her skin tingle. "Our clothing."

"Wh-what?" She took another step back and sat on the bed.

"Our clothing." He came close, took her by the shoulders, and raised her to stand. His voice turned low and silky. "Whoever loses will have to remove an item of clothing. Until we are both . . . how do you put it?" A trace of eroticism in his smile made her breath catch. "In the scud?"

This was not her idea of a wedding night. "Can we

not just take all our clothes off now?" She molded herself against his hard body and kissed him on the chin, which was as high as she could reach without his cooperation. "I will play backgammon with ye tomorrow. I promise."

"Hmm . . ." He bent his head, and his mouth took hers in a kiss that was desperately intimate, but short and unsatisfying. "I think not."

"B-but I've got the stomacher and the gown, a chemise, and stockings and garters." As well as she could in such close quarters, she eyed his velvet-clad form. "And ye are wearing that much or more. This could take all night!"

"Mmmm." He nodded thoughtfully, and his next kiss was long: a nibbling of the lips, a persuasive caress, and finally a fiery possession that left her mouth burning for more. "I intend it to take all night." When she tried to pull him onto the bed, he only resisted with a husky chuckle.

Weak with need, 'twas an effort to cross her arms. "This is not fair."

"You think not?" He stepped back, seeming to consider it. "Very well, then, I will give you an advantage." She frowned, wondering whether to be relieved when he stripped off his surcoat and dropped it to the floor.

"You're terribly untidy," she scolded, quite ineffectively considering she couldn't control the tremble in her voice.

"But I have you now." He shrugged, working on the knot in his cravat. "And you always pick up after me."

" 'Tis a reprehensible attitude, Jase. I shall have to reform ye." She bent to pick up the coat, and, confused, laid it neatly over the back of a chair. He was taking off his clothes—it looked like she had won—yet his demeanor wasn't one of defeat. When her fingers moved to the tabs on her stomacher, he shook his head and reached out to still them.

Flashing a devilish grin, he handed her the cravat, then silently unlaced his shirt and stripped it off over his head. "There." The grin widened more. "Surely now you can win. Unless . . ." He raised a brow. "Unless you find yourself distracted again by my bare chest."

The lacy cravat dangled from her fingers as she stared at him. Against that very tempting bare chest, her amulet nestled, winking in the candlelight. She swallowed hard, her hands itching to touch him, her tongue begging to taste his salty skin, her body aching to meld itself with his and convince her once and for all that he would be hers, forever. Her exasperating Englishman.

Dark as sin, his eyes captured hers as he pushed her into a chair and handed her the shirt, still warm from his body. From the folds of fabric, his distinctive scent rose to envelop her, quickening her pulse, spreading the familiar melting weakness through every fiber of her being. Unable to stop staring, she slowly wadded the shirt and cravat in her lap.

"How very untidy," he chided, seating himself across the narrow table. Their knees touched, and one of his slid between hers at the same time one long arm sneaked underneath and tossed up her skirts. Warm and tormenting, a finger trailed her thigh . . .

And he tossed the dice.

Author's Note

I always like to see the places I'm writing about, and I had great fun researching this story and visiting all the inns that lined the Great North Road—formerly the Roman road called Ermine Street—back in the 1660s. Which ones mentioned in the story are real? All of them! If an inn was mentioned by name, you can assume it was a real place that Jason and Cait could have stopped at during their travels. But a few of them have fascinating histories and deserve more than a mere mention.

In Newark, the Saracen's Head inn dated back to 1341 and was indeed run by the Twentyman family from 1590 until 1720. As told by my fictious Mrs. Twentyman in the story, their name really was originally Lydell and changed when one of them poleaxed twenty men. And the true tale of the little drummer boy saving Newark from capture is still told today. A frequent visitor, Sir Walter Scott mentioned the inn in his novels and his diary, calling the landlord "a man of the most gentlemanly manners." The Saracen's Head finally closed in 1956, and the building is now used as a bank, but a "Saracen's Head" bust on the facade attests to its previous use.

As for the tunnels under Newark's marketplace, the one supposedly haunted by the ghost of a monk does not actually lead from the Saracen, but rather from the sixteenth-century Queen's Head inn. There are no recent sightings of this ghost, but the last landlord did complain of strange noises coming from the cellar and a door that seemed to open itself in the middle of the night. Employees claim that bottles have been moved and hesitate to go into the cellar on their own. And one customer swears he saw someone "not of this world" standing on the stairs. Although the distinctive round Queen's Head sign still swings beneath the eaves of the building, it is currently operated as part of the chain of Hobgoblin pubs. A nice place to stop for lunch and—who knows?—maybe a bit of a scare!

Although it was just The Angel during the seventeenth century, Grantham's oldest inn is now called The Angel and Royal. The grounds originally belonged to the Knights Templar, and from 1212 until the dissolution of their order in 1312, it was a hostelry for royal travelers, merchants, and pilgrims. King John and his train of courtiers held court at The Angel in 1213, Richard III signed the death warrant of the Duke of Buckingham there in 1483, and the inn enjoyed a royal visit from Charles I in 1633. In 1866, Edward VII paid a visit to The Angel, and it was then that it became known as The Angel and Royal. One of the inn's most-told stories is that in 1707, the landlord Michael Solomon died and left a legacy of forty shillings a year to pay for a sermon to be preached against the evils of drunkenness every Michaelmas Day. To this day, the annual payment is made and the sermon preached. This handsome and historic inn is still a popular place to eat and stay.

The Bell Inn in Stilton dates back to 1500, and the current building from 1642, the year in which the Civil War began. There is still a Roman well in the courtyard, topped by a charming thatched roof. Alas, the inn's black cat was invented, but inspired by one who roamed the grounds during my visit. One popular eighteenth-century tale has infamous highwayman Dick Turpin hiding at the Bell for nine weeks while hunted by the law.

Supposedly, when surprised by a raid, he threw open the window and jumped onto Black Bess to gallop up the Great North Road. But the Bell Inn is most famous for Stilton cheese and the man who popularized it, Cooper Thornhill, the inn's landlord during the mid-1700s. The cheese was first made by Thornhill's sister-in-law, a housekeeper in Leicestershire. Mites and all, he served it at the Bell and named it after the village. Soon the cheese's fame began to spread, and by the time Daniel Defoe wrote his *Tour Through the Whole Island of Great Britain* (1724–27), he could say he "passed through Stilton, a town famous for cheese." In the 1980s, the inn was restored using the original plans. Today it is a charming place to stay or take a meal while absorbing some of its history, and a frequent host to politicians, actors, and pop groups.

Caithren's home was inspired by the real Leslie Castle in Scotland. Sadly, the charming little castle is no longer open to the public, but I was fortunate to stay there when it was still being run as a luxurious B&B. Set at the west end of the Bennachie Range, thirty miles from Aberdeen, Leslie was the original seat of Clan Leslie. The current castle, a turreted seventeenth-century baronial house, is the third fortified building on the site since 1070. By the time of my story, the property had fallen out of Clan Leslie hands . . . but, fanciful as I am, I like to imagine that perhaps a minor Leslie family such as Cait's might have lived there. In 1979, the decaying roofless ruin was acquired by a member of the Leslie family and restored to its former fairy-tale beauty.

If you'd like to see pictures of all these places and others, please visit my website at www.laurenroyal.com. There you can also sign up for my newsletter and find recipes for some of the seventeenth-century foods that Jason and Caithren ate—simple, delicious recipes that you can try for yourself. I adore reader mail, so I hope you will write and tell me how you like them!

Do you suppose Cait was right when she thought a romance might be brewing between her cousin, Cameron, and little Mary's mother, Clarice? To find out, watch for my novella, "Forevermore," in the upcoming anthology *In Praise of Younger Men*. Due from Signet Books in spring 2001, it also features stories by Jo Beverley, Cathy Maxwell, and Jaclyn Reding.

If you enjoyed *Emerald,* you won't want
to miss Lauren Royal's next wonderful romantic
adventure, *Amber.* Filled with the danger, the
passion, and the marvelous wit you have
come to expect from this talented author,
Amber completes Lauren Royal's
jewel trilogy, and demonstrates once again
that she is one of the brightest new voices
in historical romance today! Following is
a special preview. . . .

Amber

A Signet paperback on sale
in August 2001.

Sussex, England
June 1668

"Jason is right, Kendra. You're twenty-three years old, and 'tis high time you married."

Kendra Chase slanted a glance at the plainly dressed stranger sharing the public coach, then glared at her twin, Ford, across the beat-up interior. "Not to the Duke of Lechmere," she snapped. "I'll not be 'Your Graced' for the rest of my life."

"And what, pray tell," Jason, their oldest brother, drawled out in an annoyed tone, "would be wrong with that?" Crammed onto the bench seat between Kendra and his wife, Caithren, Jason tried unsuccessfully to stretch his long legs. "I am only attempting to see that you live a life of comfort. Would you prefer to travel like this all the time?"

As if to drive home her brother's point, the springless vehicle lurched in and out of a rut, rattling Kendra's teeth. She gritted them. Though Jason was careful with money, he was, after all, a marquess, and they did own a rather luxurious carriage. But one of its wheels had broken on their way out of London, and they'd been forced to take public transport—or else risk missing an urgent appointment back home at Cainewood Castle.

An appointment to introduce Kendra to the latest "suitable" man they planned to foist upon her.

"My comfort isn't the issue here—"

"This is your last chance to make your own choice,"

Jason interrupted her, gathering the cards from the hand of piquet they'd just played. "If you won't marry Lechmere, you will have to select one of the other men who have offered for you. Or I will do the selecting."

"The other men." Kendra tossed her head of dark red curls, not believing her brother's ultimatum for a moment. The wretched day had put him in a bad mood, but he was generally the most reasonable man she knew. "Old but well-off, or widowed and settled with children, or young but just plain *boring*. Stable, wealthy men in the good graces of King Charles, every last one of them."

Her brother's green eyes flashed. "Yes, perfectly acceptable, every last one of them."

"As it should be," Ford put in.

Mournfully shaking her head, Kendra sent Caithren an imploring glance. "They will never understand."

Cait's eyes filled with sympathy and a bit of shared exasperation. She laid a hand on her husband's arm. "I've told ye before, Kendra cares not—"

With an unnerving suddenness, the coach ground to a halt. "Stand and deliver!" a deep voice demanded from outside. Stopped in mid-sentence, Cait's mouth gaped, and Kendra's stomach clenched in fear.

Ford leaned forward and pushed open the door. A man on horseback poked in his head.

The most compelling head Kendra had ever seen.

"You again?" Jason and Ford said together.

They knew this man? Since Kendra hadn't heard of either of her brothers being hurt—or even robbed, come to think of it—most of her fear dissipated, and her heart lifted with excitement instead. Nothing like this had ever happened to her! The highwayman leaned from the saddle, one hand on the edge of the doorframe. Her eyes were drawn to his long fingers with their well-groomed, square nails. When he spoke, her gaze snapped back to his face.

"Aye, 'tis me," he said, a grin emerging—an engaging slash of perfect white in his golden face.

Well, not precisely perfect. One of his front two teeth had a small chip, but she found that tiny imperfection endearing. And he was dashing, not to mention forbidden. If any of her hopeful suitors had been like this man, she'd have married him in a trice.

She wanted to say something to make him notice her. But for the first time in her memory, her mouth refused to work.

His gaze swept the coach's dim interior as though she weren't even there. "You," he said succinctly, motioning to the whey-faced businessman seated next to Ford. "Get out."

"There be five of us in here, three of them men, likely with pistols," the man said stiffly. From his haircut, plain clothes, and the short, boxy jacket beneath his cloak, Kendra knew he was a Puritan. "Perhaps you had better think again."

"Oh . . . 'tis violence you threaten, aye?" The highwayman's voice was deep and a little husky with, curiously, the barest hint of an accent. "My friends," he said slowly, gesturing toward the hill behind him, "would make certain you cease to exist within the minute. Get out . . . Now."

Kendra looked out the door and up. Sure enough, there were a dozen or so men at the top of the hill, their guns trained on the coach.

The Puritan must have recognized the threat, for he reluctantly climbed out. Kendra shifted within the coach, the better to see out. The victim was a good foot shorter than the robber, who looked impossibly tall and elegant in a jet-black velvet surcoat. Close-faced and resigned, the Puritan emptied his pockets and handed over his money, then turned to reenter the coach.

"Not so fast . . ." The highwayman reached to grab the Puritan's sleeve. Visibly shaken, the smaller man froze, but said nothing. "Surely a . . . man of business, such as yourself, will be carrying more gold on his person than this. Where is it? Sewn into your cloak? Hidden in your luggage?"

The Puritan turned back boldly, though Kendra could see the rise and fall of his agitated breathing. "Surely *you* have no need of it," he spat out, tugging his sleeve from the bigger man's grasp while eyeing his groomed appearance and expensive, tailored suit. "A . . . *gentleman* such as yourself."

The highwayman's eyes were amber, edged in a deeper hue—bronze, Kendra decided—that now spread in toward the center as his expression hardened. But although his accent thickened, he didn't raise his voice. "Your luggage *and* your cloak, then—since ye won't cooperate." He swung his pistol in the coachman's direction. The driver scrambled down and fumbled with the ropes securing the passengers' belongings. A shove sent the Puritan's trunk to the rutted road with a decisive *thunk*.

"Your cloak." The highwayman held out his free hand, almost as if he was bored, while his victim struggled out of his plain mantle.

"What about *them*?" he sputtered, handing it over. His gaze swung toward the Chases.

The highwayman glanced inside and flashed Kendra's brothers a conspiratorial smile before answering. "They're friends. Good day."

"Good day? *Good day?*" The poor man was red as a squalling newborn, and Kendra almost felt sorry for him—until she reminded herself that 'twas his ilk who had killed her parents during the Civil War. Had it been anyone else, she was sure Jason would have jumped to his defense. But because of men like this one, her brother had been left to raise his orphaned siblings, all of them forced to spend the Commonwealth years in poverty and exile. She turned to watch the amber man remount and make his way down the road and up the hill toward his cohorts.

He'd been superb, she thought. Magnificent.

Amber. His clean-shaven, suntanned complexion. His eyes, a gold the color of the finest liquor. The black plume on his cavalier's hat riffled as he rode, and beneath it he wore a long, crimped, brown periwig that rather reminded her of her twin Ford's hair. But she was certain the highwayman's real hair wasn't brown. Though many men had shaven heads under their periwigs, he wouldn't. His own hair would be cut short, but not *off*, certainly—she shuddered at the thought—and it would be amber gold.

"Are you going to let him get away with this?" the Puritan demanded, clambering up, and glaring at her brothers, both of them armed with swords and knives and God knew what else.

One of Jason's black eyebrows rose, and he spoke for them both. "I expect so."

The coach lurched and they continued on, but the atmosphere was decidedly strained, and the Puritan got off at the next stop.

Kendra moved to sit in the now-vacant spot beside Ford. "A highwayman," she breathed as soon as the carriage resumed moving.

"Why did he not rob us?" Caithren asked. "How is it you know him? He called you a friend."

"He uses the term lightly." Jason flashed an enigmatic smile. "He's been haunting this spot for months—we've run into him before. But he's never robbed us."

"He didn't look as though he needed to rob anybody," Kendra said. "His suit was nicer than yours." He'd looked nicer than Jason all around, she mused. Not that Jason wasn't good looking, but he had the general look of her family, a look she was inured to, to say the least. This man, on the other hand, had looked . . . exotic. All golden and dressed in black   black suit, black shirt, black boots—not the look of your typical scruffy felon, that was for sure.

Jason shrugged, absently running a hand through his wife's straight, dark blond hair. "Almost anyone can afford one nice suit of clothes, if he makes it his priority. You cannot judge a man by his looks, Kendra."

But she already had. Judged him, and liked what she saw.

Restless, Jason sighed and stretched his legs, then raised Cait's hand and brushed his lips over her knuckles, earning a soft smile in return. "Perhaps we should turn him in," he suggested playfully. "This is getting to be somewhat of a nuisance."

"You wouldn't dare!" Kendra burst out. "He's . . .

well, you saw his clothes. He'd fit in at Court. And he only robbed the Puritan. I'd wager he's a Royalist."

"There's a reward. And Lakefield House is in sad shape," Viscount Lakefield, otherwise known as Ford, lamented half-seriously. "I cannot live with Jason forever."

"Oh, yes, you can."

Jason turned to Kendra. "Is it that important to you, then? I didn't realize your Royalist loyalty ran so deep."

"Well . . . it does," she declared, thanking her lucky stars that her brothers had attributed her defense to something so benign as Royalist loyalty. She herself knew not what to attribute it to.

"Well, then." Ford's deep-blue eyes gleamed with mischief. "I suppose we'll have to leave him be. At least it provides him with a stake for the card games."

Jason glared at his brother.

"What?" Kendra slanted him a suspicious glance. "What card games?"

"All highwaymen play cards," Jason said firmly. He picked up their own deck and shuffled it expertly, then dealt out new hands. Kendra's mind wasn't on the game, though, and she arranged the cards slowly.

She remembered the highwayman's voice. He'd spoken quietly and a bit cautiously, as if he was considering each word.

Not like her family. The Chases, as a rule, blurted everything that came to the minds, generally at the top of their lungs.

"What was his accent?" she asked. "Did you hear it?"

"Scots, aye?" Cait said, exaggerating the burr she was born to. "Though he sounds as if he's not been home for many a year. I'm surprised ye even noticed."

Jason looked up sharply, but Kendra studied her fan of cards. He frowned back down at his own hand. "Why do you want to know?"

She didn't want to know anything. He was a highwayman, for God's sake. "Just curious," she said lightly, leading with a jack of hearts. "Your turn."

* * *

Kendra awoke the next morning with a massive headache. Jason couldn't be serious. After her disastrous interview with the Duke of Lechmere, he'd laid down the law: she would be wed by summer's end.

He and Ford and Colin were off to a monthly house party they attended—no women allowed—and, as usual, she and Caithren would be joined by their sister-in-law, Amy, and her baby daughter Jewel for the weekend. Usually they had something of a house party of their own, playing with the babe and gossiping the long hours away until the men returned.

But this time, they'd be expecting to hear whom she'd decided to marry.

She stared up at the underside of the mint-green canopy she'd begged for in her youth. Although their parents had depleted the family fortune financing the King in the Civil War, Jason had always seen to it that she'd never wanted for anything. To the best of his abilities, he'd indulged her every whim. He wouldn't force her to marry now.

Would he?

With a huff, she rose and pulled on her new huntergreen satin riding habit. Amy would be here within the hour, but she needed to think. Alone.

She ran a comb through her hair, not bothering to call her maid in to curl and pin it, and in no time at all, she was mounted on Pandora, her mare, galloping across the Sussex Downs. Her brothers would be mightily vexed if they knew she was riding unescorted, but the three of them could go hang for all she cared right now.

Besides, they were away all weekend and would never know.

The fresh country air was helping her headache clear, but just thinking about that weasel Lechmere made her shiver. And the rest of her prospects weren't much better.

The Earl of Shrewsbury came complete with a meddling mother for which the "shrew" in her name was an all-too-fitting description. The Marquess of Rochford was kind enough, but his hair was completely gray—no doubt from dealing with his seven unruly children. Viscount Davenport didn't talk, he whined. The Duke of Lancashire lived in—well, Lancashire—which was entirely too far from her family. The Earl of Morely was wealthy and wise—but nearing fifty. Lord Rosslyn was young, handsome, and fun loving, but lacking somewhat in brains. She wondered if he could read.

Jason couldn't be serious.

Coming out of her thoughts, she slowed to a stop. She hadn't realized how far she'd ridden. In fact, she noticed with a start, she was at the same spot where she'd seen the highwayman yesterday.

His friends had been atop that hill, lying on their stomachs, training an impressive assortment of pistols on the hapless Puritan. Waiting patiently, their hats pulled down to conceal their faces.

This morning, the hill was deserted, the highwayman nowhere in sight. Kendra glanced at the sky in an attempt to judge the time, but all was clouded over. 'Twas turning into a beastly day. Not cold, but muggy, with a definite threat of rain. With no sun to confirm it, she guessed the time at about ten o'clock. Perhaps highwaymen slept in.

Plainly, highway robbery was not a full-time occupation. Not that she had any idea of what she'd have done if he *had* been here. Run for her life, in all probability. But she drifted into a vague fantasy of herself riding down the road at breakneck speed, her long, dark red hair floating on the breeze, impressing the hell out of him with her horsemanship and her grace. Him staring after her, openmouthed with disbelief and appreciation. Struck temporarily dumb by a bolt of . . . love at first sight. Well, second sight, actually—but he hadn't paid any attention before, so the first time didn't count.

Then she would turn around, ride back, stop in the middle of the road, right in front of him . . . slide off Pandora slowly . . . so slowly. He'd close his mouth and come forward, reaching her in two or three of his long strides, his large hands spanning her waist as he eased her to the ground. And then . . .

She had no idea. Inexperience didn't make for detailed fantasies. And she certainly wouldn't have anything to do with a highwayman, anyway. Her fantasy was not only boring, it was absurd.

But instead of turning back, she rode along the crest of the hill a spell, then turned away from the lane. And there, perhaps a hundred feet back, was a very mysterious mound.

It was not sculpted by nature, Kendra realized immediately. Its shape was angular, not worn smooth by beasts and weather. Its surface was dirt, not grass.

A grave. A fresh grave.

Kendra's hands tightened on the reins as she approached the tomb. Was it the highwayman? A victim of his? Either one was unthinkable. She bit the inside of her cheek, worrying the soft flesh with her teeth.

A single raindrop fell on one of her clenched fists, and a gust of wind whooshed as she reached the mound. From her perch high atop Pandora, she saw the loose dirt blow across it, revealing a sheet of canvas underneath. Her heart hammered at the sight. Was the man not buried proper, then—just covered with a spot of fabric?

She slid off Pandora, leading her forward to investigate. She leaned down, took a corner of the canvas, just a corner, in two shaking fingers. Lifted it . . .

Her shout of laughter rang across the downs as she threw back the canvas.

Twelve blocks of wood. Twelve narrow pipes of various gauges. Twelve hats with different colored plumes and a variety of hatbands.

He was clever, this man. Very clever.

"What do you think you're doing?"

She froze. She hadn't heard anyone approach, and for the barest second she thought the voice was in her head. But he was standing next to her, not three feet away.

"I'm . . . I'm . . ."

"You're letting my hats get wet."

"Oh." Kendra put a hand to her head, feeling the mass of her hair curling with dampness. She hadn't noticed the increasing drizzle " 'Tis raining."

"Very observant of you."

She turned then and looked up at him, and he was

exactly like she had known he would be. His hair *was* golden—thick, silky, and straight, the shiniest blond. 'Twas cut short, not chin-length like a Puritan's, nor cropped like a wig-wearing Royalist's, but somewhere in between, and the front was hanging in his eyes. She wanted to reach out and sweep it off his forehead, but she seemed rooted in place, and she wouldn't have dared to touch him, anyway.

His snug black breeches were wool, not velvet, and his shirt was white, not black. He wasn't here for business, then.

"I've come to put away my props. Will you help me, seeing as you're here?"

Help him? She ought to be bolting for Pandora at this very moment. "Of course."

Had she said that? She knew she shouldn't have. He turned and she concentrated on his broad back, watching the play of muscles beneath his thin shirt as he flipped over the canvas and piled the hats on top, bundled them up and tied the four corners in a neat knot to make a parcel. He hefted it, testing its weight, then turned to her. "You can carry this, aye? Before you, on your horse?" He didn't sound angry, but more as if he was simply resolved to complete his task in the most efficient manner possible. Kendra was somewhat relieved, but she still moved in a haze of unreality.

She managed to find her voice, however. "If you'll hand it up to me, yes, I'm sure I can carry it. Where are we taking it?"

"A cottage over the next hill, not too far." He gathered the pipes under one arm and lifted the bundle by its knot. "Let us be off, before it starts raining in earnest."

His horse was tied beside Pandora—amber, of course, his glossy coat a tawny golden color. Pandora's hide was a deep brown, and Kendra thought they made a handsome pair.

'Twas difficult to see over the bundle in front of her, but it was a short ride.

The cottage was unlocked, and the highwayman made short work of tethering their horses before depositing the pipes inside and returning for the bundle. After handing it to him, Kendra slid off Pandora slowly . . . so slowly . . . and a second later he was back, and his large hands were spanning her waist as he eased her to the ground.

He rested his hands on her waist a little longer than necessary, and she felt their warmth through her satin habit. She locked up at him. He had a long nose, a faint dimple in his squared-off chin. A wide mouth, the full lower lip perfectly straight across the center bottom edge. She wanted to touch him, just there.

Her eyes locked on his beneath the golden strands, and her breath caught in her throat.

A crash of thunder rent the air, and big raindrops pelted the earth. He jumped back, motioning her to follow him inside.

She should leave. Now. But it was raining . . .

The cottage looked more like a well-appointed hunting lodge, warm and cozy and very masculine. He shut the door behind them and wandered to a leather-upholstered couch, throwing his long form onto it with a surprising grace. " 'Twas close, no? Five more minutes, and my hats would have been ruined. I thank you for your help."

"You're welcome," Kendra said from over by the door where she stood in a daze. She couldn't believe she was alone in a hunting lodge with this dangerous man. 'Twas incredible—and, all of a sudden, incredibly scary. She couldn't remember ever having been alone with a man, save her brothers. And she didn't know the first thing about this one—except that he was a criminal.

Her sudden fear must have shown on her face, because he sat up, patting the cushion next to him. "Come here—I don't bite. You'll stay 'til it stops raining, aye?"

"Aye—I mean, yes." Criminal or not, she loved the way he talked, all quiet and melodic, the words slow and flowing. Her heart was pounding, but she screwed up her courage and moved to sit gingerly beside him. "I'm Kendra. Kendra Chase."

"Trick Caldwell."

"Trick?" she echoed, startled. She turned to him, forgetting for a moment that he was supposed to be frightening. "What kind of name is Trick?"

"Ahh, and that's a story." He smiled at her, a wide smile that lit up the cottage and belied the dreary day. Leaning forward, he reached out a hand and placed it on her wrist, just lightly, but a tingle raced up her arm and throughout her body, warming her in the strangest way. Something snapped inside her, and the sense of unreality was gone. She was here, really here, with the amber highwayman—no, Trick, she corrected herself—alone, and he wasn't scary at all.

Well, not very.